The Sleep

He paused, narrowing his eyes to try and make out who was there. Maybe it was nobody at all. Maybe the grisly images that he had seen in Dr Moorpath's office were making him jumpy. He had dreamed once that all of the dead from the Rocky Woods air crash had shambled into his yard one night, and knocked on the door, and stood in the moonlight, silent and accusing, waiting with terrible patience for him to give them their lost lives back. That dream had haunted him for nearly four months, and it had taken all of Dr Rice's skills to put it to rest. One night he had dreamed that somebody had knocked on his door, and when he had gone to answer it, his yard had been moonlit but empty; and it was then that he had known that the victims were no longer asking him for redemption, or resurrection, or whatever it was they had wanted him to give them. But he had never shaken the feeling that the dead can follow us, begging us mutely for help.

The Sleepless

GRAHAM MASTERTON

Mandarin

A Mandarin Paperback
THE SLEEPLESS

First published in Great Britain 1993
by William Heinemann Ltd
This edition published 1994
by Mandarin Paperbacks
an imprint of Reed Consumer Books Ltd
Michelin House, 81 Fulham Road, London SW3 6RB
and Auckland, Melbourne, Singapore and Toronto

Reprinted 1994 (twice), 1995 (twice)

Copyright © Graham Masterton 1993
The author has asserted his moral rights

A CIP catalogue record for this title
is available from the British Library
ISBN 0 7493 1576 8

Printed and bound in Great Britain
by Cox & Wyman Ltd, Reading, Berkshire

One

John O'Brien stood in the reflected sunlight in front of his dressing-room mirror and adjusted his crimson-flowered Armani necktie. He did it with precision and ceremony, not only because he was always precise and always enjoyed ceremony, but because he knew that this would be the last time he would tie it as an ordinary mortal.

He tugged down his dark blue waistcoat so that it fitted more snugly, and tugged at his cuffs, too. He liked what he saw. He had always dressed well. His father had said, 'You never know when you're going to meet your Maker; so dress every morning as if today's the day.' His father had been wearing an Abercrombie & Fitch sports coat when he died of a heart attack two years ago, almost to the day.

Eva appeared in the mirror behind him, aristocratically handsome, in her primrose-yellow Eva Chun suit. 'Is His Honour the Supreme Court justice ready yet?' she smiled.

John stuck out his jaw and turned his head from side to side. 'His Honour is ready, but His Honour isn't officially a Supreme Court justice until His Honour is sworn in.'

'His *Honour* is splitting hairs again,' smiled Eva. She came up to him and twined her arms around his waist.

'Hairsplitting is what I do, my darling. It's my job. You know what it says in the Fourteenth Amendment. "No State shall deprive anybody of life, liberty or property without splitting every hair between here and Kalamazoo."'

Eva smiled, and squeezed him, and kissed his shoulder. 'You're going to be the finest hair-splitter that ever was.'

1

'I'm going to do my damndest,' said John; and his voice was more serious now.

'You're going to be brilliant,' Eva assured him. 'You're going to give the Supreme Court all of its guts back.'

He slapped his stomach and grunted in amusement. 'You mean the Supreme Court's going to give *me* all of my guts back,' John responded. 'I've never had to eat so many lunches in the whole of my life.' He paused, and then he said, 'What do you think of this necktie? Not too showy, is it? Maybe I should wear the solid.'

'It's perfect! Showy, yes. But tastefully showy. Just like you.'

He laughed. Then, for a moment, they stood looking at each other in the mirror, pleased and proud. At the age of forty-eight, John was one of the youngest Supreme Court justices ever appointed – younger even than William Rehnquist when he was appointed by Richard Nixon in 1971. John was tall, well over six-feet-three, with wavy iron-grey hair and a broad, generously-featured face. He looked as if he had been hacked out of a single block of post oak by a sculptor who had gusto, exuberance, and terrific talent, but no truck at all with pernickety detail.

In spite of his craggy, virile, unfinished looks, however, John's career credentials were flawless – the finest that family connections and a great deal of old Massachusetts money could buy. His late father was Senator Douglas O'Brien, Boston's wealthiest and most outspoken politician since Joseph Kennedy. John and his two brothers had grown up in privileged and cultured surroundings, travelling, yachting, polo playing, skiing, and socializing everywhere that mattered from Monaco to Aspen. For his eighteenth birthday, his father had given him an Aston Martin cus-tom-painted in O'Brien Green (still in the garage today) as well as $7.2 million in stocks and bonds. For his twenty-

2

first birthday, his father had bought him this house – an ivy-fluttering redbrick English mansion overlooking the Charles River, with thirteen bedrooms, a small ballroom and a huge library.

Inside the library, there was over a mile of oak shelving and leather-bound law books. When he had first walked into it, John had closed his eyes and said, 'If justice has a smell, this is it.'

At the age of twenty-four, John had graduated *summa cum laude* from Harvard Law School, and had immediately taken up an assured position with Howell Rhodes Macklin, Boston's most illustrious law firm and his family's own lawyers. At twenty-nine, after successfully defending the Byzantine fraud action of *People vs. Bonatello*, he had been made a full partner, and during the Carter administration his vigorous campaigning for civil liberties had brought him to the attention of the Attorney General, Griffin B. Bell, who had appointed him an assistant Attorney General in the Justice Department.

Now, with the recent death from lung cancer of Supreme Court Justice Everett Berkenheim, and John's appointment in Berkenheim's place, he had reached that glory-gilded summit that he had always dreamed of – to be one of those nine men who nurtured and interpreted the US Constitution, a judge above all other judges.

Time magazine, while understandably wary of John's liberal politics – and particularly his dedicated opposition to the death penalty – had described him as 'brave' and 'forthright'. Most of the time, yes, John *did* feel brave, and most of the time he *did* feel forthright. Sometimes he could even say that he felt courageous. He loved Eva more than ever: that tangled affair three years ago with his junior partner Elizabeth seemed to have strengthened their marriage, rather than damaged it. He was wealthy and he was fit, he had a pretty daughter and literally hundreds of friends, and every day seemed to be challenging and full of sunshine.

The only thing that ever caused him any anxiety was 'Mr Hillary'.

'Mr Hillary' was only a minuscule blot in his life and yet he couldn't erase it. It seemed petty, no more significant than a single pinprick of mould on a perfectly painted wall, but it never left him alone. Ever since childhood, his nights had constantly been haunted by a single terrifying image; an image that stood silent and cold in a remote corridor in the back of his mind. It was an image that was unreachable by day. In his late twenties he had tried hypnotism, and then he had two years of absurdly expensive psychoanalysis. But the image was inaccessible to his waking consciousness – even though he knew all the time that it was there.

It was the image of a man who stood watching and waiting, nothing more, a man with features as smudged as a Rorschach ink-blot. John couldn't understand why, but the man's appearance filled him with such a sense of dread that he would wake up bathed in sweat and gargling for breath. He never moved, this man; even when John – asleep, panicking – *begged* him to move. He felt like screaming, 'Come and get me! Get it over with! Do something! Do anything! But *do* it!'

But the image remained motionless, keeping its distance, keeping its silence, biding its own malevolent time. John knew for certain that it meant him harm. It might even be the image of his own death. When he was younger, he had believed that he might be able to come to terms with it, that he might be able to go to bed at night without fearing that he would come face to face with it yet again. But his fear never diminished, and the image never went away, and every so often, as he slept, he would find himself turning that terrible, grey, familiar corner, and there it was. Watching.

4

John had named this image 'Mr Hillary' while he was still a small boy. He didn't know why – any more than he knew what 'Mr Hillary' really was. In the end he had come to accept that 'Mr Hillary' would always be there, as long as he lived, and would be watching and waiting for him when he died.

Eva said, 'How about some coffee?'

John slipped on his gold Breitling Chronomat wristwatch. It read 10:28. By this time tomorrow morning, he thought, I'll be Supreme Court Justice John O'Brien, and then the rest of my life will really begin. The glory years. The years of achievement and fame.

'I don't know about coffee,' he said, turning around and kissing Eva's forehead. 'I don't think I really need a caffeine jolt. I think I'm jittery enough as it is.'

'Oh, come on, relax. The helicopter won't be here for at least ten minutes yet. I had Madeleine brew up some of that new arabica blend from the Bentonwood Café.'

John shrugged on his coat, tugged at his shirt cuffs yet again, and then followed Eva down the curved oak staircase to the hall. The walls were oak-panelled, too, and hung with seascapes, including a huge painting of shark-fishing in the Caribbean by Winslow Homer, full of luminous greens and shimmering blues. Eva's new shoes rapped sharply on the white tiled floor. The sun shone down through the pale-tinted stained-glass window over the porch. Madeleine was waiting for them in the doorway of the morning room, a dark-haired Quebequoise maid who had been recommended by Charles Dabney, one of the senior partners. John had wanted a much younger maid but Eva's emotions had still been raw from his affair with Elizabeth, and she had been more than happy to take on an experienced domestic of a certain age like Madeleine, particularly since Madeleine walked with a slurring limp and sported a hairy mole on the left side of her chin.

The longcase clock in the hallway, as tall as a steeple, struck half-past ten, which meant that there were fewer than forty minutes to go.

Eva said, 'We'll be back Friday evening, Madeleine; about seven o'clock; and we'll be going directly out to dinner with the Kochs. Could you lay out my green Versace and ask Newton to lay out His Honour's tuxedo?'

'Yes Madame,' said Madeleine, in a flat French-accented voice.

'And could you call Bloomingdale's for me and ask what happened to that Courreges turtle I ordered? Speak to Lonnie, in Place Elegante, on two. And don't forget those new napkin-rings, will you? They should be ready by now. Call Jackie at Quadrum. You have the number already, don't you, all the fives.'

John sat down in one of the elegant yellow-striped colonial armchairs. The morning room was filled with sunshine, and sunshine was dazzlingly reflected from the polished floor. Madeleine poured him a cup of coffee, and he watched her and wondered what her mother and father had looked like, and what had attracted them to have her. Perhaps her mother had been beautiful, although he doubted it. Perhaps her father had been dashing. A violinist, an acrobat, a street sweeper. Who could tell?

Eva sat opposite him, elegantly cross-legged. 'I've been thinking about our birthday party for Sissy,' she said.

'Oh, yes?' He thought he could hear the distant *flacker-flacker-flacker* of a helicopter. Or maybe it was just the summer wind, blowing through the maples.

'She wants a theme party, a kind of fifties beatnik party.'

John frowned at her. 'She wants a beatnik party? You mean berets, and striped jerseys?'

It was a helicopter. It was very much louder now. A deep, throbbing undernote, and the *flacker-flacker-flacker* of rotor

6

blades, curving over Riverdale and turning eastwards. This was it. His appointment with destiny. A short helicopter journey to Logan International Airport and then a LearJet flight to Washington. He checked his watch: it was 10:37.

Eva had obviously heard the helicopter, too. But for some reason she seemed to be determined to ignore it.

'The helicopter,' he said, lifting a finger; and she said, 'Yes', but that was all. Perhaps she was suddenly feeling afraid of the new life to which the helicopter would be taking them. Perhaps she was afraid of John encountering another Elizabeth – an even more glamorous and sexually exciting Elizabeth, knowing what the girls were like in Washington. Girls might be attracted to rock stars; but in Eva's experience, they were always ten times more attracted to politicians, or industrialists, or judges – even if they were middle-aged and balding and fat. Girls didn't care about middle-aged and balding and fat. They really didn't. It was the aura of power that turned them on. And a Supreme Court Justice possessed not just the aura of power, but the aura of *ultimate* power. There were hundreds of rock stars, scores of eligible actors: but there were only nine Supreme Court Justices, and seven of them were over the age of sixty-five. To be perfectly crude about it, John's appointment had made him one of the most fuckable men in America.

John glanced at Eva and thought he could guess what the problem was. These days, he found it difficult to tell her that he loved her so much. He was always afraid of sounding hypocritical. In truth, he loved her in a very different way than he had when he first met her. But he still liked her, still depended on her, and he still found deep satisfaction in making love to her – although sometimes, when he climaxed, and the bedside lamps were still on, he caught her turning her face away from him, and staring at the wall

7

as if in contempt? or disinterest? or maybe pain? He really didn't know. He felt that he couldn't get close to the core of her personality any longer. But he was willing to keep on trying. Maybe one day she would let him back in.

She was, after all, very beautiful. She was the only daughter of Mr and Mrs Hunter Hamilton III, of Lynnfield, and she was a sleek, slim woman who reminded everybody she met of an upper-crust Julia Roberts. Ash blonde, impeccably dressed, impeccably mannered, wealthy in her own right. Yet John had always felt that their marriage had one piece missing, a jigsaw without that one last piece of wall, or sky, or a woman standing in the background without a face. And after his affair with Elizabeth, it seemed as if he kept discovering every day that there were more pieces missing.

The roaring of the helicopter grew louder; and after a minute or two they felt it pass directly over the house, and the antique silver coffee spoons vibrated in their saucers.

'He's early,' Eva remarked. 'It's only a quarter to eleven.'

Sissy came into the morning room – their fourteen-year-old daughter, wearing a primrose-yellow suit to match mommy's. She looked much more like her mother than her father, but her father had given her mother's features a certain broadness and generosity, so that her beauty wasn't quite so pinched. Her blonde hair was cut in a high-backed bob, and she wore huge handcrafted crystal-and-silver earrings from Rio Bahio on Commonwealth Avenue. She had sprayed herself more than generously with her favourite new perfume, L'Insolent, and anybody would have taken her for eighteen.

'My God, doesn't that noise go right through your *brain*,' she complained, as the helicopter hovered over the south lawn, its engine throbbing, its rotors whistling, and finally curtseyed and settled on the grass.

John said, 'At least we don't have to drive.'

8

'Do we really have to stay in Washington for three entire days?' Sissy asked. 'It's going to be so *hot*, and so *boring*.'

'Sissy, don't be ridiculous, darling,' said Eva. 'We have parties and receptions and media conferences and all kinds of things to go to. It's not every day of the week that a man of your father's age is appointed a justice of the Supreme Court.'

'Thank God,' Sissy retorted.

John stood up. 'You want to stay home?' he asked, with a deceptive mildness in his voice. 'You want to stay home – go ahead, stay home. I don't care; it's your decision.'

Sissy pouted and stayed silent. She knew her father well enough to guess what was coming next. A mega-boring moralistic nag.

'You can stay home,' he said. 'But think about it. You'd hurt my feelings, for sure. You'd also hurt your mother's feelings. But very much more than that, you'd be turning your back on one of the greatest ceremonies that this country has to offer: the swearing-in of an ordinary man to deliberate and give his opinions on matters relating to the country's constitution – the very heart and soul of American life.'

Sissy said, 'I'll come, okay? I'll enjoy myself, okay? I was only kidding.'

John put down his coffee cup, and brushed imaginary dust from his sleeve. 'You don't seem to realize the importance of the Supreme Court, its uniqueness.'

Sissy said, 'I'll *come*, all right?'

'In the past forty years, the Supreme Court has probably had more influence on the lives of ordinary Americans than all of the legislation passed by Congress put together.'

'I'll come!' howled Sissy, in mock desperation. 'You don't have to say another word! I'll come!'

Newton, their butler, hurried bow-legged backwards and

forwards across the neatly striped lawn with all of their luggage – six Louis Vuitton suitcases and two hatboxes. John went to the door and watched him and thought with amusement that he looked like Bill Cosby imitating Groucho Marx. The grey-and-white Sikorsky helicopter was hunched in the sunlight, its rotors drooping. The pilot, in light blue fatigues, was talking to a bespectacled young man in a badly creased linen suit, whom John recognized as Dean McAllister, a talented new assistant at the Justice Department.

As soon as John and Eva and Sissy appeared on the porch, Dean gave the pilot a quick clap on the shoulder and came hurrying towards them. He was sandy-haired, plump, and freckled. The Attorney General habitually referred to him as 'Jelly-Bean McAllister', because the pinkness of his face exactly matched the colour of watermelon-flavoured Jelly Bellies.

'Congratulations, sir!' said Dean, squeezing John's hand. 'And congratulations to you, too, Mrs O'Brien! What a great day! I can't tell you how pleased we are for you!'

'If only the President were half so pleased,' smiled John, wryly.

'Oho!' said Dean. 'Even the President has to recognize 24-carat excellence when it's right in front of his nose.' Then – to Sissy – 'You're going to have a real good time tonight. The Beaumonts are throwing a going-away party for Clarissa, and you're invited, and guess who's coming? Would you believe – dah-*dah*! – John Travolta?'

Sissy slowly wrinkled up her nose. 'John *Travolta*? He must be more than eighty years old by now!'

They all laughed. Dean said, 'You're invited anyway, even if there are one or two geriatrics coming along. Now – are we ready? The flight's scheduled to take off at 11:25 hours and that should give us plenty of time if we leave pretty much now.'

'Sure, we're ready,' said John. He turned around to

Newton, who was standing behind him, dabbing his fore-head with a folded handkerchief. 'Newton, will you make sure that Jimmy gets the message about reshoeing that grey? And keep your eye on those pool-cleaners, too. The last time they clogged up all the filters.'

'Very good, sir. You and Mrs O'Brien have a safe flight, now.'

They walked across to the helicopter. The pilot saluted them crisply and then shook their hands. 'How do you, sir. My name's Frank Coward. Welcome aboard.'

Frank was a tanned, leathery man with a cleft-tipped nose and no spare meat on him. He wore impenetrable green-lensed Ray-Bans in which John could see nothing but his own curved reflection and the white pillars of the porch behind him. There was a long white scar running down the inside of Frank's left arm, and he wore a small enamel pin in his lapel which read 'Semper Fi US Marines'.

'Shouldn't take us more than ten minutes to get to Logan, sir,' he added. 'Just relax and enjoy it.'

He closed the helicopter's door and hunched his way to the pilot's seat, where he sat down, put on his red-and-white bonedome, and ran deftly through his pre-flight checks, his scarred arm raised so that he could flick switches on the overhead panels. John and Eva sat side by side, buckling themselves into their grey leather seats, while Sissy and Dean sat facing them.

Dean said, 'The *Post* called this afternoon, Apparently they're interested in running a major analysis of all of your past defences and all of the work you did for Griffin Bell. Especially that schools legislation.'

Frank said, 'That's it, ladies and gentleman. Hold tight,' and started up the two turboshafts. The helicopter's en-gines throbbed and the rotors began to turn. John squeezed Eva's hand as they gradually rose from the lawn, and almost immediately began to tilt off toward the Charles river. They saw their own rough-mown horse paddocks swivelling below them; then a slanting view of the house, with its shining ivy and its red-tiled rooftops; then the river gleaming like molten gold, so bright that it dazzled them.

'Logan control, this is helicopter Justice Three,' drawled Frank. 'Heading sixty degrees east-north-east over Riverdale, altitude one thousand feet, ETA eight minutes fifteen seconds.'

They flew low over Highway 1 and the shining rectangular blocks of the VA Medical Center, their shadow jumping and hopping beneath them.

'What do you think?' said John. 'About the *Post*, I mean.'

Dean leaned forward and said, 'My considered opinion is that you should decline to co-operate. If they want to know why, tell them it's your *future* deliberations with the Supreme Court that they should judge you on, not your old defences. The law may be founded on precedent, but the law moves on, and you're going to be the man who makes it move on.'

John gave him a wry smile. 'I think that's what most of my critics are worried about.'

'Well, for sure,' Dean replied. 'But just remember what Chief Justice Charles Evans Hughes had to say about it. "The Constitution is nothing more nor less than what the judges say it is." And now you're one of those judges.'

'I'm *about* to be one of those judges,' John corrected him.

'Hair-splitter,' said Eva, and squeezed his hand even tighter.

Sissy said, 'John Travolta! I can hardly wait … not!'

They were flackering over the Norfolk County line when without warning the helicopter shuddered and lurched to starboard. Eva gasped and Sissy let out a little yelp. John shouted out, 'Frank! What in hell's happening?'

'Just a touch of engine irregularity, nothing I can't handle,' Frank called back. For a moment, it looked as if he might be right. The helicopter continued to fly forward at high speed, although the turboshafts were whining and rumbling in a way that they hadn't been whining and rumbling before.

'Don't you think you'd better put us down?' John shouted.

But before Frank could answer, there was an earsplitting screech of clashing metal gears, and the helicopter dropped two or three hundred feet in a bucking, uncontrolled spiral. John felt as if his stomach had been left somewhere way up in the sky. He clutched the arm of his seat and snatched for Eva's hand. He saw Sissy's face right in front of him, her jaw muscles rigid with terror, and his mouth flooded with lukewarm coffee and poisonous bile. He thought he could hear Eva screaming at him, but the helicopter was shaking and roaring so loudly that it was impossible to tell for sure.

Just when John thought they were going to hit the ground, Frank somehow managed to stabilize the helicopter's tail, and tilt the rotors to gain a few desperate feet of height. All the same, the fuselage vibrated relentlessly, punctuated by a deep, lumpy sound, and thick brown smoke began to stream across the windows.

'Jesus, Jesus, Jesus!' yelled Dean, his mouth drawn back tight as a toad's.

'We're going to crash!' screamed Sissy. 'Daddy, we're going to die!'

John, helpless and terrified, bellowed at the back of Frank's head, 'Frank! Do you hear me, Frank! For Christ's sake put her down!'

Eva was gripping John's hand so tightly that her wedding ring pressed into his nerve; but he was almost glad of the pain because it told him that he was still alive; and that while he was still alive, he still had a chance of survival.

Jolting, airsick, he tried to peer through the droplets of thin brown oil that were streaking the windows, to see where they were. He thought he recognized Jamaica Pond, and then Franklin Park. He realized that they were turning in a slow, wide circle, eastward toward the sea – Quincy Bay, most likely. He saw buildings, patches of shining water, trees, then the tawny concrete ribbon of the Southeast Expressway. The helicopter was surging up and down like a Boston whaler in a choppy surf. The roaring and grinding of the engines was so loud that, even if he survived, John didn't think that he would ever be able to hear anything again.

Eva clung to him, clung at his coat, clung at his arm. Sissy was gripping Dean's arm and Dean was staring at him in total panic, a dark stain spreading across the crotch of his linen suit. John tried screaming at Frank again, but Frank was struggling for survival in a small deafening hell of his own, and didn't have time for anything else.

They were flying so low now that John could see people on the streets and beaches below them, shading their eyes and turning around as the helicopter burped and stuttered over their heads. He saw some people running, obviously afraid that they were going to crash right on top of them. He couldn't believe that they were still airborne. They were well below the level of the rooftops and the powerlines, but somehow they managed to snatch a few lurching feet of extra lift, and cross the grey sandy diagonal of Wollaston Beach, so that they were flying out over the sun-chipped waters of Quincy Bay.

Through the oil-fogged window, John saw yacht sails shining, like fresh-laundered sheets, and for a moment he was convinced that they were going to make it, that Frank

14

was going to put them gently down in the sea, and that everything was going to be fine.

He reached across and grasped Sissy's hand, too, and said, 'We're making it, we're making it. He's putting us down in the bay. Just hold on, we're going to be fine.'

Dean could do nothing but stare at him in horror, and open and close his mouth. He turned to Eva but Eva had her right hand pressed over her face and she looked as if she were praying.

John prayed too. *Dear God save my family from death. Dear God, just this one time, let us all live.*

The Sikorsky's turboshafts let out a last hideous *grrrrrr!* like a pit-bull having its guts torn out, and then it simply dropped. It hit the water at well over 150 knots, and John felt something slamming into his back. Eva let out a scream that was so high-pitched and unearthly that he thought for a split second that it was metal tearing – that the whole fuselage was being ripped in half. Then the helicopter bounced again, and hit something much harder than the sea, although the window burst open on John's side of the fuselage and saltwater spray exploded in his face.

Jesus! Wouldn't it ever stop bouncing and crashing and rolling and bouncing? He saw sea, sunlight, the pink flurry of Sissy's face, the jolting blur of Dean's left arm, and all the time Eva was screaming and screaming *Oh God oh God we're all going to die We're all going to die We're all going to die.*

The helicopter suddenly came to a stop, three-quarters tilted, like a baseball player who suddenly stops himself on the third base, and tilts, and staggers, still full of momentum, still full of forward motion. Then it rolled with a heavy crunching onto its belly, onto the sand. As it did so, its floor buckled in, and mercilessly compressed their feet underneath their seats, where they had been tucked in the foetal position. John felt his heels forced up against the aluminum rack which held his lifebelt. Then all of their ankles snapped in unison, like a crackle of pistol fire, and they stared at each other and shouted in pain.

After that, apart from the sound of the incoming tide, and the doleful whistling of the wind, and the stray clanking of cooling metal, there was silence. The whole cabin stank of kerosene, but the smoke seemed to have died down, and there was no crackling of fire. Eva kept pulling at John's hand and whispering, 'God, oh God, John. Oh God.' Her face was grey and her forehead was badly bruised. Dean was shuddering and massaging his kneecaps over and over in pain. Sissy simply stared at nothing at all, and John guessed that she was already lapsing into clinical shock.

As for himself, his feet were on fire. He had never experienced such pain, even when he had fallen from his polo pony late last year and dislocated his shoulder. Every nerve in his ankles cringed and throbbed, and if somebody had asked him then and there if he had wanted his feet to be amputated, he would have paid them to do it.

'Oh God, John,' wept Eva. 'I think that both of my ankles are broken.'

'I think *all* of our ankles are broken,' said John. 'Keep an eye on Sissy ... she's gone into shock.'

'Where are we?' said Dean, in a clogged-up, unreal voice. He peered unfocused at the bay. 'I thought we were over water.'

'We were,' John told him. 'But we must have hit Nantasket Beach. It's kind of a spit of land that sticks out into the bay.'

'They can get to us, though? The emergency services can get to us?'

'For sure,' John shivered. 'We've made it, don't worry. They can get to us.'

'What about Frank?' Dean asked him. 'Do you think he sent out a mayday?'

John leaned a few inches sideways in his seat. It was the most that he could manage before his ankles were gripped by intolerable agony. He could just make out the back of Frank's helmet, and part of Frank's blue-shirted shoulder.

'Frank!' John called out, desperately. 'Frank, are you all right? For Christ's sake, our feet are trapped!'

Frank didn't answer. 'Maybe he's concussed,' Dean suggested.

'Maybe,' said John. From the unnatural angle of Frank's head, he suspected that Frank might be more than concussed. It looked as if his neck might be broken. But John didn't want to panic Eva, and he was suffering too much pain himself to want to speculate. As far as he was concerned, their first priority was to lift these seats off their legs, so that the pressure on their broken ankles was relieved and they could drag themselves clear.

Drag, not walk. No question of walking. He could feel the fractured bones grating inside his skin, like a smashed jelly jar full of crushed-up pieces of glass.

Eva said, with a curious note of resignation in her voice, 'John, can you hear me? I can't bear it. It really hurts so much.'

'It's all right, sweetheart,' John reassured her. 'The rescue people are going to get here real soon. You don't think they're going to leave their newest Supreme Court Justice stranded on Nantasket Beach, do you?' He winced, and his mouth filled with metallic, sour-tasting blood; but he managed to turn away from her and spit it down the side of his seat. That slam on the back must have broken some ribs, maybe punctured a lung.

'So long as we don't burn,' said Dean. The stench of kerosene was even stronger now, and John could see the fumes rippling in the breeze. 'I couldn't bear to burn.'

'It's all right,' John told him. 'Everything's going to be fine.'

'I saw somebody burn in a Volkswagen once, out on the Rockville Pike. Never want to see anything like that again. Kid went *black*, like beef.'

Dean's voice wandered from high pitch to low, and John guessed that he was going into shock, too. Sissy's eyes had rolled up into her head, and her breathing was laboured and slow.

'For Christ's sake, how long are those rescue people going to be?' John ranted, at nobody at all.

But almost as soon as he had said that, he saw the shadow of a man pass the broken window.

'Hey!' he shouted. 'Hey – we're in here!'

'Has somebody got here?' asked Eva, wincing with pain. 'Has somebody got here already?'

The shadow passed the window again. Although his image was blurred by the sunlight that was shining from the sea, John could see that he was wearing a long dark raincoat. Thank God, it must be a firefighter from the Fire & Rescue Service.

'Hey!' he yelled out, hoarsely. 'Hey, we're all in here! We're trapped! Can you get us out of here, for Christ's sake?'

There was a long pause, but no reply. In the far distance, John could hear sirens, six or seven or even more, yowling and scribbling in the chorus. The pain in his ankles was so intense now that his legs throbbed, all the way to his thighs, and a scarlet mist was blurring his vision. *Don't pass out now,* he ordered himself. *Your family needs you; Dean needs you; your country needs you.*

He heard somebody tugging away a length of bent window frame. Then a thin dark man appeared in the broken window, a man with cropped spiky hair and intensely black sunglasses. In some oblique, extraordinary way, John

18

thought that he recognized him – but it was probably no more than an overwhelming sense of relief that they had survived the helicopter crash and that somebody had actually come to get them out.

The man kicked out the last fragments of plexiglas with the heel of a high black lace-up boot. The window frame had been bent too narrow for him to climb inside, but he carefully eased his head in, and peered around the cabin, sniffing dryly from time to time.

'We're all trapped by our ankles,' John told him. 'The floor collapsed. We're going to need somebody to take the seats out – maybe jack them up or something. Can you be quick please? My daughter's in a pretty bad way.'

The man wiped his nose with the back of his black-gloved hand. Then he said, in a soft but rather strangled North Shore accent, 'This is Mr O'Brien's party?'

'I'm John O'Brien. This is my family. Come on, please. Get us out of here as quick as you can.'

The man peered around a little more, up at the ceiling, down at the floor. 'This is going to take cutters,' he announced, with great deliberation, like a house painter trying to decide which type of paint to use.

John said, 'Whatever it takes. Just do it.'

He could feel blood running out of the side of his mouth, and dripping on to his shirt collar. He coughed, and wished he hadn't, because it hurt, and because it filled his mouth with even more blood.

The man carefully withdrew his head from the window frame and vanished into the sunlight again. Eva tugged at John's sleeve and asked, 'What's happening? What's he doing? Can't he get us out?'

'He has to cut us out.'

'Oh God my legs hurt, John. I can't stand it. Oh God where are the paramedics.'

Dean said nothing. His eyes were glassy and his cheeks were grey. His breath came in little painful sips. They waited in agony that seemed to be endless. Where had the man gone now? What was he doing? Why wasn't he trying to get them out? And where were the rest of the firefighters, and the paramedics, where were the drips and the oxygen masks and the anaesthetics?

John closed his eyes and thought that he was probably going to die. And when he closed his eyes, he became aware of 'Mr Hillary', waiting and watching in the very, very back of his brain, like a grey beetle waiting motionless inside a hollowed-out nut, but ready to scuttle out at the slightest disturbance.

So you're here, you bastard, he thought. *You were here at the beginning, and now you're here at the end. I just hope that when I die, you'll die, too. It'll almost be worth it.*

John began to slide into unconsciousness, as if he were sliding down a grey greasy slope, into the grey greasy waters of a silent canal.

Perhaps it would be better, just to go to sleep. If he were asleep, then all the pain in his ankles would vanish, and he would be standing in front of the Supreme Court taking his oath, and everything that had happened this morning would be nothing more than a dream.

But – abruptly – the morning air was shattered by a loud, rasping roar, louder than a motorcycle starting up. Almost immediately, the man reappeared in the window and he was carrying a pair of huge shining steel pincers, like a grotesque parody of a giant parrot's beak.

'What's that?' asked John. 'What the hell's that?'

With a hiss of hydraulics, the parrot-beak slowly opened, revealing rows of serrated steel teeth. The man looked at John and smiled and said nothing. Then, with laconic expertise, he positioned the beak over the lower corner of the window frame, and twisted the hand-grip. The pincers cut right through the frame with a warping, crushed Coke-can noise. Then the man released the parrot-beak, and manhandled it further down, and twisted the hand-grip again. He cut again and again, and in less than a minute the whole side of the helicopter's fuselage was cut wide open, and the cabin was filled with wind and sunlight.

The man climbed into the cabin between them, hefting the pincers in his left hand. 'You're lucky you landed here, Mr O'Brien,' he told him. 'You're right on the tip of Sagamore Head, off Nantasket Beach. If you'd crashed just fifty feet short of here, you'd be surely drowned by now.'

John shivered, and gritted his teeth, and nodded his head. 'Is this going to take long? Get my daughter out first, then my wife.'

'Well, we'll have to see what's what,' the man told him. He gave him a slanted, uneven grin. 'But it shouldn't take long at all.'

'Please, hurry,' John begged him. Dean began to whimper, and then to cough.

'Let's just take a look at this pilot first,' the man suggested. He lowered his head and made his way through to the cockpit, trailing his hydraulic line after him. He peered into Frank's face, and patted his cheeks.

'Still alive,' he announced. 'Not for long, though, and he must be suffering something terrible. Tch, tch, you should see his legs, Mr O'Brien. Crushed all to mush.'

The man looked at Frank reflectively for a moment or two. Behind those tiny dark glasses, it was impossible for John to guess what he might be thinking.

'Hate to see anybody suffer,' he said, at last. 'What about you, Mr O'Brien? Don't you hate to see people suffer?'

John's vision was blotchy with scarlet and grey. He

nodded in jerky agreement. Anything to get it over with. Anything to get Eva and Sissy out of here.

'Well, then,' said the man. He lifted up the parrot-beak pincers and carefully positioned them on either side of Frank's red-and-white bonedome.

'Look at that for luck,' he said. 'Almost a perfect fit. These cutting-blades have an opening of 267 millimetres and this helmet must be no more than 263.'

John stared at him. He found it difficult to focus. 'What are you doing?' he demanded, through a crackling mouthful of blood.

'Did you ever hear of putting people out of their misery?' the man wanted to know. 'Come on, now, you're a lawyer; one of the very best. You should know all about mercy. Like, "the quality of mercy is not strained, it droppeth like a gentle rain from heaven." '

'What the hell are you doing?' John bellowed at him. He could hear scores of sirens now, and they were very much closer, and they gave him renewed hope that they were all going to get out of here alive. He just couldn't understand this casually-spoken eccentric with his dark glasses and his giant parrot-beak cutter.

The man lifted up the cutter as if he had read John's thoughts. 'This here is a Holmatro 2009 U heavy-duty cutter for general rescue tasks,' he explained, as if he were telling a small boy how a choo-choo train worked. 'It can cut through 25-millimetre round steel bar, or heavy metal plates, or metal strips 100 by 10. It's Dutch by make, but firefighters use them all around the world, because it's the best. The Jaws of Life, that's what the rescue squad calls this cutter. What's going to interest you most of all, though, is that these here blades have a cutting force of – well, guess how much?'

'For Christ's sake get us out,' said John. He could see that

Sissy's eyelids were beginning to flutter, and he prayed that she wouldn't regain consciousness and feel the pain.

'Thirty tons,' the man grinned, in triumph. '*Thirty frigging tons.*'

'What?' asked John, blurrily.

'All I have to do is twist this handle and this poor suffering man will find out what it's like, for instance, to have a thirty-ton truck run over his head.'

'For the love of God stop it!' John wept. He had no more fight left, no more strength left.

The man raised his head and listened to the wind and the ocean and the approaching sirens. 'You're right,' he said. 'I'm being dilatory, aren't I?' Then, quite matter-of-factly he twisted the cutter's hand-grip, and John saw the hydraulic lines stiffen. The thick steel parrot-beak blades closed without any hesitation at all on Frank's helmet and there was a high, brittle crack. The entire contents of Frank's head were flung at the helicopter's control panel like a sloppy handful of fish guts being thrown into a sink. John only glimpsed them for a split second before they dropped out of sight, but in that split second he saw white glistening brain tissue and clumps of bloody muscle and fragments of lower jaw, all webbed together with stringy membranes.

The man paused, and then released the cutting-blades, leaving Frank's helmet in an odd broken oval, like two dinner plates pressed together. He patted Frank on the shoulder and said, 'Come on, man. No need to go around with your face on the floor.' Then he uttered a high, asthmatic wheeze – which, even in his agony, John could interpret as a laugh.

The man clambered back into the passenger cabin. He looked from Dean to Eva to Sissy and then at John.

John whispered, 'Listen, you can have anything you want.

You can have as much money as you care to name. A million dollars. I'm wealthy, I have plenty of stocks. I won't identify you and I won't tell anybody what happened.'

The man sniffed. 'You're missing the point, Mr O'Brien.'

'Well, what is the goddamned point?'

'You don't know what the goddamned point is? Why don't you try to think about it. You're a man of intellect.' He tapped his forehead with his finger. 'You've got what it takes upstairs. Meanwhile – while you're deliberating – let's get on with it.'

He pushed in between them until he was hunched over Dean. John tried feebly to snatch at the man's black raincoat, but without warning the man whipped around and slapped John a loose-fingered backhander across the side of the head. John stayed where he was, almost blind with pain.

The man turned back to Dean. 'Come on now, friend,' the man said, 'we're going to cut your legs free. Everything's going to be fine.'

Dean stared up at him, puzzled. Because he was seated with his back to the pilot's cockpit, he hadn't been able to see what the man had done to Frank.

The man opened the parrot-beak cutting blades and fitted them either side of Dean's right thigh, snug up against his waistcoat. He grinned directly into Dean's face and Dean grinned back. *My God*, thought John. *He's going to cut his entire right leg off.*

Dean reached up and laid his hand on the man's shoulder. 'My legs hurt,' he whispered.

'Not for very much longer, I promise you,' the man reassured him, and twisted the cutter's handle. With a soft crunch, thirty tons of hydraulic cutting force went through Dean's right leg. The man opened the blades, and lifted the cutters away.

Dean's system was so shocked that he didn't understand what had happened at first. After all, he was still sitting in his seat, and his leg was still there, right in front of him, even though his beige linen trousers were suddenly flooded with blood. He stared up at the man with his mouth open and stuttered, 'What? *What?*'

But the man simply smiled, and fitted the cutting blades over Dean's left thigh, and twisted, and cut through skin and muscle and bone with no more effort than cutting cheese and crackers.

Dean screamed. But the man slapped his face and said, 'What're you screaming for? You're free to go. Just jump down off of that seat, and away you go.'

With that, he gave Dean a hefty open-handed push, and Dean toppled off the seat with his two bloody leg stumps thrashing in the air like somebody juggling with two fresh-cut joints of beef. Blood pumped everywhere; two thick arterial sprays that jetted in all directions as Dean writhed and struggled and screamed on the cabin floor, a Dean who was nothing more than a human trunk with flailing arms, while his severed legs remained neatly side by side in his blood-filled seat.

The man kicked Dean away. Dean's head was partly wedged underneath the seat, next to his own shoes, and he lay there quivering and twitching and dying right in front of John's eyes. Then, slowly, the man turned around to Eva. Eva was silent now, but John was holding her hand and he could feel her quaking – literally quaking, from head to foot.

'Don't kill me,' she asked.

The man shook his head. 'If you want me to, I'll pray for your soul. But that's as conciliatory as I'm prepared to be.'

John was openly sobbing now. He couldn't stop himself. 'Don't touch her, please! I love her, don't touch her.'

But the man said, 'I have to find out what ladies like you are made of, don't you see?'

He opened up the parrot-beak cutters as wide as they would stretch. Then he forced the lower blade deep between Eva's legs, waggling it obscenely from side to side to make sure that it thrust in as far as possible. The blades had teeth on both their inside and outside edges, and they ripped her skirt and tore her stockings and snagged the leather seat. The tip of the upper blade the man pressed into Eva's primrose-yellow jacket, just below her ribcage.

Eva clutched John's hand in a spasm of terror. She was so frightened that she couldn't even scream. John stared at the man and said, in the deadliest, most threatening voice he could manage, 'Whoever you are – I'm warning you now – if you so much as – '

But that was all he could manage. He knew the man was going to do it, whatever he said. Any threat was pointless. Any plea for mercy would only add humiliation to what was already a total nightmare. The man gave John the faintest smirk of mock regret. Then he twisted the cutter's handle and the blades disappeared into Eva's stomach, chopping her pelvic floor in half and slicing open her stomach like a crimson carpetbag. Greasy intestines slithered into Eva's lap, but all she could do was stare at them in utter horror, bewildered that this was what she actually looked like inside.

John couldn't speak, couldn't bring himself to look. His brain felt as if it were slowly imploding. But he was still clutching Eva's hand, and Eva was still clutching his. He felt every shudder and every twitch as the man began to work with his cutters with terrible swiftness. John heard him breathing harshly through his mouth as he lifted the parrot-beak higher, and cut through Eva's breastbone. He opened up her ribcage and John heard her gasp, and couldn't stop himself

26

from looking. Her lungs, bloodied and inflated with her last desperate breath, swung in her chest cavity like inflated hot-water bottles swinging on the back of a closet door.

Then the man dug the parrot-beak into the dark and bloody tunnel of her windpipe, and cut into her neck, and then split her jaw. Finally, he positioned the lower cutting-blade under Eva's palate, and the upper blade on the top of her head, in the parting of her hair, and with a single carefully-calculated crunch, he cut her head completely in half. Her hand was limp now, and John, at last, had to let it go. He couldn't look at her, couldn't, but he heard the glutinous noise of her halved skull falling apart, and he couldn't help breathing in the gassy, gunpowdery smell of human insides.

The man stepped right in front of him now, and said, 'Look at me!'

John looked up at him, his eyes wincing and flickering like a dog expecting a whipping.

'Just get it over with,' he whispered.

'You still don't get the point, do you?' the man asked him. 'What you've seen here this morning is a man who thought he was extra smart, a real achiever. But how smart can anybody be when you cut the legs from under him? What you saw here was a lady who thought she was rich and beautiful and superior and something special – but you look inside and what do you see? Blood, guts, liver and general mess. Same as everybody else. They've made you a judge of men, Mr O'Brien. They've given you control of millions of lives, millions of human destinies. And do you know something? I think you would make a fine Supreme Court judge; honest and selfless and fair. But now I'm going to see how honest and selfless and fair you really are.'

'What do you mean?' John asked miserably, bubbling blood.

The man leaned over, so that his pale pitted face filled all of John's pain-fogged vision. John could almost believe that if the man put his face any nearer, his soul would disappear inside the bottomless black holes of his sunglasses. The man said, softly, 'You can hear for yourself ... the police and the paramedics and the fire department, they're almost here. So I only have the time to deal with one of you now ... you, or your daughter.'

'I don't ... understand.' In actual fact, he did understand, but he couldn't bear it.

'Then pay attention, Mr O'Brien. I'm asking you to make a judgement. That's your job, isn't it, making judgements? I only have the time to deal with one of you, so one of you is going to die and one of you is going to live. You have to make up your mind which.'

John coughed blood. 'You goddamned maniac. You scum. If you lay one finger on my daughter ...'

'Tch, tch, tch. That's not the point, Mr O'Brien. We're making a comparison between the wildly disparate values of human lives here. We're not all equal, you know. Let's put it this way: if you survive, and you go to the Supreme Court, you're going to affect the life of everybody in the United States, not only now, but for centuries to come. You're going to affect *history*.

'On the other hand, if you die and your daughter survives, what's she going to do? Party till she drops on her old man's inheritance? Do some expensive drugs? Marry some rich dweeb from Newport and have herself some little dweebs to whom grandpa is only a gravestone?'

He paused, and slowly smiled that carnivorous smile. 'It's all down to you, Your Honour. The choice is yours. But you'd better make it quick, or I'll be forced to make it for you.'

For one catastrophic moment, John was actually tempted

by the man's argument. If he were to die, then every radical idea that he had ever dreamed of would die with him. There were social and legal injustices in America that were crying out for reform. On every level of public life there was prejudice, discrimination, corruption and brutality. The First Amendment was being strangled by bigotry and political dogma and intolerance, and the only way in which a man could say his piece to the nation was by buying millions of dollars of airtime.

He could make a difference. Only one difference in nine, perhaps; but a difference. Whereas what would Sissy do, if she were the one to survive? The man was chillingly perceptive. She would party all his money away; and the house and the family inheritance and the library that smelled like justice would be sold and scattered and dismantled.

It took John a splinter of a second to think this thought. But – like the splinter of shattered mirror in *The Snow Queen*, which flew into a young boy's eye and perverted everything he saw – it made him almost mad with shame. Sissy was his daughter. Sissy was his child. She looked so much like Eva. Yet what had he done? In the very last moment of his life he had betrayed her.

'Take me,' he said, in a thick, slurred voice.

'What?' asked the man. The sirens were very close now, and the wind was getting up.

'Take *me*,' he repeated.

'Your choice, Your Honour,' the man replied.

He came around to the side of John's seat, placed his right hand between John's shoulder blades, and pushed John forward, so that his face was pressed between his knees. Then he positioned the parrot-beak cutting-blades on either side of John's neck.

John tried to think of nothing at all. He couldn't think of a prayer. He saw in nitpicking detail the helicopter's

29

grey-flecked carpet, with a shiny black blob of chewing gum on it, and the dark rococo patterns of Dean's arterial blood. He felt the metallic teeth of the cutting-blades pinching his skin, but they were more of an irritation than anything else. He saw the shadow of a cloud crossing the carpet, or perhaps it was smoke.

Then he heard a hydraulic hiss; and his whole being detonated into blinding white pain white white white – and he heard, he actually *heard* his own head tumbling on to the floor.

But he didn't hear the parrot-beak snapping its way through the aluminum supports of Sissy's seat. Neither did he hear the man clambering out of the helicopter; and the whooping sirens and shouts that quickly followed.

Nor did he hear the softly-rumbling *whoomph* of kerosene catching fire, as the helicopter exploded in a huge balloon of flame.

Two

There was a cautious knock at the den door and Michael instantly flung away his copy of *Mushing* magazine and vaulted off the leather couch. By the time Jason opened the door and came inside, he was sitting at his desk in front of the window, his head resting on his hand, scribbling on a legal-size pad as if he had been scribbling for hours.

He kept on while Jason approached his desk. Jason trod softly because he knew Dad was busy and didn't like to have his train of thought interrupted. Jason was thirteen, skinny and gentle and tall for his age. His blond hair was cropped like a scrubbing brush. He wore black-framed Clark Kent

30

spectacles which made his ears stick out, but he had the most arresting blue eyes, clear as two lakes, and a lovely dry sense of humour. He wore a T-shirt with the red-lettered slogan Dyslexia Lures OK.

Michael swung around in his battered green leather captain's chair and said, with exaggerated patience, 'Yes, Jason, what's the problem?'

'There's a guy outside wants to see you,' said Jason.

'A guy, hunh?' Michael inquired. 'Did he say what he wanted?'

Jason shrugged. 'He just said, "Is Mr Rearden home?" '

Michael leaned back in his chair and tapped his front teeth with his Pilot pen. 'He didn't mention Games Company?'

'Unh-hunh.'

'I'm expecting somebody from Games Company. You see all this stuff on this desk? All these hundreds of little pieces of paper? This is it, this is my latest money-spinner. Project X.'

Jason glanced out of the corner of his eye at the heaps and heaps of notelets and Post-its and newspaper cuttings and legal sheets and torn-out magazine articles, all of them softly ruffling in the breeze that poured softly through the half-open window.

'You're going to start recycling paper?' he suggested.

Michael swung out his arm and gave him a feinted cuff around the ear. 'Recycling paper! Smartass!'

He swung around again, and picked up his pad. 'This, my friend, is the first major new question-and-answer game since Trivial Pursuit. This is going to make millions. No, I tell a lie, billions. In years to come, they're going to talk about this game in the same breath as Monopoly and Scrabble. That's when you and I are living in luxury in Palm Beach, with power-boats and Lamborghinis and all the babes we can handle. Well, all the babes *you* can handle. I'm quite happy with your mom.'

Jason gravely regarded the mess and said, 'It looks kind of complicated.'

Michael pulled a face. 'Oh, for sure. *Now* it looks complicated. But think about it. Before they put a clock together, it looks kind of complicated, doesn't it? All those little cogs and stuff. But by the time I've finished – ' he shuffled some more papers into order ' – well, it'll be less complicated.'

'The guy said he really had to see you.'

'Oh, the guy. Did he tell you what his name was?'

'Rocky Woods, I think.'

Michael looked up at him with a grave face. 'Rocky Woods? Is that what he said?'

'His exact words were, "I have to see your father. Ask him if he remembers Rocky Woods." '

Michael covered his mouth with his hand for a moment, and said nothing. Only his eyes betrayed what he was thinking. They were darting quickly from side to side as if he were reading from an autocue, or vividly remembering something that had upset him, in more detail than most people care to.

'Dad?' asked Jason. 'Did I do right? Do you want me to tell him to go away?'

But Michael reached out and took hold of Jason's wrist, and squeezed it, and tried to smile, and said, 'You did fine. How about asking him in?'

'Okay, if you say so.'

When Jason had gone running off, leaving the door ajar, Michael stood up and walked around his desk to the window. His den was not much more than a run-down conservatory on stilts, overlooking the grassy dunes of New Seabury beach, and the permanently blue waters of Nantucket Sound. The rest of the house was just as spartan – a three-bedroomed summer cottage that he had bought from a friend at Plymouth Insurance. It was all bare scrubbed boards and Quaker furniture and Indian-style rugs. When he had brought his family down from Boston to see how Michael was getting along, his friend had joked that it was like spending the weekend with the Pilgrim Fathers – 'all succotash and pumpkin pie and how are we going to survive the winter?'

Michael was a lean, hawkish-nosed man of thirty-four, with mousy, short-cropped hair and eyes that were blue and opaque, where his son's were blue and clear. He was handsome in the way that Jimmy Dean had been handsome; or the young Clint Eastwood; a little too drawn-looking and slightly deranged and hurt in the way he looked at people. In his blue check short-sleeved shirt, his wrists looked knobbly and treble-jointed, and his khaki hiking shorts didn't too much for his gangly legs. His movements were hesitant and shy, and occasionally almost effeminate. But there was no doubting his masculinity. Apart from the fact that he had courted and married the cutest girl at Plymouth Insurance, his interests in life were classically male: fishing, baseball, drinking beer and tinkering with things.

His greatest passion was what he called 'downwind thinking' – which meant solving problems by approaching them from downwind and jumping on them when they least suspected it. Since they had moved to New Seabury over a year and a half ago, he had invented a self-releasing weight for casting fishing lines to record distances, and converted Patsy's electro-exercising machine into a device for removing barnacles and limpets and other shellfish from the bottom of yachts. In the same way that the exercising machine caused human muscles to contract, the 'Limpet-Zapper' put the bivalves' whole bodies into spasm, so that they literally jumped off the hull.

33

But two moderately successful inventions hadn't generated anything like enough income to keep Patsy in pantihose or Jason in Adidas, and they were still living like the Pilgrim Fathers, except it was meat loaf instead of succotash and Jell-O instead of pumpkin pie and how are we going to survive until the end of the month, don't even think about the winter.

He watched the cloud shadows sailing across the sands. They reminded him of giant stingrays, gliding swiftly and silently across the floor of the ocean. He saw three children flying a red box kite, and a woman in a pink swimsuit and a huge pink hat, walking a brown-and-white spaniel. If only you could capture this scene, exactly as it was, and hang it on your wall, complete with wind and movement and sound, and the net curtains stirring at the window. He smiled to himself and realized that he had just invented television.

There was no knock at the door; but he heard it swing open a little more. He turned around and there was Joe Garboden, same as ever, in a mauve-and-green-and-cerise-and-yellow-striped blazer that looked as if it had been rejected by the Mambo Kings for being too showy. Joe was large-headed, with thick black greasy hair, and cheeks with the texture of cauliflower. His eyes were deep set and glittery, but kindly, and he smiled a whole lot – more than the average, anyway – which was what made him one of most acceptable bearers of bad news that Michael had ever known.

'Hallo, Joe,' he said, keeping his hands buried in the pockets of his hiking shorts.

Joe came and stood next to him, one hand extended. He waited; and waited; and in the end he said, 'What's the matter, Michael, playing with your dinkle more important than greeting an old colleague?'

Michael reluctantly took out his hand and shook it. Joe smiled, and then stared at the palm of his hand and said, 'I hope you *weren't* playing with your dinkle.'

'I'm not going blind, am I?' Michael retorted.

'That's only because you're not doing it right.'

Joe dropped his greasy Panama hat on to the desk, right on top of Michael's legal pad, and then he stepped right up to the window and admired the view. 'Beautiful day, isn't it? This house is heaven in summer. What's it like in mid-winter? Hell, I'll bet. How do you heat it?'

'Blankets.'

'Blankets?'

'That's right. From Thanksgiving evening to Memorial Day morning we stay in bed.'

'Hey, good deal. Especially with Patsy, if you don't mind my saying so. She still looks like everything a man ever dreamed about.'

'Oh … you saw her?'

'Sure, we talked. She's out in the yard, washing the car. Or … what shall I say? … washing the bits that hold the rust together.'

'What brings you all the way down here?' Michael asked him. 'You didn't come to show me that coat, I hope.'

Joe said, 'Mind if I park my ass?' and eased himself down on the leather couch. He picked up Michael's magazine and frowned at the cover. '*Mushing*?' he asked, in disbelief.

Michael said, 'Mushing … you know, training huskies to pull sledges, skijoring, that kind of thing. Mush! Mush!'

'People do a lot of that around here?' asked Joe, straightfaced.

'Forget it, Joe – it's just an idea I've been working on.'

'All right,' said Joe. He took out a crumpled handkerchief and wiped his forehead. 'I guess I'd better tell you why I've come.'

'You mentioned Rocky Woods. My kid thought that was your name.'

'I'm sorry. That's not a name to make jokes about it, is it?'

Michael didn't answer, but turned away, and watched the box kite ducking and weaving over the shoreline. He could guess, approximately, what Joe was going to ask him, and he wasn't sure that he wanted to look at his face when he did.

Joe said, 'You heard about John O'Brien, of course. The Supreme Court justice-to-be.'

'Of course. Who didn't? Pretty average luck, hunh? The Lord didn't mind giving it to him, but the Lord sure made sure he took it all back, in spades.'

'That helicopter was insured by us at Plymouth, and underwritten by Tyrell & Croteau. It was actually owned and run by Revere Aeronautic Services, but that day it was out on charter to the Justice Department.'

'I heard on TV that it was engine failure.'

'That's what you heard on TV.'

'You mean it wasn't engine failure?'

'I mean that's what you heard on TV. Engine failure was part of the story, for sure. Engine failure was probably the principal cause of the chopper coming down – although we still don't know *why* the engines failed, or even how, or whether it could have been sabotage. But it's what happened after it came down that's really making our heads hurt.'

'It burned, didn't it? Helicopters loaded with two hundred gallons of aviation-grade kerosene do have a tendency to burn.'

'This one didn't ignite until nine and a half minutes after impact.'

'Nobody got to the wreck for nine and a half minutes?'

'That's the mystery. The *rescue services* didn't get out to the wreck for nine and a half minutes. It was way out on the end of Sagamore Head, out on the sand – and, more than that, somebody had abandoned a beaten-up Winnebago on the track from Nantasket Beach, and it took the fire department more than five minutes just to clear *that* away.'

He folded up his handkerchief and dabbed at his forehead again. 'However ... *somebody* got out to the wreck before it exploded. Several yachtspersons reported seeing a black Chevy Blazer or similar-type vehicle parked alongside the wreckage, maybe two or three minutes after impact. One guy had actually anchored his yacht about two hundred feet off the head and was paddling ashore in his dinghy to see if he could help. He says he clearly saw a black four-wheel-drive vehicle and also a person dressed in a black coat emerging from the wreck, carrying something that could have been a bag or a sack. About twenty seconds later, the helicopter exploded and there was so much smoke and flame that he couldn't see anything more. By the time he reached the shore the vehicle had gone and the helicopter was almost totally burned out.'

Michael massaged his temples with his fingertips, like a man who feels a migraine coming on. 'So what you're telling me is, a person or persons unknown reached the helicopter ahead of the rescue services, and removed something from the wreck?'

'That's exactly what I'm telling you. Exactly.'

Michael stayed thoughtfully silent for a while. Joe watched him and mopped sweat and occasionally cleared his throat.

'Who's handling this case?'

'Kevin Murray and some new guy, Rolbein.'

'Kevin's good,' said Michael. 'He'll solve it for you.'

'Kevin's good, yes. But Kevin's not inspirational.'

Michael turned back to him. 'And that's why you've

driven all the way down here to Noplace-on-Sea to see me? To get some free inspiration?'

Joe spread his hands wide. 'I admit it.' The armpits of his striped coat were stained with semicircles of sweat. 'Aren't I a shit?'

'Nothing changes,' said Michael.

'Well, sure, Michael. But look at it from my point of view. There are hundreds of millions of dollars involved in this claim. You should see the size of John O'Brien's life insurance policy alone – it's twice the national reserves of Haiti and Dominica put together, and you can throw in Cuba's for luck. Then there's Eva O'Brien's life insurance policy and their daughter Sissy's life insurance policy; not to mention all the contingent claims for losses and damages and negligence.'

He blew his nose loudly. 'All this wouldn't be so bad if everything was straightforward, cut-and-dried. But this whole business has a very suspicious smell about it. You know what's it like when you're checking out a claim on a burned-out apartment building, and you think you can just detect the faintest whiff of gasoline, or paint-thinner, or methylated spirit? It's that kind of a smell. And there are too many weird inconsistencies. Not the kind of normal inconsistencies you get in everyday life; but inconsistencies that make you think ... now hold on, how could *that* be?'

'Give me a for-instance.'

'Well, think about it. The helicopter has engine failure, crash-lands on Nantasket Beach, and there's somebody apparently waiting for it to crash-land. If the engine failure is genuine, how does this somebody know exactly where the helicopter is going to come down?'

'Sounds like you've got yourself some kind of a problem,' said Michael, sitting down on his revolving chair, and swinging from side to side.

'Don't tell me. And I'm being pressured for a quick result. Henry Croteau is on my case seventeen times a day. And our beloved president Edgar Bedford is on my case *seventy* times a day.'

'How about the police? Are they co-operating?'

'There's another weirdness. When Commissioner Hudson first talked to the media, he promised a "full, frank and fearless investigation". But so far, the police seem to be treating the whole case with about as much seriousness as if GI Joe fell out of his plastic Huey.'

'The FAA?'

'Zip. They refuse to release even their preliminary findings. They say they have to piece the whole wreck back together again before they can come up with any whys or wherefors whatsoever. I'll tell you how cagey they're acting. They won't even admit that they *have* any preliminary findings.'

'Who's handling the reconstruction?'

'Your old buddy Jorge da Silva.'

'Really? It's not like Jorge to be cagey. How about the coroner's office?'

'Same thing.' Joe pretended to tug a zipper across his mouth. 'All that the coroner is prepared to tell us so far – and I more-or-less quote – is that "the O'Brien party was involved in a fatal helicopter incident and there were no apparent survivors." '

Michael thought for a moment, and then he said, ' "The O'Brien party". How many people was that, exactly?'

'You tell me,' Joe replied, with a gleam in his eyes. 'The plain fact is that nobody's saying. In that particular helicopter, it could have been three, it could have been anything up to eight. And what the hell is an "apparent survivor"? There's nothing apparent about surviving, not in my book. If I ever find myself in a helicopter crash, God forbid, I don't

39

want to *apparently* survive. I want to be right there on NBC evening news, live and kicking, with a smut on my snout and a Bandaid on my forehead, praising the skill and courage of the pilot.'

Michael asked, 'So nobody has yet officially confirmed the number of dead?'

'Got it in one. You know what they told me? "Physical trauma was so severe that full identification is still pending." Pending my ass. You and I were up at Rocky Woods, and there wasn't any pending up at Rocky Woods. If you wanted to know how many bodies you had, you counted heads, just like we did, whether those heads were attached to anything or not.'

Michael said, thoughtfully, 'There was John O'Brien, right? And his wife Eva O'Brien. And their daughter, am I correct?'

'That's right, Sissy O'Brien, fourteen years old.'

Michael was counting on his fingers. 'There was also a pilot, of course. Any co-pilot?'

'Unh-hunh. But there was a young hotshot from the Justice Department, Dean McAllister. He flew up from Washington the previous night so that he could escort Mr O'Brien back for the swearing-in ceremony.'

'So, five. That shouldn't have been too difficult to work out, even after a fire. Who's the medical examiner?'

'Raymond Moorpath at Boston Central.'

'Moorpath? He's in private practice these days.'

'All the same, that's where the bodies were taken, and Moorpath's doing the honours. Special request from very, very, *very* high up. But you can't deny that Moorpath was always the best, especially with fire fatalities. Good with floaters, too.'

Michael thought for a while. Then he said, 'You want a beer?'

Joe shrugged. 'So long as you're having one.'

'Come on through to the kitchen.'

They left the studio. A sudden gust of wind blew a small blizzard of paper off Michael's desk. The door banged behind them and they walked Indian-file along the narrow wooden bridge that led to the kitchen door, their feet making hollow noises on the planking. To their left, there was nothing but the grassy beach and the glittering sea. To their right, a steep flight of sunbleached steps led down to the sloping concrete front yard, where Patsy was hosing down their faded green Mercury Marquis, '69 vintage, and Jason was watching her, perched on the cinderblock wall, swinging his legs. Patsy looked up and waved and Michael waved back, and cheerfully called out, 'How's the carwash, honey?' At the same time, however, he gave her the subtlest twitch of his head and bugged out his eyes, to tell her that he didn't appreciate Joe's presence here at all.

Patsy smiled and carried on hosing. Michael had never felt so close to anybody in his entire life, man or woman. He and Patsy laughed together; worried together; they practically breathed in and out together. He loved her, but the way they lived together day by day was very much more complicated than anything that he had ever called love before. It was complete physical and emotional and intellectual entanglement.

Patsy was only a hair's-breadth taller than five-feet-two, with a shaggy carefree mane of sunbleached hair, and a sweet doll-like face, with china-blue eyes and a snubby nose and plump pink lips. Today she was wearing a tight pink-and-white striped T-shirt, which exaggerated her chubby breasts, and the tiniest pair of white cotton shorts, and fluorescent pink rubber boots.

The president of Plymouth Insurance Edgar Bedford had once disparagingly called her 'Michael's bimbo'. But

41

in spite of her Barbie doll looks, Patsy was educated and funny and determined: and it was those qualities with which Michael had really fallen in love. Of course she was eye-catching and of course she was sexually exciting, and he loved that, too. But she could hold her own in any dinner-party conversation about Mozart or Matisse or Guy de Maupassant; or the Big Bang theory; or politics and censorship; or rock'n'roll; or the ordination of women; or whether the earth was really warming up or not.

Michael and Joe went into the kitchen with its plain scrubbed table and its big old-fashioned sink and its tinkling ceramic mobiles of swans and yachts and vegetables. Michael opened the icebox and took out two bottles of Michelob, tossing one over to Joe. Then he sat astride a chair and unscrewed the cap of his beer and took a quick, uptilted swig.

'It definitely sounds like somebody's trying to cover something up,' he said. 'The question of course is what, and whether it's meaningful in terms of any insurance claim.'

Joe said, 'John O'Brien's policy covers accidental death only. It specifically excludes suicide or homicide.'

'And how much exactly is it worth?'

'Two hundred and seventy-eight million dollars and change.'

'So it's obviously in Plymouth's interest to show that he was killed deliberately, or that he planned his own death?'

Joe swallowed beer and wiped his mouth with the back of his hand. 'Not to put too fine a point on it, yes.'

Michael thought for a while, taking regular swigs from the bottle. Then he looked up at Joe and said, 'Good luck, then.'

'You realize that I'm asking you to get involved,' said Joe.

'Joe – I quit. I don't *want* to get involved. Patsy and I dropped out and we're perfectly happy the way we are.'

Joe said blandly, 'You have a bank overdraft of 6,358

dollars and no prospect of any more money until the end of October, when your next royalty is due from Marine Developments, Inc., which I can advise you in advance will be something less than 1,500 dollars.'

Michael stared at him. 'How the hell did you find that out?'

'Oh, come on, Michael, you know the routine. You don't go duck hunting without a gun, do you?'

Michael knew what Joe was talking about. It was standard practice for insurance claims investigators to check into bank accounts and credit ratings and confidential medical reports. Unlike the police, they didn't have to be so particular about search warrants or the rules of evidence. During his nine-year career with Plymouth Insurance, Michael had regularly paid off bank officials to let him take a look at private bank statements. But now that he was a victim, he felt exposed and angry, and humiliated that Joe had found out how broke they were.

'Listen,' he said, 'you had no damned right to do that, no right at all.'

'I'm sorry,' said Joe, although he didn't sound sorry in the slightest. 'But, you know, if you'd been flush, it probably would have been a waste of my time driving all the way down here.'

Michael said, 'Believe me, it *was* a waste of your time, and mine too. I may need money but I don't need it that bad.'

'Michael … I'm making a special effort to be nice here. You think I would have come down here for nothing? I hate the beach. All that sea. All that fucking sand. Look – it's a one-off job. You go in, you sort it out, you collect your money and you go home. That's all I'm asking.' He paused to see what kind of an impression he had made, and then he crossed himself and added, 'It'll be the first and last time, I promise. You have my personal guarantee.'

Michael said, 'Joe, you must have half-a-dozen guys who

are easily as good as I ever was. Not only that, I've been out of it for nearly two years. Most of my contacts have moved away, or died, or been promoted. My Filofax is a museum-piece these days. Half the numbers ring and ring and nobody answers.'

Joe swallowed beer and drummed his podgy fingers on the deal tabletop and looked out of the window. He cleared his throat. It was obvious that he had something on his mind, but he wasn't going to say what it was, not without coaxing, anyway. At last, Michael said, 'There's something else, isn't there? Something you're not telling me?'

A raised eyebrow. 'What do you mean?'

'Don't screw me around, Joe, you and I go back way too far.'

'All right, yes,' Joe admitted. 'There's something I'm not telling you.'

'Well? What is it?'

'It's grade-one confidential. I got it right from the tippety-top. I had to swear that I wouldn't tell you what it was unless and until you agreed to take over the O'Brien investigation.'

'If you told me now, do you think that it would change my mind?'

'Without a doubt.'

'So what's the problem? You don't trust me, or what? I mean, who do you think I'm going to tell?'

'Michael, Michael … of course I trust you. But, you know, even beaches have ears. If I were to tell you, and you still didn't agree to work on this investigation, and somehow this particular piece of information leaked out, then they'd hang my ass out to dry. And we're not just talking repri-mands. We're talking ass jerky.'

Michael stood up. Joe watched him without blinking as he circled around the table. 'I'm sorry, Joe,' Michael told him. 'I don't want to sound unappreciative, or anything like that. I mean, thank you for thinking of me. But, as far as I'm concerned, Rocky Woods was it. That was the finish. I'd rather be 6,358 dollars overdrawn in heaven than have an expense account in hell.'

Joe was relentless. 'I'll pay you 25,000 and one half of one per cent of whatever you save us. Twelve-and-a-half thousand upfront, now, in whatever currency you care to name. Roubles, zlotys – Zambian kwachas, if you like, they're about 2.16 to the US dollar.'

'Joe … I said no.'

'Tell me at least that you want to think it over.' Joe's face was a mask of glistening sweat.

'I don't want to think it over. The answer is no. There isn't anything that you can say or do that will make me change my mind.'

'Thirty thousand, with 15,000 upfront? And I mean 15,000 here and now, cash in your hand, no more debts, no more worries, and I'll take you all out to the Lobster Shack to celebrate.'

Michael emphatically shook his head. All the same, he had to admit that he was very tempted. He and Patsy had struggled so hard since he had quit his job and moved down here, and yet all they had managed to do was to become poorer and shabbier. Recently he had been plagued every morning when he woke up by the most disturbing of self-doubts. What was he really trying to achieve, drinking beer and dreaming dreams, the owner of very little more than a tacky, tatty seashore vacation home, two pairs of jeans and a rusting Mercury with an oil haemorrhage? He knew in his heart that he would never have the drive to finish and market his board game, not the way in which Horne and Abbott had striven to develop Trivial Pursuit. He would probably never mush across the ice to reach the magnetic

North Pole, either. He would probably never achieve anything of any significance; and he would probably die more
broke than he was now.

But the memory of Rocky Woods was bloody and dark
and pungent, like a childhood nightmare that comes loping
after you even during the hours of daylight. He couldn't
even trust himself to think about it in a downwind way.
Rocky Woods had been Hades on earth; the massacre of the
innocents; fire and brimstone and buckets of blood. On
March 17 two years ago, at 5:05 in the evening, an L10-11
of Midwest Airlines had exploded over Westwood, south-
west of Boston, three minutes after taking off from Logan
International. The fuselage had split longitudinally, and
312 men, women and children had fallen 2,500 feet into
the Rocky Woods Reservation.

For over a minute and a half, it had literally rained
people.

Joe and Michael had been assigned by Plymouth Insurance to investigate the cause of the crash. They had spent
all night and most of the next day following the ambulance
teams from one body to another, counting them and identifying them and marking their positions. Michael had
come across a birch tree that appeared from a distance to
be blossoming. It was only when he approached it that he
realized it was blossoming with human hands.

He hadn't slept properly for more than six weeks afterwards. Then one morning he had put down his phone in
the middle of a conversation with the Boston Fire Department about melting-points, walked out of the offices, and
never gone back. At first, Edgar Bedford had wanted to sue
him for breach of contract, but Joe had showed Edgar
Bedford some of the worst photographs of Rocky Woods
and that had persuaded him (grudgingly) to go easy.

Even now, eighteen months later, Michael still dreamed

of making his way through those dark and smoky woods, with flashlights criss-crossing everywhere, and helicopters roaring overhead. He still dreamed of the little girl he had found, sitting under a tree with her eyes open, as if she were still alive. He had actually shouted out, 'There's one alive here!' even as he realized that it was impossible for anyone to have survived a free fall from 2,500 feet, and that what he was looking at, in fact, was only half a girl, from the waist upward. She was still holding a blue Grover doll from *Sesame Street*, and her hair was fine and blonde like corn-silk.

More than anything else, the memory of that little girl meant that he could never go back to his old job. He had even found out her name and address: Sarah-May Williams, from Alsace Drive, Indiana, aged four. Both her parents had died, too.

Between them, he and Joe had looked at every one of the victims – all except for one, a sixteen-year-old girl called Elaine Parker. They had found her purse and her luggage and one of her shoes, but Elaine Parker had vanished for ever into Rocky Woods, as if she had never even lived.

Joe said, 'Give me a break, will you, Michael? Tell me you'll think it over.'

'I'm sorry, Joe. I don't have to.'

'Not even for old times' sake?'

At that moment, the kitchen door opened, and Patsy came in, flushed and hot, carrying an empty plastic pail. 'That's all done,' she said. Then, 'Not even *what* for old times' sake?'

'Not even nothing for old times' sake,' said Michael, putting his arm around her shoulders. 'Joe and I were just catching up on some memories.'

'He told me outside that he had an interesting proposi-tion to put to you,' said Patsy. She drew back the gingham

47

curtain under the sink and put away the pail. Then she sat down and stuck out her left leg so that Michael could pull off her pink rubber boot. He put his hand under the heel and tugged it off. Patsy wiggled her toes. 'My feet are all sweaty now. Was it anything good?'

Michael shook his head. 'Joe just thought that I might be able to help him out.'

'What with? Come on, Michael, we could use a little more money right now, couldn't we? Jason needs some new sweatshirts, and if we don't have the car serviced soon, it's going to give up the ghost for good.'

'Attagirl,' said Joe, lifting his beer bottle in salute. 'That's telling him.'

'I don't want to do it, that's all,' said Michael, defensively.

'Well, what is it? It can't be all *that* unpalatable, can it?'

'Look,' said Michael, 'I gave up insurance work because I didn't want to do it any more. I'm finished with it. Can't you understand that?'

'I told you,' Joe said, slyly. 'It's a one-off job. In and out. No strings attached, nothing.'

'No, Joe,' Michael told him. 'Absolutely and positively no.'

Patsy linked arms with him. There were tiny beads of perspiration on her upper lip. She gave his arm a squeeze and said, 'What does it pay?'

'Michael's being tough,' Joe replied. 'I offered him thirty big ones, with one half of one per cent of anything he saves us. But there you go. A moral principle is a moral principle. A no is a no.'

Patsy stared up at Michael in disbelief. 'He offered you 30,000 dollars and you turned him down?'

Michael felt himself flushing. 'Come on, sweetheart. I gave it up. If I can't make a success of doing what I want to do, then what kind of a man am I supposed to be? It's like admitting that I can't hack it. It's like throwing in the towel.'

'What are you talking about?' Patsy demanded. 'Joe's offering you a chance to do something you're very good at. How can that be throwing in the towel? And talking of towels, we could use a whole set of new ones. Most of them are worn to rags.'

Joe drank beer and grinned. 'Do you know something, Michael?' he said. 'You can never win against a woman.'

But Michael slowly shook his head. 'I'm not doing it, Joe. Not for thirty million dollars.'

'Michael –' Patsy began, but Michael raised his hand and said, 'Later, okay? We'll talk it over later.'

Joe stood up, and set his empty bottle down on the table. He picked up his hat, stared into it as if he half-expected to find something interesting inside, like money, or the answer to all of his problems, and then put it on.

'You can't say I didn't try,' he said, with genuine regret in his voice.

'It was good to see you, whatever,' Michael told him. 'Why don't you bring Marcia down sometime for Sunday brunch?'

'Well, thanks for the invite, but I don't think so. Marcia hates the beach as much as I do. Besides ... I wouldn't like to take food from the mouths of a starving inventor and his family.'

'Joe –' Michael warned him, but Joe took hold of his hand and slapped him on the back and said, 'Only kidding. Only kidding.'

Michael walked him out to his car, a brand-new Cadillac Seville, in shining midnight blue metallic. Patsy stayed up on the boardwalk, her blonde curls fluffing in the breeze. A seagull flew overhead, keening and crying.

'You know what they say about seagulls,' Joe remarked,

as he opened his car door. 'They're supposed to be an omen. Bringers of bad news.'

'That's what they say about you, too, Joe,' said Michael, and he wasn't really joking.

Joe backed up his car on the sandy roadway, gave them a wave, and then drove off. Michael stood on the sidewalk for a long time watching him go, until the sun glanced sharply off his door mirror and then he was gone. Michael climbed slowly back up the wooden steps to where Patsy was standing, and made a resigned face. 'I'm sorry,' he said. 'He wanted me to look into that helicopter crash – the one that killed John O'Brien and his family.'

'And you couldn't face it?'

Michael pursed his lips, and gave her a quick shake of his head.

'But you wouldn't have to look at the bodies, would you?'

'Of course I would. You have to know how they died, where they died … you have to check the positions where they were found.'

'And you really can't do it?'

Michael stood close beside her, grasping the splintery wooden rail. 'Ever since that night when Joe and I had to search through Rocky Woods, my head's been as close to the edge as anybody's head can get. I got out because it was either that or going totally Fruit-Loop. I can't explain what that experience did to me, and I don't really expect you to understand why I can't take a job that would solve all of our money problems with one snap of the fingers.'

Patsy took hold of his arm and kissed him. 'Michael … I don't have to understand. I *couldn't* understand, could I? Not unless I'd been there, not unless I'd seen it for myself. But I don't have to understand because I trust you. I know you would have done it if you could. I trust you and I love you, and the last thing in the world I want is for anything to hurt you. I'm not going to sell your peace of mind for the price of some new towels.'

Michael kissed her hair, and then her forehead, and then her lips. 'Something's going to turn up,' he promised her. 'I can feel it in the air.'

The seagull wheeled and fluttered overhead, balancing itself against the wind. Every now and then it cried like a baby; or a long-lost child; or a bringer of bad news.

He was lying in bed that night when the world opened underneath him and he plummeted into the darkness. For one long suspended moment he was hanging in mid-air, with the dark landscape slowly turning beneath him, and pinprick lights sparkling in the distance. There was no slipstream, rushing past his ears, only silence, but he knew that he was falling and he knew that he was falling fast.

He was aware of other people falling, all around him, a silent hailstorm of people. Nobody was screaming, nobody was crying out. They were simply dropping together through the darkness, waiting for the moment when the trees would suddenly rush up to them and they would collide with the ground.

He waited and waited. He was so frightened that he was scarcely able to breathe. Perhaps the ground wouldn't come to meet him. Perhaps he would fall for ever, down and down, into the night. But he could see the lights going out, one by one, then faster, as the hills rose up all around him. He knew then for certain that he was going to die.

Terrified, he flailed out with both arms, trying to grab hold of anything that might save him, trying to fly. He felt something against his left hand, and he snatched it, missed it, snatched it again. It was a young girl, who was falling beside him. She couldn't save him: they were both doomed to fall together. But he held her close, held her as tight as he could.

51

It was only then that he realized she was staring at him through the darkness. He could see the pale gleam of her open eyes. He thought: *Oh God, she's dead already,* and he reached down and realized that he was holding only half a girl, a child's torso with nothing below the waist but bloody rags.

He screamed and twisted, but somehow the girl's torso managed to cling on to him, and he couldn't break free. he felt her chilly blood trickling down his thighs. He heard the hollow sound of the wind, as it blew into her empty body cavity. He felt the cold, moist touch of her cheek.

Her lips came close to his ear, and he distinctly heard her whispering, *Don't let me fall! Don't let me fall!*

Then both of them slammed into the ground and he opened his eyes and he was all rolled up tight and tense in bed, slippery with sweat, his teeth clenched, his muscles so tight that his calves were racked with cramp.

He lay still for a long time, breathing deeply and trying to relax. Thank God, he hadn't woken Patsy. He hadn't had that nightmare for a long, long time, and he had never had it so vividly. He could hardly believe that he really hadn't fallen, and that he was still alive.

He climbed carefully out of bed. He felt the rough sisal matting under his bare feet. Naked, he tiptoed across the room, making sure that he didn't collide with the rocking chair in the corner over which they usually hung their clothes. It was 4:07, and the first thin light of dawn was just beginning to filter through the flowery cotton curtains.

He went into the kitchen and poured himself a large glass of cold water. He stood with his hand on the tap drinking it in large, breathless gulps. Then he crossed over to the window that faced out over Nantucket Sound, and opened up the venetian blinds. He could just make out the pale prehistoric humps of the sand dunes, and the glimmering white line of the surf.

He felt infinitely depressed. Was the nightmare of Rocky Woods going to haunt him for ever? Would he never be able to shake it off? That terrible sensation with which it always started — as if his bed had opened up right underneath him — that was more than he could take. Any more nightmares as clear and as realistic as tonight's and he felt that he could easily slip into total craziness.

Maybe he had made a mistake by quitting his job and trying to run away from it. Maybe he should have stayed on at Plymouth and faced his fears until he learned to control them. Maybe some therapy then would have helped. But he had come from a family which had always been proud and private and self-sufficient; a family that never asked anybody for help, either financial or emotional.

For twenty-eight years, Michael's father had run his own boat-making business in Boston Harbor, and his rowboats and dinghies had been famous all the way from Rockland to Marblehead for their fine traditional craftmanship. But in the early 1960s, when fibreglass boats began to supersede wood, very few of the old-fashioned boatbuilders were able to make the transition, Rearden Chandlers included.

Michael could remember the time when you could walk along Boston's waterfront and hear a cacophony of hulls being hammered together. He could also remember his father sitting on a wooden box in their empty living-room, drawn and grey, while the removal men took away the last of their furniture. He had stood beside his father and laid his hand on his shoulder and said, 'The bank would've helped you; you know that.'

But his father had simply patted his hand and said, 'You think I want to be owned body and soul by some fucking banker? Nobody owns my body and soul but me.'

Michael had inherited much of that same self-destructive

cussedness: that feeling that if you couldn't make it on your own, you were somehow less of a man.

He was still thinking about his father and watching the surfline when the telephone rang. He picked it up immediately, in case it woke Patsy or Jason.

'Michael?'

'Who is it?'

'Michael, it's Joe. Did I wake you?'

'No, no. I wasn't asleep.'

'Listen … I'm sorry to call you so late. Or maybe I'm sorry to call you so early, I'm not sure which. But I've just had a fax authorizing me to tell you everything we know about the O'Brien crash. It isn't much, but I think it'll give you some food for thought.'

Michael tiredly pressed the heel of his hand against his forehead. 'Joe … I've talked this over with Patsy, and the answer is still no.'

'Let me just tell you what we found out.'

'I'm not interested. I don't want to know.'

'But this is 24-carat, I promise you. It came straight from Roger Bannerman, of Boston Life & Trust. He and Edgar play golf together.'

'I don't care if they take showers together. The answer is still no.'

There was a lengthy pause. Michael was beginning to feel cold, and wished he were back in bed. But he could still hear Joe breathing on the other end of the line, and it was like the steady breathing of Nemesis, the chilly respiration of relentless fate. He knew that Joe was going to tell him what Edgar had found out; and he also knew that he was going to listen. He knew, too, that it would probably convince him to give up his wayward life here in New Seabury, and go back to face the nightmarish consequences of Rocky Woods.

54

'John O'Brien's daughter was missing,' said Joe.

'What?' said Michael.

'John O'Brien's fourteen-year-old daughter Cecilia ... she was travelling with her parents to Washington, DC, for the swearing-in ceremony. They found her purse on the helicopter, and they found her luggage. Strangely, they also found her shoes, under her seat. But of Cecilia herself, there was no trace at all.'

Michael said, 'I thought the coroner's office told you that physical trauma was so severe that they couldn't even tell how many cadavers they were dealing with.'

'That's what they *said*. But they've been playing for time. The actuality was somewhat different.'

'How did Roger Bannerman find that out?'

'Easy. Mrs Bannerman is a volunteer emergency medical technician. She attended the crash scene herself.'

'And she was sure that the girl wasn't there? She wasn't thrown clear, or anything like that?'

'She must have been sure or else she wouldn't have told her husband.'

'All the same, the second-hand opinion of a volunteer EMT isn't exactly evidence.'

'I didn't say anything about it being evidence,' Joe replied. 'What I did say was that it's food for thought.'

Michael hesitated, shivered. Dawn was well advanced now, and he could see the horizon, slate grey sea against lighter grey sky. Out toward Nantucket Island, it looked as if it were raining. 'What else do you know?' he asked.

'That's it. The helicopter crashed, and person or persons unknown were seen removing something from the wreck. Subsequently, when the rescue squad arrived, there was no trace of Cecilia O'Brien – even though it was known for certain that she was accompanying her parents.'

'I still don't understand why you need me.'

Joe let out a heavy sigh. 'I need you, Michael, because I need somebody sensitive. I need somebody crazy. I don't need a plodder, or an analyst. I need somebody who can jump to conclusions. What was that thing you were always going on to me about? "Downwind thinking". That's what I need.'

'What do the cops say about Cecilia O'Brien?'

'Squat. They won't even admit that she wasn't in the wreck.'

'So who's covering this up, and why?'

'Give me some guesses.'

Michael ran his hand through his tangled hair. 'O'Brien was a liberal, right? He didn't approve of the death penalty, he didn't approve of racism or segregation or police discrimination against ethnic minorities. He campaigned in favour of abortion; he also campaigned against censorship. He hated bribery and he hated featherbedding. He supported the legalization of soft drugs; but he was down on crack and heroin and snow and he was heavily down on guns. In fact, he made himself a prime target for every drug dealer and every bent politician and every redneck and every religious whacko in the continental United States.'

Joe said, 'Exactly.' But then he said, 'Remember Rocky Woods.'

'You don't seriously think that I could ever *forget* Rocky Woods?'

'No, of course not, I'm sorry. But remember who died at Rocky Woods.'

'Three hundred and forty-five unsuspecting men, women and children. That's who died at Rocky Woods.'

'Including Dan Margolis.'

'Dan Margolis?'

'That's right, Michael. Dan Margolis, who had just been selected by William Webster to head up the Drug

Enforcement Agency, so that they could strangle the Colombian coke trade before it even climbed out of its crib.'

Michael said, 'I remember Dan Margolis. He used to work in the DA's office, didn't he? All fire and shit and pepper, the way I recall.'

'The very same.'

'So what are you trying to tell me?' asked Michael.

'I'm not trying to tell you anything. If I knew the answers, I wouldn't be asking, would I? I'm just trying to think downwind, the way that you think.'

'And?'

'And – well – nothing. Except that we have two fatal air crashes within two years of each other, both involving a well-known liberal campaigner; both involving the deaths of innocent people; and both involving the complete and unaccountable disappearance of a single female. In the case of Rocky Woods, it was Elaine Parker. In the case of John O'Brien's helicopter, it was Cecilia O'Brien.'

'Joe,' protested Michael, 'this isn't downwind thinking. This is making shopping malls without straw. The most logical explanation for Elaine Parker's disappearance at Rocky Woods was that she fell way outside the search area. A gust caught her, a piece of debris deflected her, who knows? Those people fell across nine square miles. As for Cecilia O'Brien – well, we just can't tell yet, for sure. And there were at least three other people who died at Rocky Woods who could have been the target for revenge killings, or insurance scams. That's quite apart from the fact that we never discovered what caused that L10-11 to blow up in the first place.'

'Michael,' Joe retaliated, 'I'm trying to get you thinking. I'm trying to get you *involved*.'

'For Christ's sake, Joe, I don't want to be involved. I don't want to know how that helicopter crashed, and I don't want to know why it crashed; and more than anything else, I don't want to see the people who died in it.'

This time, Joe went silent and stayed silent.

'It's all finished,' Michael told him. 'I'm an inventor now, no matter how badly you think I'm doing. I'm an inventor, and I'm making things, creating things. I'm not picking through wreckage; I'm not making my living out of other people's grief. I'm not a carrion crow. I'm doing something poor, but I'm doing something honest.'

'All right,' said Joe. 'I'm sorry I disturbed you.'

He put down the phone, and Michael was left alone, naked, with that lonely continuous tone. After a while, he put down the phone, too; and looked around; and then went quietly back to the bedroom.

He was just closing the door behind him when Patsy opened her eyes and stared at him and said, 'What are you doing up? What time is it?'

'Four-thirty,' he said, climbing back into bed.

She cuddled up to him. 'God, you're cold,' she told him.

'In bed,' he replied, 'you can call me Michael.'

Three

The morning was just beginning to warm up. Lieutenant Thomas J. Boyle climbed out of his new dark-maple Caprice and buffed some fingerprints off the roof with the cuff of his coat. He crossed the sidewalk, searching in his pockets for his cigarettes, while at the same time picturing them quite clearly on his nightstand beside his bed, where he had left them. Sergeant David Jahnke was waiting for him outside the old brownstone house, wearing a cotton blouson jacket and looking more like Michael Douglas in *The Streets of San Francisco* than any sergeant had a right to. He offered Thomas a Winston; Thomas took it without even looking at him or saying a word. David lit it for him and waited for him to speak. The door of the house was open; and in the hallway Thomas could see brown-patterned wallpaper and six or seven pictures hanging in frames, although the light was reflecting from the glass so that he was unable to tell what they were.

He blew out a thin stream of smoke and looked around him. Already, there were three squad cars and an ambulance parked neatly beside the kerb. Neat parking meant dead already. No point in screeching to a halt right outside the house at whatever angle and running in with a backboard and a trauma kit, and guns unholstered in case of trouble.

'Nice area,' he remarked. 'One block away from the Public Gardens. What are we talking about? Nine-hundred-thousand freehold?'

David shrugged. 'Out of my league.'

'Asshole. I'm asking you to assess it, not buy it.'

David self-consciously brushed his hand through his swept-back hair. 'Milt Jaworski's inside, if you want to take a look.'

'In a while. Tell me about it.'

David took out his notebook and flicked through it. He paused, flicked one page forward and two pages back. Then he said, 'Okay, here it is. Caucasian female, aged about twenty. Blonde, blue-eyed, no birthmarks. She was found face down on a divan bed in the bedroom, hogtied with razor wire, which had caused severe lacerations to the wrists and ankles. There was severe bruising all over her body, including marks which looked like fingerprints and other marks which looked like cigarette burns and other burns by

59

pokers or branding irons. The divan bed was heavily stained with blood and urine.'

Thomas inhaled smoke and blew it out through his nostrils. He hated smoking, he wished he wouldn't do it. Other officers could cope with all of the blood and all of the smell and all of the chaos of human life, and they never resorted to booze or Marlboro or crack or XTC. But Thomas needed a crutch. He needed to do something obvious, to show that his psyche was wounded by what he did; and smoking was the least dangerous way that he could think of. He could still remember his mother dying in a cancer ward, puffy and yellow and shuddering with pain; and every morning he promised himself that he would smoke less. But every morning they called him out to look at gunshot victims and families burned by fire and dead molested children; and what could he do but light another cigarette?

He was forty-four years old, close to retirement age. He was handsome, in a lanky, bushy-eyebrowed, Abraham Lincolnish way. But he was unreasonably tall, almost six-feet-four, and his height had affected his whole life. At school, it had made him a target for merciless bullying and jokes. In his early years in the Boston police force, however, it had brought him respect, and assisted his promotion. He had been young, decisive and physically commanding. But in middle age, it had made him something of a dinosaur – easily picked out by aggressive young opponents both police and political, easily spotted by the press, and easily marked by Boston's criminals. Kevin Cato, who ran one of the most profitable import/export rackets from Rockland to Marblehead and back again, called him 'Giraffe'.

Sometimes, Megan teased him and called him Giraffe, too. Megan was his wife: Boston Irish, five-feet-four-and-a-half, little and dark and vivacious, despite her affliction. He never showed her that it worried him. But one day, somebody would say, 'Get the Giraffe,' and that would be the end of it. Squealing tyres on Haverhill and Causeway, or down by the Harbor; shots; and then nothing but cold concrete sidewalk; and encroaching darkness; and watching your life's blood sliding away.

Thomas took a last tight drag at his cigarette and said, 'Any identification? Pocketbook, credit cards, anything like that?'

David shook his head. 'Nothing at all. And I mean nothing at all. No clothing whatsoever, no jewellery, no cosmetics, no comb, no toothbrush, nothing. This girl was totally naked in every sense of the word.'

'You've talked to the neighbours?'

'Oh, for sure. The Dallens on this side and the Giffords on that.'

'They never saw nothing. They never heard nothing.'

David nodded. Byron Street was one of those streets where people came and went and minded their own business, where nobody would admit to domestic violence or shouting matches or scandal. The only time the residents of Byron Street ever called the police was when they needed a burglary report for insurance purposes; or if a noisy party was going on too late.

'Do you want to take a look?' asked David.

'Oh … sure,' said Thomas. 'Who called it in?'

David flipped his notebook again. 'Ms Anna Krasilovsky from the realty company. The tenants hadn't paid rent for two successive months, so she came around to check. There was no response to the doorbell; and the phone was disconnected. So she used her passkey. She smelled a smell, and went upstairs, and there she was.'

'You've talked to Ms – ?'

'Krasilovsky, yes, for sure. She's being treated for shock. But everything she says checks out.'

'What do we know about the tenants?'

'James T. Honeyman, DMD, MDS, dental surgeon; and Mrs Honeyman. Dr Honeyman apparently wanted the premises for an implant surgery practice.'

'Where did they come from, originally?'

'We're still checking their background. But the realty company records show that their permanent home address is at the Hawk-Salt-Ash resort community in Plymouth, Vermont.'

'Odd,' said Thomas. 'Who lives in Plymouth, Vermont, and sets up a practice in Boston?'

'We should have a report back from Plymouth within the hour,' David reassured him. 'My guess is that it's a bogus address. But, you know, we're just making sure.'

'Oh, you think that it's a bogus address?' Thomas asked, sarcastically. 'Maybe you'll make a detective yet.'

He knew, however, that the grisliest moment had arrived; and had to be faced. Why he had decided on a career in homicide when he couldn't even stand to look at a run-over deer on a rural highway, he could never explain. Perhaps he had imagined that it would be no more disturbing than Cluedo or reading a Sherlock Holmes story. He really couldn't remember. But there were days when he came home from police headquarters and stood under the shower with his eyes tight shut for twenty minutes on end, trying to wash away the smell of death, and trying to forget the blind bloody writhing of maggots.

He followed David up the steps and in through the open front door. He could smell death the moment he stepped into the hallway. A young woman police officer shouldered her way past him, looking pale. He didn't snap at her, or reprimand her, the way he would have done if she had pushed him back at headquarters. Instead, he watched her hurry down the steps with her hand pressed against her mouth, and thought, *Shit, this is going to be a bad one.*

David said, 'This way, sir,' but Thomas said, 'Wait.' He was studying the framed pictures hanging in the hallway – partly because he wanted to put off the moment when he had to confront the deceased, and partly because he always found other people's pictures to be most revealing. People had to think that a picture was very significant, before they decided to frame it and hang it on the wall. Sometimes they didn't realize how much their choice of pictures gave them away. Particularly nudes. And these were all nudes – sepia and black-and-white photographs of Victorian and Edwardian and 1920s nudes, wide-hipped, pale-skinned, flirtatious and coy. Only one picture was different – a curious steel engraving of formally-dressed men and women standing around a table which was covered by a heavy damask cloth. In the centre of the table lay a small, dark curled-up thing which could have been a human foetus; but the picture-glass was very grimy and it was almost impossible to tell for certain.

'What do you think *that* is?' asked Thomas.

David obviously hadn't looked at it before. He leaned forward and peered at it closely. 'I don't know ... some kind of dried-up root vegetable?'

'Then why are all these people staring it so intently? I mean, what do we have here, the Swede Fanciers of America, or what?'

David looked up at him unhappily. 'I really don't know, sir. I'm sorry.'

'Goddamned root vegetable my ass,' Thomas sneered.

Embarrassed, David glanced at the picture again. 'It could be a dead bird.'

'Oh, sure. And it could be a shrivelled-up pancake or it could be somebody's toupee, for Christ's sake. Or a quarter of a pound of Limburger cheese that's grown fur.'

'I don't know, lieutenant,' said David, trying to sound level and reasonable. 'Your guess is as good as mine.'

Thomas looked around at all the other pictures. 'I don't want guesses, David, and I sure don't want guesses that are only as good as mine. I want constructive detective work. I want *analysis*.'

David examined the pictures again, but he continued to look unhappy.

'What do these pictures tell you?' Thomas demanded. 'Look at them, David. What do they say? They're saying something! They're saying …? Come on, David, they're saying – '

Thomas circled his hand in the air as if he could coax the words out of David's larynx. 'Come on, they're telling you something clear as a bell and country simple.'

David cleared his throat. 'They're telling me that who-ever put them up was probably heterosexual.'

Thomas clapped his hands. 'Wrong! You're assuming that whoever put them up was male! Maybe a woman put them up!'

'Then what do they tell me?' asked David, in consider-able discomfort.

Thomas lifted one down from the wall, turned it over, and read the framer's label on the back. He hung it back up, and then he checked all of the others. 'I'll tell you what they tell you. They tell you that they were all framed locally, here on Chestnut Hill. They tell you that they were all framed at the same time, which may mean that they were simply hung in this house by an interior designer, and that they belong to the property itself rather than to Dr and Mrs Honeyman personally. They're also telling you that who-ever put them up sure liked their meat and potatoes. Look here: we're talking substantial women here. So did you ask Ms Krovilavsky whether these pictures belonged to the previous tenants, or whether they belonged to her realty company?'

'Ms Krasilovsky, sir. Not Krovilavsky.'

'Same difference. And, no, you didn't ask her, did you?'

'No, sir. It didn't occur to me.'

Thomas raised a single finger. 'Whenever anything sexual comes into an investigation, ask. Sex is a motive in itself.' He peered at the pictures again. 'Especially when somebody has sexual taste as wacky as this.'

He was still examining the photograph of the group standing around the table when Detective Jaworski came down the stairs from the bedroom. Detective Jaworski was short and beefy with a furry blond crewcut and eyes as tiny as two steel nails knocked into a turnip. He had been transferred to homicide only five weeks ago. He was looking grey and sweaty, and he kept swallowing.

'What do you think that is?' Thomas asked him, pointing to the hairy object on the table in the engraving.

Detective Jaworski unenthusiastically examined it.

'I couldn't say, sir,' he said, shaking his head.

'Animal, vegetable or mineral?'

'I really don't know, sir. I never saw anything that looked like that before.'

'No …' said Thomas. 'Me neither. It looks kind of unhealthy, don't you think?'

Without a word, Detective Jaworski suddenly turned around, walked three stiff steps along the hallway, pushed open the toilet door and slammed it behind him. Thomas and David waited with impassive faces while he was noisily sick.

He came out wiping his mouth with toilet tissue. He said, 'Orange juice,' as if that explained everything.

Thomas said, 'That's one reason I never eat breakfast.'

'Don't you get used to it?' asked Detective Jaworski.

'I'll tell you when I do,' Thomas replied. 'Now … we'd better take a look.'

They climbed a steep flight of brown-carpeted stairs to the first landing. In front of them was a large window of yellow and sepia-stained glass, in the pattern of orchids and wild arum. It gave the landing the same faded, brownish light as the photographs in the hallway.

On the right was a closed mahogany door. Thomas asked Detective Jaworski, 'What's in there?'

'Bathroom, sir.'

Thomas opened the door and looked inside. The bathroom was chilly and smelled of damp. The walls were half-tiled with brown majolica tiles, and the walls were painted with yellow-ochre enamel and spotted with black pinpricks of mould. A huge old-fashioned bathtub stood in the centre of the opposite wall. Inside, it was thickly ringed with greyish grease, and stained with dark brown marks. The plughole was blocked with grey human hairs.

'Forensics checked in here yet?' asked Thomas.

'Not yet, lieutenant. They got their hands full in the bedroom.'

'Make sure they take samples of that hair.' He went to the brown-measled mirror over the basin and ran his fingertip along the shelf beneath it. It was encrusted with old shaving soap and tiny black speckles. He held his finger under Detective Jaworski's nose. 'Human stubble. Tell 'em to take a sample of that, too.'

Detective Jaworski examined it with undisguised distaste. 'Whatever you say, sir.'

Thomas looked around the bathroom – walls, floor, ceiling, light fittings – then he stared at himself in the mirror for a long, thoughtful moment. At last he said, 'Okay,' and walked out, with David and Detective Jaworski closely following him.

The bedroom was the second door along the landing. Outside it stood a stocky, ginger-haired cop with his arms folded above his belly. From inside the room, electronic flash flickered like summer lightning, and Thomas heard somebody saying, 'Give me two more shots of the feet. The *feet*, for Christ's sake.'

Thomas clapped the cop on the shoulder. 'How's it going, Jimmy? Are you a grandpappy yet?'

'Not yet, lieutenant, tenth of August,' the cop replied. 'And it's a girl.'

'Well, give my love to Eileen,' said Thomas. 'And don't forget the cigars.'

Before Thomas could go any further, the cop held out his hand to stop him, and nodded toward the bedroom door. 'Take a deep breath, lieutenant. This is a bad one.'

Thomas looked at him. If Jimmy O'Sullivan said it was a bad one, then it was a bad one. 'Thanks, Jimmy,' and sharply inhaled, and stepped into the room.

Four photo-floods had turned the bedroom into a dazzling surrealistic stage set. Two forensic officers were crawling around in the far corner, on their hands and knees, carefully brushing the white shaggy rug for hairs and fibres and any other interesting minutiae. A young police photographer with a greasy quiff was adjusting his tripod to take close-up pictures at the end of the bed. And a thin, bespectacled man in a pale blue lab-coat was standing next to the bed, a clipboard tucked under his arm, a pencil tucked behind his elfish ear, looking thoughtful.

It was the bed itself that shocked Thomas more than anything else. At first sight, he thought that it had been draped with a dark brown sheet. It was only when he saw the blowflies crawling all over it that he realized it wasn't a dark brown sheet at all, but a white sheet that had been totally drenched with blood – blood which must have been vivid scarlet when it was first spilled, but which had now oxidized to the colour of a vast blotchy scab.

67

In the middle of the bed, face down, lay the naked body of a young girl. She had been hogtied with three loops of tarnished razor wire, her hands behind her back, her knees lifted. Her long hair was so thickly clotted with dried blood that Thomas was unable to determine what her natural colour might have been. Putrescence was well advanced, so that her skin had taken on a grey-green pallor, almost luminous, but she was also bruised and scarred and burned beyond belief.

Out of one pocket, Thomas took out his handkerchief, unfolded it, and laid it flat on the palm of his hand. From another pocket, he took out a small bottle of essence of cloves, which Megan regularly bought for him from a small delicatessen near Faneuil Hall. He shook the essence into the handkerchief, refolded it, and then covered his nose and mouth.

He approached the man in the pale blue lab-coat, who wasn't wearing any kind of mask at all. 'Lieutenant Boyle,' he announced himself, in a muffled voice. 'I don't think we've met, have we?'

'Victor Kurylowicz,' the medical examiner replied. 'I moved here a month ago, from Newark, New Jersey. I won't shake hands.'

Thomas looked down at the young girl's body. Her hair half-covered her face, so that he could only see the lower part of her nose and her mouth. Underneath her chin was a mass of maggots. They looked almost as if they were boiling.

'I don't know how you can stand the smell,' he said to Kurylowicz.

The medical examiner shrugged. 'It's not a question of whether I can stand it or not. It's important. It tells me stuff. You remember what Coleridge said about Cologne? "I counted two and seventy stenches, all well defined, and several stinks!" '

'Oh … you're a literary scholar,' said Thomas.

'I'm a medical examiner,' Kurylowicz retorted. Behind his black-rimmed glasses, his eyes were sharp and dark. 'What I know is bodies, and everything to do with bodies. Particularly bodies that have suffered this kind of treatment.'

Thomas looked at Kurylowicz over his handkerchief. The stench of dried blood and decomposing flesh was so strong that it even began to overwhelm the aromatic fumes of his clove-drenched handkerchief. It had an appalling ripeness that always reminded him of gas and apples and raw sewage. He thought that he was going to suffocate – or that, even if he didn't, he would never be able to smell anything but death, ever again. 'You want to tell me something about her?' he asked, his throat tight.

Kurylowicz glanced down at his clipboard. 'For sure. This unfortunate young lady is a Caucasian, about twenty or twenty-one years old, blonde hair, blue eyes. She weighed about 110 pounds I'd guess when she died, which meant that her weight was slightly below average for her age and height, but not drastically so. In other words, whoever was keeping her captive was feeding her good. On cursory examination, I'd say that life has been extinct for slightly more than two weeks.'

'Any idea how she died?'

'Oh, yes. She was tied up with razor wire, as you can see for yourself. Then her carotid, inferior mesenteric and popliteal arteries were expertly severed, which meant that she bled to death within less than ten minutes.'

'What do you mean by "expertly"?'

Kurylowicz rubbed the tip of his nose. 'I mean by somebody who knew what the fuck he was doing.'

'A doctor?'

'Maybe. They look like scalpel wounds, rather than knife wounds.'

'A dentist?'

'Whatever, who knows. Even a motor mechanic could have done it if he knew his anatomy.'

'But this perpetrator knew his anatomy?'

'For sure. All of the cuts were clean and accurate, no hesitation marks.'

Thomas forced himself to examine the girl's body. There were scores of cigarette burns, and literally hundreds of bruises, cuts and scars and even crude tattoos – triangles and circles and squiggles. Somebody had even burned a Happy Face onto her shoulder blade.

'This is serious sadism,' said Thomas.

Kurylowicz nodded. 'Maybe. On the other hand, maybe it's serious *masochism*. I've come across plenty of girls who get off on this kind of thing. And plenty of guys, too. My last job before I came up here, this guy had cut off his own scrotum, and he was walking around with his balls in a plastic bag.'

Thomas didn't want to hear about anything like that, especially not now.

'This wasn't all done recently, was it?' he remarked. 'Some of those scars look pretty much healed up.'

Kurylowicz ran his fingertips lightly over the cicatrices on the girl's bare back. 'It's hard to date them exactly – but, yes, some of these marks could be six months old, or even older.'

'So she's been systematically tortured since Christmas, and maybe longer?'

'Oh, longer. No doubt about it. Anything up to a year, eighteen months.'

'And nothing to say who she is, or what she's doing here?'

Kurylowicz shook his head. 'No identifying marks whatsoever. No rings, no earrings, no birthmarks. We'll check the dental work, obviously, but if she came from out of the area, or out of state, it could take us forever to make a match.'

'Was she sexually assaulted?'

'I'd say hundreds of times. She suffered severe vaginal and anal trauma. See for yourself. There are dozens of cigarette burns around her genital area, and other burns consistent with certain sado-masochistic practices which are rare but which I've occasionally come across before.'

Thomas breathed in cloves and death, cloves and death. Kurylowicz stared at him with glittering eyes.

Thomas said, 'You want to explain what those certain sado-masochistic practices are? You know – just for one of those dumb, innocent guys who used to think that heavy petting meant owning a St Bernard?'

Thin-lipped, Kurylowicz almost smiled. 'We're talking sodomy with a lighted candle, lieutenant, either forcibly administered or self-administered. And we're talking about not snuffing the candle out when it gets unbearable.'

Thomas slowly shook his head. 'I've heard of some pretty weird stuff, but I never heard of that before.'

Kurylowicz looked down at the girl and for a moment Thomas thought he seemed almost sad. 'People do things to themselves you can't even imagine. I'm a Catholic, you know that? "The human body is a temple." A few people treat their body like a temple. Two per cent. Most people treat their body like a shithouse. Then you get the ones who want to do more than treat it like a shithouse, they want to vandalize it – they want to tear it down, demolish it, brick by brick.'

There was a very long silence between them. The photographer finished taking his pictures of feet and packed up his equipment and waved and left. Thomas had never seen anybody move so jerkily and so fast. Talk about the Keystone Kops. The two forensic investigators, however, seemed to be unperturbed by the stench, and they were still laboriously crawling around on the rug, occasionally taking small polythene envelopes out of their pockets and inserting hairs or fluff or fragments of fibre, and labelling them, and marking the labels with felt-tipped pens.

'Irving ... There's a blue wool fibre here I haven't come across before,' one of them said.

The other took it, and peered at it closely. 'Hmm,' he said, and dropped it into an envelope, and marked it.

Kurylowicz said, 'There's one more thing ... I can't quite understand it yet.'

'Tell me,' said Thomas. He was trying very hard to be patient, but he didn't think that he would be able to stand the stench of this decomposing Jane Doe for more than two or three more minutes.

'Let me ask you to look just here,' said Kurylowicz, and pointed with his finger to two small wounds on the girl's middle back, no more than six inches apart.

'More torture?' asked Thomas, not really sure what he was supposed to be looking for, or what he was supposed to think about it even if he found it.

'I don't know what they are, frankly. But they seem to be very deep wounds, small-diameter wounds or injection-holes which have been opened up, allowed to heal, then opened up again, then allowed to heal, and so and so on.'

'Why would anybody want to do that?'

'I don't know ... maybe the perpetrator kept injecting stuff into her back to keep her quiet, or to ease the pain ... something like an epidural. Maybe it was part of the torture.'

Thomas said, 'Jesus ... You can't even imagine the suffering, can you? You can't even think about it.'

'There's one more thing,' said Kurylowicz.

'What's that?'

'I'll need to check it out back at the lab – but look at her lower legs.'

Thomas did as he was asked, trying not to focus on the girl's bruised and lacerated calves. 'I don't see anything.'

'It's the way those bones protrude. I'm not going to second-guess myself, but I think that both of her legs have been broken – not recently, but not more than eighteen months ago. They've been set, but not by a highly-qualified surgeon. See how the left calf is kind of kinked.'

'What does that mean?' asked Thomas, baffled.

Kurylowicz tapped his teeth with his pencil, and then shrugged. 'I don't know. I'm going to have to do a lot more work on it.'

One of the forensic investigators stood up and came over. He was short and fat with a Kookie Byrnes quiff and near-together eyes. His upper lip was beaded with perspiration.

'How're you doing, Irving?' asked Thomas.

'Slow but sure,' said the investigator, with an asthmatic wheeze in his voice. 'We've found seven different clothing fibres so far, and enough hair to stuff a mattress. Plus candle wax, cigarette ash, nine cigarette butts, several needles and skewers, burned book-matches, and fish hooks.'

Thomas nodded. The essence of cloves was beginning to make his eyes water, but his stomach was beginning to rebel against the stench of putrescence, and he didn't dare to take the handkerchief away from his face. From under his shirt came an audible growl, and Irving looked at him in surprise.

'Just hungry, that's all,' said Thomas. 'I didn't have any breakfast.'

'Very wise,' Irving replied. 'The first thing I did when I got here was to hurl up three cups of coffee and a double order of scrambled eggs.'

Thomas looked back at Kurylowicz and Kurylowicz said,

'It's okay, sir. I don't have anything else to show you right now. You must have plenty of other stuff to be getting on with. I'll prioritize this one, and have it on your desk as soon as I can.'

There was a detectably patronizing edge in Kurylowicz's voice. What kind of a homicide lieutenant couldn't bear the smell of death? But Thomas was too relieved that he could go to worry about reprimanding him. And anyway, it would have been pretty damned ludicrous, trying to pull rank with a clove-filled handkerchief in front of his face.

'All right, Kurylowicz. Good work. Sergeant Jahnke's going to stick around in case you need anything.'

'I'm sorry?' asked Kurylowicz.

Thomas took the handkerchief away from his mouth, and took a breath in preparation to repeating himself. But the sickly-sweet smell that immediately filled up his nose and his lungs was so thick that he couldn't say anything at all. He gave Kurylowicz a *Columbo*-like salute with his hand, and left the bedroom.

'Everything all right, sir?' Jimmy the patrolman called after him, as he hurried down the stairs.

He didn't answer. He couldn't. His mouth was flooded with warm, salty saliva, and his stomach was going into spasm.

With his hand clamped over the lower part of his face, he walked at top speed through the hallway, glimpsing jumbled images of those vase-shaped Victorian nudes, and a hatstand, and his own white face in a mirror beside the door, like speak-no-evil being hotly pursued by hear-no-evil. He took the front steps three at a time, and then he was out on the sidewalk in the warm morning wind, taking one deep breath after another.

Detective Jaworski had been talking to one of the patrolmen across the street. He came over and asked, solicitously, 'Are you okay, lieutenant?'

'No, I'm not okay,' Thomas told him. 'I'm very, very far from okay.'

Detective Jaworski reached into his pocket and produced a new pack of Marlboro. 'It's the worst one I ever saw. Even worse than that family on Otis Street, you remember that one?'

Thomas tried to light the cigarette that Detective Jaworski had given him, but couldn't. Eventually Detective Jaworski steadied his hand for him, and he lit it, and took in a deep lungful of tobacco smoke.

'You were lucky to puke,' he said; and meant it.

Detective Jaworski said, 'All those scars. All those burns. What do you think, some kind of cult killing? Maybe Satanists, something like that?'

Thomas glanced back at the house. 'It's still far too early to say. We have to find out who she is, first; and how she was tortured; and exactly how she died.'

'You know what you said to me the first day I joined homicide?' remarked Detective Jaworski. 'You said that homicide was only another kind of theft; except that a murderer was stealing somebody's time instead of their property.'

'I said that?'

'Sure. I thought it was such an incredible way of looking at it, that's why I remembered it. You said, find that stolen time and you've found your murderer.'

'I really said that?'

'Sure,' nodded Detective Jaworski, with an eager grin.

'What did I mean by it?' asked Thomas.

Very slowly, the grin faded from Detective Jaworski's face. 'You meant – well, you meant – kind of like – if somebody takes that time, you know – and if you can find it again – well, you kind of – '

Thomas laid a hand on Detective Jaworski's shoulder.

'You don't know what it means. *I* don't know what it means. If I ever talk such bullshit again, you have my permission to pour coffee down my shirt.'

'Yes, sir,' said Detective Jaworski, amazed. Then, 'Yes, sir. Whatever you say.'

He went home at a quarter past three. He knew that he had a long night ahead of him, and he wanted to make sure that Megan had everything she needed. He manoeuvred his Caprice into the awkward downsloping driveway in front of their apartment building, and opened the door carefully so that he wouldn't scrape it on the concrete retaining wall.

He was climbing the steps between the beds of fluttering geraniums when the glass front door opened and Mr Novato the super came out, in his blue cotton coat and splashy green necktie, looking more than ever like Placido Domingo's less-talented brother. Close-up, he smelled of garlic and lavender and something that Thomas couldn't quite pin down, maybe cheese.

'You're going to be long, Mr Boyle?' he asked, and you didn't have to have a PhD in sociology to detect the course that the conversation was going to take.

'Twenty minutes tops,' said Thomas.

Mr Novato looked over his shoulder at his car. 'It's just that you block the driveway for everybody else.'

'If anybody else wants to use the driveway, all you have to do is call me, and I'll move.'

'Well … I don't know, Mr Boyle. It's against the fire regulations, you know, for any vehicle to block the driveway.'

With huge self-restraint, Thomas said, 'Read my lips, Mr Novato. I am a police officer involved in a major homicide investigation. I am going to leave my car right where it is. If anybody wishes to use this driveway for any legitimate purpose during the next twenty minutes, then I shall cheerfully move it.'

'I don't want no trouble, Mr Boyle.'

'You don't want no trouble?'

'That's what I say, Mr Boyle, I don't want no trouble.'

'If you don't want no trouble, Mr Novato, the answer is easy. You don't say no more.'

Thomas went inside, leaving Mr Novato standing where he was. Thomas liked almost everything Italian – food, music, wine, fashion – but he had taken an immediate dislike to Mr Novato when they had first moved here three years ago, and Mr Novato had done nothing to change his opinion. He was bureaucratic, lazy, and creatively stupid. If Thomas hadn't occasionally needed Mr Novato's help in lifting Megan into the car, or to take messages, or to keep a special eye on Megan when he was away, he would have protested to the owners months ago, and had him canned.

Well, maybe not canned, but carpeted. Even irritating Italian supers had to make a living.

Thomas pushed the elevator button for 3 and the doors closed. For the first time in weeks, he felt really tired. He felt as drained and as empty as if he had stayed awake for two nights running; his vision blurred, his hearing stuffed with cotton wool, his sinuses blocked but dry. He closed his eyes and leaned back against the mirrored wall as the elevator carried him upstairs.

He opened the door to apartment 303 and called, thickly, 'Megan!' He took off his coat, hung it on the crowded peg in the hallway, next to the framed print of Jesus and Mary Magdalene and the view of Lough Oughter, and then went through to the living-room. There she was: sitting in her wheelchair by the window, looking out over Commercial Street and the North End Playground, writing in her notebook. Russet-haired, freckled, green-eyed, with a tip-tilted nose and the slightest hint of an overbite. She was wearing a white short-sleeved blouse, and – as always – a crucifix around her neck.

He came over and kissed her. 'How was the therapy?' he asked her.

'Oh … same as usual,' she said, closing her notebook and setting it down on the table. 'Same as usual' meant 'painful, tedious and ultimately hopeless'. 'Dr Saul gave me a new painkiller.'

He dragged over one of the two upright dining-chairs that stood on either side of the china cabinet, and sat down next to her. Since she had become wheelchair-bound, he hardly ever sat in armchairs, because they were always too low, and they made him feel as if he were lounging in comfort while Megan had to suffer the rigidity of a back brace.

'This is going to be a tough one,' he said. 'Maybe you should stay with Shirley for a while.'

She shook her head. 'I'm all right. Sometimes I like to be alone.'

'But I'm going to worry about you. You know that.'

She touched the back of his wrist and stroked it with her fingertip in an absent-minded, circular motion. 'You never used to worry before. Why should you worry now? I'm just as capable.'

'You're *more* capable,' he told her. 'But this is one of those investigations that's going to need hours of overtime, maybe nights away from home.'

'Oh, you do fuss so much,' she said, with a sudden bright smile. 'I have my television. I have my music. I have my cookbook.'

'Maybe Shirley could stay here.'

'Maybe Shirley doesn't want to stay here.'

He looked at her directly and warmly, and couldn't help smiling, too. 'You stubborn Irish colleen, you.'

'Oh, I'm not so stubborn, really,' she said. 'I just value my independence.'

'Sure,' he said; and had a sudden flash of that anonymous girl, hogtied with razor wire, lying face down on that blood-rusted bed. And smelled that smell.

'What is it?' asked Megan.

'Nothing,' he told her.

'It's a bad one, isn't it? This case you're handling.'

'It's – ah – yes, it's a bad one. I don't think I really want to talk about it.'

'It might help, Tommy. It always has before.'

He lowered his eyes. 'I don't think so, Megs. Not this time.'

She stopped stroking him and clutched his wrist tight. 'Tell me,' she said.

'Not now, please.'

'*Tell me.*'

To his own surprise, he suddenly discovered that he was crying. He sat upright on his dining-chair face-to-face with Megan and tears ran down his cheeks. He had never cried over a homicide before, not for the victim, not for himself. But here he was, weeping like a child, the first time in seventeen years.

'If you could see what they *did* to her –,' he sobbed. He bent his head and Megan put her arms around him and stroked his hair and shushed him. 'I don't understand how they could have –'

She held him tight against her bosom and kept on shushing him, her wheelchair creaking slightly as she rocked him and stroked him. She had often wondered when this would happen, when he would finally break down. She had seen him so many times with his eyes like stones, keeping it all inside of him; or staring at himself in the bathroom mirror, biting his lips. She always knew when it was a bad one, a woman or a child, or something particularly brutal. He smoked more and never sat still and stared out of the window with all the ferocious bewilderment of a caged animal.

'Tell me,' she soothed him.

He sat up straight, smeared his eyes with his fingers, then the back of his hand. 'I can't. I have to understand it first. Right now, I don't understand it. I don't understand it at all. It doesn't fit in with anything I know. It's out of my experience. It wasn't domestic. It wasn't yummies. It was so *strange*. It was like finding a sharkbite victim in the middle of town.'

Megan knew what he meant by 'yummies'. It was the acronym that Mike Barnicle on the *Boston Globe* had devised for 'young urban maggots', a permanent underclass of angry young black and Hispanic men, long on ammo, short on hope, and hell-bent on destroying themselves and each other with Uzis and crack.

'Do you want me to fix you something to take for tonight?' Megan asked him. 'I bought some of that Genoa salami you like.'

Thomas shook his head. 'I'll pick up a hot dog if I'm hungry.'

'Are you sure? How about something to eat now? A rarebit? A quick chicken sandwich?'

Again, he shook his head. He could still smell that terrible stench of decayed flesh. In fact, he could almost *taste* it. If he ate anything now, he was sure that he wouldn't be able to tell the difference between cheese and chicken and corpse.

'I'll be fine, really.' He nodded toward her notebook. 'Come on … let's not talk about me. Let's forget about homicide for five minutes at least. How's the cookbook going?'

'Oh, it's going really well! Gina called me just before I went out, and she gave me this wonderful recipe for steamship roast.'

'Is that going to be tomorrow night's dinner?'

'I have to try them out.'

He reached across and squeezed her hand. 'You know I'm not complaining. I'm the best-fed man on the force.'

Megan smiled; and he loved her smile. Ever since her accident, he had loved her more than ever, although he was always a little afraid to say so, in case she thought he was saying it out of pity, instead of genuine affection. He had realized, too, that if he told her he loved her too enthusiastically, she would begin to suspect that he was having an affair – or feeling like having an affair, or that he had met a woman who had caught his eye.

He loved her and he knew that he would never stop loving her, but there was always the wheelchair, and always the therapy, and always the pain. Once she had ski'd and swum and jogged and danced and worked out. Then, three years ago, she had gone to the farmer's market in the Webster Street parking lot in Brookline – and, happy and rushed, stepped off the kerb. A fully-laden farm truck had hit her and run over her back. Thomas had been sure she would die.

Of course, she hadn't died – although she had been irrevocably paralysed from the waist down. She had told him, just once, that she would have preferred to have died; but having said it once, she never said it again, and after that she had simply tried to make the best of things.

Thomas never could have imagined before Meg's accident what a struggle it was to have a paralysed wife in a world made for people who could walk. Even the most inconsequential shopping trips had to be carefully planned in advance (where would they park? what about stairs and escalators? what about revolving doors? were there any restrooms?). The day they first went out together, Thomas discovered the nightmarish fact that more than two-thirds of the civilized world had suddenly became inaccessible to them.

Their close friends – their police-department friends – had mostly stayed by them. But their social life had gradually dwindled away, until they counted themselves lucky if they were invited out twice a year. Even Meg's sister Joan and her cheerful husband Ray hardly ever asked them over to Framingham any more. Who really wanted to have a woman in a wheelchair drawn up to the dining-table? And hardly anybody accepted *their* invitations, either. Megan could still cook like an angel, but guests always seemed to squirm with embarrassment when she brought in the pot-roast on a special board across her wheelchair handles. As if that made it *taste* any different.

Thomas didn't have time to be bitter about it. He was too busy dealing with grisly homicides and shopping and trying to make a life for both of them. He had never burst into tears before today. He had asked himself more than once if life was fair; but he had never answered.

He stopped at the Newmarket parking lot on the corner of Massachusetts Avenue and Newmarket Square. It was four o'clock and the afternoon was oppressively humid. The sky was bright but blurry with cloud, and the traffic sounded muffled. There was a strangely dreamlike quality about humidity like this: as if everybody was walking around in a surrealistic movie, busy for the sake of being busy.

He parked his car, fastidiously locked it, and walked across to the steaming hot-dog cart that had been angled into an awkward space between an ageing Lincoln and a Winnebago plastered with National Park stickers. Ezra

'Speed' Anderson was already lifting out a hot-dog for him, and smothering it with all of his special sauces. In Speed's thumbprinted sunglasses Thomas saw two dwarfish images of himself approaching, and stretching out a lens-curved arm.

'One Speed Dog, coming up,' said Speed, laconically. 'You look like you could use some nutrition, lieutenant.'

Thomas pulled off a couple of bills and paid him. 'I've got a bad one, that's all.'

'World's a sick place, lieutenant.'

Thomas took a bite of his hot-dog. Speed's sauces were rich enough and spicy enough to obliterate the taste of death. He chewed and he didn't feel hungry but he kept on chewing just the same.

'You think I should open a chain?' asked Speed.

'What for?' asked Thomas. 'This cart of yours is one of the Hub's greatest culinary treasures. You want to spoil it all by opening a chain?'

'I don't know,' said Speed. 'Sometimes I dream of untold riches.'

Thomas said, 'Life is untold riches. You don't need more than that.'

Four

Michael said, 'I had that nightmare again.'

Dr Rice had been playing star solitaire. He looked up over his crescent-shaped eyeglasses, his lips tightly drawn together, but he didn't reply. He was waiting for Michael to tell him which nightmare, because there were several. There was the nightmare about the mortuary and then there was the nightmare about the L10-11 opening up, like a sow with a ripped-open belly, and then there was the nightmare about the trees blossoming with human hands, and the girl who was only half a girl.

And others – some of them graphic and canonical, others mysterious and obscure, jolting terrors without names or faces. Michael Rearden was a mess: a cat's-cradle of traumas and terrors and hideous experiences, played and replayed and replayed, until every thread in his psyche was stretched to the point of snapping.

Dr Rice had been trying to unravel all of Michael's traumas for over a year now, but it wasn't easy. As soon as he managed to untangle one nightmare, another would snaggle itself up. But Dr Rice was not only skilled but infinitely patient, and he reckoned that four or five years' more therapy would eventually bring Michael back to the same state of mental equilibrium in which he had been when he first landed by helicopter at Rocky Woods, eager and ambitious and unprepared for one of the messiest civil aviation disasters in recent history.

There was a difference between reliving his nightmares and dealing with them. At the moment, Michael was simply reliving them, again and again, and making very little emotional headway.

'The falling nightmare,' Michael explained. 'The girl's body. *That* nightmare.'

Dr Rice hesitated over his solitaire board. Then he picked up the last pin that he could take out of it, and said, 'Three left. Why do I never manage fewer than three?'

'I don't think I'm making any kind of recovery,' said Michael. 'It's the same nightmare, just as clear. Just as frightening. I try to handle it, but my mind doesn't *want* to handle it. It's almost like I'm trying to punish myself.'

'That's not uncommon,' Dr Rice explained. 'We've

talked about this before, haven't we? Part of your problem is survivor syndrome. "Grace of God" syndrome, Dr Leavis used to call it. "There, but for the grace of God, go I" – and don't I feel guilty about it!'

'I wasn't even a passenger on that plane,' Michael pointed out.

Dr Rice shook his head. 'Doesn't matter. You saw people killed; you saw innocent women and children smashed to pieces. You walked amongst them and you were still alive.'

Michael eased himself out of the awkward chrome-and-canvas chair. Dr Rice began systematically to put back all the pins in his solitaire board, and didn't even watch him as he crossed the office and peered out through the vertical slatted blinds at the street outside. All Michael could see was the rear end of a yellow van with Aal's Transmissions stencilled in scarlet on the side, and the corner of the Contented Cod Restaurant, with red chintzy curtains and a white mock-Colonial porch. He could also see a gingery dog sleeping in the sun, and a tricycle with a red pennant and a basket filled with groceries, bread, lettuce. It was an odd, empty scene. No automobiles passed, no pedestrians walked by. It reminded him of a painting by Edward Hopper.

Dr Rice waited for him patiently. He could afford to be patient. Michael's therapy was being paid for by Plymouth Insurance, as part of his severance arrangements, and it was up to Dr Rice himself to decide when Michael was emotionally readjusted. Dr Rice was a great believer in the effectiveness of hypnotherapy, but he was also a great believer in cashflow. 'Small and steady is better than sporadic and spectacular,' he had told his broker on the fifth green at Dunfey's Hyannis Resort. But he wasn't a hypocrite: he genuinely believed that Michael could only be cured through a very gradual and well-structured acceptance of what he had experienced.

One day Michael had to accept that witnessing a tragedy wasn't the same as causing it. People had rained from the sky, yes. Children had died. All of the private and precious detritus of hundreds of human lives had been scattered across the countryside. But it hadn't been Michael's fault. Once Michael understood that, once he had *really* come to terms with his innocence, then his healing process could begin. Up until then, there was nothing that Dr Rice could do but hold up a guiding light as he struggled through the thorns and briars of his nightmares, hoping against hope that he was travelling in the right direction.

'Do you think that anything might have triggered this nightmare off?' asked Dr Rice. 'Anything you read, anything you saw on television? Or was it simply spontaneous?'

Michael said, 'They want me to go back. They want me to do it again.'

'Who does? What do you mean?'

'Joe Garboden, from Plymouth Insurance. He came around yesterday. Unannounced, unexpected. He said they need help with this helicopter crash ... you know, the crash that killed John O'Brien and his family?'

'Yes,' said Dr Rice, 'of course I do. But why do they want you?'

Michael shrugged. 'They seem to think I have special talents.'

'But ... come on now, they know that you're still undergoing therapy.'

'I don't think they care very much about that. All they care about is the fact that they might have to cough up a great many millions of dollars.'

'They must have plenty of qualified investigators who could do the job just as well as you.'

Michael took a long last look out of the window. 'They don't seem to think so.'

Dr Rice stood up. He was very tall, at least six-feet-three, and so thin that he looked as if he were racked by some life-threatening disease, although (apart from a liver weakened in his twenties by alcohol and drugs) he was in excellent health. His dyed-black mane was combed back from a bony, horselike forehead. His eyes were so pale that they were almost colourless, like the sea washing over a stone, but they were full of expression. Fire, verve, intellect, warmth. His cheekbones were sharply sculptured and his nose was narrow and complicated and bony.

He was a survivor from the 1960s. After he had graduated in psychology from the University of Massachusetts at Columbia Point, he had headed west and lived at Sandstone and Carmel and Haight-Ashbury. He had spent long, lunatic, spaced-out nights with Timothy Leary and Ken Kesey and a Yaqui mystic who had shown him the skull that lies beneath every human face. At one point, he had *nearly* understood God. But one morning in spring, 1974, he had woken up in Balboa Park, in San Diego, ragingly thirsty and ravenously hungry and realized that the days of revelation were over. It was time to go home to Cape Cod, time to take care of his mother, time to set up in respectable practice and trade his flower-decorated VW Camper for a new gold-metallic Mercedes-Benz. Now, twenty years later, he had a fashionable and highly profitable partnership in Hyannis, helping to treat the psychological complexes of the rich, the influential, the self-absorbed and the just-plain-bored.

He draped his long fingers over Michael's shoulder. 'They can't force you to go back, can they?' he said, his voice very gentle.

Michael made a face. 'No. But poverty can.'

'How much are they offering?'

'Thirty thousand, plus expenses.'

'I think your psychological well-being is worth more than thirty thousand plus expenses, don't you?'

'I don't know. Yes, I guess. But I also have this feeling that I need to go back – that I won't ever be readjusted until I face up to it.'

Dr Rice raised an eyebrow. 'I don't think you really understand the risks. You could end up psychologically damaged beyond repair. A fully paid-up, card-carrying basket-case.'

Michael said nothing. He felt like a basket-case already. Ever since Joe Garboden had said *Remember Rocky Woods* his mind had been gradually collapsing under its own terrible weight.

'Do you want to go under?' asked Dr Rice.

'Do you think it'll solve anything?'

'It might help you to evaluate the risks. You might find out why you feel a need to go back. But you ought to bear in mind that the whole purpose of this therapy has been to help you get over what you experienced, to put it into proportion. Believe me, it's a fallacy that reliving a trauma can help you to deal with it. That's strictly for the movies. The best way of dealing with a trauma is to locate the damaged area of your psyche and see what you can do to repair it.'

Michael thought for a while. Across the street, a pretty young girl in red-and-white striped shorts mounted the abandoned tricycle, and slowly pedalled away. She looked as if she were singing, but he couldn't hear her. The sleeping dog didn't stir.

'Okay,' said Michael. 'I'll go under.'

'You're sure?'

'Sure I'm sure.'

He sat back in the canvas-and-chrome armchair. On the wall beside him, half-obscured by the light reflected on its frame, was a lavishly illuminated certificate from *Die Akademie der Hypnotismus und Mesmerismus, Wien,* 1981, testifying that David Walden Rice had graduated in advanced hypnotherapy. Underneath it hung a vaguely disturbing reproduction of Charles Sheeler's painting of the upper deck of an ocean liner – empty, like the street outside, with meticulously rendered railings and ventilators and cables. A deserted scenario waiting for something to happen.

Dr Rice tugged the chain that closed the vertical blinds, drowning his office in warm, brown shadow. 'Are you comfortable?' he asked Michael; although he had asked this question so many times before that Michael didn't feel the need to reply. 'Place your feet a little wider apart, please. That's right. Now lay your left hand on top of your left knee, palm upwards, and lay your right hand on top of your left hand, also palm upwards.'

Michael had already done what Dr Rice was asking him to do. Dr Rice came closer and Michael could smell cigarette tobacco on his clothes and that clove-scented aftershave he always wore. Dr Rice touched Michael's forehead with his fingertips and said, 'You're tenser than usual. Relax. Keep your elbows close to your sides, but not too close. Rotate your head around, let those neck muscles go.'

After a while, he reached into the pocket of his green checkered shirt and produced a small metal disc only a little larger than a quarter. He laid it carefully and almost reverentially onto Michael's open palm, as if it were a communion wafer. The disc was made of dull grey zinc, with a centre stud of polished copper. Dr Rice said, 'Fix your eyes on the middle of the disc ... on the copper spot ... keep your eyes fixed on it and don't let them waver.'

Every time that Dr Rice began to take him under, Michael was convinced that this time he wouldn't go. He wasn't at all tired; and today he felt that his resistance was stronger than ever. How could Dr Rice put him to sleep simply by making him stare at a zinc-and-copper disc? Yet he knew the disc had worked before. The disc had guided him hundreds of times into his dreams; and into the darkness beneath his dreams; and deeper still; into that Marianas Trench of the human subconscious, where forms and feelings swam in almost total darkness – forms and feelings that could never be exposed to the naked light of wakefulness.

Because of this, the disc was invested in Michael's mind with an almost holy quality – a talisman, a magical artefact. He didn't believe in it, not really. But on the other hand he cherished and respected it. It had *some* mystical aura, although he couldn't understand what. It was like the lucky glass marble he had played with at school, a sea-green sailor. He hadn't really believed that it was lucky; but he had always used it when a game was crucially close; and he had been inconsolable when he lost it.

'You feel inclined to sleep,' said Dr Rice, in a matter-of-fact voice. 'Do not resist that feeling. Allow it to make itself manifest as quickly as it likes. When I tell you to close your eyes, close them.'

Dr Rice then started to make downward passes in front of Michael's face with the palms of his outstretched hands, again and again. Each time his hands came closer and closer, until they were almost touching Michael's eyelashes.

'You are beginning to feel sleepy,' he said, in the calm, monotonous voice he always used when he was taking Michael under. 'You are beginning to feel sleepy. Your eyes are tired. You are losing feeling in your legs and your arms. Your body begins to rest. You are going to sleep. In a minute, you will be sleeping.'

Now he touched Michael's eyelids and gently closed them. 'Your eyes are closing,' he murmured. 'You find it impossible to keep them open. You are going to sleep, fast asleep. You are sleeping now. You cannot open your eyes. They are stuck fast.'

Michael felt the room darkening. He was determined this time that he was going to stay awake. But the darkness was so warm and welcoming; and after all, he had the disc to guide him – and what would it matter if he slept for just a few moments? Dr Rice would never know. He could sleep quickly, to refresh himself, and then open his eyes again, and what difference would it make? He had never really believed in hypnotism anyway. Almost every time Dr Rice had taken him under, he had felt better afterwards, but not that much better. And he had never remembered anything he had dreamed or fantasized about.

He struggled to open his eyes, just to show Dr Rice that he was still awake, but he found that he couldn't. His brain couldn't seem to find the switch to lift his eyelids. He could still hear Dr Rice intoning, 'Now your eyes are well-closed; you are going to sleep, fast asleep.' But no matter how much he grimaced, his eyes simply refused to open. God, he thought. Blinded. Helpless. He wanted to speak out. He wanted to tell Dr Rice to stop, but somehow his mouth wouldn't work either. His larynx simply refused to form words.

Even though his eyes were closed, and he couldn't open them, he saw the faintest flicker of pinkish light. He saw it every time that Dr Rice took him under, but he still didn't understand what it was. For a moment it flared like the aurora borealis, almost dazzling him, but then it died away again as it always did.

After that, after that brilliant flare of light, he felt himself sinking downward. He sank gradually at first, like a man whose lungs are slowly filling with ink. But then he began to slide faster and faster into the endless dark of his subconscious – into that world where his own terror could talk to him, and his worst fears took on flesh.

He heard Dr Rice saying, 'Deeper – and deeper – and *deeper* asleep.' He sounded like a man talking down a hundred-foot well.

Michael knew where he was: sitting in Dr Rice's office in Dr Rice's canvas-and-chrome chair. Yet he was also back at home, standing in the kitchen drinking Folger's Dark Roast coffee out of his Ross Perot For President mug, with the morning sun slanting across the table. Outside the window, red-and-white kites whirled in a tethered frenzy over New Seabury beach, and the window sash rattled – hesitated – rattled in the breeze. Jason was bent over his cereal bowl, his tousled hair shining, while Patsy was standing at the sink in her pink cotton robe, the one with the torn lace collar.

'Have you thought about it any more?' Patsy was asking him, in a blurry voice. *It* meaning death. *It* meaning John O'Brien's body. *It* meaning more people falling like heavy rainfall out of the sky, and a burned-out helicopter. Patsy turned around, and for some reason he couldn't focus on her face, although he knew for sure that it was her.

He nodded. 'I've been thinking about it all night.'

Jason looked up, and Michael found it impossible to focus on *his* face, too. 'Dad ... when you come back from Hyannis, can you fix my back brake? It keeps rubbing against the wheel.' Then he lifted his head again and said, '– rubbing against the wheel.' Then he lifted his head yet again and said, '– rubbing against the wheel.'

Michael thought *yes, I ought to keep Jason's bicycle in good working order*. But before he could answer, Patsy said, 'Have you thought about it any more?' and he began to feel that he was trapped in a loop of memory that was playing and replaying with no way out.

He was just about to say something to Patsy about Joe

Garboden when he found that he wasn't in the kitchen at all, but travelling to Hyannis along the Popponosset Beach road. He didn't know why he was going this way. He should have driven directly to South Mashpee and onto Route 28. Going through Popponosset involved an unnecessary dog-leg. All the same, he had a vague feeling that he was supposed to meet somebody at Popponosset, although he didn't know who it could be.

The odd thing was that he was standing up as he drove, as if he were still standing in the kitchen. The sunlit coast-line of Popponosset Bay unravelled past him bright and two-dimensional, in bleached-out colours, like the special effects in a cheap 1960s movie.

On the car radio, a faint, dry voice was saying, '... be meeting you later, yes. That's quite correct. He said nothing else.'

He drove past the Popponosset Inn, with its tiled beach house and its verandah and its striped umbrellas nodding in the breeze. He thought he could see a tall man in a grey suit standing by the railings watching him, but when he turned his head around to look again, the man had vanished; and the only people on the verandah were a young couple in white polo shirts.

But something had changed. Something was making him feel uneasy. Although he couldn't understand how he had become aware of it, he knew for certain that the man in the grey suit had seen him, and was intent on pursuing him. He kept turning around and around, but he couldn't see the man anywhere. All the same, the man was after him, and intended to do him serious harm.

He began to feel alarmed. The sky over Popponosset Bay began to grow rapidly darker, and the white of the break-ers began to shine in the gloom like the teeth of fierce, hungry dogs. The wind sprang up and he could actually feel it on his face, salty and warm and abrasive with flying sand.

The man was waiting for him on the beach. Strangely, it didn't look like Popponosset Beach any more, but somewhere else – somewhere that Michael was sure that he had seen before, but which he couldn't quite place. There was a scrubby headland in the distance, and a row of green-painted saltbox houses, and a curve of rocks that reminded him very strongly of Popponosset. But there was a squat, whitewashed lighthouse here; and there was no such lighthouse at Popponosset, never had been.

His car seemed to have melted away. He found himself walking across the dry, blowing sand in his Adidas training shoes. He could hear the sound of the surf quite distinctly, and the high-pitched whistling of a man calling his dog. 'Be meeting you later,' said a voice, very close to his ear; and he was too frightened to turn his head to see who it was. 'Be meeting you later – rubbing against the wheel.'

Off to his right, the Atlantic sky was evilly black, and the wind was so strong now that the sand was whipping against his ankles like snakes. He could hear his heart beating, and his lungs rising and falling, and he could even hear the faint crackling of electricity in his nerve-endings. The tall grey man was still waiting for him at the end of the beach, and Michael was beginning to feel seriously frightened. This was only hypnotism, after all; this was only suggestive therapy. He knew it was only hypnotism, even though he was experiencing the seashore so vividly. He knew he was still sitting in Dr Rice's office.

But here stood this tall grey man, and he didn't look like anyone that Michael had ever known, or anyone that Michael might have imagined. He had never appeared in any of Michael's hypnotic dreams before. Yet his presence was so distinct that Michael could almost taste it. It was like copper and thunder and something else – the metallic taste of human blood. Michael had never seen him before. He was sure that he had never seen him before, even though he thought he recognized the squat white lighthouse and the deserted, grassy beach. *Be meeting you later.*

What unnerved Michael more than anything else was the way in which he couldn't stop himself from walking so swiftly to meet this man. His legs had an urgency of their own, an urgency he couldn't control, hurrying him on, hurrying him on, even though his mind was filling up with absolute terror, like a bottle filling up with black blood.

The man had bone-white hair, long and silky and swept back, although some of it was flying in the onshore wind. He had a long sculptured face, with a straight, narrow nose and distinctive cheekbones and dark, commanding eyes. He was, in fact, frighteningly handsome, the kind of man whose presence makes husbands take a protective hold on their wives' arms. He wore a long expensive overcoat of light grey softly woven wool, which billowed and rumbled in the wind, and gave Michael the impression that he was floating just a few inches above the sand – an impression that was reinforced by the complete absence of footprints anywhere near him. Of course, Michael told himself, as he hurried nearer and nearer, the wind had blown his footprints away. But all the same the tall grey man still appeared to be floating. Not just floating, but *receding*, as if he were drawing Michael further and further along the beach, toward the dunes, and the rocks, and the squat white lighthouse on the clifftop.

Michael clenched his teeth and strained his shoulder muscles, making a huge physical effort to stop himself from walking any further. He was aware that he was hurrying across the beach, but at the same time he was also aware that he was bending the arms of Dr Rice's chair in his struggle to stay where he was.

'Come on, Michael,' the man was saying. His voice was so soft that Michael was unsure whether he was really speaking to him, or whether it was nothing more than the seductive whispering of the surf. 'You should join us, Michael. You should join us. We could ease your pain, Michael. We could give you forgetfulness. We could even grant you absolution.'

Michael grunted with the strain of trying to stop himself walking any further. His muscles were so rigidly tight that his back ached, and he felt as if his jaw would be locked for the rest of his life.

But in spite of all of his efforts he half slid, half staggered right up close to the dune where the man was standing; and it was only when he was less than three feet away that he finally managed to stop himself.

With very sharp fingernails, the man was peeling a lime. He stood watching Michael with a mixed expression on his face, partly curious, partly contemptuous, and partly sympathetic. Michael tried to back away, but he just couldn't summon enough strength. The tall grey man wanted him there, and that was that. Michael opened and closed his mouth, and realized that he had never been so terrified of another human being in his life. This man scared him so much that he couldn't even *breathe*.

Whoever he was, whatever he wanted, this man was Death itself. And the most frightening part about it was that Michael knew with total certainty that he was Death.

'Do you want to live like half a man for the rest of your life?' the man whispered, his voice sounding almost sad. 'Do you want all of your dreams and all of your ambitions to sift through your fingers, like sand?'

He finished peeling his lime, and lifted the thin corkscrew of dark green peel so that it twisted in the breeze. Then he bit into the lime itself, deeply; and he didn't even flinch.

96

'You should know me, Michael,' the man told him, with juice running down his chin. 'My name is –'

Michael clamped his hands over his ears. He didn't want to hear the man's name. If he heard the man's name, then he would know for certain that he was real. And if he was real, he could come after him, not just in dreams and nightmares and hypnotic trances, but in cars and buses and along the sidewalk, until he reached his door and Michael opened it and there he stood, tall and grey and terrifying.

Michael thought: he's going to kill me. Somehow, somewhere, I'm going to meet this tall grey man, and when I do he's going to kill me. He would probably kill me here and now if he could, on this beach, in this office, with the sea whispering and the traffic bustling outside the window.

'You don't want to live like half a man, do you?' the man whispered, with a smile.

Then he said, '*Wake up.*'

'We can cleanse you of all of your guilt, you know.'

'*Wake up, Michael. When I count to six I want you to open your eyes and look at me; and then you will be fully awake. You will recall everything that you have thought about, and you will tell me about it immediately.*'

'What?' asked Michael. He didn't understand.

'*Wake up,*' insisted Dr Rice, and it was then that Michael looked around him and understood which of his parallel existences was real. The sound of the sea died away, and the tall grey man faded away, and the very last thing that he was conscious of seeing was the squat white lighthouse, which remained as a dark triangular image on his retina for nearly ten seconds, before that faded away, too.

Dr Rice looked concerned. 'Michael? Are you okay?'

Michael blinked. Although the blinds were closed, the office still seemed uncomfortably bright. 'Sure, yes … I think so. That was one of the weirdest sessions I've ever had.'

97

'You don't have to tell me. Take a look at the arms of your chair.'

Michael cautiously lifted both hands and examined the arms. The right-hand one was twisted into an S-shape, where once it had been completely straight. The left-hand arm wasn't quite as badly bent, but it still had a noticeable double kink in it. Part of the canvas seating was torn away, too.

'What's happened?' he asked, incredulously. 'What did I do?'

Dr Rice said, 'You pulled and you twisted and you shouted out, and you tried to turn my best Oggetti chair into a pretzel, that's what you did.'

Michael took hold of one of the chair arms in both hands and tried to bend it back again, but he couldn't. He looked up at Dr Rice in perplexity and embarrassment.

Dr Rice shrugged. 'I don't think you'll be able to straighten it out. Most people exhibit some degree of enhanced physical strength when they're under deep hypnosis, but you really went off the scale. That chair is 6mm tube steel. Normally, you'd need a heavy-duty pipe wrench to bend those arms.'

'I was trying to stop myself,' Michael explained. 'I was trying to stop myself from – *walking*, from walking toward this –' He suddenly realized that the back of his shirt was soaked in sweat, in spite of the air-conditioning, and that he was shaking like a man who has just survived an auto wreck.

The trouble was, he didn't understand *why* his trance had been so strenuous; or *why* it had been so traumatic. He had dreamed of meeting a tall grey bogyman on a beach, but that was all. He couldn't even remember why the man had terrified him so much – although he was still very aware that he *had*. In fact he hoped he never dreamed about him again, ever.

98

'You want to tell me about it?' asked Dr Rice, sitting down on the edge of his desk.

'I don't know … I don't know whether it has any relevance at all to Rocky Woods.'

'It sure shook you up, though. You were pulling that chair around and shouting like a madman.'

'I was shouting? What was I shouting?'

Dr Rice got up, walked across to his Bang & Olufsen recording deck, and rewound his tape-player. 'It was unusual for you … you were talking in several distinct voices. I have quite a number of patients who talk in three or four different voices. It's quite a common symptom of extreme emotional trauma. Many people are so distressed by what they've experienced that they can only deal with it by acting it out through the eyes of others; or through their own eyes when they were children. That's why they use a variety of voices. But you, up until now you've strictly been a one-voice guy.'

'That makes me sound pretty dull and worthy, doesn't it?'

Dr Rice smiled. 'Believe me, it makes treatment a whole lot simpler. When you have a multiple-voice situation, it can take a therapist years to sort out one voice from another. I had one guy last year – white guy – whenever he was under hypnosis he always used to talk like Eddie Murphy. It turned out that he believed that somebody like Eddie Murphy would see the funny side of what he had done, whereas he himself was incapable of laughing about it.'

'And what *had* he done?' asked Michael.

'Oh … doused his wife and children in gasoline and set them on fire.'

'Jesus.'

It was then that Dr Rice located the beginning of the session on his tape.

'Here, listen to this.'

There was a moment's hissing and then Michael recognized his own deep breathing. The breathing continued for two or three minutes, and he could hear rustling noises in the background as Dr Rice walked around his office and rearranged his papers.

Then, without warning, he heard a strange, high voice, almost like a woman's voice, but slightly harsher.

'*Have you thought about it any more?*'

Michael turned and stared at Dr Rice. 'Who the hell was that?'

'That was you.'

'That was *me*? That didn't sound like me at all.'

'You want to hear it again?' Dr Rice leaned over and rewound the tape a short way. The breathing returned, then the same strained, high-pitched voice.

'*Have you thought about it any more?*'

Michael said, 'I remember that now. I thought I was back at home. Patsy was asking me whether I was going to take that insurance job or not.'

'Well … you may have thought it was Patsy,' said Dr Rice. 'But in actual fact it was *you*.'

'I don't understand it. Why should I try to talk in Patsy's voice?'

'It's not unusual. It's a way of discussing the problem with yourself, that's all. Like you're trying to see the situation from her side as well as yours.'

The tape continued. Next, Michael was talking in a much closer approximation to his normal voice, except that he sounded dreamy or drugged – the way most people do when they're under deep hypnosis.

'*I've been thinking about it all night.*'

But then his voice changed again – higher, lighter.

'*Dad … when you come back from Hyannis, can you fix my back brake? It keeps rubbing against the wheel.*'

'Jason,' said Michael. 'I'm trying to talk like Jason.'

Next, he heard the telephone warble, and Dr Rice quickly answer it. '*Hallo? Yes, this is he. Oh, Dr Fellowes. Yes. For sure. I'll be meeting you later, yes. That's quite correct. No, Dr Osman didn't mention it. He said nothing at all.*'

Michael said, 'I remember some of that conversation from my trance. Not all of it. I thought it was part of what was going on.'

Now there was a longer pause, although Michael could distinctly hear himself breathing. To begin with, the breathing was slow and measured. But all of a sudden, it grew harsher, as if he were jogging; and then harsher still, as if he were running. He heard the squeaking of his hands on the arms of the chair, and the ripping of canvas.

'*Come on, Michael,*' he heard a voice urging him, in a breathless whisper.

He frowned, and leaned forward in his chair so that he could hear better.

'That was you, too,' said Dr Rice.

Michael shook his head. 'That doesn't sound like me at all. That doesn't even sound like me pretending to be somebody else.'

'Believe me,' said Dr Rice, 'you were the one who was moving his lips.'

Panting, and gasping, and – '*You should join us, Michael, you should join us.*'

'That can't be me,' Michael protested.

'*We could ease your pain, Michael, we could give you forgetfulness. We could even grant you absolution.*'

'This is incredible,' said Michael. 'There was this guy in my trance ... this really tall guy, in a greyish kind of a coat ... This voice isn't my voice ... this is *his* voice, I swear it. Listen to it – it doesn't sound anything like me!'

Dr Rice leaned back and crossed his legs. 'I know you

find it hard to believe, but when you're in hypnosis you're capable of all manner of extraordinary achievements. People often demonstrate talents that normally they're too inhibited to show off. Or maybe they never even knew they had them. They're also capable of changing their vocal cords so that they can speak in very different voices.'

'*Do you want to live like half a man for the rest of your life?*' the voice asked.

'*No!*' Michael heard himself shout.

'*Do you want all of your dreams and all of your ambitions to sift through your fingers like sand?*'

'*No!*' Michael screamed; and he couldn't believe that he had screamed like that. He hadn't been conscious of screaming – only of struggling to keep himself away from the tall grey man in the long grey coat. '*Don't touch me! Don't touch me! I want to wake up! I want to wake up! I want to wake up!*'

There was a confused, jostling, knocking noise. He heard Dr Rice saying, '*Michael! Michael! Wake up, Michael! When I count to six I want you to open your eyes and look at me and then you will be fully awake.*'

'*Don't touch me!*' Michael screamed, again and again. '*Don't touch me!*'

There was more jostling, and a blurting sound. Then the voice whispered, '*You should know me, Michael. My name is* –' But the name was blotted out by another blurting sound.

Dr Rice switched off the tape. He looked at Michael for a long time without saying anything. Michael dragged a handkerchief out of his pocket and wiped the sweat from his face and his neck.

'You say you saw a really tall guy in a greyish coat?'

Michael cleared his throat, and nodded. 'He was down on the beach.'

'Any particular beach?'

'No, I didn't recognize it. There was a lighthouse in the background, that's all I remember.'

'But it wasn't anyplace you'd been before? Nowhere you'd carried out an insurance investigation, say? A drowning, or anything like that?'

Michael shook his head. 'I've done drownings, but nowhere like that.'

'Was there anything familiar about this guy in the greyish coat?'

'Never seen him before, never.'

'He said, "*You should know me, Michael.*" '

'I didn't know him.'

'But you were frightened of him, weren't you? Why were you frightened of him?'

Michael folded his handkerchief into a pad and wiped the back of his neck again. 'I don't know. I guess it was just one of those irrational things that happen under hypnosis. You know … like in nightmares.'

'He told you his name.'

'I couldn't hear him. I don't think I *wanted* to hear him. I put my hands over my ears.'

'Why didn't you want to hear him? Were you afraid that you might know him, after all?'

'I didn't know him, okay? He was a spooky character out of a dream, that's all.'

Dr Rice made a few jottings on his pad, and then said, 'All right. I guess that'll do for today. It seems like this job offer may have stirred up some feelings that you've been keeping under wraps. It's just possible that they could lead us in some new directions … help us to tackle your trauma from another angle, as it were.'

'What does that mean?'

'I'm not sure yet. It kind of depends who this tall guy in

the coat actually is, or was … and, as you say, whether he has any relevance to Rocky Woods or not.'

'Does it mean that I should take the job?'

Dr Rice tapped his pencil on his teeth and looked at Michael seriously. 'Do you want to take the job?'

'I don't know. Yes and no. I'd like the money, I'd like the respect. I also feel that it might help me to get back in touch with the real world, if you know what I mean. When you spend every single day on your own, with nobody to bounce your ideas off … well, you tend to get a little screwy.'

'Those are the plus points,' agreed Dr Rice. 'What about the negative points?'

Michael turned away and stared at the picture of deck rails and ventilator pipes and masts. A ship waiting for passengers. A moment waiting to begin.

'I'm afraid,' he said, so quietly that Dr Rice could scarcely hear him.

'What are you afraid of, more than anything else?'

'Everything. Nothing. Jesus – I'm afraid that I'm going to take one look at those dead people and my brain's going to collapse and I won't be able to think or speak or move or do anything at all, ever again.'

Dr Rice said nothing for a very long time. But eventually he made another jotting on his pad, and asked, 'What about that tall man in the greyish coat? Do you think he might represent that particular fear? What I'm saying is, do you think he might be some kind of symbolic figure? Your own trauma, in the flesh?'

Michael looked back at him. 'Would that make a difference?'

'It might. After all, you've shown me quite clearly that you're capable of resisting him – that you're fighting him with all the mental and physical strength at your disposal … and then some. Visualizing your single greatest fear in the

104

form of an actual man might be the most important step that you have taken toward your recovery since you were very first traumatized.'

'So you think I ought to take the job?'

'Aha! I'm sorry, Michael. No can help. Nobody can take that decision except you.'

Back at home, seated at his drawing-board, Michael sketched a picture of the seashore where the man had been standing, and the squat white lighthouse. With its grassy headland, its ocean-weathered cliffs and its curving sands, it could have been any bay from Pigeon Cove to Horseneck Beach. It might not even have been in Massachusetts, although he was irrationally convinced that it was. It might not even have been a real beach at all.

On a separate sheet of paper, he tried to draw the tall grey man in the long grey coat. It was curiously difficult. Although he could remember very distinctly what impression the man had made on him; and that he was tall; and grey-haired; and narrow-nosed; he found it almost impossible to assemble all of these features in a recognizable face. He pencilled and shaded for nearly two hours, and in the end he managed to produce a vaguely similar figure, but he was very far from satisfied.

He sat back, frowning, and looked out at the clouds crossing New Seabury beach. The sands were deserted. There were no swimmers, no walkers; nobody flying kites. A landscape waiting for something to happen.

All the way back from Hyannis, he had known with complete certainty what he was going to do. He lifted a sheaf of papers under which his telephone had been concealing itself like a burrowing crab, and lifted the handset. He punched out the number which even hypnotherapy could never have erased from his memory, 617–999 9999.

When the girl answered, 'Plymouth, first and finest, how can I help you?' he hesitated for only a moment before saying, 'Joe Garboden please.'

He heard Joe's extension ringing, and he knew then that there was no turning back.

Five

'That's him!' barked Detective Ralph Brossard, the instant that the lanky black man appeared in the doorway and started to lope across the sidewalk. He flicked his freshly-lit cigarette out of the car window and reached for his r/t.

'Newt – Newt, Jambo just exited the front door. He's crossing the street and he's headed for his vehicle. He's carrying the sports bag. It's a go.'

Next to him, Detective John Minatello reached inside his cream cotton windcheater and lifted out his .38. He gave Ralph a quick, pale, sweaty grin and said, with nervous satisfaction, '*Nailed* the son-of-a-bitch. Geronimo!'

Ralph started the Pontiac's engine, and quickly glanced behind him to make sure that there were no civilian cars coming up the street. With the flat of his hand, he spun the wheel over to left-hand lock, until the power steering whistled. Then he licked his lips and tensely waited.

'Come on, you mother,' he breathed.

It was six minutes after eleven a.m. on Seaver Street, in the Combat Zone. The brick tenement buildings were brown and the sidewalks were brown and even the air was brown. The day smelled of cooking fats and automobile fumes and dried-out water traps. Ralph had been sitting by the kerb in his Grand Prix since fifteen minutes before dawn, waiting for Jambo to emerge from 1334. He and John Minatello had breakfasted on Egg MacMuffins and tepid coffee, and the vinyl seat was still cluttered with the debris of their meal, along with crumpled biscuit wrappers and empty cartons of Winston Lights and a dog-eared copy of *Islands in the Stream* by Ernest Hemingway.

Ralph was a plaid-shirt and twelve-bore Hemingway enthusiast. A man's man.

All his life (well, ever since his divorce four years ago from Thelma) Ralph had been preparing himself for a Hemingway-like retirement in the Caribbean, fishing for shark and marlin in deep blue waters, listening to the rain rustling on a dried-palm roof, beachcombing, drinking whisky, letting one warm tropical day slide into the next. He had even grown to look a little like Hemingway, although police department regulations forbade a beard. He was broad faced and bluff, with a black-and-white moustache and eyes that crinkled up and focused way beyond Boston, even when he was sitting in cars for days on end waiting for suspects, or typing out reports.

Two years and seven months to go, and Ralph could hang up his gun, hand in his badge, and take the plane south for Miami and then Bimini, leaving behind him the sweating brown summers and the ball-cracking winters, the air pollution and the grimy crime. He could leave behind the supercilious rich on Newbury Street and the snarling poor on Blue Hill Avenue – and everything else he detested about this pretentious, squalid, quaint and dangerous city.

He had been following Jambo DuFreyne for over a year now, through five tedious seasons. Leaves had budded, ice had melted, sun had filled the streets. Every two weeks Jambo brought exhibition-quality cocaine in a sports bag from Atlanta, Georgia, to sell it in Boston, and Ralph and John had seen him open that front door and lope across that same street in rain, in snow, in sunshine, in freezing fog – thin and spindly-legged, in the same brown woolly tom and the same knee-length leather coat, and climb into the same dented brown Buick with the squealing bearings.

Up until today, they had let Jambo well alone. Jambo, after all, was nothing more than a carrier. But here, in this apartment building, fifth floor back, lived Luther Johnson, one of the evilest faces in Boston, the Spider of Seaver Street; and from Luther Johnson's apartment Ralph had patiently followed Jambo's cocaine to a crack factory in Cambridge; and from the crack factory in Cambridge to most of its major outlets, which included Harvard University and MIT and Harvard Med School, where rich kids were willing to pay well over the odds for good-quality produce.

Ralph already had sufficient evidence to arrest the sons and daughters of some of America's wealthiest and most influential families on charges of drug trafficking, conspiracy, extortion and tax evasion. He had videos and wiretaps on Belmonts, on Woolleys, on Pembrokes and Cabots. Jambo DuFrayne was the final connection. This morning he was carrying a sports bag of used $100 bills, in payment for his latest delivery – all of which, unknown to Jambo, were marked and all of which could be traced conclusively back to the golden young men and women on five different campuses. Ralph had nicknamed it the Ivy Connection.

Jambo climbed into his car, and for a few moments Ralph was unable to see him, because he was parked about 150 feet further up the road, on the opposite side, behind a large green van.

'Come on, you mother,' he repeated, drumming his fingers on the steering wheel.

'He's coming, he's coming,' said John Minatello. 'He's started his engine. I saw the exhaust.'

'Newt, you there Newt?' Ralph called, into his r/t.

'I'm here, Ralph, don't sweat it.'

'When I say hit it, Newt, you hit it, and you ram that mother up the rear end so that he doesn't know whether it's tomorrow or Christmas.'

'I got it, Ralph, don't you worry.'

'Come on, you mother,' Ralph repeated.

He glanced in his driver-side mirror. The street was clear. He gently revved the gas, then glanced again. A powder-blue Volkswagen Beetle had appeared from nowhere at all, was slowly approaching. 'Shit,' he said. The very last thing he wanted now was any civilian presence. It was inconceivable that Jambo wasn't armed. He could be carrying anything from a .44 to an Uzi, or both, and he wouldn't hesitate to use them. Jambo had a history of armed robbery and violent assault that made Saddam Hussein look like St Francis of Assisi.

Ralph could only pray that the Beetle would reach the far end of the street before Jambo decided to pull out of his parking space. He could pull out himself to block the Beetle's progress, but then he would have to keep on going right past Jambo, or Jambo would immediately twig that he was being ambushed. And if he kept going and passed Jambo by, he would be giving the son of a bitch an open route to make his getaway.

On the other hand, if he didn't block the Beetle off, Jambo might pull out immediately – when the Beetle was still halfway between Jambo and the end of the street, where Newt was waiting. There were vans and automobiles parked on both sides of the street, and with the Beetle obstructing him, Newt wouldn't be able to come speeding down from the far end of the street to rear-end Jambo and box him in.

Apart from that, there would be an unacceptably high risk of the Beetle's driver being injured or even killed.

'Civilian vehicle approaching,' Newt remarked, flatly.

'I'm aware,' Ralph replied.

'What do you want to do?'

'Pray to St Philip that it clears the street.'

'You could block it?'

'Jambo's not moving yet. If he senses that something's going down, he won't move. He'll make a run for it.'

The Beetle chugged closer and closer.

'We could let him go,' Newt suggested. 'We could hit him on Washington Street instead.'

'Unh-hunh. We have to hit him here. Remember *DeSisto.*'

DeSisto vs. Commonwealth of Massachusetts was a notorious case in which a drug-runner's conviction had been overturned because the police had momentarily lost sight of his vehicle in traffic. During those few lost seconds, DeSisto's defence attorney had argued, anybody could have tossed the package of incriminating evidence into his client's car. Whether it was *likely* or not was immaterial. It was *possible,* and DeSisto had walked. Ralph was determined that Jambo wouldn't walk, because if Jambo walked, then all of those snotty overbearing Ivy Leaguers and all of those arrogant MIT technocrats would walk, too. Ralph spent most of his time picking up small-time pushers and crackheads and crazies with pissy pants. As far as he was concerned, it was a deep moral principle that the law should be applied with equal vigour to those who wore Calvin Klein and Nino Cerruti and spent their summers in Newport or the Caribbean.

The Beetle crawled slowly past him. He glanced quickly at the driver. A black girl, aged about twenty-three, with cornrow hair and silver hoop earrings. On the Beetle's door was painted a cartoon crow from *Dumbo* doffing a straw hat and saying Brush My Feet! Ralph noticed that the licence plate was out of date, and that the rear wheel-arches were severely rusted and patched with fibreglass.

'Come on, baby,' Ralph urged her, under his breath. She had almost reached Jambo's car now. 'Come on, baby, keep your foot down.'

But the Beetle crawled slower and slower. When it was almost alongside Jambo's parking place, it stopped completely, and a cloud of brown smoke belched out of its exhausts. For a moment, Ralph thought that the girl might have broken down; but then he realized that she had paused only because she was searching for some particular building. The Beetle stayed where it was for nearly a minute, juddering and pouring out smoke, while Ralph sat drumming and sweating and *praying* that the girl would move on.

'What the fuck is she *doing*?' Newt asked, over the r/t.

'Looks like she's checking the street numbers,' Ralph replied. 'She must be lost.'

'Why the fuck doesn't she get herself lost someplace else?'

Ralph didn't reply. He was far too tense. The girl was lost because she was lost; and because every surveillance that Ralph had ever arranged was plagued by innocent glitches: people who wandered bewildered and unknowing into the line of fire, trucks that parked in front of windows they were watching, road menders who would suddenly decide to hammer-drill right next to phone booths that they were tapping.

'Come on, baby, *move*,' he breathed; but still the Beetle stayed where it was, puffing smoke.

He heard Jambo blasting his car horn, and that got the girl moving. She chugged a few feet further down the street, and now Jambo was manoeuvring his black Electra out of his parking space. Through the purplish tint of his windshield, Ralph could see the silhouette of Jambo's woolly tom and his sunglasses black and expressionless as an insect's eyes. But the Beetle had stopped again, just behind him, which meant that Newt was faced with a high-speed run along 120 feet of street, culminating in a 50 mph 'squeeze' between the dawdling Beetle and the cars parked along the kerb – a 'squeeze' which would allow him less than six or seven inches on either side.

'Newt, you going to try it?' asked Ralph.

'Never say never,' Newt replied.

Jambo's car had cleared the parking space now, and was driving towards Ralph at quickly increasing speed. Jambo's Electra was an '81 model, unwashed but mechanically well maintained, with stiffened suspension and widened wheels. Ralph knew for certain that if he didn't stop Jambo now, he would have God's own job to stop him on Washington Street, or the turnpike, or whichever way he chose to speed to the airport. And he couldn't let him out of his sight, not for an instant, not for the blink of an eye; or else it was *DeSisto* all over again. This was one case he couldn't even think of losing. He couldn't bear the idea of those Ivy Leaguers laughing at him. He had to nail them and arraign them and lock them up and that was all that mattered. He had to bring them low, because they *were* low, they were shit.

'This is it,' he said, so matter-of-fact that John Minatello was taken by surprise. He slammed his foot on the gas and swerved the Grand Prix out into the middle of the street with an operatic screaming of tyres.

Jambo didn't even have time to hit the brakes. His 4,000lb Electra was travelling at nearly 30 mph when it collided head-on with Ralph's Grand Prix. Ralph heard a devastating smash and his head was slammed backward against the seat and his left leg was jammed against the door. Then he was screaming, 'Out! Out!' and he was kicking the door open and rolling into the street. He tugged his non-regulation .44 out of its holster and cocked it and kept on rolling, underneath the back of a parked car, so that when he finally scrambled to his feet he was holding the .44 in both hands and he was shielded by the sagging rear end of an ancient Le Sabre.

He saw John Minatello crouched behind the passenger door of their wrecked Grand Prix, brandishing his .38 and screaming, 'Show me your hands! Show me your fucking hands!'

He saw Newt in his sea-green Plymouth, roaring toward them down Seaver Street with his red beacon flashing, blurred by sunlight and smoke. There was a split second when he really thought that Newt would make it through the narrow gap between the Beetle and the cars parked on the side of the street. He actually mouthed the words, *Done it, you beautiful s.o.b.* – but then he saw pieces of door-mirror flying in the sunlight, and heard that terrible wrenching, *bosh*-ing noise of cars colliding, and the Beetle was tilted and dropped, and Newt's Plymouth was wedged in tight against a rusty brown pick-up.

Jambo – half-out of the driver's door – turned around and looked behind him with extraordinary grace, almost as if he were performing in a ballet. Ralph saw his thin chest lean back, his hips pivot.

'Show me your hands!' John Minatello raged. But Jambo ignored him and it was then that Ralph realized that Jambo was holding a very large handgun.

God, he wanted Jambo alive. He *needed* Jambo alive. He roared at John Minatello, '*Don't!*' but the morning suddenly boomed with two heavyweight shots, and then *boom!* another heavyweight shot, and then *snap! snap! snap!* which was John Minatello's .38.

Ralph saw the Beetle's rear window explode, and a burst of blood spray out of it – almost as if the driver had tossed a cup of coffee into the street. *Shit*, he thought, *he's killed her*. Then he saw the windshield of Newt's Plymouth starred and shattered; and a quick, consistent cracking as Newt returned fire. The street was suddenly filled with smoke, and theatrical shafts of light, and Jambo was gone, like a conjuring trick.

Ralph, panting heavily, leaned to one side of the parked car, then to the other. The fucker had gone, the fucker had gone. He stayed where he was, utterly tense, his knees slightly bent, his gun held upward in both hands, his blue T-shirt darkly circled with sweat.

'Where's he gone?' he shouted to John Minatello.

John Minatello's face was as pale and long as a calf's-brain sausage. 'I can't see him. I thought I hit him.'

'Newt!' yelled Ralph, in a harsh, high voice.

'It's okay, Ralph!' Newt shouted back.

'Where the fuck is he?' Ralph demanded.

'I don't know. I didn't see where he went.'

'What the fuck do you mean, you didn't see where he went?'

'I mean, I didn't see where he went.'

There was a lengthy silence. Seaver Street was oddly hushed, apart from the ambient murmuring of traffic, and the sound of an L10-11 taking off from Logan, and making its way south-westward.

Ralph reluctantly edged his way around the back of the car. He held his .44 two-handed, way out in front of him, and he knew that the barrel was trembling, but he put that down to adrenaline.

'Mr DuFreyne!' he called, glancing over at John Minatello. 'Mr DuFreyne, we're police officers here, and we have a warrant to arrest you. Now – either you make it easy, or else you make it hard.'

The smoke began to drift away; and as the smoke cleared,

the silence began to fill up, too. Suddenly there were crowds talking and music playing and dogs barking and trees rustling.

Ralph leaned down and looked under the car which he was using for protection. He looked all the way across the street. There were plenty of gum wrappers and bottles and squashed drink cans, and a black thing that looked like somebody's discarded bondage suit, but that was all.

'Mr DuFreyne, you're under arrest but if you co-operate this whole thing could go very easy on you!' Ralph shouted. 'Do you hear me? We're after your buyers, not you! We're not even interested in Luther! You just tell us who's been bankrolling this little bit of business, and you can have the deal of a lifetime. Come on, it's election year! The DA's pretty sweet on people who act in the public interest. You know that. Look what happened to Mack Rivera.'

Again, there was silence. Ralph taxi-whistled to John Minatello to catch his attention, and then indicated with an urgent wave of his gun so that John should leave the comparative safety of a car door, and make his way slowly up the sidewalk until he could see where Jambo DuFreyne had concealed himself.

The only real worry he had was whether Jambo had done a Harry Lime on him – opened a manhole cover and gone to ground down the sewers.

He edged along the sidewalk, ducking down now and again to see if he could catch a glimpse of Jambo's legs. 'Newt!' he shouted. 'Your radio still working?'

'It's working, Ralph,' Newt called back. 'I called for an ambulance already.'

'Shit,' said Ralph, under his breath. He had a sick sensation in his stomach. He should have let Jambo go, he should have let him get away. The death of a single innocent bystander was too high a price to pay for any bust – even the most spectacular drugs bust in the history of Massachusetts. Even if that girl with the cornrow hair and the hoop earrings wasn't dead, she was seriously hurt, and her family and her friends and her lawyer and every TV station and newspaper in New England was going to want to know why Detective Ralph Brossard had initiated an ambush when she was still puttering along Seaver Street in the line of fire.

'Shit,' he repeated, 'shit, shit, shit.' He was angry and shaken and bitterly regretful; and frightened, too; and all he could taste was shit.

'I don't see him!' called John Minatello.

'Then where the fuck?' Ralph demanded.

Newt said, 'Look under the cars, for Christ's sake. Look under the cars.'

'I did,' John Minatello protested.

Crouching as low as he could, Ralph made his way up the left-hand side of the street. Every now and then, he leaned over sideways, his hand flat on the hot, gritty sidewalk, so that he could check beneath the parked cars for any sign of Jambo's ankles. An elderly black woman watched him dispassionately from an open window, her eyes magnified by her spectacles, so that they looked like two freshly-opened oysters.

'Get the hell inside!' he snapped at her.

'What for?' she wanted to know. 'I seen men die before now.'

'Police!' said Ralph. 'Now get the hell inside!'

At that moment, when he was distracted, Newt shouted out, *'There he goes!'* and Ralph was conscious of a dark shadow flickering between the cars, all arms and legs, and the showy glitter of a nickel-plated gun.

'Freeze!' he screamed, lifting his .44 and aiming it two-handed along the sidewalk, right to the point where Jambo's next leap would take him. He saw Jambo's woolly tom bobbing up and down behind the peeling vinyl roof of a brown Sedan de Ville. He saw Jambo suddenly appear, diving down onto the sidewalk, twisting around, dark glasses and flashing teeth and flashing gun.

He also saw the young woman push the baby-buggy out of the apartment entrance right behind Jambo, as clear and as plain as anything that he had ever seen, as clear as watching Thelma on a summer's morning, when he first began to realize that he didn't love her. Thelma had been smiling, contented, while all the time her days of happiness were already over, and there was nothing left for her but loneliness and tears.

And this girl smiled, too, as she leaned forward to wipe her baby's dribbly chin. As Jambo fired, a heavy, swelling, booming shot. As Ralph fired back, a .44-calibre bullet that left the barrel of his gun at 770 feet per second – and blew apart the baby-carriage like a bomb, mattress, blankets, plastic pony-rattles and bloody flesh.

Jambo scrambled to his feet, turned, stunned. Newt came stalking across the street with his gun held out stiffly in front of him. He practically pushed the muzzle up Jambo's nose, and screamed at him, 'Drop it! Freeze! Face down, you fuck!'

Ralph stood with his gun still lifted high, and the girl with the baby turned and looked at him, and nobody had ever looked at him like that, never, not even wives whose husbands he had been compelled to kill; nor men whose sons had hanged themselves in jail.

John Minatello came over. 'Ralph,' he said. 'Give me the gun.'

'What?' said Ralph.

'Give me the gun. I saw what happened. It wasn't your fault.'

Ralph stared at him. He had never realized before how pale John Minatello was. His skin was white like wax, with large and obvious pores. He had big sad brown eyes and a mole on his right cheek. And that stupid silky brown moustache, the kind that kids grow to show that they're men. And that ridiculous pink-and-silver Hawaiian shirt, with palm trees and hula girls.

Newt had forced Jambo flat on his face on the sidewalk, and was handcuffing him, jerkily, silently, like a man trussing a turkey. The girl with the baby-carriage was staring at all of them in disbelief.

'My baby,' she said. She sounded almost as if she were singing, rather than talking. '*My ba – a – a – aby.*'

Ralph walked up to her, hesitant, wary. He continued to hold his gun up high, to show her that he didn't mean her any harm. She was a young pale-skinned black, oval-faced, pretty, with stiffly lacquered hair and thinly plucked eyebrows. She wore a red-and-yellow smock and black leggings. Her eyes were glassy, and she was shaking, and it was obvious to Ralph that she was in shock. As he was, too.

'My baby,' she said; and she reached inside the wrecked baby-carriage and lifted out something that looked like a bloodied rolled-up towel. Except that a small chubby arm swung lifelessly from one side of it, and blood dripped from tiny fingers.

'I –' Ralph began. But his larynx constricted, and his mouth locked, and he was totally unable to speak. He wanted to apologize, he wanted to explain. He wanted to beg her forgiveness. But what was the point of apologizing? What was the point of explaining? And how could he expect her to forgive him, after what he had done?

John Minatello reached up and eased the .44 out of his hand.

'Come on, Ralph, it's all over.'

'I – didn't mean to –' he choked.

'It's okay, Ralph.'

The hot brown air was warbling with sirens. An ambulance

turned into the far end of Seaver Street, followed by another, and then two squad cars. Ralph allowed John Minatello to usher him back to their Grand Prix. He sat in the passenger seat, with his head bowed, staring at the asphalt pavement. He heard people hurrying backwards and forwards. He heard a window break, but he wasn't aware of its significance. He looked up after a while and said, 'John? How was the girl? The girl in the Beetle?'

John was leaning against the open door, looking around him anxiously. He glanced at Ralph and said, 'Hard to say. The EMTs are checking her out now. There's a lot of blood. Brains, too. Doesn't look hopeful.'

Another window broke. Ralph heard shouting and arguing, and somebody drumming. A brick sailed through the air without warning, and bounced off the back of his car. He raised his head, groggy, shocked. Something was happening but he couldn't work out what. Another brick flew over, and shattered close to his feet, then another, then a bottle, then a length of piping, which landed on its end and danced on the pavement like Fred Astaire's cane.

He stood up. He couldn't believe what he saw. Seaver Street, which only a few moments before had been sultry and suffocating and deserted, was now crammed with a jostling, screeching, jumping crowd of young blacks. They were tossing bricks and bottles and hubcaps and lengths of timber, and one young blood with a wide-brimmed hat and dreadlocks was whamming out a ferocious reggae rhythm on the hood of a parked car with two metalworking hammers, and yelling, '*Latomba! Latomba!*'

'What the hell?' Ralph wanted to know. But at that moment Sergeant Riordan came storming toward him, bull-faced, thick-necked and snorting.

'Get your ass out of here, Brossard, you stupid dumb bastard!'

'What the hell's going on?' Ralph demanded.

'You're going on, that's what,' Sergeant Riordan retorted. 'You and your fucking cack-handed ambush! You've only gone and blown away the first and only son of their beloved local hero, that's all. Even if they don't kill us, they'll wreck this fucking place, and that means eleven years of racial diplomacy and softly-softly and equal policing for all goes down the toilet, one flush, gone for ever. Now get your ass out of here before you get burned or beaten or blown away.'

'What are you talking about, Riordan?' Ralph yelled at him. 'We just pulled off the biggest drugs bust this godforsaken city ever saw! And I'm sorry about the baby, all right? I wish it hadn't happened, but it happened, and there was nothing at all I could do!'

John Minatello took hold of his arm. 'Come on, Ralph, we have to get out of here.'

Ralph turned and stared at him. 'Certainly we have to get out of here. But Jambo comes with us.'

'Newt already took Jambo.'

'Newt took Jambo?'

More bottles and bricks smashed all around them, and suddenly – over by the steps that led up to Luther Johnson's apartment building, a gout of orange fire rolled up, and the sidewalk started to blaze.

'Come on, Ralph,' John Minatello urged him. 'They're throwing Molotov cocktails. We're not equipped to deal with anything like this.'

'Give me my gun,' Ralph insisted.

'Ralph … you know I can't do that.'

A huge piece of plaster coving burst on the pavement beside them, and almost choked them with dust. So far, two uniformed officers with pump-guns had been keeping the crowd well back, but when the medics lifted the tattered remains of the baby-carriage into the back of their ambulance, and everybody could see for themselves how bloody and burst-apart it was, a shriek of outrage went up, and bottles and bricks landed all around the squad cars in a thunderous, shattering cascade. It was a monsoon downpour of grief and frustration and fury.

Sergeant Riordan was hit on the shoulder by a triangular lump of concrete; and a bottle clouted Ralph on the back of the head.

'Give me my goddamned gun, John!' Ralph yelled at him. 'And that's an order!' John Minatello hesitated, and glanced at Sergeant Riordan, and hesitated some more, and then handed it back. Ralph snatched it impatiently and cocked it. Sergeant Riordan, smacking concrete dust from his shoulders, snapped, 'Get your ass out of here, Brossard, and if any one of my men suffers so much as a single fucking scratch, then I'll be looking out for you myself, and don't you forget it.'

'Newt got the sports bag?' asked Ralph.

'That's the point,' said John Minatello.

'What's the point? What do you mean, "that's the point"? What's the fucking point?'

'The point is that we lost the sports bag.'

Ralph stared at him. On every side of them, bottles and cans and bricks and rocks were hurtling and bouncing down, but Ralph stayed completely still, his shoulders slightly hunched in disbelief, not shielding himself, his gun hanging down by his side.

'You lost it?'

John Minatello shrugged, embarrassed – and then ducked, as a bottle flew past his face.

'Jambo must've thrown it someplace. There's not a sign of it.'

'What the hell do you mean he must have thrown it

someplace? Where? How far could he throw? Ten feet? Twenty feet?'

'I'm sorry, Ralph. There's not a sign of it. We've searched way back to the buildings; and underneath all of the cars.'

Ralph bit his lip. He was too chagrined even to swear. They had lost the sports bag, and all of the marked money – which meant that more than a year of painstaking surveillance and wire-tapping and intelligence-gathering had all gone completely to waste. More than a year of his life had been futile. All those stultifying hours of sitting in cars, eating congealing hamburgers and drinking coffee out of polystyrene cups; all those numbing hours of waiting at courthouses for wire-tap warrants; all those seasons; all that ingenuity; all those hunches; all that seat-of-the-pants detective work; everything.

Another Molotov cocktail exploded in the middle of the street, and the front tyres of a Mazda pick-up truck began to blaze. The crowd were screaming now – a weird, high-pitched ululation, and Sergeant Riordan said, 'Come on, Ralph. It's time to get out of here. They'll be tearing us limb from limb before you know it.'

A young uniformed officer came running across the street, crouching low. 'Orders are to pull out, sir. They're sending in back-up.'

'Okay, O'Hara,' said Sergeant Riordan. He barked some instructions to the rest of his men, although his voice was almost drowned out by the wailing and whooping of the ambulance sirens.

'*Death to the pigs! Death to the pigs!*' screamed the crowd. Further down the street, they were bouncing a Chevy pick-up on its suspension, and then turning it over. It exploded with a splintering roar, and a huge cloud of oily smoke rolled into the air. The crowd screamed even louder.

Sergeant Riordan grasped Ralph's arm, too fiercely to be comfortable. 'You'd best be coming with us, Brossard. It's your ass they're after, and you'll never get your vee-hickle out now.'

They ducked back across the street through a blizzard of rocks, bricks, planks, bottles, and even coins. Newt had managed to get his car started, and was backing up the street with a howl of tortured tyres. Three young men ran after him, shouting and hopping and beating at his windows with baseball bats and steel bars. They smashed his side windows and starred his windscreen. But somehow he managed a screeching handbrake turn, and sped off northward, the tail of his car snaking wildly from side to side.

Sergeant Riordan wrenched open the back door of his squad car and pushed Ralph roughly inside. 'Put your foot down, O'Hara,' he ordered. 'We've got the albatross on board.'

He was opening his own door when Ralph felt him stagger heavily against the side of the car. Blood gushed down Ralph's window as if it had been emptied from a slaughterhouse bucket. '*Sergeant!*' screeched O'Hara, like a frightened woman.

'Back up!' Ralph yelled at him.

'What?' asked O'Hara, white-faced. A half-brick bounced off the squad car's roof.

'Back up, for Christ's sake!'

O'Hara revved the engine until it screamed, and then reversed the squad car up the street. 'Now, stop!' Ralph ordered him.

O'Hara jammed on the brakes. Ralph kicked open his door, and ran back through the blizzard of debris to Sergeant Riordan, who was lying on his back with his hands drawn up like a begging puppy and his legs twitching. His face was varnished dark scarlet with blood, and when Ralph knelt down beside him, he could see at once that the top of his head had been blown off.

Sergeant Riordan stared up at him helplessly. He probably didn't even realize who he was, or what was happening. Ralph had seen too much of this, too much blood, too much helplessness, and he had no doubt at all that Sergeant Riordan would die.

The crowd were now swarming all around him, screaming at him and taunting him and yelling, 'Kill the fucker! Kill the pig!'

Ralph gradually stood up, his .44 raised in his right hand, saying nothing. There was a moment when he was stocky but all coiled-up, tense and determined, with all the virile menace of a real Hemingway.

The crowd shied back a little, but he wouldn't be able to keep them away for long. He found himself looking from one face to another – mostly young men, but women and children, too – and he felt a rising sense of dread and disbelief at the hate which distorted their faces. How could they hate anybody so much – especially a man they didn't even know?

A brick came tumbling through the air and hit him on the shoulder, knocking him off balance. With a whoop, the crowd shifted forward. He levelled his gun two-handed and shouted, '*Freeze!*' but they kept on coming.

He shouted, '*Freeze!*' a second time, but they still kept on coming, and one young man in a red baseball cap came dancing towards him, bare-chested, beads and feathers around his neck, and whipped at his arm with a radio aerial.

Ralph swung around and shot him. The noise was deafening. The young man danced, slipped, and fell to the pavement, still staring at Ralph in surprise. There was a hole in his chest bigger than a baseball, jetting arterial blood.

The crowd shrieked – really *shrieked* – with a sound that could have cut plate glass. Ralph backed away, shocked at the shrieking and shocked at what he had done. He might have been Hemingway – he might have been the hottest, hardest, ballsiest detective on the narcotics squad – he might have seen blood and guts and whores sliced up with razors; but at the age of forty-three this was the first time that he had ever killed a man face to face, deliberately shot him, just like that, and he was appalled and astounded and excited, too, adrenaline pumping around him so fast that he felt he could have jumped back twenty feet.

But then the crowd surged toward him and they were swinging bats and hurling bricks and a rusty elbow-pipe hit him on the forehead and almost concussed him. He fired in the air, twice, but the crowd took no notice, so he fired again, and a young girl toppled, and he fired again, and another young man went down.

The crowd didn't stop. His shooting didn't deter them, it enraged them even more. Every shot gave them another martyr. Every shot added another credential to their cause. *Kill the pigs!*

He thought that they were going to rip him apart. But then somewhere in his consciousness he heard the deep *booofff!* of a pump-gun loaded with buckshot, and then another *booofff!*

He had never imagined what it was going to be like, to see people shot. But pieces flew off them, whole muscles flapped in the air, faces were blasted into raspberry fool.

Then the squad car came slewing in beside him, with its door flapping open, and John Minatello shouted, 'Ralph! For God's sake, Ralph!'

Ralph fired one more shot, deliberately high, and then tumbled backwards into the squad car. O'Hara slammed his foot on the gas and spun the wheel and the car collided with

Jambo's Electra. He backed up, and they could feel the soft, heavy jolt of hitting people. Then the crowd were beating on their roof with hammers and lumps of concrete, and the side-windows caved in, and John Minatello screamed at O'Hara, '*Get us the hell right out of here!*'

There was an instant he was convinced that they were going to die, and shouted, 'Mary, Mother of God, forgive me!' The end of a scaffolding-pole exploded through the right-hand side of the windshield, and dug its way into the seat. If Sergeant Riordan had been sitting there, he would have been impaled. But then the squad car bounced and skidded forward, hitting parked cars and debris and bricks, and suddenly they were swerving right at the end of the street and heading north.

Ralph sat in the back of the squad car feeling totally shocked and detached. He heard sirens whooping as police and fire-trucks sped past them; he heard helicopters clamouring overhead. But it wasn't long before they were driving past normal streets where normal people were walking and shopping and kids were skateboarding, and suddenly it was an ordinary summer morning in the suburbs of south Boston.

His .44 lay across his lap, no longer warm but smelling strongly of burned powder. John Minatello glanced at it once or twice, but made no attempt to take it away from him. Ralph said nothing, but watched the trees and the buildings and the traffic pass him by, all of it seen through the red gelatinous filter of Sergeant Riordan's blood.

Matthew Monyatta was talking to a young single mother about her tenancy rights when the door of his office burst open.

'Hold on just a minute, I'm busy here!' he called out, raising his hand.

But his unexpected visitor wasn't deterred. He rapped with his knuckles on the open door, said, 'Sorry to butt in like this, Matthew … but –' and waited with an expectant face for Matthew to ask him what he wanted.

Matthew said, 'This must be important, right?'

'It's important,' nodded his visitor. 'In fact, it's critical.'

'How long's this going to take?' asked Matthew.

His visitor made a face. 'As long as it takes, I'm afraid.'

Matthew turned around to the young woman with the haunting almond-shaped Ethiopian face and the huge gold earrings and the red satin dress and said, 'Elizabeth … I'm sorry about this, but I'm going to ask you to excuse me for just a while. Don't you worry … you won't be put out on the street. I won't let that happen. You have the right to stay where you are; and you have the right not to be harassed. So don't you worry. The Lord is with you; the law is with you; and so am I.'

The young woman took hold of his hand and squeezed it. She looked as if she would have been quite prepared to kneel down on the floor and kiss his feet. Then she rose from her chair, and without even looking at Matthew's visitor, she left the room with a rustle of silken skirts.

The visitor came in and closed the door firmly behind him. He was a broad-shouldered white man with a florid face and wiry blond hair and eggshell eyes that stared just a little too widely, as if he were slightly unhinged. He was built like an old-fashioned wardrobe. He wore a loud check sports coat in mustard and blue and a poached-salmon shirt that was almost the same colour as his face.

'Haven't you heard the news?' he asked Matthew, abruptly.

'Of course I've heard the news,' Matthew replied, tilting himself back in his chair, so that the springs squeaked. He was a lion-headed black man of fifty-five – handsome now that he was older, because his eyes had sunken a little and his cheekbones were more pronounced and his jaw had taken on a biblical sharpness. His hair was thick and very white. He was wearing a loose oatmeal-coloured djellaba, a hooded North African robe, which not only gave him the appearance of a prophet or a mystic, but which also concealed his considerable bulk. He wore three heavy gold rings on each hand.

The visitor sat down. He had been in this room before, so he was no longer intrigued by the prints that hung on the beige-painted walls: sand dunes and pyramids and strange stylized African faces with slanted eyes. Matthew Monyatta was the founder and president and chief guru of Boston's Olduvai Black Consciousness Group. He had been a protégé of Malcolm X in the days of the Black Muslims, but after the shooting of his wife and children in 1973 in a bloody struggle between black political factions, he had become far less fanatical, far more interested in racial reconciliation, while at the same time trying to show that black civilization was as ancient and as deeply rooted as white.

Hence the name 'Olduvai', from the gorge in Tanzania where some of the earliest fossils of *Homo erectus* were discovered.

'There's a full-scale war going on down there,' said the visitor.

'Are you surprised, Mr Deputy Mayor?' asked Matthew. 'A white police officer shot and killed the three-month-old son of one of the ghetto's greatest heroes. Four other black brothers also died, and one black sister. It was a massacre, right on our doorstep. And this was supposedly part of an exercise to catch a drug-running ring run by wealthy white Ivy Leaguers who never even drove down Seaver Street with the windows closed and the air-conditioning turned to "purify".'

128

Kenneth Flynn pursed his lips tight and looked away. He had never liked Matthew Monyatta and he knew that he never would. He wasn't racially prejudiced: one of his closest buddies at college had been black, and was now running for state treasurer. Kenneth just didn't happen to like ethnicity, period. Irish ethnicity was just as bad as African ethnicity: they both added up to ugly handmade pottery and monotonous songs with a lot of amateurish harmonizing and dopey young people with sandals on their feet and stars in their eyes.

Meanwhile, down on Seaver Street, apartment blocks were burning and markets were being looted, and Hieronymus Bosch had come to town.

'I talked to the mayor and the mayor asked me to come across to see you,' said Kenneth.

'Of course he did,' said Matthew. 'He sent you across to see me because you're good at persuading people to do things they don't want to do. And he wants me to go down to Seaver Street to tell all the black folks to stop rioting and looting and start acting peaceable because that's what I'm good at. There are times, though, when I wonder what *he's* good at.'

'Delegating,' said Kenneth. 'He's a great hands-on delegator.'

Matthew glanced up, and gave Kenneth a wry smile and a nod of the head. 'This time, Mr Deputy Mayor, I'm not at all sure that I want to go. This is police business. This is an ambush that never should have happened, not on Seaver Street – even if it *had* gone right. If I go down there and raise my hands and say people, people, stop your rioting, stop your looting, don't be angry no more the pigs didn't mean it, what does that make me? An Uncle Tom? A traitor to my race? Or just an honorary pig?

'Maybe I don't see eye to eye with Fly Latomba, but I

129

bleed for Fly Latomba's shot-dead baby just like everyone else on Seaver Street, and I bleed for all those other lives that were lost this morning; and for those who have suffered; and for Boston, too.'

Kenneth ran his finger around inside his collar, and grimaced. 'I really don't need the rhetoric, Matthew. Unless you talk to these people, we're looking at major bloodshed. This city's going to burn, Matthew, and you're the only person who can put out the flames.'

Matthew eased his 265lb bulk out of his armchair, which rock – *squikked* – rock – *squikked* two or three times, as if in relief. He came around his desk and stood over Kenneth like Mt Monyatta, blocking out the sunlight from the window. Around his neck there were six or seven strings of African beads and bronze discs and amulets fashioned from goat's hair and copper wire and glass.

' "Can you lift up your voice to the clouds," ' he quoted, ' "so that an abundance of water may cover you? Can you send forth lightings that they may go and say to you, 'Here we are?' Do you know the ordinances of the heavens, or fix their rule over the earth?" '

Kenneth slowly raised his eyes until he was looking Matthew straight in the face. ' "I have heard of Thee by the hearing of the ear," ' he quoted back. ' "But now my eye sees Thee." '

Matthew stared down at him for a very long time. Then he reached across his desk, picked up his portable telephone, and dropped it into the capacious pocket of his robe, along with his wallet and his car keys.

'You're a very clever man, Mr Deputy Mayor,' he said. 'You'd better direct me down to hell.'

Six

As he climbed out of the car, Michael could see the smoke rising from the Roxbury district, and he stood in the parking lot watching it for a while, and listening to the distant, muted wailing of sirens. Helicopters flackered overhead, circling the Combat Zone in a stilted aerial dance, and then flackering away again.

The day was humid, with scarcely any breeze, and the air tasted coppery, like pennies. This morning's forecast had warned of electric storms, with heavy rainfall.

Michael locked the car and walked across to the entrance of Boston Central Hospital, jangling his keys. He had driven up from New Seabury yesterday afternoon, and spent the night on Joe Garboden's couch. This morning, he had turned up at Plymouth Insurance with a dull headache caused by the high atmospheric pressure, aided and abetted by the bottle of Maker's Mark that he and Joe had finished off between them, to celebrate his return. He had officially been welcomed back to Plymouth Insurance, and handed the saddle-brown ring-binder marked O'BRIEN.

He had read most of the file over a solitary lunch at Clarke's Saloon, opposite Faneuil Hall, cheeseburger and ice-cold Mick. He had wanted to bone up on all of the background before he talked face to face with Kevin Murray and Artur Rolbein, the two investigators who had been representing Plymouth's interests up until now.

He was aware that they would probably resent his being brought in; Kevin Murray had done what he could, but the police and the coroner had supplied him with only the sketchiest information, and an FAA spokesperson had doggedly replied to all of his enquiries that 'as of this time, we are not in the business of speculation.'

There was an interesting note in the file from Artur Rolbein. Rolbein had talked to the yacht owner who had paddled ashore in his dinghy after he had seen John O'Brien's helicopter crashing on Nantasket Beach. He was a New York advertising director called Neal Masky who owned a small summer home at Cohasset.

'Masky: *After the helicopter hit the beach everything was incredibly quiet for quite a long while. I don't know, three or four minutes at least. I tacked around and it was then that I saw a black or dark blue pick-up parked not too far away from the wreck. I wasn't sure how it could have gotten there ... I hadn't seen it drive up since the crash, although maybe I could have missed it because I was busy turning against the wind, and the helicopter was obstructing my view.*

'*All the same ... I was so concerned about the people in that helicopter that I kept glancing over toward it to see if there was any sign of life, and I'm sure I would have noticed a truck approaching. I can't really see how I could have missed it.*

'*I can only assume that it was already parked there .. you know,* before *the helicopter crashed.*

'Rolbein: *You said you saw somebody around the wreck. Somebody wearing a black coat.*

'Masky: *That's correct. I couldn't give you any kind of detailed description, it was a very bulky coat. Well ... I'm not too sure that bulky is the right word. Maybe voluminous.*

'Rolbein: *What was this person doing, as far as you could discern?*

'Masky: *He or she had some kind of cutting machinery, some kind of cutting gear, the same kind the fire department uses in traffic accidents. I could hear the generator, and I saw him or her lifting up the cutters like a huge kind of metal crab-claw.*

'Rolbein: *The Jaws of Life.*

'Masky: *Is that what they call them? I don't really know. They looked like a crab-claw to me.*

'Rolbein: *Then you saw this person carrying something out of the wreck? Am I correct?*

'Masky: *That's correct, yes. I couldn't hazard a guess as to what it was. I shouted but I was still too far away to make myself heard. I started to row harder, but of course when you're rowing a dinghy you have your back toward your direction of travel, and the next thing I knew, I heard a huge whoomphing noise, and I felt a blast of heat on the back of my neck, and the whole damn helicopter was afire from end to end.*

'Rolbein: *And you didn't see where the pick-up went?*

'Masky: *There was only one way it could have gone, back along Sagamore Head and then either north or south on Nantasket Road. North, of course, takes you to Hull and Stoney Beach and no further, unless you can catch the passenger-ferry.*

'Rolbein: *But you didn't see it?*

'Masky: *No, sir. I didn't see it.*

Underneath this transcript, Rolbein had Biro'd a question to himself: '*It's conceivable that the pick-up could have been parked on Sagamore Head completely by chance and the driver taken advantage of the wreck to loot it. But the pick-up driver was carrying what appears to have been professional metal-cutting gear, Holmatro or similar – a fact which the police briefings to the press have all failed to mention (why?). The driver used this cutting gear to gain access to whatever he or she wanted. So he or she was not only at the right place at the right time, he or she was fully prepared for what must be regarded with a great deal of doubt as an accident. According to our computers, if anybody were to stand at any random point on the Massachusetts shoreline in the hope of having a helicopter crash nearby, the chances of it happening would be 87,234,000:1, and you could be standing there for 239,000 years without any luck. So let's assume our pick-up driver must have*

133

known that the O'Brien helicopter was going to crash there. How? Unless it was crashed there on purpose? By a missile, so far unreported or undetected? By rifle or anti-aircraft fire? (Still wouldn't make such an accurate crash-landing ... only a few feet short and it would have dropped straight into the sea.) By a suicide pilot? NB: Check the pilot's personal medical records ... query ME's report. Maybe he was suffering from a terminal disease but wanted his family to benefit from accident insurance. Remember Pan American Airlines vs. Roddick.'

Michael had thumbed through the rest of the binder but Rolbein's meanderings were by far the most provocative thoughts in the whole file. He had called Rolbein and left a message on his answerphone, requesting a meeting within the next few days. Meanwhile, he was visiting Boston Central Hospital to meet Dr Raymond Moorpath, who had carried out the medical examination on the victims of the O'Brien helicopter crash at the specific request of Boston's police commissioner, Homer T. Hudson.

Boston Central had once been a shabby, run-down metropolitan hospital, with junkies nodding in the corridors and blood in the toilets and alcoholics screaming on every floor. It had closed in 1981 for lack of funding, but six years later it had been taken over by a powerful consortium of financiers, property developers and wealthy doctors. Its redbrick Gothic grandeur had been restored. Every room was a luxury room. For those who could afford it, or who had adequately protected themselves with TAHPS or Bay State or Blue Cross, Boston Central offered state-of-the-art treatment for heart and vascular disease, diabetic complications, cancer, AIDS and transplantation. At Boston Central, you could have photopheresis to fight off your autoimmune disease, or neutron capture therapy to frizzle your brain tumour, or radio frequency catheter ablation to quell your irregular heartbeats.

Boston Central was the gilded temple of modern medicine, and Dr Raymond Moorpath was one of the most exalted of its priests.

Michael had to wait in the downstairs lobby for nearly fifteen minutes, pacing the shining mosaic floor and peering at the oil-paintings of eminent Boston doctors, and then sitting on a huge tan-coloured leather couch and flicking through leaflets for liposuction that offered 'body contouring for a more desirable you ... we eliminate "saddle-bag" thighs, "protuberant" abdomen, "love handles", redundant chins and enlarged male breasts.'

Her eyes glowing violet in the light from her desk lamp, the brunette receptionist with the dinky little mock-nurses' cap suddenly leaned forward and said, 'Mr Rearden? Dr Moorpath will see you now. Eighth floor, room 8202.'

The hospital was deeply carpeted in eau-de-Nil and smelled of hotels rather than hospitals. The walls were hung with hesitant, messy abstracts, which looked as if they had been painted by neurotics and purchased by Philistines. Michael passed a white-haired man in a wheelchair who stared at him wildly and demanded, 'Are you Lloyd Bridges?'

He found Dr Moorpath playing golf in a huge, high-ceilinged corner office. The view through the windows was hazy and blurred, but only a few miles away Michael could see the terrible orange glittering of fire, and brown smoke rising thickly and lazily into the air, and helicopters hovering like dragonflies. None of this seemed to perturb Dr Moorpath, even if he had noticed it. Michael had the feeling that he would derive a certain amount of malicious enjoyment out it. Anything that the poor and underprivileged did to inflict yet more misery upon themselves was only further evidence of their stupidity, that was Dr Moorpath's opinion. 'Nobody has ever considered that they might

135

actually enjoy being underprivileged. It gives them a sense of importance.'

The office was furnished in a style that was supposed to capture the grandeur and solidity of an English country house, with oak-panelled walls and a massive stone fireplace, and a leather-topped desk that was almost big enough to house one of the poor and underprivileged families that Dr Moorpath was always complaining about. On the opposite wall was a vast oil-painting of the Quorn Hunt, in England, a blaze of hunting-pink jackets and shining top hats and polished boots.

Dr Moorpath himself was gigantic, the kind of man who could overcrowd an elevator on his own. He had a big, jowly face and bushy black eyebrows, and his shiny raven-black hair was combed severely back from his forehead. The black of his hair was so intense that it must have been dyed: a crude and obvious vanity that was quite at odds with his complex personality, and which Michael had never been able to understand. Dr Moorpath was swathed in a very expensive maroon shawl-collared cardigan, and he was wearing baggy tan corduroys and Jesus sandals with dark green socks.

Dr Moorpath had graduated from Harvard Med with honours in pathology, and for two decades he had been one of the most dedicated medical examiners in the state. He had written the definitive book on forensic entomology, pinpointing the time and date of death by the development of flesh-flies within the body, *The Life-Cycle of Sarcophaga Carnara in the Establishment of Time of Extinction* – more usually referred to by medical students as *Moorpath's Flies*.

But the ferocious internal politics within the coroner's office had denied him promotion again and again; and twelve years ago, angry and frustrated, he had accepted an offer from Brigham & Women's to move to their pathology department; and when Boston Central had opened, he had taken over as Head of Pathology. He had become wealthy, respected, thoroughly disliked, and twenty times louder than ever.

'Michael!' he boomed. 'This is a wonderful surprise! It must be all of five years!'

'Near enough,' said Michael. He shook Dr Moorpath's enormous hand and, just as they always had before, those banana-sized fingers made him feel like a small boy.

'I heard that you quit,' Dr Moorpath queried, as if quitting were as distasteful as urinating in public.

'Well, yes, I did, kind of,' said Michael, glancing around the room. 'I had a little nervous trouble.'

'I heard that, yes. I guess there are some psyches that can take the strain and others that can't. Death isn't attractive at the best of times, is it? I'm doing some interesting work on gangrene at the moment – especially gangrene caused by crushing or burning. Fascinating ... but, no, not attractive.'

'Quite an office you've got here,' Michael remarked.

'Hmph, thank you. I like to think that it lends some dignity to a profession that's notoriously lacking in dignity. The proportions are slightly different, lower ceiling, but apart from that it's almost an exact replica of the main drawing-room at Foxley Hall, in Huntingdonshire, in England. Except, of course, for the hi-tech equipment.'

He approached a fine Jacobean-style dresser, and opened it up to form a desk. Inside were three telephones, an Apple desktop computer, and a fax.

'And look at this,' he laughed. He swung open a narrow oak cabinet next to it, to reveal a CDI. 'I like the interactive golf ... means I can practise in between cases.'

'I'm impressed,' said Michael.

Dr Moorpath closed the doors, and said, 'Drink? I have

some very good dry sherry. Or there's Scotch; or beer if you want it. Have you tried Singha Beer, from Thailand? It's very good. Six bottles of that and you can understand Thai, no tedious learning necessary. "Do not be infatuated with honour", that's a good old Thai proverb.'

'I'm trying to keep a clear head,' said Michael.

'Well … you're probably wise,' said Dr Moorpath. All the same, he poured himself a large tumbler of Glenmorangie and held it to his nose for a moment, as if it were an oxygen mask, breathing in whisky fumes. Then he said, 'Ahh … there's nothing like it.'

'You're probably wondering why I wanted to see you,' said Michael.

'My secretary said something about reviewing some of my old cases. You're writing your memoirs? Or reliving your nightmares? Which particular cases did you have in mind?'

'None of them, I'm afraid. I wasn't being one hundred per cent truthful.'

Dr Moorpath parked his large bottom on the arm of his sofa. 'We worked on some good ones, though, didn't we? What was that last one? That powerboat accident off Spectacle Island, wasn't it? The lovely Mrs Deerhart III, rich enough to buy anything and everything, except her own amputated feet.'

Michael smiled wryly, and nodded. 'She got $7.19 million, which almost made up for them. And she can dance pretty well these days.'

'Well, good for her,' said Dr Moorpath. 'That's more than I can. My wife says that I dance like Godzilla. That's my fourth wife. You haven't met Jane, have you? We were married last April in Santa Cruz Huatullo. Beautiful girl – bright, young, brilliant hostess. She was shortlisted for Playmate of the Month.' He thought for a moment, then noisily cleared his throat. 'I wouldn't have *minded* her doing it,

Playmate of the Month, don't get me wrong, but I'm glad she didn't.'

Michael said, 'The real reason I'm here is, Plymouth have retained me to investigate the John O'Brien accident.'

Dr Moorpath covered his eyes with his right hand. He remained masked like this for almost a minute, saying nothing, but when he did take his hand away, he stared at Michael with deep revulsion and mistrust, as if Michael had just reported him to the welfare department for abusing his daughters.

Taking a shallow breath, Michael said, 'I'd like to ask you one or two questions, if I could.'

Dr Moorpath's tone was already hostile. 'I've already spoken to somebody from Plymouth. What was his name? Ballpen, something like that.'

'Rolbein,' said Michael. 'And, fine, yes. Rolbein reported that you were very co-operative, as far as you were prepared to go. The trouble was, you weren't prepared to go very far. You've held back a whole lot of very critical information. Like, a preliminary post-mortem report. Like, copies of death certificates. Like, how many individuals died in this wreck, and whether there was any discrepancy between the number of individuals who were found in this wreck, and how many individuals boarded the helicopter at Mr O'Brien's home. I mean, we're talking a very substantial insurance claim here, Raymond, a real ball-breaker, and we need that information.'

'Why do you think the commissioner asked *me* to conduct the post-mortem?' said Dr Moorpath. 'And I mean he asked me *personally*.' He lifted his hand to his ear, thumb and little finger extended, miming a telephone-call.

'I expect he asked you for the sake of discretion,' Michael replied. 'If they'd taken those bodies to the city morgue, the *Globe* would have front page pictures of them by morning, lying on their respective slabs. "O'Brien Family United In Death", or whatever.'

'Exactly,' said Dr Moorpath. 'He sent those remains to me because the bodies of John O'Brien's family are not just carrion, not just street-meat. John O'Brien was a Supreme Court Justice, and John O'Brien's father was a friend of my father; and this whole tragic business calls for privacy, and dignity, and restraint, and the suppression of wild and idle speculation.'

'Some people are going to say that the only time that people insist on privacy is when they've got something to hide.'

Dr Moorpath thought about that, and made a growling, humming noise in his larynx. Michael could tell that he was deeply irritated. But it was very difficult to resist the temptation to irritate him even more. Dr Moorpath had never welcomed fools or dissidents; and he had always been driven into a rage by anyone who questioned his clinical judgement. But Michael had quickly realized that the angrier he became, the less certain of his ground he really was; and that an outburst of fury was the sign not to back off but to prod, and prod, and keep on prodding.

'Have you completed your preliminary examination?' he asked.

'When I have, it will go through the proper channels.'

'So you haven't completed it yet?'

'I didn't say that.'

'So you *have* completed it?'

'I didn't say that, either.'

'Raymond … for God's sake. You have a job to do and I have a job to do. The man's dead; his family's dead. Who are you going to harm?'

Dr Moorpath gave him one of his famous glittering looks. 'You really wouldn't understand.'

'Try me, Raymond. My employers are facing the prospect of paying out millions and millions and *millions* of dollars, which means that my employers will have substantially less money to invest in the interests of other clients, and substantially less money to buy themselves Maseratis and marble-tiled jacuzzis. They'll be seriously pissed. And so will I, because they won't be seriously pissed with you, they'll be seriously pissed with *me*.'

Dr Moorpath swallowed whisky, and shivered slightly, as if somebody had walked past his burial plot and paused and smiled at it. 'You haven't changed, have you?' he said, with a humourless smile.

'Let me see the report,' said Michael. He didn't want to see the report. He kept thinking of burned, shrunken bodies. Masklike grins, flame-exposed teeth.

Dr Moorpath shook his head. 'You really wouldn't understand, Michael. When a man like John O'Brien is suddenly killed … well, it has repercussions. Political, legal, financial … it's not like some homegoing suburban family rolling over their station wagon on the VFW Parkway, or some wino dying in an alley. It's a sensitive issue. It has to be dealt with on many different levels.'

'I understand that,' said Michael. 'But Plymouth have as much interest in John O'Brien as anybody else. If not more.'

Dr Moorpath shrugged. He was behaving as if he were marginally drunk, and it was plain that he didn't feel helpful. Michael sat and looked at him and thought, how are the dedicated fallen. There isn't anybody more bitter and stubborn and self-absorbed than an idealist who has abandoned his ideals.

Minutes went past. Outside the window, smoke kept piling into the summer sky. It looked like heaps of filthy cauliflower. Dr Moorpath finished his Glenmorangie and didn't even bother to talk. Michael sat watching him, knowing that he wasn't going to make any progress, yet strangely reluctant to leave. As if Dr Moorpath would suddenly relent, and tell him everything. Or some extraordinary sign would manifest itself, like a shimmering dove from heaven.

'You have a boy, don't you?' asked Dr Moorpath, unexpectedly conversational.

'Jason, yes. He's fine. He's thirteen now. He's had some reading problems, but – '

'I have children,' said Dr Moorpath. 'Juniper – that's my oldest, she's twenty-seven now, older than Jane. I think, on the whole, that she hates me. Well, she's a feminist. It's strange how feminists hate men. I would have thought that the first job of a feminist would be to make friends with men … make them her allies, rather than her enemies.'

'Are you going to let me see that file?' asked Michael.

Dr Moorpath looked up and raised an eyebrow and said, 'Mmh?' and it was then that Michael realized he wasn't particularly drunk, he was making a point. He was telling Michael in not so many words that the subject of John O'Brien was way off limits, and that he wasn't going to discuss it under any circumstances whatsoever, and he didn't even want to be asked.

Michael said, 'I think I'll try that Thai beer after all.' His throat suddenly felt like thistles. He sensed danger – danger from an unexpected direction, as if he were a swimmer, and something very big and dark and amorphous were rising up beneath him, like a huge black octopus rising through the sea.

Dr Moorpath opened up an icebox that looked, on the outside, like a Victorian walnut davenport, a little desk for 'young ladies of learning.' He took out a frosted bottle of beer and opened it. 'Looks like Armageddon, doesn't it?'

142

he remarked, nodding downtown toward the rising smoke. 'What was it they used to say? "Armageddon, Armageddon, and Armageddon oudda here."'

'We're having real problems making any headway with this O'Brien investigation,' said Michael, watching carefully as Dr Moorpath poured out his beer.

'Well ... under the circumstances, that's only to be expected.'

'I'm not even sure what the circumstances are.'

'The circumstances are that John O'Brien's appointment was finally going to tip the balance against the right-wing justices that Richard Nixon first installed. And much more than that. John O'Brien's appointment was going to change America for ever.'

'Did you support him?' asked Michael.

The true expression on Dr Moorpath's face was disguised by light and shadow. 'I'm a pathologist,' he replied. 'I deal in meat; not political ideals.'

Michael was about to pursue Dr Moorpath further when there was a quick, token knock at the door, and a swarthy, bearded, harassed-looking doctor hurried into the office. 'Dr Moorpath, I'm sorry to interrupt you. But they just brought in some victims from the street-fighting; and the police commissioner and the deputy district attorney are very anxious that you should look at them. Apparently there's some –' He saw Michael and stopped in mid-sentence, but Michael could guess what he had been just about to say. *Apparently there's some question about who killed them, and how.* The cops in the Combat Zone were almost as trigger-happy as the yummies.

'Very well,' said Dr Moorpath, and stood up. He turned around to Michael, and asked, with consummate dismissiveness, 'Yes, Michael? Was there anything else?'

'As a matter of fact, yes,' Michael told him. 'I wanted to

143

ask you about times and procedures, and what you did when the bodies arrived here, and who handled them.'

'Can't that wait till tomorrow?' asked Dr Moorpath, impatiently, tugging on his white coat.

'I could buy you lunch,' said Michael.

'Thank you, Michael, but all my lunches are booked.'

'Jasper's?'

'Thank you. I'm tempted, but sorry.'

'Okay …' said Michael, standing up. 'I'm not sure how old man Bedford's going to take it, but – what? You still play golf together, don't you, you two?'

Dr Moorpath checked his glittering Jaeger-le-Coultre wristwatch. 'Listen, Michael … I won't be long. Give me twenty minutes. Read some magazines. Janice will bring you some coffee.'

Michael sat down again. 'Raymond … Edgar's going to appreciate this.'

But Dr Moorpath had already swept like a low-pressure storm-front out of the door, leaving Michael alone in his eighth-floor country house, with nothing but silence and air-conditioned coldness and a view of Boston burning.

He circled the room, picking up a china shepherdess and reading the label on the base. 'Oliver Sutton Antiques, London. Staffordshire, *ca* 1815. Guaranteed genuine.' He carefully replaced it. He didn't like antiques very much. He didn't like to think that the people who had fashioned them, and the people who had first bought them, were long since dead and forgotten, their names unrecorded, their lives blown away like dust.

He went to the window and watched the smoke rising and the traffic sparkling. Eight floors below, in the hospital parking lot, he saw two miniature doctors walk up to each other and hold an ant-like conversation. He saw both of their heads turn as a nurse walked briskly past.

He was still staring out of the window when the door opened behind him.

'Oh, I'm sorry …' said a girl's voice. 'I was looking for Dr Moorpath.'

He turned around. A tall brunette girl in a grey pin-stripe suit was standing in the doorway, holding three manila folders.

Michael said, 'It's okay … Dr Moorpath was called down to emergency.'

'I have these photographs, that's all. He wanted them urgently.'

'You can leave them here. He'll be back in a couple of minutes.'

The girl held the envelopes protectively close to her chest. 'I'm not so sure … I was told to give them to Dr Moorpath personally.'

'Well … you can wait, if you want to. He won't be long.'

The girl anxiously glanced at her watch; then stepped into the office; and waited, fidgeting from one foot to the other. Michael thought she was very attractive: rather like Linda Carter when she used to play *Wonder Woman*. In spite of the severity of her suit, she had a very full figure, and her eyes were brilliantly hyacinth-blue.

'I have a lunch appointment at twelve,' she said, with a quickly-evaporating smile.

'Dr Moorpath shouldn't be too long,' Michael reassured her.

'These are blow-ups, you see,' the girl explained. 'Dr Moorpath wanted computer-enhanced blow-ups.'

Michael nodded. He wasn't really interested. 'Quite a war going on out there,' he remarked, inclining his head toward the rising smoke and the circling helicopters.

The girl smiled, and fidgeted, and checked her watch a second time. Eventually, she said, 'Listen … I'm really tight for time. If I leave these here, could you make sure that Dr Moorpath gets them? I mean, right in his hands? They're real important.'

'For sure,' said Michael. 'Just leave them on the desk. I'll make sure that he gets them.'

'Thanks,' flustered the girl. 'You saved my life.' And with that, she laid the envelopes on Dr Moorpath's leather-topped desk, blew Michael a kiss, and left. Michael sipped his beer and smiled to himself. Before he was married, he would have asked her out by now. Or at least asked her what her star sign was. Sagittarius, he guessed. A beautiful, flustered ditherer.

Ten minutes went by. Then twenty. Still Dr Moorpath didn't return. Michael heard sirens down below, and saw three more ambulances arriving, their red lights flashing. Doors opened, miniature paramedics rushed around miniature casualties. He didn't want to look. He had a sudden sense of vertigo, of falling down to the concrete apron two hundred feet below him. He had a sudden memory of broken bodies and trees that grew human hands.

He prowled around Dr Moorpath's office some more, staying away from the window. Eventually, maybe inevitably, he arrived at Dr Moorpath's desk, where the envelopes lay. The top envelope was labelled ROOSA, followed by a long serial number. Michael knew all about Democratic state senator George Roosa. He had been discovered hanging from a roller towel in a gas station men's room in New Brighton, Watertown. Some said homicide, some said suicide, some said sexual peculiarity. Michael decided that he didn't want to look at blown-up photographs of George Roosa, dead or alive.

He lifted up the ROOSA envelope and underneath was one labelled ZERBEY. Michael had never heard of anybody called Zerbey, and he reckoned that he could probably live quite comfortably for the rest of his life without finding out

146

who Zerbey was – particularly if he or she had suffered a horrifying death.

He heard distant ambulances wailing. Then he lifted up the third envelope and it was labelled O'BRIEN.

For a long time, he held the envelope in his hand and his hand was trembling as if he had been carrying a heavy suitcase from one end of Park Street subway station to the other.

O'BRIEN, 343/244D/678E/01X. He even knew what the numbers meant. They were file numbers from the coroner's office, and the '01X' suffix meant that the contents of this envelope and everything connected with the O'Brien case were strictly confidential, and only for the eyes of authorized personnel. '01X' meant 'you talk to about this to *anybody* – even your wife – you're going to end up jobless and poverty-stricken and maybe worse.'

Michael looked around, and then listened. The office was silent; he couldn't hear elevators whining; he couldn't hear footsteps.

He waited for a moment longer, keeping his breathing slow and shallow and very quiet. He couldn't hear anybody. With chilly sweat trickling down inside his shirt, he turned the O'BRIEN envelope over, and started to unwind the waxed thread that held its flap fast.

He paused again, and listened. He heard somebody quickly approaching along the corridor outside, but just as quickly their footsteps Dopplered into the distance, and the office was silent again.

He eased the glossy colour photographs out of the envelope. There were eleven in all, and he laid them out on Dr Moorpath's desk in a fan shape. He stood and stared at them and for a moment he felt that he was going to lose his grip, and that the floor beneath his feet was going to open up like the belly of the L10-11 over Rocky Woods, and that he was going to go plunging into darkness and trees and rocks and smash, and be shattered into bones and blood.

He saw a burned man, hunched over, a man with no legs. He saw a burned woman, her body opened up from her crotch to the top of her skull. He saw a burned man lying between the burned seats of a helicopter, a man with no head.

He saw a man in a broken flying-helmet, what was left of a man, his face oddly and frighteningly distorted, like a gruesome Picasso, his cheekbones raw and sooty from fire.

Jesus Jesus Jesus –

Michael closed his eyes. He could still see the images, even with his eyes closed. Staring eyes, exposed jawbones, contorted arms and legs. He said to himself: *steady, for Christ's sake, steady.*

He examined each photograph again, one by one, comparing, frowning. His breath sounded harsh and ragged, and his hands were trembling. He could feel that dark amorphous shape rising beneath him. He could feel that huge black octopus rising out of the ocean to entwine itself around his sanity. But he stopped, and held his breath for a moment, and said to himself: *keep a grip on yourself ... this is important.*

He studied the photographs with the slow, analytical care of somebody who knows what to look for. How were the bodies lying? How had they fallen into those positions? Had they been mutilated by impact or by explosion or by fire? Why was one of them hunched on the floor? How had the woman's body been cut open so violently? What had happened to the headless man's head?

Michael could see at once that the burning of the bodies was far less severe than the press had obviously been led to believe. He thought: we're not talking 'unrecognizable' here. We're not talking 'wizened black monkeys'. These are four distinct and identifiable cadavers that have been momentarily flash-flamed by the explosion of several hundred gallons of kerosene, but not totally incinerated. Anybody could have counted how many corpses there were. Those first official reports that had claimed that 'physical trauma was so severe that full identification is still inconclusive' – they simply hadn't been true. Michael could easily pick out four separate bodies; and he could easily see who each of them was. Frank Coward, pilot. Dean McAllister, assistant at the Justice Department. Eva Hamilton O'Brien, wife of John O'Brien; and despite the fact that his head was missing, John O'Brien himself, Supreme Court justice-as-never-quite-was.

To Michael, something else was glaringly obvious: these corpses must have been corpses *before* they were burned. The stumps of Dean McAllister's legs had been partially cauterized by flame. Mrs O'Brien's intestines had been shrivelled by heat, which was a clear indication that she had been disembowelled *before* the fire. Frank Coward's face was scorched scarlet – but only those parts of his face which were exposed *after* his helmet had been crushed.

John O'Brien was headless, yes, but only the back of his suit was burned, which was evidence that he had been sitting bent double in his seat when the wreck exploded.

Michael lifted up one photograph after another, checking and comparing. No wonder there was so much secrecy surrounding this crash. No wonder Murray and Rolbein had been stonewalled by the police department and the coroner's office. He had seen this kind of 'accident' dozens of times before, in burned-out buildings and skeletal automobiles.

There was no question about it: Somebody had killed the O'Brien family – and somebody had killed them so gruesomely that it was almost more than Michael could take.

He closed his eyes for a moment. He heard sirens

shrieking and chorusing in the street. Then, decisively, he shuffled the photographs back together, and carried them over to Dr Moorpath's mock-Jacobean dresser. He opened the front of the dresser, and switched on Dr Moorpath's NEC fax machine. Quickly, he punched out his own fax number at Plymouth. His mouth had been dry before, but it was even drier now. His hands wouldn't stop shaking as he inserted the photograph of John O'Brien's headless body and waited for the first transmission.

The fax chirruped, warbled, and accepted his call. He felt the sweat gradually chilling in the small of his back. The first photograph slowly edged its way through the scanner. It seemed to take hours. He drummed his fingers on the edge of the dresser and prayed under his breath that Dr Moorpath wouldn't come back until he had finished.

Just as the first transmission was completed and he was taking the photograph out, the door of the office was flung open and a tall black doctor in a white coat appeared.

'Dr Moorpath?' he asked, perplexed.

'Down in emergency,' said Michael.

The doctor looked around the office. Then he said, 'May I ask what *you're* doing here?'

Michael nodded toward the fax. 'Maintenance,' he replied.

'Oh ...' said the doctor. 'Okay,' and left, closing the door behind him.

As quickly as he could, Michael inserted a second photograph into the fax.

It took him nearly fifteen minutes to transmit all eleven photographs, but Dr Moorpath didn't return from emergency for almost a half-hour, and by that time he had switched off the fax and returned the photographs to their envelope.

Dr Moorpath looked pale and distracted. 'Everything all right?' Michael asked him.

'It's like Viet Nam out there,' said Dr Moorpath. He went to his liquor cabinet and poured himself another large Scotch. He drank it all in three gulps, and then coughed.

'Maybe I should come back tomorrow,' Michael suggested.

'Yes, why don't you? Make an appointment with Janice. I think I'm free after four o'clock.'

'I'll do that. Thanks for your time.'

Michael shook Dr Moorpath's hand; and for a split second Dr Moorpath looked him sharply in the eye, and frowned.

'Something wrong, Michael?' he asked, still tightly clasping Michael's fingers.

'Nothing at all. I'm just a little tired, that's all. Not used to working nine-to-five.'

Dr Moorpath kept hold of his hand for a few moments longer, and Michael sensed that he suspected something, but plainly didn't know what.

'Take care of yourself,' he said, at last, and went over to his desk and picked up the envelopes of photographs.

'Oh ... some girl came in just after you'd been called away, and left those for you.'

Dr Moorpath checked the labels on them. 'O'Brien,' he said, holding up the last envelope. 'I've been waiting for these.'

'Are you going to let me take a look at them?' asked Michael, boldly.

Dr Moorpath shook his head. 'Not yet. All in good time.'

Michael shrugged, and left the office, closing the door very quietly behind him.

Patrice Latomba finished his muesli and stacked the bowl

on top of all the other dirty crockery in the sink. He parted the venetian blinds with his fingers and stared out of the window for a while, at the smoke rising. There was a lull in the rioting. The police had encircled most of the neighbourhood, but the fire department had stayed away and allowed the fires to burn themselves out, and only one or two helicopters occasionally circled, unlike the swarms that had roared overhead yesterday for hour after hour until Patrice had begun to believe that he was going mad; and Verna had crouched behind the white vinyl sofa and screamed and screamed at the top of her voice.

He couldn't blame her. She had seen little Toussaint shot, right in front of her eyes. He hadn't seen the body but he had seen the pram, a burst-open carcass with a shredded foam mattress, soaked in blood so that it looked like strawberry angel-cake. A white doctor had said something to him, so softly that he hadn't been able to understand. But then a black male nurse had repeated the doctor's words with awful clarity. 'There was no way that anybody could have survived that shot. Even Mike Tyson couldn't have survived that shot. All we can say is, he wouldn't have known nothing. Nothing at all.'

'No pain?' Patrice had asked him; and the nurse had emphatically shaken his head, and that had been worst of all. Toussaint must have been catastrophically wounded for the nurse to be quite so sure. Patrice had walked out into the hospital parking lot and whooped and screamed and cried like an injured wolf.

That night, he had run long-legged and hysterically inexhaustible through the streets of the Combat Zone, smashing automobile windshields with an aluminum baseball bat, tossing bricks and chunks of kerbstone, helping the wild whooping crowds to turn over trucks. Helicopter searchlights had criss-crossed the streets, and at one stage, shortly after midnight, Seaver Street had been flooded with tear gas. Patrice, choking, had found it exhilarating, a huge natural high. *Terminator*! *Universal Soldier*! *New Jack City*! Rifles had crackled in the darkness, bullets had ricocheted everywhere. Music had throbbed and pounded from every apartment, warcry music; *this is it, brother, this is the revolution*! Store windows had smashed, and panes of plate glass had rung out like peals of discordant bells. Young boys had gone running off into the smoke and the darkness, toting video recorders and Adidas shoes and food mixers and stacks of CDs and all the leather jackets they could carry. Grim-faced brothers with crowbars had torn away the security bars that covered the windows of liquor stores, and then rampaged among the shelves, stealing everything they could and smashing what they couldn't. Whisky had coursed across the sidewalks and vodka had gurgled down the gutters. They broke into the Seaver Square Launderette and tore the washing-machines from their mountings, and hurled them into the street. In their joyful and uncontrollable rage, they even set fire to their own apartment buildings, and their own atuomobiles, and broke thousands and thousands of windows.

On television this morning, the mayor had said, 'I fail to understand the mentality of people who express their sense of social injustice by destroying their own neighbourhood.'

But Patrice understood. Patrice knew that they had wanted to tear down everything that their history in America had forced them to be. Patrice knew how constricted they felt, how poor they felt, how powerless and threadbare they felt, living out their lives in this impoverished suburb of a white man's prosperous city. Patrice knew that they wanted to go naked again, and free, that they needed to breathe, that they needed to dance. Patrice knew that they wanted to build up their *own* civilization, from scratch if need be. They had destroyed the neighbourhood, yes – but they weren't destroying their *own* neighbourhood. They were destroying the neighbourhood that white people thought was good for them.

Patrice was thirty-three, a former boxer with a hard, lithe build that was just beginning to soften with age and lack of constant training. His hair was shaved short, a flat-top with closely-razored sides, but his face was handsome enough and strong enough to carry it. His nose had been broken twice but it was still straight, and although his eyebrows were swollen from constant punches, they didn't conceal the brightness and the dark intensity of his eyes. His boxing had made him a neighbourhood hero (in 1986 he had knocked out Lightning Gary Montana in five rounds, in hosepipe sprays of blood and sweat, and had appeared on television, and thought to himself: this is it – fame, fortune). But then he had discovered the writing of Matthew Monyatta, *Black Identity*, and it had turned him overnight into an active revolutionary, a streetfighter, a black man with an attitude so ferocious that even *The National*'s reporters had refused to talk to him without bodyguard. At Madison Square Garden, after knocking out Lenny Fassbinder in two devastating rounds, he had pummelled both his fists at the TV cameras and screamed at them, 'One down, the rest of you ghosts to go!' He had been banned from professional boxing for life – but this had almost sanctified him on Seaver Street; and from then on he had lived his life as a political leader, and father-figure, and eccentric, and lover, and (as far as the *Globe* was concerned) a useful source of extremist black quotes.

Today he wore black, a simple black shirt, a black bandana, and jeans, and a mojo round his neck of spices and herbs and the ashes of his brother Aaron. He was in

154

mourning for little Toussaint, seventy-eight days old, who hadn't had a chance when Detective Ralph Brossard's .44 bullet had hit his baby-carriage, and who was now in heaven, singing with all the other dead babies, sweet and plain.

Verna wore black, too, a simple black ankle-length dress, and her hair brushed back, and fastened with an ebony comb. She was very thin and very beautiful, and grief made her look more beautiful still.

'You going to eat?' Patrice asked her.

She shrugged, her shoulder rising sharp and angular like Picasso's painting of a woman ironing.

'You have to eat, Verna,' he told her.

'I will,' she promised. 'But not yet.'

'You want me to call the doctor?'

'The doctor won't come. Nobody won't come, not till they stop the fighting.'

'They're fighting for little Toussaint, honey. They're fighting in memory of our baby. Every gunshot you hear, that's one more brother saying, *no more children killed, no more children killed.*'

She looked up. Her eyes were liquid. 'Little Toussaint wouldn't have wanted fighting, would he? He wouldn't have wanted all this burning, and killing, and looting.'

'They murdered my baby, Verna. They set up an ambush in a goddamned suburban street, where women and children were bound to walk, and they *murdered* him. No two ways about it.'

Verna lowered her head. Her finger traced a pattern on the red formica-topped table, around and around, the same pattern over and over.

'It doesn't make no difference, does it?' she asked. 'He's dead now, and nothing aint never going to bring him back, never.'

Patrice stood with his hands resting on his hips, looking

around the kitchen. It wasn't much to show for all of the training and all of the fighting and all of the years of political struggle. It was poky and dark and painted sunflower yellow in an attempt to cheer it up, but somehow the yellow made it seem all the gloomier, and all the more depressing. Polaroid prints of little Toussaint were thumbtacked onto the cheap orange-formica cabinets, and his elephant teething ring lay beside the icebox. Patrice shivered, as if Toussaint's little spirit had passed momentarily through the kitchen, touching his father and mother one more time, before leaving them for ever.

'Maybe you should stay with your momma for a while,' Patrice suggested.

Verna shook her head, distractedly. 'I couldn't do that, sweetheart. That would be just like leaving him. I mean, supposing he looked down from wherever he was … and saw that I wasn't even home no more?'

Patrice laid his hand on her shoulder. He understood what she meant.

'Can't we just stop all of this fighting?' she said. 'Toussaint would never have wanted fighting.'

' "The black American can never stop fighting," ' Patrice replied, in a flat voice, quoting from *Black Identity*. ' "The black American has to fight and fight and fight, every day of his life, just to keep what he already has; let alone win anything more." '

'But not *now*, Patrice!' Verna begged him, her eyes sticky with tears. 'Not now, and not like this, and not because of little Toussaint!'

Patrice shook his head, quick and negative, like a dog shaking away a wasp. Outside, he heard tyres squealing, and – in the distance – the heavy, deliberate cracking of a high-powered rifle, three shots altogether. He hated the whites more than he could ever articulate. He hated the ones who scowled and he hated the ones who looked right through him and he hated the ones who smiled and tried to make friends.

If Boston burned from end to end, he would show the white man once and for all that his days of supremacy were numbered, and he would be gleeful, and glad.

'Patrice,' Verna begged, 'this isn't the way! We want justice, don't we, not revenge!'

'Oh, yeah? Whose justice? *Their* justice?'

'Patrice, for my sake. This isn't going to solve anything at all. Patrice, please ... for little Toussaint, even if not for me.'

He knew, logically, that she was right. Looting and rioting would only make things worse. The cause of Black Identity had already lost what little public sympathy it ever had. And after days of burning and shooting and vandalizing property, where would they find a jury who would be willing to find Detective Brossard guilty of anything more than negligence? If Detective Brossard was ever brought to court at all. More likely the police commissioner would give him a bawling-out, and then buy him a drink at the Brendan Behan Club and crack jokes about exploding black babies.

'I don't know ...' he told Verna. 'I got to think about it.'

At that moment their doorbell rang. They glanced at each other questioningly, but then Patrice said, 'That'll be Bertrand. He wants me to meet some brother from LA. Apparently he helped to spark off that Rodney King thing.'

'Patrice,' Verna repeated. 'No more fighting. I'm begging you, on our dead child's broken heart.'

Patrice was right: it was Bertrand – an itchy, jumpy, dreadlocked figure in coal-black sunglasses and a crimson suede cowboy jacket with fringes. But Bertrand had another message. 'Matthew Monyatta want to see you, man.'

'Matthew Monyatta? What's he doing down here?'

'He was here last night, man, looking for you, excepting

nobody knew where you was. He says he wants to talk about what's going down.'

Patrice glanced at Verna, and then back to Bertrand. 'Where's he at? Can't he come up here?'

'He's waiting for you down at the Palm Diner. Says he won't wait too long.'

'Why doesn't he come up here?'

Bertrand didn't reply, but both of them knew the answer. It was a question of seniority, a question of protocol. Seaver Street was Patrice Latomba's turf, but Matthew Monyatta was the elder statesman, and Patrice had to show him respect.

'How about the other brother?' asked Patrice.

'He can wait,' Bertrand told him.

'Okay, then … let's hit the bricks.'

Patrice gave Verna a quick kiss, squeezed her hand to reassure her that he was going to be safe, and left the apartment. Seconds later, he unlocked the door and called, 'Don't forget to put on the chain! And don't answer the door to nobody!' He slammed the door again, but seconds later he unlocked it again, and Verna heard him cross the living-room, open the bureau drawer, and take out something which sounded metallic. She knew what it was: his .45 automatic.

Matthew Monyatta was sitting in the back of the Palm Diner, wearing a brown velvet cap and a loose brown djellaba. The diner was dark, because all the windows had been smashed and boarded up; but there were still twenty or thirty young men playing pool, smoking and laughing, and Kenny the proprietor was still serving up barbecued ribs and Southern fried chicken, and the air still throbbed with reggae music.

'Long time, Matthew,' said Patrice, as he approached, holding out his hand.

158

Matthew kept his arms folded. He eyed Patrice up and down with wary disapproval.

'What's the matter, man?' Patrice wanted to know, pivoting around on his heel. 'No need for you to get heavy on me, you know? You heard what those bastards done to my child.'

'I heard, and I'm sorry.'

'You're sorry? You're *sorry*? If you were real sorry, you wouldn't have come on down here, running errands for no ghosts.'

'Running errands?' Matthew demanded. 'You know me better than that. I don't run errands for nobody, ghosts nor brothers, nobody. I work for black pride, and I work for black identity, and I work for the black man's place in history; and what do you call this? You burn your own houses, you loot your own stores, you fuck up your own neighbourhood, and then you complain that you was put upon, that you was oppressed, that nobody never gave you no chances.

'They killed your baby, man, that was a tragedy. But a tragedy like that – that's no more than a symptom of what you've allowed to happen here, by your own carelessness, by your own stupidity. By your own wilful rebellion.'

'You sold out, man,' Patrice told him, dismissively. 'You just totally sold out.'

'Sit down,' Matthew told him; but Patrice remained standing. 'All right, then,' said Matthew, 'let me tell you something. I came down here yesterday to talk to you because the mayor asked me; and nobody could find you. You were running wild, weren't you? You wanted to see some fires burning, didn't you? You wanted to see the sky all lit up, so that everybody would know that Fly Latomba was suffering, and that Fly Latomba was wronged. Well, I saw that sky lit up, and I wasn't impressed. But here I am again, and I want all of this burning and all of this rioting

159

and all of this goddamned carry-on to stop; and I mean *now*. You're hurt; I know that. But don't hurt your friends and your kinfolk just to show them how badly you've been done by. They're looking to you, Fly, same way they used to look to me.'

Patrice sniffed, a dry coke-nosed sniff; and looked away.

'You hear me?' asked Matthew.

Patrice whipped around and glared at him, his eyes wide. 'What are you, Matthew? Some goddamned saint or something?'

Matthew looked down at him sadly. 'I'm a black man, Fly, that's what I am. My soul was born in Olduvai and my body was carried here.'

'Bull*shit*,' sneered Patrice.

Matthew said, 'Listen, Fly … I saw it in prophecy … I saw it in the bones.'

Bertrand began to look nervous. To him, the name of Matthew Monyatta was legendary, as it was to most young blacks, and he didn't like the sound of African soothsaying; not so close to home.

Patrice said, 'Forget it, Matthew. It's all bullshit. The only two things that will get you ahead in this world are (a) money and (b) white skin. Look at Michael Jackson, for Christ's sake. Got the first, still working hard on the second – and which is more important?'

Matthew said, 'You're tempting fate, Fly. There are people in this world who want nothing more than to see you destroy yourself. I know it.' He touched his forehead with his fingers. 'I know it *here*.'

'Bull*shit*,' Patrice repeated.

Matthew gave him a bulky shrug, as if he were disappointed but not surprised. 'I'm a black man, Fly, just the same as you. But this aint the point.'

'So what *is* the point?' Patrice challenged him. 'You want

us to stop rioting? You want us to stop burning? You want us to be good little domesticated black people, singing sweet and low? You want us to roll with the punches, little black boy, is that it? You want us to ro – o – ooll with the punches?'

Matthew lowered his head, saying nothing, but he was clenching his fists and his massive chest was rising and falling and Bertrand began to back away; as if he expected a major eruption.

'Fly,' said Matthew, 'you are up against more than you even know. Why do you think those cops were here?'

Patrice nervously sniffed. 'Making a drug bust, that's what I heard.'

'A drug bust,' Matthew repeated. 'A simple, ordinary, common-or-garden drug bust?'

'How the hell should I know? They killed my baby.'

Matthew Monyatta stared at Patrice for a long, tense moment. Then he said, 'You should call off the riot, Patrice. Tell your people, hush up, go on home. Don't do it for the mayor; and don't do it for me. Don't do it for the Boston Chamber of Commerce, neither. Just call it off, for your own sake, and for all of our sakes. You aint up against white society. You aint up against whites.'

'Oh, yes?' Patrice challenged him. 'If not the whites, then who?'

'The whiter-than-whites,' said Matthew, cryptically. 'The real white ones.'

Patrice fixed him with narrowed eyes. Bertrand was jumping and hopping and looking distinctly uneasy. 'Come on, man, this is seriously bad karma.'

'I don't know what the hell you mean,' Patrice told Matthew.

Matthew raised a single finger. 'You'll find out, Fly. You'll find out. But you won't care for it, when you do. I warn you now.'

161

'You trying to scare me, what?' Patrice wanted to know.

'I can't scare you, but *they* will. Oh, boy ... they'll scare you good.'

Patrice stared at Matthew for nearly a minute, fearful, uncomprehending. Then, slowly, he backed away between the tables, through the ganja smoke and the throbbing reggae music, and Bertrand backed away with him.

It was only when he had reached the door that he turned around and screamed at Matthew, 'You're crazy, you know that? You used to be my hero, you know that? And look at you now! Whiter than fucking white!'

Matthew stood where he was, and watched Patrice go. Eventually, Deputy Mayor Kenneth Flynn came out of the shadows beside the juke-box and stood beside him with his hands in his pockets.

'Nothing doing, hunh?' asked Kenneth.

'I don't know,' said Matthew. 'He may come around.'

'What was that he was shouting at you? Whiter than effing white?'

'You don't come from the Holy Lands,' said Matthew. 'You never walked with Aaron.'

With that, he scraped back his chair, and walked out of the diner. Kenneth went over to the counter and peeled off three twenty-dollar bills.

'Don't come back on your own, man,' the proprietor warned him.

Outside, Matthew walked back to Kenneth's dark-blue Buick, and climbed in, so that the whole suspension bounced up and down, and waited patiently for Kenneth to drive him home.

Kenneth stood outside the diner for a moment and watched Roxbury burning, and heard the flat rattle of semi-automatic gunfire in the middle distance, and the barber-shop quartets of ricochets. For the first time in his political career, he realized that he didn't understand what was happening in Boston; or anywhere in America. For the first time in his life, he felt a genuine sense of fear.

Seven

Joe Garboden dropped the faxes onto his desk and eased himself back in his tan leather chair.

'They're pretty damned dark,' he remarked. 'This one here looks like midnight in a Bible factory.'

'But you can make out O'Brien's body,' Michael insisted. 'Look ... that's the curve of his back ... that's where his head should have been.'

'Well, these are clues,' Joe admitted. 'But they're a long way from being proof.'

Michael said, 'O'Brien's policies with Plymouth covered him for accidental death or injury, but not for acts of war, terrorism or homicide. He had his head cut off, for Christ's sake. What kind of an accident is that?'

Joe said, 'People have been known to lose their heads accidentally. Think of poor Jayne Mansfield. To think I used to have the hots for her, when I was fifteen.'

Michael gathered up the faxes and slid them back into an envelope. 'There's enough here to challenge the coroner to show us the originals.'

'Come on, Michael, we have to tread a little careful here. Those photographs were police evidence. I'm not so sure that you weren't infringing the law by copying them. Let's check with our lawyers first. We don't want to jeopardize our case by acting illegally.'

'If a Supreme Court justice has been murdered, don't

you think that everybody has a right to know about it, regardless of how that information was obtained? I mean, this is quite apart from Plymouth's interest in it.'

'Those faxes are not conclusive proof that he was murdered. Any more than the photographs you copied them from are conclusive proof that he was murdered. You *say* that McAllister's severed thighs were cauterized and that Mrs O'Brien's viscera were shrivelled ... but that's not an expert opinion. We need to see Moorpath's post-mortem and the FAA's crash report before we can say for sure.'

Joe cleared his throat, and then he said, 'I agree with you ... it looks pretty likely that O'Brien and his family *were* murdered. But we can't risk compromising Plymouth's case or Plymouth's reputation by screwing around with the law.'

Michael knew that Joe was right. Judges were becoming far more critical about the lengths to which insurance companies would go to save themselves from paying out on disputed claims. Plymouth had already been humiliated once this year when an appeal judge had disallowed a tape-recording of a telephone conversation held by a woman who was supposed to have been struck dumb in an auto accident, because her phone had been tapped illegally.

'Okay,' he told Joe. 'I'll just keep chipping away at it.'

'There's one thing ...' said Joe. 'Did you notice if Cecilia O'Brien appeared in any of the photographs? You know – Sissy, the daughter?'

Michael thought about it, and then shook his head. 'No ... she didn't. There were only four bodies ... O'Brien, his wife, McAllister and Coward. No pictures of Cecilia.'

'That's something else that might be worth looking into,' Joe suggested.

Michael lifted the envelope in a wave. 'Do you have time for a drink tonight?' he asked.

'Unh-hunh. Mildred's sister is coming over. I call her The Alien. In Brookline, nobody can hear you scream.'

'Goodnight, Joe,' said Michael, and left the office.

He pushed his way out through the smoked-glass revolving doors of the Plymouth Insurance Building and into the heat and jostle of Huntington Avenue. He felt suddenly alone. He had called Patsy before he left the office, but the phone had rung and rung and she hadn't answered. He had tried to imagine where she could be, what she was doing, and unexpectedly he had found himself missing her – much more keenly than he had ever missed her before.

Last night, he had stayed with Joe and Mildred on the roll-out bed at their apartment in Brookline, but Joe had already found him a single-bedroom apartment over the Cantina Napoletana on Hanover Street. He had always liked North End, with its noise and its shabbiness and its pungent little neighbourhood shops, and so he knew that he was going to feel at home. Except that Patsy and Jason weren't with him; and he really had to work, and work hard. No more dreaming by the sea.

He walked across Copley Place, beside the concrete flowerbeds of splashy red geraniums and the breeze-ruffled pool. Behind him soared the gleaming spires of Back Bay: the Prudential Tower and the Plymouth building and the Marriott Hotel. But ahead of him, far to the south, dark brown smoke still stained the sky, as Seaver Street and twenty blocks of surrounding suburbs were looted and burned.

Two huge National Guard helicopters roared overhead, their twin rotors flashing in the sunlight. Michael shaded his eyes to watch them fly southward. When they had disappeared over the buildings, he turned around – and his attention was caught by a sudden movement among the neatly-planted rows of trees nearby. It looked as if somebody had seen him turn, and had quickly stepped into the shadows between the trees so that he wouldn't be noticed.

Michael wasn't sure why he thought that. But there was something furtive about the way in which he had stepped out of sight, and in the way in which he hadn't emerged from the shadows back into the sunlight, as he would have done if he had been strolling along normally. It could have been a *she*, of course, but it had seemed too tall for a woman.

He paused, narrowing his eyes to try and make out who was there. Maybe it was nobody at all. Maybe the grisly images that he had seen in Dr Moorpath's office were making him jumpy. He had dreamed once that all of the dead from the Rocky Woods crash had shambled into his yard one night, and knocked on the door, and stood in the moonlight, silent and accusing, waiting with terrible patience for him to give them their lost lives back. That dream had haunted him for nearly four months, and it had taken all of Dr Rice's skills to put it to rest. One night he had dreamed that somebody had knocked on his door, and when he had gone to answer it, his yard had been moonlit but empty; and it was then that he had known that the victims were no longer asking him for redemption, or resurrection, or whatever it was they had wanted him to give them. But he had never shaken the feeling that the dead can follow us, begging us mutely for help.

He walked further, occasionally glancing over his shoulder. At first he saw nothing, but as he neared the end of the flowerbeds, he thought he glimpsed the swirl of a coat behind the trees. He stopped, and waited, but nobody appeared. He stepped to one side, and then to the other, trying to catch his shadow out. But there was only the sun-dappled shadow, and the thundering and squealing and honking of the traffic, and the warm south-westerly breeze.

He started to walk diagonally across the concrete path toward the trees. If somebody were following him, he wanted to see who it was. He climbed over the low retaining wall, and then walked faster and faster toward the trees.

As he entered the shadow beneath the leaves and branches, he saw an old blind man in a washed-out linen jacket, tapping his way toward him. The blind man wore a beret and very black sunglasses and he was accompanied by a bored-looking black-and-white mongrel.

There was nobody else. Michael turned this way and that, but there was no sign of anybody wearing a coat; or anybody who might have had any reason to follow him – either real, or imaginary, or out of his nightmares.

The blind man stopped a few paces away. 'Have you lost something, sir?' he asked, in a voice as dry as crushed crackers. His mongrel licked its lips.

'I thought I saw somebody I knew,' Michael lied. Then, 'How did you know I was looking for anything?'

'Hmh! The way your feet were turning – this way, then that way, then back again.'

'You must have pretty sensitive hearing.'

'Too darn sensitive sometimes. Occasionally, I hear things that I wish I hadn't.'

'Well … thanks for your interest,' said Michael, and turned to go.

'He was here, you know,' the blind man told him.

Michael stopped, and turned. 'Who was? What are you talking about?'

'The man you were looking for. He *was* here, you know.'

'How do you know? I don't even know what he looks like myself.'

'Thought you said it was somebody you knew,' the blind man retorted.

'I wasn't sure.'

'But he knew you all right. He was following you, stopping when you stopped, and keeping himself hid.'

Michael quickly looked around. 'So where is he now?'

The blind man smiled. 'There are other places to go, apart from "away".'

He's mental, thought Michael. *He's not only blind, but crazy.*

There was a strange pause between them. For a moment, Michael wondered if he had accidentally spoken aloud. But then the blind man said, 'I was hypnotized too, you know. When I had eyes. I was hypnotized six or seven times.'

Michael didn't answer. This had to be some kind of game; some kind of tortuous joke. How could this man possibly know that he was undergoing hypnotherapy? It wasn't as if it showed on his face – not that this man could even *see* his face. It wasn't as if it affected the tone of his voice.

The mongrel whined in the back of its throat, anxious to be off.

The blind man said, 'There are people who live here and there are people who live there, and there are people who live both here and there.'

'I don't understand you, I'm afraid.'

The blind man smiled, and raised his hand, palm outward. 'Here's hoping you never do.'

'You *heard* somebody following me?' Michael persisted.

The blind man nodded. 'Your old friend Mr Hillary.'

'I don't know anybody called Mr Hillary.'

Without another word, the blind man went shuffling and tapping off between the trees. Michael watched him go, brushing back his hair with his hand. He felt peculiarly disturbed, as if he had discovered by chance that the world wasn't at all the way he had always believed it to be – as if there were invisible doors everywhere, through which people could come and go, but which he had never noticed or known about before.

But – *nah*, the blind old man was just a blind old man, with a wandering mind. 'Mr Hillary' was probably somebody he had known when he was young – a schoolteacher or a storekeeper or a family friend. All the same, it was pretty unsettling that he had guessed that Michael was undergoing hypnosis. He had actually said, 'I was hypnotized *too*.'

Michael reached Columbus Avenue and hailed a cab. When he was in central Boston, he almost always rode the bus or took the T; but this evening he felt as if he needed to get away from the office as quickly as possible. He said '346 Hanover,' and the grizzle-haired black cab driver in the Red Sox baseball cap pulled out into the traffic without a word.

Another two National Guard Chinooks thundered overhead. The cab driver glanced at Michael in his rear-view mirror and Michael saw that one of his eyes was darkly bloodshot. 'Looks like it's war,' the cab driver remarked.

'I didn't hear the latest,' Michael told him. 'Is the rioting still going on?'

'The cops are still shooting innocent bystanders, if that's what you mean.'

'Hey,' said Michael, 'I'm not getting political here.'

'Who's getting political?' the cab driver retorted. 'This is the day of atonement, aint it? This aint political, this is biblical.'

'Whatever it is, it's a crying shame,' said Michael.

'It's the day of atonement,' the cab driver repeated. 'I always knew it was going to come, and now it has.'

He dropped Michael outside the Cantina Napoletana. The late afternoon sunlight filled Hanover Street with molten gold. The Cantina Napoletana was a small old-style restaurant with a red-and-green awning and a shiny window with shiny gilded lettering, and two lollipop bay trees on either side of the front door.

The cab driver handed Michael his change, fixing him

with his one good eye and his one bloodshot eye. 'It's a burnt offering, that's what it is,' he said, with aggressive over-emphasis. 'An offering by fire of a soothing aroma to the Lord.'

'A what?'

'A so – o – oothing aroma,' the cab driver replied, and steered off into the traffic.

Joe had done him proud. The apartment was large and airy, with a newly-sanded and varnished oak floor, and white-painted walls. The living-room overlooked Hanover Street, with a cast-iron balcony just wide enough to accommodate two folding chairs, an upturned terracotta planter which served as a table, and a plastic potful of dusty geraniums. The furniture in the room was bland and oatmeal-coloured. There was only one picture: a travel poster of a bone-white grassy beach, under an inky blue sky.

Michael hauled up the white linen blinds and opened the balcony doors, and the room was filled with noise and the warmth of the afternoon, as well as the smell from the restaurant downstairs – onions and garlic and tomatoes and basil, gently sweating in golden panfuls of virgin olive oil.

Joe had fetched around Michael's battered tan leather suitcase and left it in the corridor. Michael carried it through to the bedroom and hoisted it onto the bed. He unbuckled it, and looked at his crumpled polo shirts and corrugated slacks with resignation. He had never been very good at folding and packing, and he always packed far too much. He didn't know why he had brought that huge maroon fisherman's sweater that he had won from John McClusky the fishbait-seller down on the beach; or maybe he did know. Maybe it was a kind of security blanket – a reminder of home, and the seashore, and Patsy, and Jason, too, and all of that love and all of that freedom that he had been obliged to compromise for money.

He hung up his clothes in the white closets with the louvred doors. The closets smelled of new chipboard. He wedged his empty suitcase under the bed. The bedroom was just as plain as the living-room, with a white night-table in *faux*-bamboo and a warehouse bed covered with a white-and-oatmeal bedspread. There was so much oatmeal in this apartment that Michael began to wonder if it had been decorated by a horse. But there were fine net drapes at the bedroom windows, and he could see through them to the brick-paved yard behind the restaurant, where the chefs emerged from time to time to wipe their necks with tea-towels and smoke a cigarette and shout and laugh.

He washed his face and hands in the small white-tiled bathroom, and then he called Patsy again.

'I just got to Hanover Street.'

'How is it? Is it okay?'

'It's terrific. A big living-room, a bedroom, a bathroom, and a kitchen. It's everything I need. Well, let's put it this way, it's everything I need for now. It's a good thing I like Italian food, though. It's right over a Neapolitan restaurant.' To the tune of 'Pennies from Heaven', he sang, 'Every time I breathe, I breathe *pollo abruzzese*.'

She laughed, but then she said, 'How's it going? The job? You sounded kind of tense at the office.'

'Fine, the job's going fine. The trouble is, I miss you guys already.'

'You're not having any problems?'

'Problems? What problems?'

'Well, you know … stress or anything.'

He thought of the fleeting figure that had seemed to be following him through the trees of Copley Place, and the blind man who had known that he was looking for someone. *Mr Hillary*, whoever he was.

He thought of the cab driver who had talked about

171

atonement, and biblical punishment, and that offering by fire of a soothing aroma to the Lord.

He said, a little stiffly, 'Everything's fine. I'm keeping my head together.'

Patsy said, 'You won't try to keep it from me, will you, Michael, if things start to come apart? It's not your fault. It's nothing for you to feel ashamed about. All you have to do is call me, and we can talk about it. Or call Dr Rice. I know we need the money but we don't need the money that bad.'

He cleared his throat. The net curtains rose and fell in the sunshine. 'It's okay, everything's fine. Joe's been taking care of me. He even fetched my case around.'

'The riots are all on television.'

'Well, there's smoke, and a whole lot of helicopters going over; and when I went down to Boston Central this morning they were bringing in casualties. But everything else seems normal. It's one of those long hot summer things, that's all.'

'Just take care,' said Patsy. 'I'll see you at the weekend, okay?'

'I could be working.'

'Then I'll come up to Boston to pay you a visit. You won't object to a little company when you're working, will you?'

He smiled. The *Boston Globe* lay on the corner of the bed where he had dropped it. The headline read: 'Monyatta Appeals For Calm: Death Toll Rises to 23'. His smile faded as the light through the window faded. He felt strangely responsible, as if the rioting, obliquely, were *his* fault – as if his unexpected arrival in Boston had disturbed the city's equilibrium.

Patsy said, 'Michael?'

'Still here,' he reassured her. Downstairs, they were starting to fry fish.

It was still light outside when the telephone woke him up. Not daylight, not moonlight, but the floodlight that illuminated the back yard of the Cantina Napoletana, while the dishwashers clattered and the chefs laughed and smoked and talked about girls with fettucine-fed figures. (In an hour, they would be home, in pyjamas, snoring next to their wives.)

He couldn't find the phone at first in the unfamiliar apartment; but it kept on ringing, over and over, and eventually he discovered it on the canvas sling chair in the corner of the bedroom, under his discarded coat. He picked it up and said, 'Yes? What is it?' He felt dizzy, disoriented. He couldn't even remember what he had been dreaming about. It had been something to do with trees. Something to do with coattails, flapping out of sight. His tongue felt as if it had been sprinkled with salt.

'Mikey? Is that you?'

'Who is this?'

'Joe … who else do you think?'

'Oh, Joe. What do you want? What the hell time is it?'

'Three-oh-seven. I was watching the news. Weren't you?'

'Are you kidding? Who the hell watches the news at three-oh-seven? I was asleep.'

'Oh, you were asleep, that accounts for it. You took so long to answer, I thought you'd packed your bag and gone back to New Seabury. I was worried you were homesick. I was worried you'd quit.'

'I think I might quit, if you keep on calling me at this time of night.'

'Michael … this is a one-time-only. Switch on the news.'

'I don't have a television yet. You'll have to tell me.'

'Oh … in that case, listen to this. They just found Sissy O'Brien.'

Michael sat down on the edge of the bed. 'They found her? Sissy O'Brien? Who found her? Where? Is she alive?'

'The coastguard found her in Nahant Bay. She's very much dead.'

'They found her *where*? In Nahant Bay? That's more than a dozen miles north of Nantasket Beach.'

'That's right. And if her body had floated from the helicopter crash site on Sagamore Head to East Point, just where they found her, she would have had to float through Hingham Bay, or Quincy Bay, missing Peddocks Island and Long Island and Georges Island and all the rest of the islands and all the rest of the tides – out across Massachusetts Bay, and then back into shore.'

'Was that all they said? That they'd found her; and that she was dead?'

'That was the length and breadth of it.'

Michael caught sight of his skinny pale naked reflection in the mirror, tousled brown hair, loose-wristed arms and legs, cock hanging down. He cleared his throat, and then he said, 'Nahant Bay, that's Essex County, right? So who's handling it? Not Wellman Brock, surely?'

'I don't know yet,' said Joe. 'But I very much doubt it. Poor old Sheriff Brock couldn't find a turd in a sewage plant.'

Michael said, 'Pick me up in twenty minutes. Let's go take a look at Nahant Bay.'

'What? It's only a quarter after three.'

'What are you worried about? It'll be light by the time we get there.'

Michael and Joe parked at an angle amongst the dunes and climbed out of the car. Joe turned back and said, 'Shit. You know what that goddamned sand can do to your paint finish?'

They slid – walked – slid down the dunes. Joe cursed when the sand got into his Gucci loafers. He cursed when the sand blew into his eyes. Michael was used to the sand, and had a way of turning his face away when the wind gusted.

For two hundred feet north of East Point the beach had

been cordoned off with fluttering orange pennants, even though there was nothing left for anyone to see. The morning sky was pale mauvish. The Atlantic Ocean was mauvish, too, but broken up, and a little angry, and it bitched at the shore, and sulked, and bitched again, and dragged up seaweed, and dragged it back again.

Michael's nostrils were all scoured out with salt, and cold, and the air-conditioning of Joe's Seville. He was wearing his maroon fisherman's sweater and he was glad of it, while Joe was shivering in his emerald-green Italian jacket and his sand-stained Gucci shoes.

Two patrol cars from the Essex County Sheriff's department were still parked here; as were three unmarked automobiles, including a dark-maple Caprice and a pea-green Buick Century with a spectacular dent in the offside fender. Close to the shoreline stood a very tall man in a crumpled fawn raincoat, and a younger man with a sweptback hairstyle and a suit, and a heavy-built, blodgy-looking man with a Boy Scout hat, whom Michael recognized almost at once as Sheriff Brock.

Joe lifted the pennants and an acne-blotched deputy came toward him and lifted his hand.

'I'm sorry, sir, restricted area.'

'Tom!' Joe shouted, and gave a wide-sweeping wave to the very tall man in the crumpled fawn raincoat.

The very tall man in the crumpled fawn raincoat waved back, and Joe dropped the pennants behind him and continued to walk across the sand.

'Hey, I'm sorry,' the deputy repeated. 'This area is really restricted. I mean, that means that it's – '

Joe turned and glared at him and snapped, 'Screw you,' and continued to walk towards the shoreline. He turned again, and snapped again, 'Screw you!' The deputy shouted, 'Stop!' and unfastened the snapper on his holster,

175

but Michael came up and laid a hand on top of the deputy's hand. In spite of the cold – or because of it – the boy was trembling.

'Listen,' Michael told him, out of the side of his mouth, as if he weren't talking to him at all. 'We all get caught in no-win situations. This is one of them. You're doing your duty and you're doing it good, but none of those people will see it that way. That tall guy in the raincoat is Lieutenant Thomas Boyle, right?, of the Boston Police Department; and that's your boss Sheriff Wellman Brock, right?, whose every whim is your command; and that's Joe Garboden of Plymouth Insurance who doesn't actually *own* me, balls and all, but everything but. So let's think of our pensions, you and I, and let the big guys tromp around the sandbox. Our turn will come, believe me.'

The young spotty deputy stared at him as if he were mad. But then he said, 'Okay ...' as if he hadn't quite understood, and fastened up his holster.

Michael squeezed the boy's arm. 'Your time will come, believe me, when those guys are all sitting in sunset homes, and forgetting they ever ate food out of aluminum saucepans.'

The deputy nodded, and toothily grinned. 'Right,' he agreed. He turned right around on his heel, and kept on grinning.

Michael walked across the moist sand towards the shore, his left cheek turned against the wind. 'Giraffe,' he said, extending his hand to Lieutenant Boyle. 'How's Megan keeping? I saw her article in *Boston* magazine. The one on pot roasts, or whatever.'

'Well, well, Mikey Rearden,' said Thomas, smiling. He looked tired. His cheeks were white and his nose was pinched red by the wind. 'They told me you'd given it up.'

'Psychological problems,' Michael admitted. 'A simple case of the fruitcakes.'

Thomas sniffed, and dragged out his handkerchief. 'I heard that,' he said.

Michael tapped his forehead. 'It wasn't too serious. I just couldn't stop the outside from getting inside. Know what I mean? But I'm pretty much cured. I've been going through hypnotherapy.'

'Yeah? Does that really work?'

'It depends. I guess you have to want it to work.'

'I was wondering about hypnotherapy for Megan,' said Thomas. 'You know, just to make her feel more positive. She gets pretty damn down sometimes. She doesn't tell me. But *I* would, if I were her.'

'I don't know,' Michael shrugged, and he really didn't. 'I guess she could discuss it with her doctor. But sometimes I think that hypnotherapy can open up more cans of worms than it's worth. I didn't even know that I was afraid of the dark until I was hypnotized.'

Joe looked uncomfortable. So did Sheriff Brock – a huge, wobbling jelly of a man in a sandy uniform and a blatantly artificial toupee. His eyes flicked from side to side and he looked like a man who desperately wanted his breakfast, and his office chair, and a lengthy continuation of last night's sleep.

Thomas squeezed Michael's elbow. 'Let's talk about this later, okay? These guys have been up since three.'

'Where'd they find her?' asked Joe, in an unnaturally loud voice.

Thomas led the way down to the smoother sand of the shoreline. There was a simple wooden marker in the surf – a stick, no more. Every trace of Sissy O'Brien's arrival here had already been washed away by the sea.

'Did you talk to the coastguard?' asked Michael.

Thomas looked up at him and nodded. 'You're thinking about winds and tides and currents, right?'

'That's right,' said Michael.

'Well ... the coastguard have promised me a tidal survey right from the moment the helicopter came down. They may even try floating a dummy body from Sagamore Head to see what happens ... you can judge the winds and the tides mathematically, but a floating body won't always do what you expect it to do.'

'You're telling a fisherman,' said Joe.

Michael looked around. There was something oddly familiar about this curve of beach, although he couldn't think why. He walked down to the shoreline until the surf seethed around the welts of his shoes. He shielded his eyes with both hands and stared out toward the horizon. He had been here before, he was sure of it. When he was a child, maybe, with his father. Every time his father completed a whaler that he really liked, he would sail it up to Marblehead, or down to Plymouth, and take Michael along with him. They carried hot chocolate in Thermos flasks, and brown bags of cheese and baloney sandwiches, and they had sung sea-songs together, old traditional shanties, or silly sea-songs that they had invented themselves.

> We sailed on the good ship Bum
> With a huge supply of rum
> The Bum didn't sink but it sure did stink
> We should have called her some-
> -thing else that wasn't so rude
> But that's our problem, we're just crude.

He smiled to himself, although he felt like crying, too. He looked back up the beach towards Joe and Thomas and Thomas was lighting a cigarette.

'Have they taken her away yet?' he called.

Thomas turned around. 'No ... the meat wagon's still

178

here. We're having a little difference of opinion over where to take her. Commissioner Hudson wants her over at Boston Central with the rest of the dead O'Briens. I want her back with us ... with the other young lady we found Tuesday.'

Michael frowned. 'What other young lady?'

'Didn't you see it on the news? We found a girl in a house on Byron Street, up by the Public Garden. She'd been hogtied with razor wire, tortured, you name it.'

'So what's the connection here?'

Thomas beckoned him up the beach. Michael took a last quick look at the ocean and followed him. It was hard going up the dunes, and Thomas began to cough before they reached the summit.

'You ought to quit smoking,' Joe remarked.

'Tell me about it,' Thomas retorted.

The ambulance from the Essex County Coroner's department was parked at angle on the sandy roadway. Its red lights silently rotated, as if they were lighthouses, warning of death. One of the rear doors was still open, and a young medic with a blond downy moustache was leaning against it, looking tired and bored.

'Any word, lieutenant?' he asked Thomas, as they all approached.

Thomas shook his head. 'This is one of those cases where politics takes precedence over common sense. These gentlemen represent Plymouth Insurance, they're investigators. You want to let them take a look?'

'You *really* want to look?' the medic asked them, with an incredulity that made the palms of Michael's hands tingle.

'Just open up, will you?' Thomas asked him, impatiently.

'Whewff,' said the medic, clearly implying that anyone who wanted to look at this particular item of human flotsam was out of their tree.

He opened wide the second door, and climbed into the ambulance. A grey body bag lay on the folded trolley, with an identification label already attached. The medic tugged open the zipper, all the way down, and a greenish-grey arm suddenly flopped out of the bag and made Michael start in alarm. The medic must have seen him, because he said, with amusement, 'She's dead, don't worry. She aint going to jump up and chase you round the beach.'

'Thank you,' said Thomas, and climbed into the ambulance. Unlike most of those who had to clear up the dead, he didn't like graveyard humour – particularly when the dead had suffered in the way that this poor girl had suffered. Death could sometimes be funny, just as life could sometimes be funny. But for some reason he could never get used to it, and it hardly ever made him laugh.

Michael climbed into the ambulance beside him, ducking his head down. The girl's body smelled strongly of seawater and decomposition. A young, slim girl, no more than fourteen or fifteen years old, judging by her figure. Her hair was short, blonde and bedraggled, and flecked with seaweed. Her visible ear was filled with sand, although she was still wearing a decorative earring that looked as if it were made of glass and some tarnishable metal – possibly silver.

Her eyes were open, and she was staring up at the ceiling. Her irises, however, were all milked over, like a poached codfish, and of course she didn't blink. There was sand in her nostrils and sand in her slightly-parted mouth.

It was her body that horrified Michael the most. Her small breasts were criss-crossed with deep open slices, as if she had been cut with a craft-knife. Her nipples had each been stapled six or seven times, with a paper-stapler, so that they were distorted and twisted. Her bare stomach was covered with scores of burns and scratches and lacerations, most of them pale and puffy because of her long immersion in the ocean. Her upper thighs were also decorated with burns and cuts.

'This is Sissy O'Brien?' asked Michael, his mouth swimming with saliva.

Thomas took a colour photograph out of his coat pocket and held it up in front of him. The photograph shook and Michael had to hold it still so that he could see it clearly.

Thomas said, 'Sissy O'Brien, no question about it. See for yourself. Pending formal identification, of course.'

'Jesus Christ, who could have done this?'

'We think the same people who killed our Jane Doe on Byron Street. Same perverted *m.o.*, same cuts and whip-marks and torture-burns ... and we released none of that stuff to the media, so we're not talking copycat.'

'What is it, some kind of s/m cult or what?'

Thomas shook his head. He could have used another cigarette, but he knew that he wasn't permitted to smoke inside the ambulance. Not that it mattered, the patient was dead already.

Michael, with huge reluctance, pulled down the body bag zipper a few inches further. There were livid burns and scars between Sissy O'Brien's legs, all around her vulva and her inner thighs.

'Some joker had fun with a Zippo,' Thomas remarked, his voice totally flat. He didn't want to think how much Sissy O'Brien must have screamed. Or maybe she hadn't been able to scream. There were bruises around her mouth that indicated that she had been gagged – probably with one of those inflatable rubber gags that fetishists used.

Michael leaned over, and it was then that he saw something that made him recoil with total horror, and stare at Thomas wide-eyed. Something dark and bushy and wet, draped between Sissy O'Brien's thighs.

'There's something there,' he said, and his voice didn't sound at all like his own.

Thomas swallowed, shrugged. 'They gave her a pretty hard time, believe me.'

Michael didn't dare to take a second look. He could see that Thomas was tired; but he couldn't understand how anybody could take madness like this for granted. There was something *there* – something dark and disgusting and bushy, thickly matted with blood, protruding from Sissy O'Brien's deathly white buttocks.

'Damn it, Thomas, she's got a *tail!*'

Thomas said, 'Let's get out of here.'

'What?'

'Let's get *out* of here!' Thomas barked at him, and jostled him down the steps of the ambulance and onto the sand. Joe was standing a few feet away, talking to Sergeant Jahnke, and both of them looked across at Michael and Thomas with concern.

'I'm sorry,' said Thomas. He took a deep breath. 'I keep telling myself not to let this stuff get to me but it always gets to me.'

'She has a *tail,*' Michael repeated. He knew that he was sounding hysterical but he didn't particularly care. 'Thomas, she has a goddamned *tail!*'

Thomas took out a book of matches from the Sunset Grill & Tap and spent a long time lighting a cigarette, cupping the flame against the breeze.

'I told you they gave her a pretty hard time. They've done something to her … with a cat, as far as we can make out. We can't really tell yet.'

'A *cat?* What the hell are you talking about, a *cat?*' Michael was seriously upset.

The wind whipped sand between them. Somebody shouted, 'Jack! Jack! Get on down here!'

At that moment, a thin young bespectacled man in a dark blue windbreaker appeared around the side of the ambulance. He approached Thomas and said, 'It's okay, lieutenant. We can take her. I talked to the coroner and the coroner talked to the commissioner and the commissioner talked to the governor.'

'The *governor*? What did you say, for Christ's sake?'

'I said it was probably a serial killing, and there could be more; and how would it look on television if the police department had tried to keep it under wraps.'

'You've got some nerve, Victor,' said Thomas, with grudging admiration.

'Anybody can have nerve, so long as they know what they're doing.'

Thomas said to Michael, 'Here, Mikey ... this is Victor Kurylowicz, our new medical examiner. Moved here from Newark, New Jersey. Victor's an expert on floaters, and fire victims, too.'

Michael extended his hand. Victor's handshake was cold and yielding and limp; like shaking the hand of a man recently dead. 'Pleased to know you,' he said. 'I'm Michael Rearden, Plymouth Insurance. Well, actually, I invent board games for a living, and marine supplies. But Plymouth asked me to check all this out ... this O'Brien case.'

'Well, I wish you luck,' said Victor. 'This is a pretty strange case.'

'What's this about a cat?' asked Michael.

Victor glanced at him quickly. 'I don't really want to discuss it just yet. I haven't had a chance to make any kind of detailed examination.'

Michael's voice was shaking. 'The girl has a *tail* for God's sake.'

'Listen,' said Victor. 'I have a pretty clear idea of what they did to her, but I won't be able to say for sure until I carry out a post-mortem. It's too damned horrible to start speculating about it.'

Michael took three or four deep breaths. His head was beginning to feel as if it were filling up with deep, black blood. 'This doesn't make any sense. How did Sissy O'Brien get here? And who would have wanted to hurt her this way?'

'I don't have any idea,' said Thomas, flatly.

'How can anybody even have *thought* of doing something like that?'

'Mikey ... really, I don't have any idea. But we're working on it. If we can find a link between Sissy O'Brien and that girl who was killed on Byron Street ... well, we might begin to make some positive progress.'

'There's a link,' said Victor, with complete, unemotional certainty. 'In fact, there's more than a link. These two killings are completely interwoven, believe me. I can smell it.'

'Detective *manqué*,' Thomas remarked. 'Could have made the grade, too, if he hadn't been far too intelligent. They don't like eggheads on any force, right, Victor? But they grit their teeth and tolerate them in Boston.'

Michael glanced back towards the ambulance. The young moustachioed medic was zipping up the body bag and grinning at him. Jesus. Sometimes the saviours were just as hard-hearted as the killers.

'If the O'Brien family were deliberately killed, we don't have to pay out, you know that, don't you?' asked Michael.

Thomas blew smoke. 'The only O'Brien I'm concerned about is Sissy; and she was killed, no doubt about it.'

'Somebody was seen carrying something from the wreck of their helicopter,' said Michael. 'That something could have been Sissy, injured or unconscious.'

'That's a possibility,' Thomas agreed. 'In fact, that's the most likely possibility. I don't believe she floated here from

184

Sagamore Head, not for a moment. I believe she was dumped here, late last night, by the people who killed her.'

'So what's the next step?' asked Michael.

'The next step is to tie her in conclusively with the Byron Street victim, and at the same time start interviewing everybody and anybody who might have seen somebody throw something into the ocean. House-to-house questioning, but it shouldn't be too hard, way out here. Nahant has a population of 4,200, and that includes cats.'

'You think you can tie her in?'

Thomas nodded. 'The girl we found at Byron Street had two puncture marks in her back, just above her pelvis. Sissy O'Brien had very similar marks.'

Michael wiped cold sweat from his forehead with the back of his hand. 'Puncture marks?' he asked.

Victor said, 'We don't know what they are, but they're much less brutal than any of her other injuries. I mean they're almost clinical.'

Michael watched Thomas smoke for a while, and then he said, 'What the hell do you think this is all about?'

Thomas flicked his cigarette into the surf. 'Your guess is as good as mine.'

'Do you mind if I see the other girl? The one you found on Byron Street? Not in the flesh necessarily. Pictures would do.'

'For sure. Give me a call and I'll fix it for you.'

Victor said, 'She looks as bad as this, believe me ... and she was dead a whole lot longer.'

'How long do you think Sissy was in the water?' asked Michael.

Victor pulled a face. 'I don't know yet. Eight, nine hours, maybe longer.'

'Was she drowned?'

'Doesn't look like it. It won't be hard to find out.'

Michael narrowed his eyes and looked up the pale, windswept beach. 'Somebody took her from Sagamore Head and tortured her and brought her here, and threw her in the ocean. Now why do you think *that* was?'

'They wanted something,' Thomas suggested.

'They wanted something? What did they want?'

'I don't know … but nobody ever gets murdered for nothing. *Ever.* Maybe a husband wants peace and quiet, and kills his children. Maybe a clerk wants promotion, and kills the only guy who's standing in his way. Maybe a mistress gets jealous, and kills her lover's wife.'

'So what could anybody have wanted from Sissy O'Brien – especially since her parents were already dead and nobody would have a paid a ransom for her?'

'Well …' said Thomas, grasping Michael's shoulder and giving him one of his famous crooked smiles. 'They didn't want money and they didn't want sex and they didn't want blood. You tell me what else they might have killed her for.'

A seagull flew past, very low, screaming at them. 'Maybe I shall,' said Michael.

It was time to go. Joe was beckoning, and Sergeant Jahnke was lifting his r/t up into the air, to indicate to Thomas that somebody was calling him, somebody urgent.

Michael and Victor trudged up the dunes together. Victor said, 'They're hiding something, you know.'

'Who?'

'The powers that be. The coroner, the commissioner, the governor. Maybe higher still.'

'How do you know that?'

'I saw the same thing happen in Jersey when they killed anybody important in local government, or in in the law enforcement agencies, or in the mob. The bodies were always

186

whisked away, the evidence always went missing. The only murders that ever ended up with straightforward convictions were the murders of people who didn't matter.'

Michael thought for a moment, and then he said, 'I saw some photographs of John O'Brien's helicopter, after the crash.'

'It was burned out, right?'

'It wasn't as burned out as the media obviously thought. You could still identify the bodies.'

'I thought they were charred so badly you couldn't tell one from the other.'

'Unh-hunh, no way. There must have been a flash-fire, but that was it.'

'Are you kidding me? The coroner told me they were burned up beyond recognition. Charcoal, he said.'

'There were four people in that wreck – the pilot, a man named Coward; plus a young assistant from the Justice Department, Dean McAllister; plus Mrs O'Brien; plus John O'Brien himself. When I first saw the pictures, I wondered if there were two or three missing ... you know, pictures of Sissy O'Brien. But now I know that she wasn't even there.'

Victor said, 'Why should the commissioner lie about it?'

'I don't know. But I have some copies of those photographs and I'd like you take a look at them. The quality's average-to-shitty. I had to fax them out of Dr Moorpath's office while Dr Moorpath was patching up victims from Seaver Street. As I say, they're pretty smudgy and pretty dark. But maybe you can see something in them that I can't.'

Victor stopped, and took off his spectacles, and polished them thoughtfully with a small piece of crumpled-up kitchen-towel.

'You're taking a risk, aren't you, telling me about this? How do you know that Dr Moorpath and me aren't bosom-buddies. Medical examiners of a feather tend to stick together, don't you know. And Dr Moorpath and I are both members of the Massachusetts Association of Practising Pathologists.'

'Sure I'm taking a risk,' said Michael. 'And that's because you look like the kind of guy who wouldn't be seen dead playing eight holes at Chestnut Hill with Raymond Moorpath. Besides which, there's no such association.'

Victor replaced his spectacles. 'Okay,' he said at last. He checked his watch. 'Today's wiped out. But meet me tomorrow – say, eleven o'clock. I have to have a haircut first.'

Michael wasn't sure if he'd discovered an ally in Victor Kurylowicz or not; but he liked Victor's combination of self-mockery, toughness and weirdness. It took all three to make a good medical examiner. Michael had been totally psyched out simply by the sight of dead bodies; Victor had to spend all day cutting them up, and handling their internal organs, and lifting out their brains, and trying at the same time not to think of them as somebody's mother, or somebody's child – somebody who could have been talking to him, only a few hours before.

He plodded up the dunes, and took one last look around. Joe was waiting for him, talking impatiently to Sergeant Jahnke. Behind him, he heard the ambulance drive off, with a sudden abbreviated whoop of its siren that made all of them jump.

It was then, in the middle distance, that he saw something white. Something that shone in the gilded morning haze, like a sail.

He shielded his eyes against the glare, but still he couldn't be sure what it was. He turned to one of the coastguards who was standing nearby and asked him if he could borrow his binoculars.

'Okay, sir, but treat them with respect, okay? They're Zeiss, seven hundred bucks and change.' The coastguard had a cluster of bright scarlet spots on each cheek and Michael hoped they weren't catching.

He took the binoculars and focused them on the white shape in the distance. It was still blurry, because of the summer-morning mist that was rising from the sea. But there was no doubt about what it was. What he had taken at first for a sail was well inland, on the top of a rough, grassy headland. On top of the white triangular shape was a black lattice balcony, and a gleaming glass lens.

It was a lighthouse – but not just any lighthouse. It was the same squat white lighthouse that he had seen in his hypnotic trance.

And off to the right, behind the windswept trees, a row of green-painted saltbox houses. The same houses that he had seen in his trance.

With gradually-rising thrill of dread and discovery, he turned this way and that, and it was then that he knew for sure that *this* was the bay – *this* was the bay that he had seen when Dr Rice had last taken him under.

This was the bay and that was the lighthouse; and it was here, where Sissy O'Brien had been taken from the ocean, that his life was going to change. He could feel his destiny swinging around the way the weathervane swings. He could hear the sand sizzling in the sea-grass. He looked back toward the lighthouse with excitement, with fear, and when Joe came across and took his elbow and said, 'Come on, Michael, I'm starved. Let's grab some breakfast,' his eyes were wide and staring, he knew it, and Joe instinctively let him go.

'Michael? What's the matter?'

'Nothing. But something's beginning to come together.'

'Want to tell me about it?'

'I don't know … not yet. Let's find some breakfast.'

'Hey!' shouted out the coastguard, as they walked away. 'Those are my goddamned binoculars!'

Verna Latomba was standing in the kitchen pressing her black skirt when the doorbell rang. She reached over and turned down the television. She had been watching Oprah Winfrey talking about incest. A man with a very white face had been confessing that he had fallen in love with his sixteen-year-old daughter. Verna frowned, and listened. She wasn't expecting anybody. She knew that Patrice wouldn't be back till nightfall, maybe very much later, and in any case he had a key, and could let himself in.

She propped her iron on its base and walked through to the living-room. She saw that she had forgotten to put the chain on the front door. She lifted her hands towards it, but before she could do so, the doorbell rang again, startling her. She hesitated, listening, waiting, but it didn't ring again, so she went right up to the door and called, 'Patrice? Is that you?'

There was a long silence. Nobody spoke. But Verna was sure that there was somebody out there – and not just because she hadn't heard footsteps retreating along the landing. She couldn't hear talking. She couldn't hear breathing. But somehow she could *feel* the presence of somebody waiting, somebody with infinite patience and unimaginable intentions.

'Who's there?' she called.

No answer. She took hold of the knob on the dangling end of the door-chain. Beside the doorframe, on the yellow-papered wall, a picture of Jesus stared at her sadly – Jesus depicted as a black man, with yellow eyes.

'We're friends,' said a young man's voice, from the hallway outside.

Verna stood with the chain half-lifted toward the latch.

'Friends?' she demanded. 'What friends?'

'Friends,' the young man repeated, as if that were quite enough.

'You aint no friends that I know,' said Verna.

'Friends of Patrice.'

'Patrice said not to let anybody in.'

Another long pause. Then, 'You can let *us* in.'

'I can't do that, I'm sorry.'

'Patrice said you could let *us* in. We met Patrice in the street, just outside of the Palm Diner.'

'Patrice told me nobody.'

'You really won't open the door?'

'I can't, Patrice would go crazy.'

'If you won't open the door, do you know what we'll do?'

'Don't you go making no threats.'

'If you won't open the door, we'll huff and we'll puff and we'll blow your house down.'

'What are you, sick or something? Go away!'

Another pause. She thought she heard whispering, and the shuffling of feet. She could have sworn she heard a young man giggle.

Then – without any warning at all – the lock clicked, and the door was pushed open.

'Out!' she screamed. 'Get out!' She flung herself against the door, bruising her shoulder, but she didn't stand a chance. Two young men in sunglasses forced their way into the room, shoving Verna ahead of them with the heels of their outstretched hands. One of them slammed the door behind him, and fastened the security chain.

The other pushed Verna, push, push, push, into the living-room, and then pushed her back onto the sofa. It was an old sofa that a friend of Patrice's had given them, and it was covered with a beige-and-white durry. Verna jarred her

191

hip on it as she fell backward. She tried to get up, but the young man pushed her back down again.

'What do you want?' she asked them, trembling with anger and anxiety. 'You aint no friend of Patrice's that I know.'

'What are you going to do, Verna?' one of the young men grinned at her. 'Call the cops?'

'The cops?' she retaliated, even though her voice was off-pitch. 'The people I'm going to call are going to make you a whole lot sorrier than cops ever could.'

She tried to get up a second time, but the young man pushed her back, harder this time, and said, 'Sit, Verna, sit! There's a good bitch!'

The young men were skinny and lightly built, no flesh on them at all, and at first glance she had thought they were twins. But as they looked around the apartment, she could see that they were very unlike each other, and it was only their floury-white faces and their tiny, impenetrable sunglasses that had made them appear so similar.

One of them was tall, his greasy black hair brushed straight back from his forehead and tied in a small, lank pony-tail. His nose was large and fleshy, and his cheeks were sunken. His lips were so bloodless that they were almost mauve, and he had a mole on the left side of his chin from which a single long hair sprouted.

He wore a silky black coat, with a black T-shirt underneath, and baggy black trousers. He reminded Verna of a rock manager she had once known – fashionable and hip but self-interested to the point of cruelty to everybody who depended on him, and infinitely sleazy.

He had a strange and distinctive smell about him: like stale pot-pourri mingled with some kind of burned cooking oil, maybe walnut oil or sesame oil.

The other young man had short-cropped hair and a short, pointed nose and a permanent wolfish grin, his lips stretched back over his teeth. He was shorter than his companion, wirier, and far more hyperactive, dodging from one side of the apartment to the other, picking things up, putting them down again. He was wearing a black polo-neck sweater and black leather trousers that were decorated with hooks and chains and safety-pins; and black rubber-soled combat boots. He had a black canvas bag slung around his shoulder, a bag that bounced on his hip as he circled the room.

'We going to do it, then, Joseph?' he wanted to know, ducking and weaving.

'Certainly,' said the one called Joseph. 'Certainly we're going to do it.'

'We going to do it *now*?' the young man asked, impatiently.

Joseph smiled a mauve, bloodless smile. 'Certainly, Bryan. Certainly we're going to do it now.'

Bryan lifted the black canvas bag over his head and set it down on the tile-topped coffee table. Joseph bent over and unbuckled it, and rummaged around inside. Verna heard metallic jingling and clinking; and then Joseph produced two chromium-plated lengths of thin wire, each about two feet long; and then a pair of pruning shears, the kind that gardeners use for dead-heading roses.

Joseph turned back to Verna and smiled. 'Have you ever panicked?' he asked her. 'I mean – have you ever *totally* panicked?'

Verna stared at him, terrified, unable to understand the question.

Joseph released the catch on the pruning shears, and snipped at the air with menacing snips, as if he wanted to cut the very morning into shreds. He whooped with laughter. 'You never totally panicked? Never in your life? Well – *no – o – ow's* your chance!'

Eight

Michael held the photograph up to the window and studied it for almost a minute without saying anything, even though he had recognized the girl at once.

Six floors below, sirens still howled south on Cambridge Street.

In the last photograph that he had seen of this girl, she had been just about to smile – one eye closed against the summer sunshine.

This one had been taken in the morgue. A portrait in bruises and scars and encrusted burns.

'Dear God,' he breathed.

Victor had been poring for the past ten minutes over the fax-blurred photographs that Michael had transmitted from Dr Moorpath's office, making painstaking little pencil crosses here and there, and writing neat, intense little notes on a yellow legal pad. At the same time, he had been taking quick, wolfish bites from a salt-beef and dill-pickle sand-wich, and swigging tomato soup out of a polystyrene cup.

Suddenly, however, Victor realized that Michael had something important and painful to say, and he lowered his pencil and looked up at him, his eyes magnified behind his spectacles, his jaws chewing more slowly.

'This is Elaine Parker,' said Michael, and lowered the photograph with shaking hands.

Victor laid down his pencil altogether, and swallowed. 'You *know* her?'

'I should do. I've seen enough pictures of her.'

'But, who is she?'

Michael came away from the window and sat down on the opposite side of the desk. 'You remember the Rocky Woods air disaster? The L10-11 that came down?'

'Who doesn't. You were one of the insurance investigators, weren't you? The Giraffe told me.'

Michael dropped the photograph of Elaine Parker onto Victor's desk. 'Three hundred and twelve people died that night. The airplane split open like a goddamned peapod and they all dropped out of the sky. All except her.'

'I don't follow you,' said Victor.

'She was on the passenger manifest – Elaine Patricia Parker, twenty-one years old, an arts student from Attleboro, Massachusetts. She was on her way to see some exhibition that was touring from Europe. Turner, Gauguin, I don't recall. She checked in to the Midwest Airlines desk at nineteen minutes after three that afternoon. Her only luggage was a single plaid valise.

'As far as we know, she had a cup of coffee and a Danish in the airport coffee lounge before going to the gate. In the coffee lounge several people saw her talking to a young man. Dark hair, smiling, that was the only description we ever got. But then, so what? The world is full of dark-haired, smiling young men, and young girls like to talk to them.'

Victor looked down at the dark and blurry fax in front of him. He had already traced the outline of a sprawled and distorted body, and part of another. John O'Brien, bent double, headless. Dean McAllister, with his legs cut off at the thigh. He took another bite of sandwich.

Michael said, 'We searched eleven-and-a-half square miles – way beyond the perimeter of any wreckage – and we never found her body. We found her purse, we found one of her shoes. But we never found her.'

He leaned over the table and stared at the photograph. The girl's face was puffy from decomposition and horribly scarred. There were fish hooks penetrating her lips and cigarette burns on her eyelids. He hadn't seen the photographs of the rest of her body and from the way that Victor had described it, he didn't want to. He had never realized that it was possible for a woman to be hurt in so many ways.

'She suffered, didn't she?' he said. 'She really suffered.'

'What? You want to believe it,' Victor replied, with his mouth full.

Michael stood up again and paced around the office. A human skeleton was dangling in the corner and he went up to it and stared into the dusty hollow sockets of its eyes. He touched it, gently, and it danced a little jig for him, its kneebones knocking.

'We call him Idle,' Victor remarked. Michael managed half a smile.

'The question is – ' he began, but he was interrupted by the office door opening and Thomas walking in. Thomas looked tired and hot. Half of his shirt tail had come out of his crumpled fawn slacks and his necktie was all skewed. He said to Victor, 'How's it going?'

Victor held up his half-eaten sandwich. 'Nutrition break. It's hard work, cutting people up. We've opened the thorax and the abdominal cavity, Keiller's retrieving the stomach contents. I'll send you up a quick preliminary report as soon as I can.'

'*Before* dinner, preferably,' said Thomas. 'My digestive system is never too happy about this kind of thing.'

He looked at Michael, and sniffed, and then wiped his nose with the back of his hand. 'Well, Mikey – Victor tells me you've been giving us a little assistance with this case.'

'More than a little,' said Victor. He pointed to the photography lying on the desk. 'Michael thinks he's ID'd our Jane Doe from Byron Street.'

196

'You're kidding me,' said Thomas. He picked up the photograph. 'You know who she is?'

Michael nodded.

'You're *sure* you know who she is?'

'Absolutely. Her name's Elaine Patricia Parker,' said Michael. 'She was the only one on the passenger-list in the Rocky Woods air disaster whose body we never found.'

Thomas was head-and-shoulders taller than Michael. He stared down at him for a long time, breathing harshly through his open mouth. 'Elaine Patricia Parker?'

'That's right. She was an art student from Attleboro.'

'And you can recognize her, after all this time, in spite of the fact that she's been tortured like that, and beaten like that, and facially disfigured?'

Michael nodded. 'Thomas, believe me, I studied every available photograph of that girl a hundred times over. I'm a professional.'

Thomas raised an eyebrow.

'I'm *still* a professional,' Michael insisted.

Victor briskly drummed his fingers on his desk, stood up, and reached for the green surgical gown that was hanging on the hatstand next to the chart of lymph glands from *Hewer's Histology*. 'Listen,' he said. 'I'd better get back to it.'

'Okay,' said Thomas, without taking his eyes off Michael. 'Let me know soonest, won't you?'

Victor went out of the door and Michael and Thomas and Idle the skeleton were left together in uncomfortable silence. Thomas picked up the photograph of Elaine Parker and held it up, close to Michael's face. Michael glanced at it quickly from time to time, but couldn't stand to examine it too closely. He could feel that dreadful familiar sensation of vertigo, as if the floor were just about to open up underneath his feet – as if he were just about to plummet 20,000 feet into freezing darkness. Then whipping branches, and bruising trees. Then straight into solid ground, like a swimmer diving into concrete.

'You're sure this is her?'

Michael cleared his throat. 'I'll pull her file at Plymouth and bring it over. She had distinguishing marks, too, as far as I can remember. A small strawberry birthmark underneath her right armpit.'

'I'll tell Victor to look for it,' said Thomas. He kept the photograph raised in front of Michael's face. Michael looked pale and distracted, and he kept swallowing, and Thomas was very interested to know why.

Michael said, 'Her parents are still living in Attleboro, as far as I know. You – uh – you could ask them to identify her, couldn't you?'

'I'll have to, if I'm persuaded that it *is* her,' said Thomas. With his left hand, without lowering the photograph, he reached into his shirt pocket and took out a cigarette. 'But you can see my point of view. I'm not going to expose anybody to viewing this girl's remains if there's any serious question that it isn't her. What was done to that girl – that gave *me* nightmares, and I've seen plenty of very unpleasant things done to plenty of people.'

'It's her, I'm sure of it,' Michael insisted. And he *was* sure.

'If you're right, Mikey, you're giving us some pretty damned difficult questions to answer,' said Thomas. 'Like – how did she survive a high-altitude air disaster that nobody else survived?'

'There are several possibilities,' said Michael. 'It could have been one of those freaks of physics, one of those million-to-one chances. Some of the Lockerbie victims were still showing vital signs when they were found, and *they* fell from 31,000 feet. Admittedly, they didn't survive for very long. But when a human body falls from a great height, it reaches a terminal velocity of 110 mph, and then wind resistance prevents it from falling any faster. When it hits the ground, it's no worse than a head-on smash between two automobiles travelling at 60 mph.'

'And no better, either, I presume,' put in Thomas.

Michael shrugged. 'The other possibility is that she wasn't on the plane at all. She checked in, she was *seen* to check in – and her baggage was found on board, as well as a shoe and a purse. But of course we have no surviving witnesses to say that they actually saw her on board.'

Thomas put the cigarette between his lips, and it waggled, unlit, when he spoke. 'If you're right about what's-her-name, Elaine Parker, then we have two girls – both in the Boston area – who have both survived air-crashes in one way or another – and who have both subsequently been abducted, imprisoned, tortured and killed. And the whys and the wherefores and the whodunits of *those* particular questions – well, God only knows.'

Michael said, 'Of course we do have the pinprick connection – those scars that were made on both girls' backs.'

'For sure,' Thomas agreed, tiredly. 'But it's not a whole lot to go on, is it? Somebody stuck needles in their backs. But so far we don't have any idea *why* they should have wanted to. Part of the problem is that Jane Doe's insides were too badly decomposed for Victor to determine what her assailant was trying to achieve – that is, apart from causing her extreme pain.'

'When you say decomposed …?'

'Maggots,' said Thomas. 'The larvae of the common flesh-fly. Ask Victor about it, he's the expert. They ate her insides out like a condemned building.'

'It's all right,' said Michael. 'I'm pretty much up on maggots.' He pressed the back of his hand against his forehead. He was feeling chilled and sweaty at the same

199

time. It might be a good idea for him to call Dr Rice this afternoon, just to talk things over, just to re-orient himself. The real world was beginning to take on a cold and menacing cast, and he was beginning to feel very far away from Patsy and Jason, and Dr Rice's quiet, reassuring office in Hyannis.

The phone rang. Thomas picked it up and snapped, 'Boyle.'

He listened, and then he put down the phone and said, 'Victor wants me down in autopsy. He says there's something I ought to see.'

He paused, and then he said, 'Do you want to tag along?'

Michael hesitated for a moment, and then he nodded. 'I guess I'll have to.'

It had been a clamorous two days at the City Morgue. Twenty-two men and three women had already been killed in the rioting on Seaver Street, and worse was expected tonight. Apart from that, the medical examiners were having to deal with the usual daily quota of shootings, stranglings, knifings, burnings and drownings. Boston was a Mecca for drownings. The mayor had once indiscreetly boasted that more people had drowned in Boston Harbor since the turn of the century than the casualty lists of the *Lusitania* and the *Titanic* put together.

Michael had to squeeze himself back against the wall while a green-sheeted corpse was rolled past them by a dwarfish black porter. The porter was singing to himself, 'When a man ... loves a woman ...'

Victor was waiting for them outside the swing doors of the mortuary. He was holding up his bloodstained gloves as if he were making a blessing. 'This is not at all pretty,' he warned them. 'But it's *very* interesting.'

He pushed his way through the doors and into the

chilled, brightly-lit room. The air was strong with the smell of antiseptic and bile and unfresh human flesh. Thomas, just behind him, was vigorously shaking his essence of cloves into his handkerchief. He turned around and said to Michael, 'Want some?' but Michael shook his head.

On the white ceramic table in front of them, under a penetrating battery of surgical lights, lay something that looked like a huge burst-open sack of exotic fruits – browns and yellows and purples and reds. It was only when Michael walked around to the other side of the table that he could make any kind of sense of what he saw – because this burst-open sack of exotic fruits had a head and a face and two arms and two legs. It was the body of Sissy O'Brien, opened up from crotch to clavicle, split wide apart by a vast suprapubic incision, so that Victor Kurylowicz could find out just what her abductors had done to her.

Michael found himself staring at her face. Her eyes were closed, and her skin was an odd pearly-grey, almost phosphorescent, but in death she had taken on a calm, mature beauty, and Michael found it almost impossible to believe that there was nothing at all inside that head, beneath that silky hair. Only darkness, and nothingness, a young life hideously ended for no earthly reason that he could imagine. He looked across the gaudy gruesomeness of her insides, and saw Thomas with his watering eyes and his handkerchief over his face and Victor watching him with light-reflecting spectacles.

'Here,' said Victor, beckoning. 'You'll have to come closer.'

Michael came closer. He felt the darkness beginning to rise up beneath him. Victor said, '*Closer* – she's not going to jump up and ask you to dance the watusi.'

Michael edged as close to the table as he dared. Victor picked up a stainless-steel speculum and used it to push aside the beige, gelid heaps of Cecilia's intestines. 'Now here – ' he explained, ' – here are her kidneys.'

Cecilia's kidneys were so kidney-like that Michael silently swore to himself that he would never eat kidneys again. Brown and curved and shiny – just slightly dulled from their recent exposure to the air. Victor prodded them and they wobbled slightly in their bedding of off-white fat and loose, veiny, connective membrane.

In a matter-of-fact, lecturer's tone, Victor said, 'As far as I've been able to work out so far, the major injuries are all consistent with torture or sadistic gratification. They're terrible – and when I say terrible, I mean that they're far more extreme than anything I've ever seen before. But what I wanted to find out first was what those two needle-punc-tures in the lower back were all about – since obviously they might establish some connection between our Byron Street victim and this poor young girl here in front of us. I don't think that the prime purpose of the needle-punctures was to cause pain. They *might* have caused pain, but compared with having a lighted cigarette touched against your bare nipples, forget it.'

'So what did you find out?' asked Thomas, growing nauseous and impatient.

Victor looked up, and raised an eyebrow in self-satisfaction. 'What I found out was that those needle-punctures led directly to the suprarenal glands, *directly*.'

Thomas, in a muffled voice, asked, 'Would that be diffi-cult?'

'Extremely. You can see for yourself that the kidneys are pretty mobile.'

'So whoever stuck those needles directly into those par-ticular glands did it with skill – '

'Oh, yes.'

' – and accuracy – '

'Fantastic accuracy ... remember that the left kidney is always slightly narrower, and higher in the abdominal cavity than the right.'

' – and forethought.'

'For sure.'

'A surgeon, maybe?' asked Michael.

'It's a possibility. It sure wasn't a darts player.'

Thomas took a deep clove-soaked breath, and then he said, 'So what are these supra-what's-their-name glands, then? Why would anybody want to stick a needle into them?'

Victor took a scalpel and cut away the fibrous outer layer of the glands that clung to the top of the kidneys. A little blood and fluid seeped out, but Sissy was long dead, she wouldn't embarrass him by bleeding very much.

'Here, look – ' said Victor, and opened up one of the kidneys so that Thomas and Michael could see for themselves. Thomas couldn't stop himself from thinking about that brunch he had eaten three weeks ago at Barrett's, all those kidneys lying in a silver chafing-dish, wrapped in bacon. 'This is the suprarenal gland, there's one on top of each kidney, about two inches long and a little less than two inches wide. Inside it you can see this firm, deep-yellow layer, okay? This is what we call the cortical layer. And right inside the middle, here – this soft, dark-brown portion, this is what we call the medulla.'

'Okay,' said Thomas, swallowing. 'But what does it do? Is it important?'

Victor stood up straight. 'If you took out anybody's suprarenal glands, they would suffer from muscular prostration and death within a few days. Inside that soft brown part, the medulla, that's where adrenaline is produced.'

'You mean the same adrenaline like when you get all hyped up?'

'That's right. Whenever you're threatened or excited or

stressed, your suprarenal glands pump out adrenaline – and it causes your eyes to widen, your hair to stand on end, your heart to beat faster, and your liver to fill your bloodstream with extra sugar.'

Michael could feel the darkness closing in, but he tried to keep himself rational. 'What are you trying to say here? You mean to say that somebody deliberately stuck needles into these girls' suprarenal glands, in order to tap their adrenaline? Is that it?'

Victor made an amused, dismissive face. 'How should I know? That's Lieutenant Boyle's job.'

'But somebody purposely stuck needles into their suprarenal glands?'

'That's correct – right into the middle, where adrenaline is produced. And, of course, under the circumstances, their suprarenal glands would have been producing a great deal of adrenaline.'

Thomas said, 'You're talking about the fear – the pain – the threat of imminent death?'

Victor nodded. 'This can only be theory, of course. But it does suggest an alternative motive to simple sadism.'

Michael said, 'Alternative motive? What alternative motive? Why the hell would anybody want anybody's adrenaline?'

'Hard to say,' Victor replied. 'Usually, we get all the adrenaline we need from animals, or produce it artificially. We use it in eye and nose operations, and all kinds of medical emergencies, because it raises the blood pressure, and constricts smaller blood vessels, and reduces bleeding. Sometimes we apply it directly onto a serious wound on a piece of gauze or lint, and it helps to stop a haemorrhage. It can be helpful in relieving asthma, too.'

Thomas stared down at Sissy O'Brien's plundered body. He felt baffled, and he felt sickened, but most of all he felt sad. Megan, his wife, had been tragically hurt by fate, but Megan at least was alive. This poor girl's life had ended for ever, in shock, and agony, and to satisfy some greed that nobody could understand.

They stood around her in the bright, uncompromising light of the mortuary, and each of them wondered in his own way about pain. Not only that, but about God, and whether there was one.

After two or three minutes, Thomas suddenly said, 'The tail.'

Michael glanced at him. This was one revelation that he hadn't been looking forward to.

Victor raised the surgical sheet that covered the lower half of Sissy's body. Michael didn't want to look, but he couldn't help it, and with a terrible feeling of sickness and prurience he glimpsed the bushy, bedraggled fur between Sissy's thighs.

'I haven't cut into the lower gut yet,' Victor explained.

'But you do have a pretty good idea of what they've done to her?'

Victor nodded. 'Yes.'

'Are you going to do it now? We really need to know.'

'You don't have to stay here.'

Thomas looked at Michael over his handkerchief and thought: my God, this guy's right on the edge. He knew Michael from way back. He knew that he was good, and that he was special, especially when it came to tangled, deceptive investigations. But Joe Garboden had warned him that he wasn't quite the same, not since Rocky Woods. And he could see for himself that Michael was collapsing under the weight of his own traumas. His face was grey, his eyes were dilated, and as he stood beside Victor Kurylowicz's dissecting-table, he was exhibiting all the signs of imminent shock.

'Victor …' said Thomas. 'Maybe we'll skip this part. You can send me up the pictures later.'

But Michael wanted to see. Michael *needed* to see. He was sure that there was some connection between what had happened to Sissy O'Brien and what had happened at Rocky Woods. He was sure that if he could solve one case, he could exorcize the other. His whole sanity depended on it. His whole soul depended on it.

'It's okay,' he told Victor. 'Go ahead.'

Victor looked at Thomas, but all Thomas could do was say, 'Sure … if that's what he wants.'

Victor beckoned over two young medical examiners and spoke to them quickly under his breath. One of them, a black girl, kept shaking her head, but Victor laid his hand on her shoulder and said, 'This is as bad as it ever gets. If you can deal with this, you can deal with anything. Think about it.'

Michael felt perspiration sliding slowly down his back. He kept sniffing, as if he had a cold coming, but it was nerves. He was overwhelmed with dread. He felt as if the whole building were pressing down on him, while the darkness was rising up to engulf him. He watched Victor bend over Sissy O'Brien's remains, his scalpel glinting, and he couldn't turn away. It was too terrible to watch: but it would have been even more terrible not to watch.

Only Victor spoke as he began to cut open the coiled pink large intestine – lower and lower, fat peeling apart, skin peeling apart. He was tape-recording his impressions so that he could give Thomas an accurate preliminary report. Later, on his own, he would spend hours dissecting and analysing and preparing a complete catalogue of everything that had happened to Sissy O'Brien, and in what sequence, and which particular event or events had finally killed her.

'We can see that the rectum and the lower section of the large intestine has been grossly distended by the forcible intrusion of a foreign object – an object approximately two feet in length and four inches in diameter.'

Michael knew what it was, and from the bloodied lacerated bulges in Sissy O'Brien's intestines he could see what it was. But he still prayed that none of this had happened; and that nobody could have perpetrated such an act. He didn't realize that his face was as bloodless as ivory, like a martyred saint in some medieval chapel. He didn't realize that tears were streaming down his cheeks.

This should never have been. This cannot be. Oh God in heaven, please tell me that it never was.

'There are several perforations and intrusive lacerations of the lower bowel any one of which could have caused fatal peritonitis,' Victor was saying. Michael could hear his voice only from a long way away, as if he were talking through a tin megaphone in another room. He felt cold and distant, and he could feel the blood draining out of his head. He was aware that he was probably going to faint.

Victor held out his hand and the black girl slapped a scalpel into his palm. He bent over Sissy's body, and carefully sliced into the dark, bulging section of her rectum.

The whitish tissue parted, and Michael heard Thomas say, 'Jesus,' and that was all. He didn't faint. He didn't fall. But he couldn't move either. All he could do was to stare at the fierce dead eyes of the cat which had appeared between the sliced-open folds of flesh.

He found himself sitting on a hard chair. He wasn't sure how he had got there. Somebody was holding his hand, a woman. He was staring down at an empty paper cup. He heard Victor's voice, Thomas's voice. He heard the squeaking of wheels.

He was suddenly aware of the thick, pungent odour of death.

Victor was saying, ' – don't know what you're dealing with, lieutenant.'

'Insane,' Thomas kept repeating. 'Whoever did this is fucking insane.'

' – wrapped it up tightly in razor wire – wrapped it up tight like a baby – you know, like a goddamned round of beef – then *forced* it – Jesus – '

He was still standing by the window in Victor's office when Victor came back. It was almost nine o'clock. The sky over southern Boston was thick with smoke, turned dramatically purple by the setting sun, and fires burned all along the horizon like the fires of a besieging army of barbarians, the Huns or the Goths or the Visigoths.

He didn't turn around when Victor came in, but he heard Victor collapsing into his tilting captain's chair, and swivelling around, and opening up his desk drawer. He heard the chink of shotglasses and the liquid *galoop* of a whisky bottle.

'How about you?' Victor asked him. 'You want one?'

Michael shook his head.

'You want to talk to anybody?' Victor asked him.

'I, er – I'll be talking to my therapist later tonight.'

'You can phone him from here if you want to.'

'I did. He's out right now, making a housecall. Hypnotizing some woman in West Yarmouth who wants to get thin.'

Victor came across to the window and stood beside him, leaning against the frame, swilling the bourbon in his glass around and around.

'Looks like you Bostonians are destroying your own city pretty good, doesn't it?' he remarked.

'Don't ask me,' said Michael. 'After what I've seen today, I think that people are capable of absolutely anything. I mean, how can people – '

Victor waited for him to finish his sentence, but he didn't, so Victor finished it for him.

'How can people torture an innocent young girl to death, and then kill her in a way that you or me couldn't even dream up in our sickest nightmares?'

Michael looked at him, expressionless. Victor took off his glasses and smiled at him. 'There's one thing I learned in Newark,' said Victor. 'If somebody doesn't give a shit for human life, then he doesn't give a shit for human life. It doesn't affect him, *how* he kills people. Shoot, stab, strangle, what difference does it make? So long as they end up dead. It's only people like you and me who care *how* people died. Killers don't care. They're taking away somebody's very existence – what does it matter if they suffer?'

Michael said, 'You don't think it mattered to the people who killed Sissy O'Brien or Elaine Parker, how much they suffered?'

Victor sipped his whisky. 'I'm beginning to think that it did – but not in the way you mean it.'

'I don't understand.'

'Okay, then, let me put it this way. I'm beginning to think that these needle marks are critical to the whole case. We don't have any hard physical evidence that they were inflicted on Elaine Parker in order to penetrate her suprarenal glands. All of her internal organs were too badly decomposed. But Elaine Parker's external needle marks are identical to Sissy O'Brien's needle marks. They could even have been inflicted by the same needles. So – for the moment – I think that we can safely speculate that we've established some pretty strong connections between Elaine's death and Sissy's death. They were both sadistically tortured. Both of them went through hell, believe me – and Elaine went through hell for almost a year before they finally killed her. If you can stomach the post-mortem report, I'll send you a copy. There's a lot of razor wire involved, and a lot of lighted cigarettes, and cockroaches, and a live rat, too.'

'Oh God,' said Michael. He really didn't want to hear any more.

But Victor persisted. 'The question is, *why* were they tortured? They couldn't have been tortured for money, because nobody demanded a ransom for either of them, did they? They couldn't have been tortured for information. Neither Elaine nor Sissy could have known any earth-shattering secrets, could they – and Sissy couldn't have influenced her father's legal opinions. They weren't used for any kind of extortion, they weren't used to twist anybody's arm to do something they didn't want to do.'

'So why?' asked Michael.

Victor swallowed whisky. 'I always used to say that there were only three great motivating forces in human life – money, power and sex. But if this isn't about money, and it isn't about power, and it isn't about sex – what *is* it about?'

Michael stared at him, too numb to say anything sensible.

'It's about life itself,' said Victor, slapping his arm. 'Not *just* the money, not *just* the power, not *just* the sex, but life itself.'

'I don't get you.'

'I don't get me, either. I don't know what the hell's going down here. But the minute people start tampering with human bodies, you can bet your ass that somebody, somewhere, is looking for *life*. Look at the Third World – India, Africa – people are selling all kinds of body-parts, and people in the West are buying them. There's a market for kidneys, there's a market for livers, there's even a market for testes. Come to Dr Snipgood and have a ball. I mean, for Christ's sake! And when people in the West can't buy the organs that they want, they do the next best thing which is arrange for what we morticians call "a forcible donation". Find a match, kill him, and take what you want.'

'Are you serious?' asked Michael.

Victor nodded emphatically. 'Nobody in their right mind should ever register for organ or bone-marrow transplantation. There's always the risk that one day, somebody richer than you is going to want your liver, or maybe your lungs, or even your heart – and, man, if you just happen to match ...'

'But this is adrenaline we're talking about,' said Michael.

'That's right,' Victor agreed. 'Human adrenaline. And maybe cortisone, too. I don't know why anybody should want it so bad ... but I have every intention of finding out.'

'Did you tell Thomas about this?' Michael asked him.

Victor nodded.

'What did he say?' asked Michael.

'Not much. Thomas is what you might call a pragmatist. Apart from that, Thomas has a sensitive stomach and doesn't like to talk about physiological realities. Thomas doesn't mind hearing how bad things are, as long as you don't tell him that they're probably a damned sight worse.'

Michael couldn't stop remembering that cat's horrific eyes, staring at him out of Sissy O'Brien's remains. It was like something out of Edgar Allan Poe or George Fielding Eliot – *The Black Cat* and *The Copper Bowl*.

But now he looked at Victor in a very different light, and he was surprised, and disturbed; and in a strange way, he was pleased, too. The thin, prickly medical examiner from Newark, New Jersey, had suddenly shown a willingness to think obliquely, to use his imagination. Victor looked back at him darkly, intently, without any suggestion of a smile, but there was strong professional empathy between them, and some kind of personal understanding, too.

'I don't know,' said Victor. 'I can't be sure. But some kind of pattern is coming out of this – some kind of reason, some kind of motive. I'm just thinking aloud, really. But I've dealt for most of my professional life with death. My uncle was a mortician, and when I was nine I helped him to lay out my own father. How about that for an education? I know about death, Michael. To me, death is like an empty house, when everybody's moved out, and all the furniture has been toted away. I can walk around in it, it makes me feel regretful, but it doesn't scare me. But plenty of people never want to die, never, and I mean *never*, and what they'd do to stay alive ... well, just stick it up there in your brain in that pigeonhole marked "possible motives", okay?'

Michael looked at his watch. 'Are you busy tonight?' he asked Victor. 'I wouldn't mind talking this over some more.'

'I have some notes to write up.'

'And then?'

'Then nothing, I guess. A TV dinner and some sleep.'

'In that case,' said Michael, 'you're invited for supper. I live right over the Cantina Napolitana on Hanover Street. They serve a veal saltimbocca that will make you cry.'

Victor had a short think, and then he nodded. 'Okay, you're on. I could use a good weep.'

The shades were drawn down in Matthew Monyatta's living-room in the Mission Hill housing project, so that only a thin triangle of sunlight fell on the left-hand wall. The room was bare, except for large black beanbags and a low black Japanese table. In the middle of the table, three sticks of sandalwood incense smouldered in a copper bowl. Matthew Monyatta himself was reclining on the floor next to the table, dealing out the bones. His face was serious and sweaty. His CD system was playing 'Jah Africa', a hypnotic tip-tapping Afro-Caribbean rhythm, very quietly.

The bones had been read by witch-doctors long before the slave trade. Originally, they had always used human bones – people had been specially killed for the purpose of providing bones, and human bones still gave a better prophecy. The secret of the bones had been carried across the Atlantic on the slave ships, and in the Southern plantations the same predictions had been made with chicken bones, or pig bones, or better still, with the bones of miscarried babies.

Matthew had been taught by his grandfather how to read them; and he was reading them now. Bones that fell in a star-shape meant bad times to come. Bones that fell in a criss-cross pattern meant conflict. Two parallel bones meant white men. Three parallel bones, and bones that fell like a goat with horns, that meant more than white men. That meant white-white men. That meant sacrifice men. That meant horror and horror and horror; and the world turned upside down.

He had sensed the growing activity of the white-white men for more than ten years now. Each time he read the bones, there was always something to suggest their presence, no matter how insignificant. Maybe he was wrong: but he had begun to draw a parallel with the gradual erosion of Jamaica Plain and Roxbury and other areas of southern Boston. Roxbury had once been a solid middle-class Jewish community, with excellent shops and exemplary schools. Now it was riddled with crack and crime and drive-by shootings. The last supermarket had closed its doors, and the last bank had just closed down.

And however Matthew cast them, the bones said: the white-white men. The men who never closed their eyes. This was the world they wanted. This was Armageddon come to pass.

Matthew was gathering up the bones when he heard the

phone ringing in the kitchen. After a moment his daughter Yasmin came in, slender and graceful in her scarlet sari.

'Papa, it's for you. Patrice.'

She handed him the phone. Matthew said, 'Patrice? I thought I was whiter than fucking white.'

Patrice sounded strange and scared. 'Matthew ... you have to help me.'

'What are you talking about, Patrice? What kind of help could you want from me?'

'Listen, Matthew ... what I said earlier, I'm sorry, okay? I'm sorry I said it. I came home two o'clock and the door's locked and somebody's holding Verna hostage.'

'Are you serious? Who would want to hold Verna hostage?'

'I don't know, man. There's two of them, they're both white. I seen them looking out of the window.'

'Have you talked to them?'

'I asked them what they wanted, that's all.'

'So what did they say?'

'They said they wanted their money.'

'What money?'

'How the hell should I know? I don't have anybody's money.'

'Maybe you robbed somebody and forgot.'

'Listen, man, this isn't no joke! I never robbed nobody! There's two white dudes in my apartment and they've got hold of Verna and they're going to *hurt* her, man, that's what they said!'

Matthew glanced up at Yasmin and gestured that he wanted a Coke. Yasmin went to the kitchen, while Matthew said, 'What can I do? This is a crime thing, Patrice. This is nothing to do with black identity. You need help, you call for a cop.'

'How can I call for a cop? This is a goddamned war zone,

man. There are buildings burning and they won't even send in the fire department.'

Matthew knew what he was going to have to do. No matter how much Patrice Latomba irritated him, no matter how much Patrice Latomba undermined his credibility and his work on black self-sufficiency, Patrice Latomba was a brother in need, and Matthew was going to have to go.

'You going to drive me down to Roxbury?' he asked Yasmin. 'Reckon I can just about squeeze into that itty-bitty Volkswagen of yours.'

Yasmin said, 'You break my car, you die.'

Followed by Patrice and Bertrand and two other brothers, Matthew cautiously approached the doorway of Patrice's apartment. The building was thick with the stench of woodsmoke and burning rubber, and something else, too – the stink of burned potatoes.

Matthew hesitated for a moment, and then pressed the doorbell.

The answer was almost instantaneous, as if somebody inside had been waiting for them. 'Who's that?'

'Matthew Monyatta,' said Matthew. 'I'm a friend of Patrice. I came along to see what I could do. You know – to see if I could make things easier.'

A few moments' pause, and then: 'We want our money, that's all.'

'Ask him what money,' hissed Patrice.

'Patrice says what money,' Matthew repeated.

'The money that was taken, after his baby was shot.'

'What are you talking about?' Patrice screamed out, in fear and frustration. 'I never took anybody's money!'

'Oh, no ... we know that,' the voice replied. 'But one of your friends did, Patrice. One of your so-called brothers. Look around you, see who's missing. Ask some questions,

Patrice. Somebody picked up that money and it wasn't the cops and it wasn't our man so it must have been one of yours.'

'Can I talk to you face-to-face?' Matthew interrupted.

There was another pause. Then the voice said, 'Okay ... you want to come in? So long as it's you and nobody else.'

'That's my wife you've got in there!' shouted Patrice. 'If you just touch her – '

Matthew grasped Patrice's arm. 'Stay cool, okay? It's all for the best. Please.'

Patrice thumped his fist against the wall and cracked the plaster. He was close to tears. 'That's my wife they've got in there. First of all they kill our baby – now this.'

'I'll be doing my best for you, man,' Matthew reassured him, and gently knocked at the door.

The door was opened, but only by an inch.

'Everybody else stand well clear,' the voice demanded.

Bertrand had been edging closer to the door, but Patrice jerked his head to indicate that he should do what he was told, and keep away.

The door opened wider. Matthew turned around to Patrice and gave him a long, sympathetic look. Then he pushed the door wider still, and stepped inside the apartment.

The door swiftly closed behind him. He found himself in the living-room, confronted by a tall, thin, white-faced man in black sunglasses.

The white-faced man looked him up and down. 'Heavy reinforcements, huh?' he said, with a sloping smile.

'I don't think this a time for jokes, do you?' said Matthew. 'What have you done with Verna?'

'Not very much, as yet. But we will, if provoked.'

'I want to see her.'

'You want to see her? For sure! We've got her in the kitchen. Come on in. By the way, my name's Joseph, and this is my friend Bryan.'

Uneasily, Matthew followed the white-faced man into the kitchen. What he saw made him immediately turn away. Verna had been stripped naked, and hogtied face down on the formica-topped kitchen table, her feet raised up into the air.

Bryan was as white-faced as Joseph. He didn't look up when Matthew came in. He was concentrating on holding a lighted white candle over Verna's bare back. Every now and then, when it brimmed with molten wax, he tipped it carefully sideways, and the scalding white wax dropped and solidified on her dusky bare skin. She winced with every drop, and let out a soft, small cry. There were twenty or thirty drops on her back already, all across her shoulders and down her spine.

'What, are you *sick* or something?' Matthew breathed, his voice shaking with emotion.

' "He who steals my purse doesn't steal trash," ' Joseph misquoted. ' "He who steals my purse is going to suffer, and suffer, and suffer some more, till I get back my cash." '

'This woman's done nothing to you!'

'I don't think that's very relevant,' said Joseph. 'She's a victim, that's all, and we can't help that, can we, Bryan?'

'No,' said Bryan, dropping more wax onto Verna's back. 'We can't help that.'

'You realize that Patrice will kill you,' said Matthew.

Joseph circled around the table, gently trailing his fingertips across Verna's wax-measled back. 'I don't think so, Mr Monyatta. In fact, quite the reverse.'

'Let Verna go,' Matthew insisted. 'You have to ... she's totally innocent.'

'Oh, we won't hurt her very much, unless it's necessary,'

Joseph replied. 'But, you know, somebody picked up our bag when Jambo was arrested – and there was a whole lot of money in that bag, as well as cocaine and ammunition. That's all our property, and we want it back.'

'I don't think Patrice knows who took it,' said Matthew. 'Somebody just picked it up and ran off with it, as far as I can tell.'

Joseph took off his dark glasses, and Matthew froze at the sight of his eyes. They were blood-red, like the eyes of a demon, and they were filled with contempt and hatred that he couldn't help himself from shivering.

'I want that bag back and this lady will stay here with us, enjoying our attentions, until I do.' He smiled, and produced a double-edged razor blade between his index finger and his middle finger, like a conjuring trick. 'You don't think she's enjoying it? Let me show you.' And with that, he reached down between Verna's buttocks and spread them wide with the fingers of his left hand, exposing her dark wrinkled anus and her curly-haired vulva.

'You see this?' he said, dipping the tip of his fingers into the soft scarlet flesh of her vagina. 'She's wet, she's ready for sex. Terror always does that, it turns women on. If you want to excite a woman, Matthew, I mean *really* excite a woman, then frighten her to death. She'll be soaking, I promise, before you can say "Monyatta".'

He took the razor blade, and very carefully drew a noughts-and-crosses-grid on her left buttock. It scarcely drew blood; just a few fine beads, which congealed almost at once.

'Tell your friend that we want our money, Matthew. Otherwise, Verna's going to suffer very much more than she needs to.'

Matthew walked around the table. He was so shaken that he had to lean against the kitchen hutch. Verna's face was pressed against the red formica. Her eyes were blotched with tears, and her lips were swollen and bruised.

Matthew leaned over her, and said gently, 'Verna … can you hear me? My name's Matthew … Matthew Monyatta. Maybe you've heard Patrice mention my name.'

Verna didn't seem to register. Her eyes flickered up at him but they didn't focus.

'Verna … we're going to get you out of here, I promise.'

Bryan said, 'You'll get out of here, Verna, don't you worry about that. Cut up like hamburger, probably … but you'll get out.'

Matthew reared up, furious. But Bryan instantly lifted his left hand to him, with his index-finger and his little finger stiffly raised, and all of his other fingers folded down, the *cornu*, the goat-sign, and it was then that Matthew was quite convinced that he was right – and that what the bones had been warning him about was all true.

He felt an awful shuddering coldness in his stomach. The bones had been warning him, night after night, stronger and stronger, year after year. The white-white men. The men who never closed their eyes. In Ethiopia, and in Egypt, centuries ago, they had called them watchers, the sleepless angels.

Matthew had never been so frightened in his life. Hoarsely, he said, 'I know you.'

'You *know* us?' asked Joseph, replacing his sunglasses, and smiling.

'You're watchers, aren't you? Seirim.'

Joseph laughed. 'Sounds like you've been imagining things, Mr Monyatta. You've been dreaming dreams. We're honest tradesmen looking for our money, that's all.'

Matthew said, 'Tell me how much money. I'll see if I can find it for you.' Although it was warm and stuffy in Patrice's kitchen, Matthew was beginning to shake with cold.

'Four hundred and fifty.'

'Is that all?' Matthew asked, incredulous.

'Four hundred and fifty *thousand*.'

Matthew touched Verna gently on the head; a blessing; a hope; a saintly wish. 'God keep you,' he said. Then he turned to the white-white man and said, 'Give me some time, will you please? I can raise your money, if you give me time.'

'It's not *just* the money, Mr Monyatta,' chipped in Bryan.

'What else?' Matthew demanded.

'It's the rioting,' the man explained, whirling his hands around in the air. 'It's the looting, it's the shooting, it's the chaos.'

'You want it to stop?'

Joseph laughed, a harsh, cracking laugh. 'Stop? Are you crazy? We want it to carry on! We want it worse! We want windows smashed and cars torched and pigs shot down with no provocation!'

'I can't allow that,' said Matthew, trembling, ashy-cheeked.

'Why not? Tell me why not?'

'These are my people ... this is where they live. You're asking them to ruin their own community. Christ knows – Christ *knows* – it was bad enough before.'

Joseph said, coldly, 'Don't you invoke the name of Christ against *me*, Mr Monyatta. If there's one thing I hate more than a mediator, it's a saint, and if there's one thing I hate more than a saint, it's a mediator who thinks he's a saint.'

'I'm just a man,' said Matthew. 'You don't have anything to fear from me, except that.'

'We're not afraid of you, Mr Monyatta,' Joseph breathed. 'Maybe we're watchers, maybe we're not. But if I were you, I wouldn't take any chances. Mmh?'

He said, 'Here,' and held out his hand to Bryan, who passed him the lighted candle. Without taking his eyes off

Matthew, he twisted the butt of the candle into Verna's bottom, and left it there.

Matthew stared at the candle in horror, and then at Joseph.

'You don't have very long, Mr Monyatta,' Joseph told him. 'Maybe an hour, maybe an hour and a half. Then the pain is *really* going to begin. Oh … and don't think of trying to persuade the police to help you. One *sniff* of pig, one single *sniff*, and Mrs Latomba will be rocking her baby in heaven above. And I kid you not.'

Outside in the streets, Matthew heard a volley of gunfire, and the sound of windows breaking. He crossed himself, and said, 'God protect me. And God protect that innocent woman. And God damn you two to hell.'

Bryan said, in a voice loaded with infinite menace, 'I think it's time for you to leave now, Mr Monyatta. Joseph and me, we're not famous for our inexhaustible patience.'

Matthew took one last desperate look at Verna, with the candle-flame dipping and bobbing between her buttocks. Then he edged toward the kitchen door, and out through the living-room. He tugged open the front door and he was out in the hallway, sweating and shaking, before he knew it.

Patrice immediately snatched at his sleeve. 'So what's happening?' he wanted to know. 'They're letting her go, what?'

Matthew stared at him, his upper lip beaded with perspiration. 'I can't do nothing for you, man. You brought this on yourselves. You let them in, man. You let them in. You don't have nobody to blame but you.'

He blundered his way along the landing, and started to tromp down the stairs. Patrice hesitated, shocked, and then ran after him.

'What about Verna?' he screamed, over the banisters.

'God keep her safe, that's all I can tell you.'

'But what am I supposed to do?'

Matthew stopped halfway down the stairs. 'They're going to hurt her, Patrice. They're going to hurt her in ways you never even thought of.'

'That's it! That's it!' Patrice screamed. He dragged out his .45 automatic and cocked it. 'I'm going to blow their goddamned brains out! Bertrand! I'm going to blow their goddamned brains out!'

'They'll kill her before you get through the door,' said Matthew. 'Believe me, Patrice, you don't know what you're up against.'

'Then what the hell do they want?' Patrice shrieked down at him.

'They told you before. They want their money.'

'I don't have their money, for Christ's sake!'

'Then you'd better find out who does; or else you'd better whip up four hundred and fifty g's, and whip it up now.'

'Say *what*! Where am I going to get that kind of money?'

'That's what they want, Patrice.'

'So what are you doing?' Patrice demanded. 'Are you walking out on me, or what? You're just leaving me here, to deal with these cockroaches all on my own?'

'Patrice – I want Verna safe and free as much as you do. But there's nothing more I can do, not here, not unless you find that money.'

'What about the man? Couldn't you talk to the man? Listen – we'll stop the rioting, stop the whole thing.'

'They say if you bring in the man, they'll kill her just like that.'

'So what are you going to do? You're just going to walk out?'

'There's only one thing I can do, and that's to find out who and what we're up against here. Then I'll come back.'

With that, he continued down the stairs.

'Matthew!' Patrice howled at him. 'Matthew, you can't leave me! I need you, man!'

Matthew gripped the banister rail and roared up at him, 'They're here! The white-white men! They're here! Because of you! You gave them everything they wanted! You gave them everything they needed! And now you're asking me to save you?'

With that, Matthew hurried heavily downstairs, and was out of the door before Patrice could answer him.

Patrice turned to Bertrand and said, 'The white-white men? What the hell are the white-white men?'

Bertrand shrugged. 'I never heard of no white-white men.'

Patrice went up to his apartment door, and beat on it furiously with his fists. 'You bastards! You lay one finger on my wife, I'm going to ice you bastards!'

There was no reply. Patrice turned to Bertrand and said, 'Who took that money, man? Where the hell's that money?'

Bertrand scratched, shrugged. 'Guess we'd better ask around.'

Patrice smashed his fist onto the banister rail. 'Whoever took that money, I'll kill them! I'll kill them!'

And then Verna started to cry out, 'Patrice! Patrice! Patrice!'

Just before dawn, Michael saw the cat crawling out of Sissy O'Brien's insides, yellow-eyed, skinny with human mucus, and snarling, and he woke up screaming.

Victor, who had been dozing on the couch in the living-room, ran into the bedroom to find Michael wedged in between the bed and the wall, pummelling wildly at the wallpaper.

'Michael!' he shouted at him. 'Michael! For Christ's sake, Michael!'

He caught hold of Michael's elbow and tried to lift him up, but Michael was struggling too fiercely.

'Michael!' he repeated. 'Michael, listen to me!'

At last, Michael stopped thumping the wall, and turned, and stared up at him. His pupils were pinpricks and his face was frighteningly white.

'Michael, it's Victor. Are you okay?'

Slowly, painfully, Michael eased himself up. 'I'm okay,' he said, after a while. 'I just had an experience, that's all.'

'An experience? What kind of experience?'

Michael tried to give him a wry smile. 'If you had it, you'd call it a nightmare.' He tapped his forehead. 'Because of my particular psychological condition ... I virtually *experience* it. It's called post-traumatic re-enactment, something like that.'

'Do you want some coffee?'

Michael nodded. 'I'm sorry about this. I guess I shouldn't have come down to the morgue yesterday. Triggered something off.'

'No problem, forget it. Why don't you talk to your shrink?'

'That's probably a good idea. But I'll have to see him in person. I have hypnotherapy; and hypnotherapy doesn't seem to work on the phone.'

Victor looked at his watch. 'Listen – why don't I drive down there? I could use some time off. Where did you say he was? Hyannis?'

Detective Ralph Brossard was nodding in front of *Genghis Khan* when the telephone rang. At first he thought it was a dream, and expected somebody else to answer it. But it went on and on, and at last he opened his eyes and realized where he was and what was happening.

He cleared aside the half-empty boxes of chow mein and chili beef that cluttered the small table next to his La-Z-Boy armchair, and picked up the telephone. 'I'm not here,' he said, thickly.

'Ralph? Ralph, this is Newt.'

'I just told you, Newt. I'm not here.'

'Ralph, something weird's come up.'

Ralph looked around his boxy, brown-wallpapered apartment for cigarettes, but couldn't see any. Through the curtainless window, he could see the endless flow of early-morning traffic on the John Fitzgerald Expressway, and the gradually greying dawn over Boston Harbor, and in the window itself he could see his own ghostly reflection – even more like Ernest Hemingway now that two days' suspension from duty had allowed him to grow some stubble.

'I've, er, I've had a contact from Patrice Latomba,' said Newt.

'Latomba? Are you kidding me? Hold on a minute, Newt, I've got to find myself some smokes.'

In spite of Newt's diminutive protests, Ralph dropped the receiver and collided around the living-room, picking up books and magazines and dropping them down again. At last he found a half-crushed pack of Winston in the narrow green-varnished kitchen, and he bent over the gas ring, eyes narrowed, to light himself one.

He picked up the phone again, blowing smoke. 'Okay, Newt, I'm with you. What's this all about?'

'Patrice Latomba says his wife Verna is being held hostage by two white guys, right in his own apartment.'

'Shit! Are they *crazy*?'

'It doesn't seem like it. They've been there since yesterday morning.'

'Does he know who they are?'

'He doesn't have any idea. But he thinks that *you* may.'

'How should I know who they are? I spend my life in a little box marked "Narcotics"; I don't have anything to do with Black Muslims or African Uprising or whatever it is that Latomba's into.'

'These two white guys are saying they want their money back.'

'Money? What goddamned money?'

'Listen, Ralph – the money that was lost when we ambushed Jambo. It seems like somebody picked up the bag during the ambush, and now these people want it back.'

'So that's what happened to it,' said Ralph, with smoke seething out from between his teeth. 'Then why doesn't he give it to them? Who gives a shit, once that money's been out of our sight, it's no longer admissible anyway. I mean, the department's down four hundred and fifty big ones, but say-la-vee.'

'No way, Ralph. Apparently the brother who picked it up decided it was too much to share with his other brothers, and is now somewhere where his other brothers can't immediately find him. Like, who knows, Bermuda maybe; or Las Vegas.'

'So, tell Latomba to call the cops.'

'Come on, Ralph, Latomba's apartment is right in the middle of the battle zone. Latomba's people are shooting at cops on behalf of Latomba's dead baby, and cops are shooting back. Officially, we couldn't mount a hostage operation on Seaver Street without an unacceptable risk to officers and civilians. Unofficially, they wouldn't give squat what happens to Mrs Latomba or to anyone else called Latomba.'

'So what am I supposed to do about it?'

'You're supposed to give Patrice Latomba an expert helping hand in getting Mrs Latomba away from the hostage-takers, alive and well. I don't know *how* well. Patrice says there's been some screaming.'

'Patrice wants *me* to help him? Who the hell is he trying to kid? I shot his baby.'

'Exactamundo. That's why he reckons you owe him one.'

Ralph watched Genghis Khan's hordes galloping wildly

across the Universal backlot, swords flashing.

'Newt,' he said, 'there is absolutely no way. If you ask me, this whole story is nothing more than a goddamned clumsy stupid trick to get me down to Seaver Street, so that Latomba can ice me. Tell him to send me a bomb in the post, it'll save me driving down there.'

'He says if you can save his wife, he'll stop the riots and won't take out any complaints against you for what happened to little Toussaint.'

'And what if I can't save his wife? What if the hostage-takers blow her away? What's he going to do then? Shake me by the hand and buy me a soul-food dinner?'

There was a lengthy, hollow silence. At last, Newt said, 'I believe him, Ralph, as a matter of fact.'

'You believe him? Good! But you're not the one who has to put his mouth in the lion's den, or whatever.'

'Ralph – those guys have threatened to torture and kill Latomba's wife unless they get their money.'

Ralph smacked his forehead with the heel of his hand. 'What does he expect me to do? I can't do any more than he can do, not without a SWAT squad. Tell him to kick the door down and go in with guns blazing. He might save his wife, he might not.'

'You can negotiate with them, that's what Latomba said. You can offer them some kind of deal.'

'What deal? I'm on suspension, in case you'd forgotten. I can't even offer them a sandwich.'

'Okay, Ralph … no need to get sore. I was just passing on the message.'

'Yeah … thanks, Newt. I'm sorry. I guess I'm feeling sorry for myself, more than anything else.'

'It's my day off tomorrow,' said Newt. 'Why don't you and me go to the Sunset and see how many different beers we can get through?'

Ralph looked across at the photograph of Hemingway propped over the fireplace. No wonder the poor bastard had blown his brains out. In a world of fake and fear and cowardice, sometimes it seemed like the only course that a real man could take.

Nine

They drove southward down the Pilgrims' Highway in the blurry, sunlit morning, with 1970s rock'n'roll on the radio, 'Staying Alive' and 'The Air That I Breathe' and 'Reasons To Be Cheerful'.

Victor said, 'I should take a vacation. I haven't taken a vacation in years. Every day, another dead body. You know what I mean?'

'It must be pretty depressing,' said Michael.

'Oh, no way, it's not depressing. It's just boring. You know what I mean? You've seen one pancreas, you've seen them all.'

They drove into New Seabury just before eleven, and Michael turned into his own yard and blasted the horn. Patsy immediately opened the kitchen door and came running down the wooden stairs, dressed in tight jeans and a pink checkered shirt, her hair pinned back. Michael held her tight and she felt just as warm and sexy as she'd ever felt, and she smelled of Lauren, just like she'd always smelled.

'This is Victor Unpronounceable,' he said at last, turning around.

'Kurylowicz,' said Victor, holding out his hand.

Patsy shook his hand and smiled at him. 'It's good to meet you. Michael told me all about you, on the phone.'

'Not the truth, I hope.'

'He said you were a friend.'

They climbed the steps to the kitchen, and then walked through to the living-room, with its two worn-out sofas and its jumble-sale chairs; its stunning blue-and-white view of the ocean. 'You want coffee?' Patsy asked Michael. Her eyes were bright because she was so pleased to see him.

'That'd be great,' said Michael.

After Patsy had gone through to the kitchen, Victor said, 'Look at this place. It's beautiful. God knows why you want to work in the city.'

'Lack of income,' said Michael. 'Otherwise, wild horses couldn't drag me away.'

'How're you feeling?' asked Victor.

'Unbalanced, if you want to know the truth.'

'You're going to see that shrink of yours?'

'Sure, this afternoon.'

'That hypnotism … that really helps?'

'For sure. It's like living out your worst nightmares. You live them, you walk around in them, you get to know them, you learn to deal with them … the same way that you learned to deal with death.'

Victor smiled, and looked out toward the sea. 'You know what my old man said to me, before he died? He said, "For Christ's sake, don't let Uncle Kazyk put lipstick on me. I don't want to be buried looking like your Aunt Krysta." We laughed so much we practically cried; then we cried anyway. Well, he had cancer.'

'What made you move here from Newark?'

'Nothing, in particular. This job was on offer, so I came.'

'You're not married?'

He shook his head. 'When you've seen what's inside of people, it's difficult to have any kind of physical relationship with them. It makes you kind of distance yourself, if you know what I mean.'

Patsy came back with the coffee. She poured it out, and then she sat close to Michael and kissed his cheek. 'I called you this morning,' she said, 'but you'd already left.'

'Oh, yes?'

'I was a little worried. There were two guys hanging around on the opposite side of the street. They looked as if they were watching the house. I thought of calling the police, but I looked out about ten minutes later and they were gone.'

'What did they look like?' asked Michael.

'I don't know … strange. One of them was dressed all in black and the other one was dressed in grey. They both wore sunglasses so you couldn't really tell what their faces looked like. All I could really see was that their faces were terribly pale. You know, almost albino.'

Michael shrugged. 'Ah well, we get all kinds around here. A whole limousine-load of mobsters came down once, and sat on the beach in their vicuna overcoats and their Gucci shoes and smoked cigars. Then they all drove away again.'

'These two didn't look like burglars or anything,' said Patsy. 'But they worried me, I'm not sure why.'

'Well, call the cops if you ever see them again.'

'There was something else. Late last night somebody phoned three times, a man. I told him he had the wrong number, but he kept calling back.'

'Did he say what number he wanted?'

Patsy said, 'No, he didn't.'

'Did he sound like anybody you know?'

'Unh-hunh.'

'He didn't say anything obscene?'

'No, not at all. But he was so insistent. he kept on asking for Mr Hillary.'

Michael stared at her. A chilly prickling feeling crept down his back. 'Mr Hillary? Are you sure?'

'That's what he said. "I want to speak to Mr Hillary." '

Michael frowned. *Mr Hillary.* That was the name the blind man had mentioned, when he was walking across Copley Place. It was too much of a coincidence for *two* references to have been made to 'Mr Hillary' accidentally, in such a short space of time, and so gratuitously, too.

'Anything wrong?' asked Victor, sipping coffee.

'I don't know ... I've heard that name before, that's all.'

'Weird,' Victor remarked.

Victor and Patsy went shopping in Hyannis while Michael went to visit Dr Rice. It was a sparkling, sunny afternoon, with a brisk wind blowing, and the clouds racing across the sky like frisky sheep. Dr Rice kept him waiting for over twenty minutes, and when he opened the door of his office, a middle-aged woman with a scarlet face and an orange linen suit came hurrying out, her eyes red and her mascara blotchy.

'Sorry to have kept you, Michael,' said Dr Rice. He was looking unusually casual today, in a yellow short-sleeved shirt and checkered blue golfing trousers and white loafers with tassels. 'Excuse the attire. I'm playing at Chatham this afternoon. Psychiatrists vs. dentists. We should lick them hollow.'

Michael sat down in the chrome-and-canvas chair. The arm had been straightened since his last therapy. Dr Rice went to the window and adjusted the blinds so that the office was plunged into brownish gloom.

'How have you been, then, Michael?' he asked, perching one buttock on the edge of his desk. 'You sounded somewhat panicky on the phone.'

'I've been ... unsteady, to tell you the truth,' Michael confessed.

'Unsteady?'

'It's this job, no question about it. I keep having action replays of Rocky Woods. And other things, too. Really strange incidents in the street: incidents I can't understand.'

'Are we talking about nightmares?'

'No, no. They're definitely daymares. Or anytime-mares. I keep experiencing these sudden feelings that I'm falling out of that airplane – that I'm just about to die.'

'Well,' said Dr Rice soberly, 'I know you need this job, but maybe you should think of quitting. Just like I said before – your sanity is worth a whole lot more than any amount of money. No good being a millionaire if you're too screwed-up to enjoy it.'

'I don't want to quit. I *can't* quit. There are too many questions, too many puzzles … if I don't find out what happened to John O'Brien and his family, I think I'll be more screwed-up than I ever was before.'

'Do you really think that finding out what happened to John O'Brien is of any great significance? He's dead, nothing can bring him back. It may matter to Plymouth Insurance how he died; but what does it really matter to you? I mean, psychologically?'

'It matters a lot,' said Michael. 'I guess you've seen on the news that O'Brien's daughter was washed up dead at Nahant Bay?'

'Of course,' said Dr Rice, warily. He reached over and switched on his tape-recorder.

'I went to Nahant Bay myself, and saw the body. But more than that, I saw Nahant Bay … and Nahant Bay is the same bay that I saw, the last time you took me under.'

Dr Rice looked surprised. 'You're sure about that?'

'Absolutely. Same beach, same lighthouse, everything.'

'And had you ever been to Nahant Bay before?'

'Never.'

232

'You've never seen it in a guidebook, or a magazine?'

Michael emphatically shook his head.

'Well … that's remarkable,' Dr Rice admitted. 'I've heard of patients having flashes of insight under hypnosis … but I've never heard of a patient seeing into the future.'

'I want you to take me down again,' said Michael.

Dr Rice stood up, and walked around his desk. The muted sunlight shone from his bony, freshly-shaved cheeks, but his eyes remained circles of impenetrable darkness.

'Are you sure about this?'

'I'm sure … why do you ask? You never asked me before.'

'The reason is, I'm worried about you. Normally, patients use their experiences under hypnotherapy to come to terms with their psychological traumas. In your case, it seems as if you're doing the reverse … as if you're creating more psychological traumas while you're under hypnosis, and bringing them back to disturb your everyday life.'

'I saw Nahant Bay. I saw the lighthouse, I saw the beach. I saw these green saltbox houses. They were *there*, for Christ's sake. They were really there. I have to know how I managed to see them, before I went there; and why.'

Dr Rice lowered his head. 'You must understand that hypnotherapy can only reveal things that are already dormant inside of your brain. It can't tell you something that you don't already know.'

'Please,' said Michael. 'I'm right on the edge as it is. I'm clinging by my fingernails. I'm seeing things that I shouldn't be seeing. I'm having all kinds of peculiar experiences. In Boston, I had this feeling I was being followed; and then this old blind man started talking to me; and then my cab driver started spouting the Bible.'

'Sounds like normal Boston to me,' said Dr Rice, with a small, arch smile.

'I need to go under,' Michael insisted.

Dr Rice, at last, said, 'All right. But the tape-recorder is running, and I want it on record that I hypnotized you at your own request, and at your own risk, and that you totally absolve me of any responsibility.'

Michael hesitated. He had never heard Dr Rice talking like this before. 'You're scared,' he said.

'I'm just concerned. Hypnosis isn't a party trick. You could be severely traumatized.'

'I'm already having waking visions of falling out of airplanes. I mean, waking visions, right in the middle of the day, like the floor's opening up, right beneath my feet. I see bodies. I see pieces of bodies. I *see* them, for Christ's sake! What could be worse than that?'

'All right,' agreed Dr Rice. 'If you think going under can really help. But let me tell you again: you won't experience anything under hypnosis that you don't already know. And maybe you'd better think about what it is that you already know.'

'Hunh?' Michael asked him, turning his head around as Dr Rice circled behind him.

'I like you,' said Dr Rice. 'I can't say any more than that.'

'Please …' said Michael. 'Take me under, okay?'

Dr Rice dragged over a chair and sat down next to him. Michael could smell the Binaca on his breath. 'Are you comfortable?' he asked, and Michael nodded.

Dr Rice said, 'Lay your left hand on top of your left knee, palm upwards, and lay your right hand on top of your left hand, also palm upwards.

'Relax …' he said. 'You're anxious, you're frightened, you don't know what to do … but you've come to find help, and I'll give you help. Rotate your head around, let those muscles go. Relax.'

Michael relaxed – really relaxed. He let his soul flow out

of his feet, until he was nothing more than a marionette, slumped in the armchair, stringless, empty, completely suggestible, ready for anything.

Dr Rice took out his hypnotizing disc of zinc and copper, and pressed it into Michael's open palm.

'Fix your eyes on the middle of the disc, on the copper spot. Keep your eyes fixed on it and don't look away.'

Michael stared down at the copper spot, and saw it dancing in front of his eyes. *This time,* he thought, *he'll never get me under. This time he's going to fail.*

'You feel like sleeping,' said Dr Rice. 'Do not fight the temptation to sleep … allow sleep to cover you, as soon as it wants to. When I tell you to close your eyes, close them.'

Dr Rice passed his hands in front of Michael's face, over and over. 'You feel sleepy,' he said. 'Your eyes are so heavy that you can scarcely open them. You don't have any feeling in your arms or legs. Your body is numb. Your eyes are closing, you are going to sleep.'

He touched Michael's eyelids, and then he murmured: 'You find it impossible to keep your eyes open. You are going to sleep, sleep, sleep. You cannot open your eyes: they are stuck completely fast. You are sleeping now. You are asleep.'

Michael didn't want to fall asleep. Not so easily, anyway. This time, he wanted to show Dr Rice that he could resist him. But even while he was thinking *no, not this time, no*, he was sliding into unreality, sliding into that warm, dark welcoming ocean of unconsciousness, and he couldn't open his eyes, no matter how much he tried. He simply couldn't. And didn't really want to, because the ocean was deep and the ocean was so relaxing, he could swim deeper and deeper, and sleep as he swam.

He saw that bright, pinkish flare that he always saw before Dr Rice put him completely under, and this time it seemed brighter than ever. Then, he was enveloped in darkness.

He knew that he was standing on the beach. He still didn't want to open his eyes, but he knew that he was standing on the beach. He could hear the surf tirelessly dragging itself all along the shoreline, and he could feel the salt wind blowing in his face, and he could hear the seagulls screaming. He heard Jason saying, ' – *bicycle* – ' and then he opened his eyes.

A tall man was standing close by, watching him. The man had bone-white hair, long and silky and swept back, although some of it was flying in the onshore wind. He had a long, sculptured face with a straight, narrow nose and distinctive cheekbones and dark, commanding eyes. He was frighteningly handsome, the kind of man whose presence makes husbands take a protective hold on their wives' arms.

He wore a long, expensive overcoat of light grey softly-woven wool, which billowed and rumbled in the wind. He was meticulously peeling a lime, and letting the fragments of peel drop onto the sand.

'You've come to join us, then, Michael,' the man said, smiling, although his voice didn't seem to be synchronized with his lips, like a badly dubbed foreign-language movie.

Michael was flooded with fear, from his head to his feet, but the man laid his arm around his shoulders and said, 'Come along ... you shouldn't be frightened ... you're among friends now ... friends and relations.'

'I don't understand,' said Michael. He looked around at the seashore, at the wind-whipped dunes, at the small crouched saltbox houses, at the gulls silently circling. In the middle distance he could see something greyish and pale lying on the beach, something that could have been a washed-up mail sack or a slimy collection of flotsam or something worse. Some of the seagulls were stalking proprietorially around it, snatching at it with their beaks.

The man gently guided Michael away. His coat kept on

236

curling around Michael's legs, making it difficult for Michael to walk. He said, 'You're very privileged, you know. Not many of you still have any memory of what you are …'

They climbed the dunes, their legs sinking into the soft sand. Michael couldn't help turning around one more time, to stare at the shape that was lying on the beach. It couldn't be Sissy O'Brien, could it? He didn't like the way the seagulls were tearing at it, and the way in which one seagull lifted off into the air with a huge chunk of something wet and shredded dangling in its beak.

'Come on, now,' the man urged him. 'We don't have much time.'

Michael said, 'Where are we going?'

The man said nothing, but took hold of his elbow with a strong, clawlike hand, and pushed him on. They mounted the top of the dunes together, with the wind whipping at their backs, and then they began to descend a wide sandy slope toward the white lighthouse that Michael had seen in his last hypnotic trance.

'I'm dreaming,' said Michael. 'Tell me I'm dreaming.'

The man turned to him, and his face was angular and white, like a chalk quarry, and his eyes were as red as liquid rubies. 'No, Michael, you're not dreaming. This is real … this is the here-and-now. If you were dreaming, then I would have to be dreaming, too, and you and I would be sharing this dream.'

'I'm not really here, though,' Michael insisted.

'Of course you're here! Can't you feel the wind? Can't you hear the sea?'

'I'm in a trance. I'm sitting in Dr Rice's office in Hyannis. He's hypnotized me.'

'You're *here*, Michael. Why try to pretend?'

Michael stumbled in the sand as the man dragged him nearer and nearer to the whitewashed lighthouse. The wind whistled and sizzled in the grass. The lighthouse was so white that even on a dullish morning like this he could scarcely look at it, because of the glare.

'Will you quit pulling me!' he shouted at the man, and snatched his sleeve away. 'I don't want to go here anyway!'

The man stopped and stared at him, his legs planted far apart, his back straight, his hands resting on his hips. He looked biblically stern.

'You must,' he commanded.

Michael shook his head. 'I'm not going anywhere. This is a dream.'

The man leaned over him. 'I never sleep. Because I never sleep, I never dream. This is no dream. This is reality. You are *here*, Michael, out on the shore; and you are coming along with me.'

He seized Michael's arm and dragged him forward. Michael was partly aware that it was Dr Rice who was dragging him forward. He was partly aware that he was still in Dr Rice's office. Yet the sea breeze was strong and salty; and he could feel the sand sliding under his feet, and the man's coat wrapping itself around his legs, and he thought to himself: *How can this be? how can this possibly be? Where am I, for God's sake? Am I hypnotized or dreaming or am I dead?*

The man pulled him yard by yard to the base of the lighthouse. Close up, Michael could see that it was constructed out of brightly whitewashed concrete, although it was much more stained and weathered than it had appeared from a distance.

'Come inside,' the man ordered him, and pulled him around to a low, heavy door of brown-stained oak. He turned the iron handle, and swung the door back. Then he grabbed Michael's arm again, and jostled him inside.

Michael looked around him. He was standing in a large, gloomy, damp-smelling chamber, with a high ceiling and thickly-rendered walls. All around him, in a semi-circle, stood sixty or seventy young, white-faced men, dressed in blacks and greys and thunderstorm greens. They stared at him without surprise. They stared at him with chilly curiosity. He turned from one to the other, and all he could see was expressions of cruelty and hostility; as if they were almost too dismissive of him to pinion his arms and skin him alive.

'This is a dream,' he insisted, turning from one arrogant white face to another. 'This must be a dream.'

'No dream,' the man insisted. 'You want me to prove it to you?'

'It's a dream,' said Michael. 'I'm in Hyannis, not in Nahant Bay. I'm sitting in Dr Rice's office in a hypnotherapic trance. Can you hear me, Dr Rice? I want you to get me out of this! I want you to get me out of this now!'

He didn't know whether he was speaking coherently or not. Perhaps his waking self was talking gibberish – in which case, Dr Rice would probably let him continue. But he needed to be out of this trance. He couldn't stand the wind; and he couldn't stand the coldness on these young men's faces; and he couldn't stand the idea of the mail-bag bundle on the seashore suddenly rising to its feet, and coming after him, because he was sure it was Sissy O'Brien, with her grey face and her weed-flecked hair and the terrible cat that was hidden so deeply inside her, ferocious and vengeful, and ready to tear out his eyes.

'You frighten me,' he told the white-faced man. 'You frighten me, and I have to leave now.'

The white-faced man laid a restraining hand on Michael's arm. 'Everything's fine now, Michael. Everything's fine. All you have to do is go right back to your family, and forget about us. You wouldn't want anything *bad* to happen, would you?'

'No,' said Michael, nervously.

The white-faced man came toward him and stared into his eyes. Michael had never seen blood-red eyes like this before, and he backed away.

'What are we frightened of?' the man asked him, teasingly. 'We're not frightened of blood-red eyes, are we? Did you never see the eyes of a man who hasn't slept in three thousand years? Did you never see the eyes of a man who has stayed awake night after night, month after month, year after year, while Caesar rose and Caesar fell, and the pyramids were built, and Vikings rowed across the ocean, and Pilgrims landed at Plymouth Rock?'

'I'm dreaming,' said Michael. He closed his eyes, and repeated, 'I'm dreaming.'

When he opened them again, the white-faced man was still leaning over him; and all the other men were still clustered around, staring at him, as if they would rather see him dead.

The white-faced man prodded him forcefully in the chest, so that he could feel it. 'Do you know who I am?' he asked. Michael shook his head.

'You've been looking for me, you've been searching for me, although you don't know it yet.'

'What do you mean?' Michael shivered. 'If I don't even know who you are, or *what* you are, how could I possibly have been searching for you?'

'They call me Mr Hillary,' the white-faced man told him. 'And you have been looking for me without even knowing it. But now – '

He paused, and stood up straight, and slowly walked around the room, with his long grey coat billowing out behind him like a trail of smoke. 'Now you know who I am, now you have *sensed* who I am ... and I am here to warn you to leave me undiscovered; to forget that you saw me, to forget that I spoke.'

He said, almost regretfully, 'The world has never been easy, Michael. Neither easy nor virtuous. You can't get rid of your sins by praying to God. You can't get rid of your sins by wrapping all of them up into one person's soul, and then sacrificing that one person to the Lord your terrible God. You can't get rid of your sins by confession or absolution or saying you're sorry.

'A sin is a sin is a sin, whether you enjoy it or not. It's there to stay, and you have to live with it. And even if you manage to absolve yourself somehow, that absolution can only be temporary ... do you understand me? ... because no matter how much you try to hide your sins or forget your sins or pretend that you never committed them, they will always, always, *always* find you out.'

He pointed to his eyes. 'Do you know why? Because we've got them. *We've* got them, and even if you've forgotten them, we remember them. We never sleep, we never forget. For us, there is no "feeling better in the morning". For us, there is no saying "well ... it was just like a dream". For us, there is nothing but pain and punishment, until we give you your wickedness back, and return you to all that chaos and cruelty in which you lived before Aaron atoned for your sins. You haven't paid, Michael. You haven't paid! But the day is soon coming when you shall!'

Michael backed away, but 'Mr Hillary' came after him, his eyes blazing red.

'This is a trance,' Michael reminded himself. 'I'm sitting in Dr Rice's office in Hyannis and this is all a trance.'

'Mr Hillary' came closer and closer, until Michael could feel the coldness of his breath. Behind him, all the white-faced youths began to rustle and stir, like albino bats dislodging themselves from the walls of a long-undiscovered cave.

'You haven't paid, Michael. None of you have. But the day is soon coming, when you shall!'

He lifted his left hand and stroked Michael's cheek with infinite softness. Then he leaned forward with his lips slightly parted and it was suddenly obvious that he was going to kiss him on the mouth.

Michael pushed against him, and swung his fists, and shouted out loud. 'Get off me! Get off me! You goddamned pervert, get off me!'

He struck his right knuckle against the metal-banded side of Dr Rice's desk, and opened his eyes, and realized at once that he was right. It *had* been a trance. It *had* been a dream. He hadn't visited Nahant Bay. He hadn't walked up the dunes, and into the lighthouse. He hadn't seen those clustering boys with their deathly-white faces.

He had been here, in this chrome-and-canvas chair, in this gloomy brown office, all the time. There was Dr Rice's framed certificate from Vienna, and there was Charles Sheeler's painting of an ocean liner – deserted, silent, meticulous.

A deserted scenario waiting for something to happen.

Dr Rice was standing with his back to the window. He looked unhappy.

'Are you all right?' he asked Michael.

'I don't know,' Michael told him. 'I had the same experience as last time ... the man on the beach. Only this time it went much further.' He described his trance in short, jerky sentences, trying not to leave anything out.

When he had finished, Dr Rice said, 'Something's disturbing you badly.'

'I don't even begin to understand it,' Michael told him. 'I never even heard of "Mr Hillary" before.'

'You're creating this whole thing in your subconscious imagination,' said Dr Rice. 'It's like a metaphor for what you're doing in real life. The human mind doesn't like the idea of meaningless accidents, like the O'Brien disaster –

especially *your* mind, which has been trained to look for answers and explanations. This "Mr Hillary" is just like one of those imaginary friends which kids have when they're little ... except that "Mr Hillary" is your imaginary enemy. He's somebody that you can blame for John O'Brien's death.'

'Like a scapegoat,' said Michael.

Dr Rice looked up with unexpected suddenness, and stared at Michael as if he had touched a nerve. Then he pursed his lips, and nodded. 'Yes. That's right. Like a scapegoat.'

He shuffled and tidied his papers. Michael watched him, and then said, 'What do you think?'

'I don't know, it's up to you. But in my opinion, the only way you're going to get better is by resting, and by staying away from anything that involves violent and accidental death. You just don't have the mental strength for it, Michael. You don't have to be ashamed; very few people do.'

Michael stood up. For some reason, he felt that he couldn't completely rely on Dr Rice to tell him the truth about 'Mr Hillary', although he didn't know why. He had always trusted him before. It was just that, this time, Dr Rice seemed to be trying extra hard to persuade him not to give up his job at Plymouth Insurance. Dr Rice had never actually tried to persuade him not to do anything before – even manifestly dumb things, like sailing round the world, or mushing to the North Pole.

'I'm going back to Boston tomorrow morning,' said Michael. 'Maybe I can call by and talk to you one more time before I go.'

Dr Rice nodded. 'Very well ... make it a quarter to ten. Not later, I have one of my lady slimmers every Thursday morning, and she doesn't like her cellulite to be kept waiting.'

243

Michael left Dr Rice's office and walked out into the windy sunlight. He caught sight of Patsy and Victor across the street, looking into the window of the Raven Bookstore. He called out to them, but a heavy truck was passing and it drowned him out. As he was just about to step off the kerb, he saw a white-faced man in dark glasses standing in a hardware-store doorway, only a block-and-a-half away. It looked very much as if he were watching Patsy and Victor – although as soon as Michael crossed the street to join them, he left the doorway and began to walk quickly north-ward.

Michael took hold of Patsy's arm. 'You see that guy there? The one just disappearing up the street?'

'What about him?'

'He wasn't one of the men who was watching the house?'

Patsy shaded her eyes with her hand. 'I'm not sure ... I can't see his face. He had the same kind of clothes ... but no, I couldn't be certain.'

'You want me to go after him?' said Victor. 'I used to play for my high school football team.'

Michael shook his head. The man had already vanished around the next corner, and Michael had the strangest feeling that even if they ran after him, they wouldn't be able to find him.

They walked back to Michael's car. Victor said, 'How was your hypnotherapy?'

'I'm not sure yet. Kind of confusing. It doesn't always leave you feeling better.'

'If it doesn't leave you feeling better, then what's the point of it?'

'It's supposed to help you to explore your subcon-scious.'

'I'm not too sure I'd want to do that,' said Victor. 'I've got a subconscious full of demons.'

'Don't we all. But today was kind of weird. I'm going back tomorrow morning, just to see if I can make some sense of it.'

'I've never been hypnotized,' said Victor. 'I don't think I could be.'

'Oh, you'd be amazed,' Michael told him. 'Sometimes I go into Dr Rice's office quite determined that he's not going to put me under, but he still does it.'

He unlocked the car and they all climbed in, Victor in the back. Victor leaned over and said, 'I saw a hypnosis show on stage, once. They had people standing on one leg, taking their trousers off, all kinds of stuff. And that was after they were supposed to have woken up, and left the stage.'

'That's what they call post-hypnotic suggestion,' said Michael, backing the Mercury into the street. 'I never believed it could work, but it does ... provided the suggestion is simple and clear.'

'What if the suggestion is something destructive?'

Michael was about to answer when a bus blew a devastatingly loud horn-blast at him. By the time the bus had manoeuvred around the back of them, and Michael had finished yelling at the bus driver out of the window, they had forgotten the thread of their discussion.

All the same, as they drove back towards New Seabury, Victor began to look thoughtful.

Patsy turned around in her seat and said, 'Penny for them?'

'I don't know. Something just occurred to me, that's all.'

'Something good? Something bad?'

'Something that begins to make sense out of something that doesn't make sense.'

Ralph Brossard was noisily frying some bacon for himself when the phone rang.

'I'm not here,' he announced, wedging the receiver under his chin. 'You want to leave a message, leave it after the doot. *Dooott.*'

'Are you Detective Ralph Brossard?'

'That's right, who wants to know?'

'Detective Brossard, you know who I am, you killed my son.'

Very, *very* long silence.

'Did you hear me, Detective Brossard?'

'I heard you. Detective Newton called me last night, told me what you wanted.'

'They've had her for nearly twenty hours now, Detective Brossard. I've managed to buy some time by telling them I know where the money is. But they've been hurting her, man. They've really been hurting her, and I don't know what to do.'

Ralph turned his bacon rashers over with his fork. 'Mr Latomba, you're going to have to deal with this situation yourself, or else you're going to have to call 911. I'm on suspension pending internal investigation, which is normal procedure after a fatal shooting. I couldn't do anything, even if I wanted to.'

Patrice sucked in his breath. 'Detective Brossard, I hate you, I hate your guts, but then I hate all white people equally, and just because you shot my baby son, that doesn't make me hate you any more than I would have done already. It just wouldn't be possible.'

'Nice to know you're such a fair-minded kind of guy,' Ralph replied. 'But that doesn't change anything, does it?'

'What I'm saying is, man, that whether you help me or not is down to your conscience. You shot my son, you killed my little Toussaint, and because of that you owe me, man. You *owe* me.'

Ralph turned off the gas. 'Mr Latomba, your son's death

was tragic. If there was any way I could go back in time and make sure it didn't happen, I would. It was tragic, it was terrible, and I feel totally bad about it, but it was an accident. Jambo fired at me and I fired back. Your son's baby-carriage just happened to get in the way.'

'Man, you *owe* me!' Patrice shouted at him, close to tears.

'I'm sorry, Mr Latomba, but I don't owe you anything except respect as a human being.'

'My wife, too?' Patrice's voice was shaking.

'Your wife, too,' said Ralph, dully.

'All right then. Listen to this. It's a tape-recording, made on my own hi-fi equipment, which the hostage-takers pushed out of my apartment just an hour ago.'

'Mr Latomba, I don't really think – '

'*Listen*!' Patrice demanded, with such fury that Ralph was silent, and listened.

He heard some rattling noises, as Patrice switched on his tape-recorder. Then he heard some echoing, distorted conversation, as if two people were talking in a bathroom, or a kitchen. Somebody laughed, a man's laugh. Then a voice came breathily close to the microphone and said, 'We know you're doing your best to find our money, Patrice, but we just thought you might respond to a little foretaste of what might happen if you don't.'

Another voice, more echoing, said, 'Some fancy knife-work to start with.'

There was a momentary pause, followed by the sound of a woman screaming. She screamed and screamed and didn't stop. The hair prickled on the back of Ralph's neck, and after a few seconds he put down the receiver and covered the earpiece with his hand. He had heard women screaming in pain before, and he knew this was real. Not only was it real, it was the most agonized screaming that he had ever heard – and he had heard women who had been doused in gasoline by their jealous husbands, and set fire to. He waited until he was sure it was over, and then he lifted the phone again and said, 'Mr Latomba?'

A clicking noise, as Patrice turned off the record-player. 'Mr Latomba?'

'I'm here. Did you hear that, man? They were cutting her, man. They were *cutting* her.'

'Do you have any idea where that money is?' Ralph asked him, his voice very serious.

'I got seven guys out looking. But one of them thinks that a brother called Freddie picked it up, and nobody's seen hide nor hair of Freddie ever since.'

'Freddie probably opened that bag and thought it was Christmas, come early.'

'What am I going to do, man? You heard what they're doing to Verna. They're going to give her so much pain. They're going to kill her.'

Ralph reached across the kitchen for a cigarette. 'Tell me something about your apartment,' he said.

'What do you mean?'

'Is it first floor, second floor, what?'

'Second floor.'

'Does it have a service door as well as a front door?'

'Unh-hunh. Front door's the only way in.'

'How about balcony?'

'Kind of a narrow balcony, out in front.'

'How about the apartment immediately above it? Does that have a balcony, too?'

'That's right. They all got balconies.'

'And how can you get out onto that balcony? French doors, something like that?'

'That's right. Hey – why are you asking me all these questions about my balcony, man? What the hell does my balcony have to do with anything?'

248

Ralph lit his cigarette by the gas ring, almost singeing his eyebrows off. 'Does your balcony have french doors or what?' he repeated.

'Yes, it does.'

'Do they open outward or inward?'

'I don't know, man,' Patrice protested. 'Outward, inward, what difference does it make?'

Ralph said, 'I'm going to ask you one more question. Do you give me your word that if I try to rescue your wife for you, but I fail, you'll guarantee that I get safe passage out of Seaver Street?'

He could hear Patrice swallowing in emotion. 'You mean you'll do it?'

'Give me your word, Mr Latomba. And all of those gooks and pinheads you call your security force – make sure that they know you've given your word, too.'

'You got my solemn oath, man.'

Ralph checked his wristwatch. 'Give me twenty minutes, okay? I'll be driving a tan Volkswagen.'

He put down the phone. *I must be out of my mind*, he thought. But at the same time, he felt a ferocious kind of pleasure surging through his veins. This was going to be dangerous, and dramatic, and best of all, unauthorized. This was real Hemingway stuff. This was real man's stuff. This was what he had joined the police force for, but rarely found. He had always craved action, but what had they given him? Paperwork and more paperwork, relieved only by hours of mind-numbing surveillance, or even more mind-numbing hours in court, waiting to give evidence.

He opened the drawer of his night-table and lifted out a nickel-plated .44. Then he went to the bureau, unlocked it, and took out two boxes of shells. He went back into the kitchen, and there was his bacon, lying in the frying-pan.

He picked up a rasher in his fingers and crammed it into his mouth, followed by a second rasher.

With his mouth full, sucking his fingers to get off the bacon-fat, he left his apartment and sallied forth to be a hero.

Ten

To Michael's surprise, Joe Garboden's metallic blue Cadillac was parked outside the house when they returned home from Hyannis. At first, there was no sign of Joe, but when Michael unlocked the front door and walked across to the window, he saw him standing on the beach, two or three hundred feet away, his coat slung over his shoulder, staring at the ocean.

Victor came up the steps with the shopping, and laid it on the kitchen table. 'Who's that?' he wanted to know.

'My immediate boss,' said Michael. 'I wonder what the hell he wants.'

He went back down to the yard and across the sand. Joe heard him coming, because he turned around and raised an arm in greeting.

'Hi, Michael. Terrific day. How was your therapy?'

'I don't know. Strange. Revealing, in a way – but definitely strange.'

Joe didn't really seem to be interested. 'I thought I'd better come down here in person,' he said.

'Oh, yes? Beginning to get a taste for the seashore, are you?'

Joe looked around. The surf glittered white, the houses sparkled in the sunshine. Michael looked around, too, and saw Victor watching them from the living-room window, with a can of beer in his hand. When he saw that Michael was looking his way, he lifted it up in a silent toast.

Joe said: 'We've just received the results of Dr Moorpath's post-mortem examinations. I've brought an advance copy down with me, it's in the car. The press get it at four o'clock this afternoon, in time for the evening news.'

'Well, progress at last,' said Michael.

'I'm not so sure.'

'What do you mean, you're not so sure? There was only one conclusion that Moorpath could have come to.'

'Oh, yes?'

'Joe – those people were murdered. You saw the pictures, for Christ's sake. John O'Brien was beheaded, his wife was gutted, Dean McAllister had his goddamned legs cut off. Maybe the pilot died accidentally, but I wouldn't have thought so. His head was beaten into bolognese. It was homicide. It was assassination. What else could it have been? I mean, it sure as hell wasn't *suicide*, was it?'

Joe shook his head. 'You're way off beam, I'm afraid. Dr Moorpath in his infinite wisdom has concluded that all of the occupants of the helicopter suffered fatal injuries as a result of the crash. Their bodies were burned in the subsequent fire but not so badly that Dr Moorpath wasn't completely satisfied that "their varied and catastrophic injuries" were all caused by accident.'

Michael stared at him in disbelief. 'John O'Brien was *beheaded*! His wife had her bowels dragged out onto her lap!'

'John O'Brien was decapitated by a sheared bulkhead. Mrs O'Brien was eviscerated by a broken-off seat support.'

'But I showed you the pictures! There was no sheared bulkhead anywhere near John O'Brien's body! There was no broken seat support!'

Joe stared out to sea. Michael suddenly thought how

much older he looked, how much more round-shouldered. He could remember times when he and Joe had been really hot – when they had solved case after case together, arson, automobile wrecks, yacht-scuttlings, you name it. In 1989 the two of them had saved Plymouth Insurance more than $78.5 million in fraudulent claims. The Golden Boys, the quickest, the most intuitive, the very-best paid. But now he was scared of falling through the sidewalk and Joe was all worn-down, like an old sofa that three generations of kids have been jumping on.

He laid his hand on Joe's shoulder; but he felt the muscle stiffen, and he took it away again.

'What do the police have to say?'

'Commissioner Hudson will issue a statement later this evening to the effect that he has read Dr Moorpath's post-mortem report and accepts it.'

'And the FAA?'

'Jorge da Silva examined the turbines and the gear mechanisms with a boroscope. The direct cause of the crash was a gear failure. Worn gears, which led to a sharp decrease in backlash, and dramatic overheating.'

Michael felt as if he were drunk, or mad. 'You mean the entire crash was completely accidental?'

'Jorge da Silva is willing to let us examine the entire wreck. His exact words were, "You can go over it with Japanese chopsticks, if you want to." '

'Joe – if that crash was completely accidental, how come that pick-up was waiting for it on Sagamore Head? What about the statement that Neal Masky made to Artur Rolbein?'

Joe gave a dismissive shrug of his shoulders. 'The pick-up was coincidental. The pick-up was there by chance. That's if Masky didn't invent it.'

'Why the hell should he have invented it?'

'Maybe he was rowing ashore to loot the helicopter himself.'

Michael raised his hands to the sky, in supplication for something that sounded like sense.

'*Maybe he was rowing ashore to loot the helicopter himself?* Can I believe what I'm hearing? Joe, the emergency services were homing in from every direction. He had to row across three hundred feet of open bay in a stiff south-westerly wind in a dinghy the size of my bathtub. The chances of his reaching the helicopter before the police or the fire department were absolutely minimal. And he was thinking of *looting?*'

'It was one of the alternative theories that was put forward.'

'By whom? Who put it forward?'

'Mr Bedford suggested it, as a matter of fact.'

Michael stared at him. 'Mr Bedford suggested it? Mr *Edgar* Bedford, our lord and master?'

Joe nodded. He seemed embarrassed, and he wouldn't catch Michael's eye. 'It was a fresh way of looking at it, that's all. You know yourself that when you're dealing with a complex investigation, you can get too close. Can't see the wood for the trees.'

Michael felt a sharp snap of fury. 'Woods? Trees? What the hell are you talking about, Joe? Edgar Bedford is supposed to be the – what's-it's-damn-name? the guy in charge, the custodian of Plymouth's assets. That's the whole goddamned reason he employs you and that's the whole goddamned reason *you* employed *me*. Our whole case depends on establishing that John O'Brien was killed deliberately. Yet here's our own president, blithely putting forward a theory that undermines the integrity of our best and practically our only witness.'

Joe didn't answer at first. He took out a crumpled white

handkerchief, folded and refolded it, and then blew his nose. 'There's not a lot more I can say,' he admitted. 'Why don't we walk on back to the house … I can show you Dr Moorpath's report, and the faxes I got from Jorge da Silva at the FAA?'

'Joe …' Michael insisted. 'What's going down here? What's wrong?'

They started to walk. A seagull hovered very close to them, and kept pace with them, and even when Joe flapped his hand at it, it refused to fly away.

Joe said, 'Somebody's applying some very heavy pressure.'

'What do you mean?'

'Exactly that. Somebody wants the O'Brien case closed and filed away. Somebody with the kind of influence that you and I can only dream about.'

'Like, who?'

Joe made a face. 'I don't have any idea and I don't think it pays to think about it too deeply. Use your brains, Michael. If Edgar Bedford is suddenly showing willing to cough up several hundreds of millions of dollars, without even a fight in court, then somebody is squeezing him with the kind of force that could turn a man's gonads into pâté-de-foie.'

They circled around the house and began to climb the wooden steps.

'Is this political?' asked Michael.

'I don't know,' said Joe. 'I didn't ask. There are times in a man's career when he decides that it's wiser to look the other way.'

He paused, and looked down at Michael with a very sad and serious face. 'I'm not saying it's honorable. I'm not saying it's professional. But it's wiser.'

'What about Sissy O'Brien?' Michael asked him. 'Where does she fit into this "complete accident" scenario? How is Edgar Bedford going to explain away what happened to her?'

'Sissy O'Brien's case is still being investigated.'

'I know it is. By me – and by Lieutenant Thomas Boyle of the Boston Police Department – and by Mr Victor Kurylowicz from the coroner's office. As a matter of fact, Mr Kurylowicz is down here with me today.'

Victor appeared at the top of the steps, holding up his can of Bud. '*Nasdravye*,' he said, and bowed his head.

'Victor, this is Joe Garboden, of Plymouth Insurance. Joe's brought down an advance copy of Dr Moorpath's post-mortem on the O'Brien crash.'

Joe and Victor shook hands. Joe was looking uneasy, and checked his watch. 'Listen, Michael – maybe this isn't the time.'

'Come on, Joe, Victor performed the post-mortem on Sissy O'Brien. I saw her myself, although I wish to God that I hadn't. Everything the TV and the papers said was true. She was sexually assaulted and tortured, and she was sexually assaulted and tortured when she was still alive.'

Victor nodded, and took off his spectacles, and said, 'This is true.'

Michael went on, 'If she was tortured, then she must have survived the helicopter crash. You can commit sexual assault on a dead person, but there's no point in torturing them, is there?'

'That would be the logical conclusion,' Joe agreed.

'The logical conclusion? This is Michael talking to you, Joe. Michael, your old buddy Michael. *Of course* she survived the helicopter crash. And this is where Raymond Moorpath's post-mortem starts to look distinctly ramshackle. Although they didn't find her body in the wreck, Sissy O'Brien would have been sitting right next to Dean McAllister – so it was pretty goddamned peculiar that *his* legs were cut off by a piece of sheared bulkhead that cut across both seats whereas *hers* weren't.

'The appearance of Sissy O'Brien's body also makes a total nonsense out of Edgar Bedford's theory that Neal Masky was trying to loot the helicopter, and that there was no pick-up truck.'

Very softly, his voice almost inaudible in the ocean wind, Victor told Joe, 'She survived the wreck, but she was unable to leave her seat. The only way she could have got out of the helicopter was if somebody had prised her free and carried her.'

'What?' Joe demanded.

'This is true, too,' Victor told him. 'Her feet and ankles had been crushed beneath the seat. I can only presume that somebody used a lever of some kind of prise her free, and then carried her away. She wouldn't have been able to walk or even to crawl.'

Joe was looking very upset. His face was almost beige. 'Michael ...' he said, 'I don't really want any difficulty here. Whatever happened to Sissy O'Brien ... I'm sure that Commissioner Hudson can sort that out.'

'There's nothing to sort out,' said Michael, and he had never sounded so cold before. He startled even himself. 'All you have to do is go back to Edgar Bedford and tell him that we dispute Raymond Moorpath's post-mortem, and that we dispute Jorge's technical investigation, and that we're intent on saving him more money in the next ten days than anybody saved him in ten years.'

Joe said, 'I think Edgar's already considered that option, and turned it down. Reluctantly, I might add. I mean, *real* reluctantly.'

'All right. Tell him we'll go the media.'

'Aw, come on, Michael,' Joe protested. 'Have you seen the media so far? It's all Tragic Accident Kills Youngest

Supreme Court Justice. That's all they want to know. So Sissy O'Brien was washed up on Nahant seashore. So what? She could have floated out of the wreck: she could have jumped out before it hit the ground. Who knows? She's dead now. She's not going to say anything: she can't. And nobody else can find out.'

'How do you account for her torture?' Victor asked him.

'Who knows?' said Joe. 'Anybody could have picked her out of the bay. Maybe she wasn't really tortured at all. She'd been in the sea for quite a long time, hadn't she? You know what predators can do. Sharks, crabs, they're none of them fussy what they lunch on.'

There was a long silence between them. Eventually Joe couldn't take the silence any longer and lifted up his hands in exasperation and said, '*What?*'

Michael was trying hard to control his temper. 'What you don't know, Joe, is that Sissy O'Brien was tortured with cigarettes, with weird iron instruments, with knives, with fish hooks, with all kinds of things you don't even want to think about. The ultimate torture was a stray tom-cat, bound up tight in razor wire, and inserted by force in the same damn place that you and Edgar Bedford are talking out of.'

Joe's lips were white. He clung onto the wooden banister rail to steady himself. 'Jesus,' he whispered. 'I'm sorry.'

'So what's this all about, Joe?' Michael wanted to know. 'All these excuses, all these phony post-mortems and all these hoked-up accident reports?'

'I don't honestly think we need to know,' Joe told him. 'The word from the top is that the O'Brien investigation has been satisfactorily closed, accidental death, and that Plymouth Insurance is going to pay out. That's all I came here to say.'

Michael took hold of his arm. 'Joe?' he said, suddenly worried.

'It's okay, it's fine. It's all under control. Listen – why don't you come to the car, and I'll give you Dr Moorpath's report. Then we can call it a day.'

'Joe – '

Joe twisted around, quite violently, and Michael heard the underarm seam of his coat ripping. His face was sweaty and contorted, more like a puppet's than a man's.

'For Christ's sake, Michael, I know it's a crock. You don't have to make it more difficult for me than it already is.'

'Then why?'

'Because survival sometimes comes before glory, that's all.'

'What about truth?'

'Truth? Hah! That's a good one. You and me, we work in insurance, don't we? In insurance, there's a pretty un-affordable premium on truth.'

Michael realized that there was very little more he could say. He had never seen Joe like this before – humourless, worried, *shifty*.

'Okay …' he said. 'If that's the way it is.'

Joe walked across to his car. Michael hesitated for a moment and then followed him. Joe opened the door, reached across to the passenger seat, and picked up a green cardboard file marked O'BRIEN.

'Use your head, Michael,' he said. 'This thing is way too big for the likes of you and me. If somebody didn't hesitate to total an influential and well-connected guy like John O'Brien, do you think they're going to bat an eyelid about doing the same to us?'

'You're trying to tell me this is all a set-up?'

'I'm not saying nothing. I'm trying to tell you to use your head, is all.'

He was just about to hand over the post-mortem report when something caught his eye, across the street. Michael

258

looked up, too. A black Camaro was parked on the wrong side of the road, next to the Anstruthers' front yard. Its bodywork was streaked with dust and its windshield was smudged with fly-spots. All the same, Michael could see that two young men were sitting in it, their eyes concealed behind dark glasses.

'You know those guys?' he asked Joe.

Joe said, 'Unh-hunh, just checking. You can't be too careful, if you know what I mean.' He reached inside his coat and unclipped his pencil. 'Here – this is my mobile number, if ever you need me.'

He opened the back of the post-mortem folder and quickly scribbled. Then he handed the folder to Michael, slammed the door of his car, and started up his engine.

'You'll be back in the office tomorrow?' he asked.

Michael nodded. 'Round lunchtime, if that's okay. I just have one more session with the shrink.'

Joe waved, and then pulled away from the house, and along the street towards South Mashpee. Michael stood in his front yard watching him disappear around the corner. Almost immediately, the dusty black Camaro started up its engine, a deep, aggressive burble, and set off in the same direction.

Something wrong here, thought Michael. He turned back to the house and Victor was still standing at the top of the steps, watching him.

'Trouble,' said Michael, as he reached the landing.

'Is that the post-mortem?' Victor asked him.

Michael gave it to him, and Victor flicked through it. 'This is bullshit,' he said, running his finger down the report on John O'Brien. ' "*Mr O'Brien was decapitated by the horizontal guillotine action of the sheared aluminum bulkhead immediately behind his seat.*" Oh, come on, Dr Moorpath, who are you trying to kid? I'll tell you something, Michael, those faxes you showed me were pretty indistinct, but you could clearly see that the bulkhead was still intact. And even if his head *had* been cut off when he was sitting upright, his collar and coat would have been drenched in blood. As it was, he was bent forward in his seat *before* he was decapitated, must have been, because all of the blood spurted out in front of him, onto the floor. His collar was spotless, his shoulders were spotless. Somebody executed him, for God's sake.'

'The trouble is,' said Michael, 'the powers that be don't want us to say that somebody executed him. The powers that be want us to accept that this was all an accident.'

'What about Sissy O'Brien?'

'Oh, don't you worry about Sissy. They'll find a way to explain that, too. Hauled from the sea by a fishing-boat, accidentally snagged her lips on a row of fish hooks, accidentally fell over and burned her eyelids in an ashtray, then accidentally sat on a cat. I can see it all now.'

Victor quickly leafed through the rest of the post-mortem report in disgust. But when he reached the back cover, he suddenly stopped, and frowned.

'Did Joe write this?' he asked.

'It's his mobile phone number, in case I need him in a hurry.'

'I don't think so. Here.'

Victor raised the folder, and Michael peered at the hastily-pencilled lettering. It wasn't a telephone number at all. It simply said, *Mushing December '91*.

Michael frowned at it. *Mushing December '91*? Why on earth had Joe written that? And why on earth had he been so insistent that he used it only in an emergency?

'Don't you have any idea at all?' asked Victor. 'I mean, you're the great mushing expert.'

'It's a magazine, that's all.'

'Do you have a copy?'

'I don't know. I may do.'

'Why don't we take a look?'

They went back up to Michael's study. When he had first moved in here, Michael had put up two long bookshelves across the back wall, and these were now crammed with books and scientific journals and coffee mugs that he should have taken back to the kitchen.

'You look up on the top shelf, I'll take the lower shelf,' Michael suggested.

Even with both of them looking, it took over ten minutes before Victor suddenly tugged out a copy of *Mushing* magazine and triumphantly held it up. 'December '91 ... special feature on disciplining your dog team.'

He handed the magazine to Michael and as he did so, a large manila envelope dropped out onto the floor. Michael picked it up and turned it over. It was sealed, and there was nothing written on it except the pencilled word *Parrot*.

'Joe must have hidden this here,' said Michael. 'I wonder what the hell it is?'

'There's an easy way of finding out.'

Michael carefully tore open the envelope. Inside, he discovered more than a dozen photostats of black-and-white photographs, most of them blown up to the very limits of clarity. Most of them showed a group of people, men and women, standing in front of a fence, some of them out in the sunlight, others shaded by trees.

Michael passed one to Victor and Victor examined it closely, but all he could do was shake his head. 'This doesn't mean anything to me.'

'Me neither.'

'No – look, wait a minute. There's something written on the back of this one.'

Victor read the long, faintly-pencilled inscription and

then he gave it to Michael without a word. Michael read it, too, and then stared at Victor and said, 'Holy shit.'

'Do you think these are genuine?' asked Victor.

'Joe seems to think they are, and Joe won't even believe that it's daytime unless you give him a notarized affidavit.'

'So what are you going to do?'

'I don't know. Change my name, go into hiding, and make out I never saw them.'

Joe had kept his eye on the dusty black Camaro in his rear-view mirror ever since leaving New Seabury. He knew who they were. The same white-faced young men who had walked into his office this morning and handed him the post-mortem folder, with clear instructions that the John O'Brien insurance inquiry was closed, as of now.

He had started to argue with them, but one of the white-faced young men had asked him in the silkiest of tones how much he enjoyed his wife the way she was. Unmarked, undefiled, untouched by skewer or pliers or blow-torch.

Shaken, he had called 'upstairs' and asked to speak to Mr Bedford.

Mr Bedford was in a day-long conference, but Mr Bedford had left instructions that the young men from Hillary Underwriters had his complete approval.

'They threatened me,' Joe had protested, to Mr Bedford's personal assistant.

Mr Bedford's personal assistant had replied, 'Tongue-in-cheek, Joe. Tongue-in-cheek.' But the tone of his voice had told the whole story. *Keep your mouth shut, Joe, and do what you're told.*

He switched on the car radio. A band called the Red House Painters were singing a mournful, West Coast kind of song that made misery sound almost attractive. He checked his rear-view mirror and the white-faced young men in the black Camaro were still there, clinging to his tail with sinister doggedness – not so close that they wanted to overtake him, not so far that they had any intention of letting him go.

He had originally planned to take 130 to join Highway 6 at Sandwich, and then whack straight back north to Boston. Instead, he turned due west on 151, a winding state highway that would take him south of Johns Pond, through Hatchville, eventually to turn north again on 28. Now he would see if they were really following him or not – and, if they were, how well they could drive.

He took the first long curve into 151, between a blurred, multi-coloured kaleidoscope of oaks and maples and larches, and as soon as the black Riviera was out of sight, he slammed his foot on the gas so that his Cadillac surged forward through 50 – 60 – 70 – 80.

With a late-model company automobile, however, he didn't stand a chance. The Riviera appeared almost instantly in his mirror, and it may have been dusty and beaten-up, but it was powered by a turbocharged 5-litre engine and it was fitted with T-type stiffened suspension and wide-oval tyres. It came after him with all the power and predatory hunger of a mountain lion, and the next time he glanced into his mirror it was right *there*, less than half a car's length behind his rear bumper, and the white-faced young men were smiling at him, mocking him, and daring him to try driving faster.

Joe dragged out his handkerchief and wiped the sweat from his face. 'All right, you bastards, you want to make a race out of it?' he breathed. He slammed his foot down again, and the Cadillac picked up speed. But not enough. It wasn't a muscle car: it didn't have the guts. The next thing he knew, the black Riviera was knocking and nudging at his

263

rear bumper, only lightly, but enough to taunt him, and to send his steering askew.

Joe swerved from one side of the highway to the other, praying that nobody was coming the other way. The Riviera nudged him again and again, and his tyres screamed like frightened children.

He tried to slow down, but the Riviera kept on knocking him and knocking him, and in the end he slammed his foot back down on the gas, and tried to outrun them. He'd been driving for thirty years, for Christ's sake. Okay, his reactions were slower – okay, his cold-blooded nerve had deserted him. But he was skilled, and he was experienced. And there was no young punk in the world who could out-drive Joe Garboden – never, not ever, never.

Locked together, the two cars whinnied around the curves that carried them south of Johns Pond. The Riviera kept on nudging and taunting, and again and again Joe felt his steering turn to watery slop.

I'm experienced, I can handle it. But he knew that he was terrified. He knew that he couldn't cope. He looked in his rear-view mirror and he saw the two young men laughing at him, really laughing. Their eyes black, their faces white.

Laughing at him.

The police call it 'red mist' – that over-stimulated sense of rage and fear and unreality when a driver ceases to act like a reasonable human being, and loses all control. Fired by anger, fired by adrenaline, fired by a burning sense of competition, he will do anything and risk anything. His job, his life, and the lives of everybody else around him.

Joe was overtaken by "red mist". And stood on his brakes.

The Cadillac slewed, skidded and circled. The Riviera clipped the Cadillac's rear end, took off its nearside brake lights and trim and half of its bumper, and snaked off, howling, up the grassy embankment, and into the maples.

It struck a stand of trees, and rolled over. There was a moment's solemn silence, and then it blew up, fifteen gallons of gasoline rolling and blazing into the sky.

Joe's car skidded around and around and finally came to a halt beside the highway. The Riviera was already fiercely ablaze. Smoke obliterated Joe's windscreen: fragments of blazing vinyl floated past, black, like dancing bats: then sparks. Joe managed to unbuckle himself and climb out. The Riviera was softly roaring, like a gas ring.

Joe managed to walk fifteen or twenty feet towards the wreck. But without warning his knees turned to bags of transparent jelly, and he had to turn back, and lean over the hood of his car for support. His stomach gurgled. The stench of gasoline and burning plastic filled the afternoon air. A flock of sparrows suddenly burst from the hedgerow across the highway, startling him.

'Jesus,' he said to himself. 'Jesus.' He felt shocked and relieved, both at the same time.

He leaned over the Cadillac's polished hood and saw his own distorted, distraught reflection. He closed his eyes, breathing deeply. He had killed them, right?, those two white-faced men in their dark, dark glasses. He felt sick but he couldn't feel guilty. They would have killed him, for sure. They would have hurt his wife. He had seen people like this before – not just once, but many times. He hadn't noticed them until he had first noticed them – but once he had, he began to realize that they were everywhere – at every social function that really mattered, at every important business conference, at every political get-together. He had seen them come and go from Plymouth Insurance in their black-windowed limousines. He had seen them at parties in Milton and Duxbury and Canton, white-faced, reticent, evasive. Nobody ever spoke about them but nobody ever argued with them, either. They were accepted in Boston society in the same way that people accept dry rot in an antique house. You don't like it but once it's taken a grip, there's nothing very much that you can do about it, except cut out the house's heart.

Joe was humorous and vulgar and good at his job. He drank too much but he always took a roll of mints with him. One of the reasons he drank too much was because he had seen something happening in the world around him which he didn't understand. He had seen white-faced young men, anonymous, unannounced, in the company of Boston's wealthiest and most influential men and women. He had seen Edgar Bedford opening doors for them, and shaking their hands, and smiling. He had seen them at the mayor's inauguration ceremony.

He had seen two of them leaving the FAA offices on the morning of John O'Brien's fatal helicopter crash, and he had seen others at police headquarters, and one talking with indecipherable earnestness to the mayor. What proof was that? No proof at all. But Joe had decided to keep his butt well covered, and that was why he had chosen Kevin Murray and Artur Rolbein to investigate the crash. Kevin and Artur were intelligent, persistent and unemotional, not to mention independently-minded. Both of them were healthily sceptical of Edgar Bedford and the whole of the Boston political establishment.

That was why he had been so disconcerted when Edgar Bedford had abruptly directed that he ought to have Michael back on the job.

He knew that Michael hadn't yet been able to come to terms with Rocky Woods. In his last quarterly report to Plymouth Insurance, Dr Rice had said that Michael wasn't even halfway to getting over it – and another investigation that brought him face-to-face with human mutilation could easily make him feel even more angry and even more guilty, and totally alienate him from useful social functioning. How could you smile and say 'good morning' to people when you knew what people looked like when they were ripped apart? One more job like Rocky Woods could send Michael right over the edge, next stop the Casa del Coconut.

He had argued for over an hour, but Edgar Bedford had insisted. 'The fellow needs another chance ... it's like being involved in an automobile wreck ... the sooner you get back behind the wheel and start driving again, the better.'

Edgar Bedford had paused, dryly rubbing the palms of his hands together. Then he had added, 'You'll make it seem like your idea, won't you? You won't say that I wanted him. If you tell him that I wanted him – well, he probably wouldn't come, would he? You know how cussed he can be.'

Joe had been left with no choice but to drive down to New Seabury and persuade Michael to take the case. For sure, Michael was a skilled and intuitive investigator with 100 per cent integrity. He was eccentrically brilliant, too – an investigator capable of understanding that woods weren't made up of nothing but trees, but of the spaces in between the trees, too. Good insurance investigators saw what wasn't there, as well as what was.

But Joe had needed somebody who didn't suffer from nightmares – somebody who didn't think that they were being hounded by dead, dismembered accident victims.

Joe had needed somebody who wasn't afraid of those white-faced men.

He took a deep breath, and opened his eyes. Then he felt as if somebody were slowly pouring ice-water down the back of his shirt. His reflection on the Cadillac's hood was flanked by two other reflections – two curved, distorted

267

images of white-faced men, their eyes blacked out, their clothes smoking.

He turned around. They were standing only six or seven feet away from him, their hair singed, their coats charred, their faces as white as death. Their eyes were blood-red.

Joe was so frightened that he had to clench his muscles to prevent himself from opening his bowels.

'Thought you'd seen the last of us, did you?' called one of the white-faced men. 'Thought you'd seen us roast?'

Joe edged away, reaching behind him to feel the security of his car. 'Come on, pal,' he reasoned. 'That was an accident. You were bumping me, right?'

The white-faced man wagged his index finger from side to side. 'That was no accident, my friend. That was deliberate. That could have been manslaughter, under other circumstances.'

'Accident,' Joe repeated, his voice wobbling.

'We don't think so,' his friend smiled, and smoke came out of his mouth.

Joe stayed where he was for just a moment, his back pressed against the Cadillac, wide-eyed, sweating, tense. He prayed that another car would come by, and frighten these two charred zombies away. He prayed that a helicopter would pass, and notice the burning wreck of their Riviera, and call for the highway patrol.

He prayed most of all that they wouldn't hurt him.

One of the white-faced men reached inside his coat and drew out two long metal tubes, each as thin as a ballpen refill. 'Do we frighten you, sir?' he asked, in a matter-of-fact voice.

'Do we make you feel like you're going to *die*?' asked the other.

As they came closer, Joe could see that one of them had a tarnished silver goat's skull on his left temple. Not just on his left temple, but *in* his left temple – because the only way in which such a decoration could have been fixed would have been by drilling a hole into his forehead. Smoke-blackened saliva dribbled from the sides of his mouth.

'Do we frighten you, pal?' the white-faced man asked him, and then whooped a terrible whoop, like a hog-calling whoop, and more birds burst from the bushes.

Joe slowly circled around his car, and then, without warning, he suddenly began to run. He ran diagonally up the slope toward the woods, across the stumbling, tufted grass. If he could make the woods, then they wouldn't stand a chance of finding him. Joe had fought with the 3rd US Marines at Phu Bai. Joe knew what fear was but he also knew how to survive.

He reached the top of the slope and glanced over his shoulder. They were still sixty or seventy feet below, but they were coming after him, and they may have been burned and they may have been shocked, but they were young, and young legs can run. He crashed through the bushes and bracken and saplings, and thin branches whipped and stung at his face. He could hear his breathing, harsh and quick. *On! on! on! on!* He could almost hear Sergeant Jackson screaming at him now.

Shielding his face with his upraised arm, he slid down the side of a gully, and then ran along it, his shoes storming up last year's leaves. *On!* he gasped, and *on!* he gasped, and *on!*

He reached the end of the gully, and then he had to scramble up a steep, loamy slope, clinging onto roots and weeds to stop himself from sliding back. He heard footsteps churning through the leaves in hot pursuit, but he didn't look back. Sergeant Jackson had always told him, *don't look back, it slows you down, and it gives you The Fear, and it gives them your honky white face as a target.*

Gasping, seriously winded, he dragged himself up between the branches of two silver birches, and then started to run flat-out. The ground was more level here, although it gradually sloped off to the right, and Joe found himself following its natural inclination, which took him further and further away from the highway.

Behind him, he could hear the white-faced men tearing at the roots and tubers as they scaled the loamy slope. He ran and he kept on running.

Although their leaves completely obscured the sky, the trees in this wood were oddly far apart, so that Joe had the impression that he was running through a gloomy, pillared ballroom. It was difficult to determine distance and scale, because the woods were deserted, and there was nothing manmade to give him any sense of proportion. *On! on! on! on!* demanded Sergeant Jackson, but Joe was sweating and trembling and all of a sudden all those years of beer and cigar-smoking and *spalla di vitello brasata* began to tell.

He heard a whoop very close behind him – very much closer than he had believed they could be, those two burned men with their blood-red eyes. His fear gave him wings for just a few more feet. His feet brush-drummed through the leaves, his heavy thighs churned, his belly leaped up and down and from side to side.

Jesus, where was Marine Joe Garboden, tough and young and fit as shit? Who was this wheezing, perspiring clown, with his rhumba-dancing gut and his weak and watery knees? He fell before he realized he was falling. He snagged his foot on a root and crashed to the ground without even raising his hands to protect himself. He was winded and bruised and *hurt*, for Christ's sake. He could have burst into tears and curled himself up and begged for mercy. But Sergeant Jackson insisted it was *on! on! on!* and so he heaved himself onto his feet and tried to keep on running.

Just as the white-faced men caught up with him – silent this time, not whooping, not laughing, and brought him thundering back down to the ground like two lions bringing down a wildebeeste.

'Please,' Joe begged. He didn't even know what they were going to do. He was sure, however, that they were going to kill him, in one way or another.

They kept him pressed against the leaves, face down. One of them sat astride the small of his back, while the other stalked about and made fussy preparations.

Joe sweated and sweated and tried to catch his breath. Only two or three inches in front of his nose, a tiny amber spider was trying to climb along the ridge of a dried-brown leaf. Joe's panting breath set the leaf trembling, and so the spider had to cling on to it tightly. My God, thought Joe. How the strong can terrify the weak – and how they don't even realize they're doing it, most of the time.

But he almost wished that he could have been that spider, because all that spider had to worry about was balancing, and whether it would rain, and what it was going to eat.

The white-faced man who was sitting astride his back was surprisingly light, although his knees dug into Joe's hips so viciously that Joe was unable to move. His trousers were crusted with burnt patches, and he smelled strongly of scorched cotton and sour body-odour and something else: something that reminded Joe of hospitals or funerals, he couldn't decide which.

'You asked for this, friend,' said the other man, hunkering down beside him, so that Joe could see his face. White, so white, with a spotty, blotchy complexion, the wings of his nose crowded with massive blackheads and his eyes filled with blood.

'I have a family,' Joe croaked, and then spat fragments of leaves out of his mouth.

'You have a family? That's even better. People who have families always get much more frightened. And – of course – the more frightened you are – the better we like it.'

'You think you're – scaring me? I served in Nam.'

The white-faced man crouched right down amongst the leaves and kissed Joe's lips, and then licked the sweat from Joe's forehead with his tongue.

'You're *alive*, though, aren't you?'

'You disgusting son-of-a-bitch,' Joe retorted.

The white-faced man laughed, a kind of high-pitched whinny, and then he stood up, and paced around. 'You know something, friend, I'm glad you ran into the woods. It's so much more private here, don't you think? Listen! You can't hear anything. Not even an airplane. Not even a bird. A dead place, this, like a mausoleum. Kind of spooky, aint it?'

He circled around Joe's prostrate body, kicking leaves. He began to hum; a high, quavery hum, and after a while, with his face pressed hard against the loam, Joe recognized the song he was humming. He had learned it in grade school – everybody had learned it in grade school.

> *What is your five-o?*
> *Green grow the rushes-o!*
> *Five for the symbols at your door*
> *And four for the gospel-makers.*
> *Three, three, the rivals …*
> *Two, two, the lily white boys*
> *Dressed all in green, ho-ho*
> *One is one and all alone and ever more shall be so.*

Joe listened and closed his eyes and tried to believe that he wasn't here at all – that he was back in grade school, with the morning sun shining through the upper windows, and children's voices lifted all around him in song.

For a split second he believed that he could escape from his nightmare just by the power of his imagination alone.

But then the man who was sitting astride him yanked up the back of his coat, and his shirt, too, his uncut fingernails scratching Joe's skin.

'Bastard! Get off me!' Joe raged at him. But the other man knelt down beside him again and helped his friend to tug Joe's coat right up over his shoulders. Joe shouted, 'Bastard!' again, and without hesitation the man scooped up a handful of dirt and leaf-mould and pine-needles and crammed it into Joe's open mouth.

'No need to be rude, my friend,' he admonished him. Joe coughed and spat out dirt, and struggled to get up. But now the two men began to assault him with terrible strength and animal-like earnestness. One of them hit him with his knuckles three or four times on the side of his head, while the other one kicked him in the thighs and the ribs. Joe screamed and breathed in leaf-mould and almost suffocated.

'Think he's scared?' whooped the man who was sitting astride his back. 'Think he's good and scared?'

'I'll make him good and scared,' said the other man. He seized Joe's belt and dragged his trousers down over his buttocks. The belt scraped painfully against Joe's hips and thighs, and he shouted out 'Help! Don't! Listen – whatever you want!' but the men took no notice of him. They dragged his trousers right off him and threw them into the bushes.

Half-naked, stunned, Joe made one last effort to get to his feet. But one of the white-faced men walked around him and kicked him right in the bridge of his nose. The kick was so unexpected that he didn't even realize what had happened at first; but then he felt blood flooding down the back of his throat, blood mixed with pine-needles and leaf-mould – blood that tasted fresh and metallic, like death.

It suddenly occurred to him that they were going to kill

him. It suddenly occurred to him that today was the day he was going to die.

Oh God, forgive me, he thought. *Oh God, don't do this to me, please. Not here, not now. Not at the hands of these terrible white-faced men.*

The man who had been sitting astride Joe's back now dropped on his knees onto Joe's shoulders, pinning him down to the ground. At the same time, the other man groped his hand between Joe's legs, and took hold of his testicles. He gave them an agonizingly hard squeeze, and Joe yelled, '*No!*' and tried to twist himself around.

'It's your choice, my friend,' said the man who was kneeling on his shoulders. 'Life ... death, it's all up to you.'

'I have a wife,' Joe told him, with nose-blood running out of the side of his mouth. 'I have a family.'

'Should this make a difference?' the man asked him.

'I'm asking for a little compassion, that's all.'

'Compassion! That's rich! You would have gladly seen us fry!'

'For God's sake,' Joe choked.

'I don't think so,' the man replied.

At that moment, the man who had been squeezing Joe's testicles ferociously burrowed his head between Joe's thighs, dragged his penis backward and downward, and gripped it in his mouth. Joe grunted in terror, and humped his back, but the man clung on, his teeth clinging tenaciously to the rim of his glans.

Joe was shaking with shock and disgust. 'What the hell do you want?' he kept repeating. 'What the hell do you want?'

'You want it bitten off?' the man asked him, in a suggestive, oily tone. 'My friend just adores to bite them off.'

To make his point, the white-faced man sank his teeth into the sensitive skin of Joe's penis just a little deeper, and lasciviously licked around the end of it. Joe's stomach knotted up with fear and revulsion and the taste of blood.

He could hardly think. His mind was like a television screen filled with static, turned to top volume. He couldn't see, he couldn't hear. Every one of his senses seemed to be blotted out by an endless crashing roar.

He had been frightened for his life before: once in an automobile crash, and once on a flight to Niagara Falls, when his plane had been struck by lightning. But nothing like this. This was misery and terror and utter humiliation, all mixed up together. He found himself praying that his family would never find out what had happened to him. Better to be lost forever, in a shallow grave in the forest, than for Marcia to discover what these white-faced men had put him through.

He was still praying when the man who was sitting astride his shoulders slid two long metal tubes out of his inside pocket. Without a word, without any hesitation at all, he positioned one of the tubes above the middle of Joe's bare back. It made an indentation in his white, plump flesh.

'You know what it says in the Bible,' the man told Joe, conversationally. 'Man cannot live by bread alone.'

'Wha-?' said Joe; and it was then that the man pushed the tube so hard that it penetrated Joe's skin, and Joe felt it run cold and sharp right into his body. It touched him somewhere right inside him, and he felt tissues snag and nerves thrill with unexpected agony. He tried to fight, but teeth crunched into his penis, so deep that he felt as if they would bite it in half. In spite of the agony that the needle was inflicting on him, in spite of the sheer exquisite pain of having that thin tube sliding into his body, pricking and digging at his kidneys, he gripped the soil with both hands and squeezed his eyes tight shut and tried to think of anything else but pain.

Which was impossible, of course – because the next thing he knew, a second tube had been pushed into the other side of his back, deep through skin and muscle and fatty tissue. He screamed, although he couldn't hear himself screaming, and then his sinuses exploded in a hideous sneeze – blood and earth and twigs and vomit.

He thought he heard somebody laughing – a high, shrill, maniacal laugh. He thought he heard thunder, but it was only the blood roaring through his brain.

He felt a sweet, intense agony in his kidneys, an agony that convinced him that he was dying. He didn't know whether to join in the laughter or to sob with pain.

He dived deep into unconsciousness, and as he lay unconscious, the two white-faced men bent over him, sipping with intense concentration at the thin metal tubes that protruded from his bare back. All that disturbed their sipping was an occasional twittering from a bird in the trees above, and the distant droning of an airplane.

Joe could feel their sipping, but he remained comatose. He thought that he was walking along a beach somewhere, with the breeze blowing steadily into his eyes, and gulls circling all around him. He was aware that somebody was following him, very close behind his right shoulder, so close that he felt he couldn't turn around and confront him.

'You could join us, you know,' a voice whispered, a voice half blown away by the breeze.

He stopped, and whoever was following him stopped too.

He heard somebody say, 'Mr Hillary? Mr Hillary?'

He turned around. He found himself face-to-face with a tall, angular man in a soft grey coat, a man with bone-white hair which whipped and curled across his face.

The man's eyes were filled with red, like two glass inkwells brimming with blood.

'Mr Hillary,' he heard somebody say; and that somebody was him.

The man nodded, and slowly raised his right hand, so that his sleeve fell away from his arm. His wrists were thin and his skin was unhealthily white. 'You could join us, you know,' the man smiled, although he spoke like a stage ventriloquist, without moving his lips. 'All the world is our dominion. The sins of the fathers, and of the sons, they all belong to us.'

Joe was cold with absolute terror. His heart was bumping slower and slower. Nobody had ever frightened him so much in his entire life.

'Mr Hillary' kept on smiling, and held his arm closer. It appeared that his skin was wriggling. Joe didn't want to look, didn't want to find out why, but he couldn't help it. The man terrified him so much that he didn't dare to look away.

'Do I alarm you?' the man asked. 'Is there something about me which makes you feel uneasy?'

Joe stared at the man's arm and realized that the wriggling movement was right inside his veins. In fact, on the inner side of his wrist, where his skin was thin and almost transparent, he could actually see what was causing it. Through the man's veins, in a constant and sickening stream, grave-worms were crawling. They oozed and waggled down the inside of his arm, and around his elbow, and bulged through the veins on the back of his hand.

Joe slowly raised his eyes, toward 'Mr Hillary's' face, and saw that the worms were even squeezing their way through the arteries in the side of his neck.

'Mr Hillary' grinned. 'Do I frighten you, Joe?' he asked him.

Joe took a sharp, cataclysmic breath. He breathed in blood and earth and ragged shreds of sinus. He tried to breathe again, but he couldn't. His lungs were clogged. His trachea was blocked with leaves and fibre. And he was far too frightened.

His heart clenched, like a man clenching his fist, clenching it tight, and refusing to open it.

Oh God. Oh God.

But his heart refused to beat. And his lungs refused to breathe.

Oh God. Oh God. Oh God.

And then death came rushing in. Like black wings beating. Like a cellar door opening. And then there was nothing at all.

Eleven

Ralph pulled his car into the kerb at the end of Seaver Street, followed nose-to-tail by the metallic-purple '82 Eldorado which had escorted him all the way southward through the Combat Zone. He climbed out and locked the door, even though he realized how absurd it was, to lock the door of a three-year-old Volkswagen parked on Seaver Street. Absurd because (a) nobody on Seaver Street would want to steal it; and (b) even if they did, police department statistics showed that even models with factory-fitted alarms were broken into and moving within 1 minute 58 seconds, usually quicker.

Somehow, however, he felt that his car wouldn't be stolen today. Patrice Latomba was waiting for him on the sidewalk, flanked by six or seven of his lieutenants, including Bertrand, dreadlocked and black-spectacled and jumpy and wild, and a totally handsome young black man with a bald-shaved head and silver hoop earrings and a sleeveless leather jerkin, and an ex-boxer with puffy eyes and a squashed nose whom Ralph (with some sadness) recognized as Henry 'The Hammer' Rivers, one of his heroes from the days of black-and-white television with rounded corners. The Cassius Clay days: the Kennedy days.

He walked around his car and onto the sidewalk and Patrice was waiting for him, stony-eyed.

Ralph said, 'I'm sorry. I want you to know that, before we say anything else at all. It was an accident, no more than that. But, your son's dead, and I shot him, and I'm sorry.'

Patrice said, 'Don't let's talk about it, okay? Talking won't bring him back. Aint nothing won't bring him back.'

Ralph said, 'Which is your apartment?'

Patrice turned around and pointed. 'Right up there. Third storey. But they've drawn the drapes. You can't see nothing.'

Ralph stepped back on the sidewalk and examined the stained, redbrick apartment block. The balconies were much narrower than he had expected – scarcely wide enough to accommodate a couple of chairs. But he knew that front-door assaults were always murderous. He had seen far too many uniformed officers shot down on Roxbury landings, and he wasn't at all keen to be the next in line.

'Have you talked to them lately?' he asked Patrice.

'I tried. But they don't seem to show no sense of reason, man. They say they want their money and that's it. They don't care who's got it. *I* have to find it for them. Shit man, I've tried, I've put all the feelers you can think of. But I don't know who's got it. Jesus, if I did, they could have it now.'

Ralph said, 'They're on the phone?'

'That's right.'

'And there's two of them?'

'No more than that, for sure.'

Ralph said, 'How long since they slept?'

'Not since yesterday, man. We've been talking to them all of yesterday; and all of last night; and all of this morning.'

'Both of them?'

'Sure. They both got different voices. One of them sounds like Salem or Marblehead, know what I mean? Upstate, classy. That real weird drawl. The other one sounds more like regular Boston.'

'They must be pretty tired.'

'You tell me, man. They don't *sound* tired. Neither of them.'

Ralph thought for a while, and then he said, quite sharply, 'You don't know where the money is, right?'

'Man, if I knew –'

'Okay, okay, I believe you,' Ralph interrupted him. 'But you don't know who these guys are, either? I mean, you have no idea at all? Not even a clue?'

'Nobody I ever heard of, and that's the 18-carat truth.'

Ralph rubbed his forehead with his fingertips. 'I didn't even know that anybody else was involved in this operation, apart from Jambo DuFreyne and Luther Johnson and all of the preppie connection, Harvard and Harvard Med and MIT.'

'Man, I didn't even know *that*,' said Patrice. 'I knew that Luther was dealing; but everybody knew that Luther was dealing. I mean, that's his job.'

'So what's the situation now?' Ralph asked him. Tense, anxious, out of place. The good-looking black was watching him with eyes of unwavering hatred, and Henry 'The Hammer' was shuffling and ducking his neck and punching his fist into the palm of his hand.

'They've been hurting Verna,' said Patrice, in a tight, off-key voice. 'I don't know how much, I don't know how. I heard her on the phone and she was screaming. I never heard nobody scream like that. They say they're going to kill her if I don't bring the bag by twelve o'clock, no ifs or buts.'

Tears suddenly sprang into Patrice's eyes; and Ralph looked at him, and got caught by something completely unexpected. For the very first time in his entire career he understood that the people he was policing were human; and that they were just like him; and that they wept and cared, even if they were burglars and racketeers and drug dealers and pimps. It wasn't a question of forgiving. It was up to juries to forgive. But it was a question of understanding; and Patrice cried; and Ralph understood; and this was the man whose baby he had killed.

Ralph said, 'I'll get her out. I've got some rope and a hook in the car.'

'And that's it? Some rope and a hook?'

'That's it. Provided somebody can direct me into the apartment directly above.'

Verna suddenly opened her eyes and felt excruciating pain in her wrists and ankles with her cheek pressed against the kitchen table, she could just see the square yellow electric clock on the kitchen wall and she found it both distressing and relieving that she had slept for less than twenty minutes. Distressing because she had needed to sleep for very much longer; and while she was asleep, she had at last been free from the prurient tortures that Bryan and Joseph had kept inflicting on her. But relieving because there were still two and a half hours to go until noon, when Patrice had promised to return the money.

She thought for a moment that Bryan and Joseph might be dozing, too. But the moment she opened her eyes, and tried to wrestle herself into a more comfortable position, Bryan appeared, blood-eyed, white-faced, filing his nails with the kind of file that you usually found in Christmas crackers.

'Hungry?' he asked her.

She swallowed dryly. 'I could use a drink of water. And my wrists hurt something terrible. I can't even feel my hands.'

Bryan nodded, as if he quite understood. 'These things are sent to try us.'

Joseph appeared, frowning distractedly. 'I lost one of my pipes,' he said.

'You probably left it in the living-room,' said Bryan. 'You want to fetch Verna some water?'

'I'm sure I left it in here.'

'Fetch Verna some water, will you? We don't want her dehydrating. Bad for the system. Thickens the blood. Sours the adrenaline.'

'Couldn't you just untie me?' Verna pleaded. 'I promise I won't try to get away.'

Bryan shook his head. 'We'll be needing some nutrition pretty soon.'

'I could cook you something. I've got plenty of pork chops in the icebox.'

Joseph was filling up a cup at the sink. He yelped with laughter.

'We don't eat pork,' Bryan explained.

'I got steak, then, and beans. I got tuna.'

'We don't eat steak and we don't eat beans and we don't eat tuna,' said Joseph. He brought the cup of water across the kitchen and lifted Verna's head so that she could drink. Most of the water poured out of the side of her mouth, but she managed to swallow enough to relieve her thirst.

She rested her head on the table again. Joseph stayed close beside her, so close that she could *smell* him, a dimly decaying, floral smell, like dying roses in a dried-up vase.

They didn't eat steak and they didn't eat beans and they didn't eat tuna. Verna didn't care to ask them what they *did* eat, in case she didn't like the answer. Besides, she had already learned not to provoke them, either of them. They were strangely formal in their behaviour, but they had already inflicted enough pain on her for Verna to know that their capacity for cruelty knew no limits whatsoever.

She couldn't understand how anybody could want to hurt another human being so much – especially since neither of them seemed to derive any pleasure out of it, not even a faintly sexual pleasure. Whenever they hurt her, whenever they touched her, they did it in such a matter-of-fact way that she felt completely characterless, a piece of flesh that they were torturing not because they bore her any ill will, but for some incomprehensible ritual of their own.

They didn't hate her, she could sense that. They didn't even dislike her. In fact, they talked to her in such a teasing, friendly way that she could almost believe that they had grown fond of her.

That was what made their cruelty all the more terrifying. That was what scared her more than anything.

There was something else that disturbed her. Something else that had penetrated her consciousness like a shard of broken glass stuck in her foot. Most of the time she had been too confused and too hurt and too exhausted to think about it. But it kept digging into her mind again and again.

They hadn't slept. She had seen them together, she had seen them apart. Just when she thought that one of them might be resting, he reappeared, smiling, his eyes as blood-red as rubies.

She had the oddest feeling that they *never* slept.

The big black woman in the blue floral dress opened her

french windows for Ralph and showed him out onto the narrow balcony. At one end of the balcony was a wicker chair with a half-collapsed seat and a frayed cushion. 'This is where I habitually sit,' she told him. 'That's when the fires aren't burning and the bullets aren't flying.'

At the other end of the balcony was a collection of earthenware pots, filled with a mixture of brightly-coloured flowers and herbs – thyme, Italian parsley, cilantro, basil and sage. 'And this is my garden, my pride-and-joy.'

'That's real nice,' Ralph remarked. 'Nice to see something grow.'

He leaned over the edge of the balcony and he could see the balcony of Patrice Latomba's apartment, fifteen or sixteen feet below. There was a red bicycle on it, and some tall nettle-like plants growing in rusty cooking-oil cans, plants which looked suspiciously like *cannabis sativa*. He gripped the metal railing which surrounded the balcony, and shook it. It seemed firm enough.

'I think they've got her tied up in the kitchen,' said Patrice. 'She was screaming a couple of times and that's where the screaming was coming from.'

'Okay,' Ralph nodded. 'And your kitchen is in the same location as the kitchen in this lady's apartment, right?'

'That's right.'

'Okay,' Ralph repeated, trying to sound cheerful. 'Nothing to do then but do it.'

He went back into the woman's apartment, and picked up the heavy grey rope which he had brought downtown in the trunk of his car. Patrice and the woman watched him in silence as he deftly tied a clove hitch around the railing, and tugged it hard to test it. Then he lifted his .44 from its shoulder holster, opened the chamber, spun it, closed it, and cocked it.

'You'll take care who you're aiming at, won't you?' asked

Patrice. 'You already took my child, don't take my woman, too.'

Ralph looked at him hard-eyed and said nothing. He could have refused to come down here altogether, and he could still turn his back on this situation here and now, although he wasn't going to say so. His adrenaline was rushing and he was ready for anything. All he wanted to do was swing off this balcony and kick ass; and even uppity talk from Patrice Latomba wasn't going to stop him.

'Say a little prayer,' he said; and the woman crossed herself and said, 'Hallelujah, hallelujah,' and Patrice stared at him as if he were truly mad, which he probably was.

He wrapped the rope around his left wrist. Then he climbed up onto the railing, and balanced there, with his legs apart, his back to the street, which was nearly seventy-five feet below him. He kept his .44 raised in his right hand. This was it. This was what being a man was all about. He heard the distant knock-knock-knocking of a semi-automatic rifle, and looked around, and Seaver Street was all devastation and thick brown smoke, and *this* was what he wanted, this danger, this warlike landscape, this overwhelming sense that he could make a difference.

He let out a scream which frightened even himself. Then he jumped backward off the balcony rail, launching himself into space. He kicked out once against the wall, to throw himself out even further, then he was swinging down onto Patrice's balcony, still screaming like a madman. He caught his ankle on Patrice's balcony rail, knocked over his bicycle, spun, swung, but then he went right through Patrice's french windows, with a splintering explosion of glass and glazing-bars, and found himself tumbling across the living-room, wrapped up in white net curtains like a shroud.

He struggled to his feet. His left cheek was cut, and there was blood dripping steadily from a long laceration on the heel of his right hand, all across the rug. But – coughing – he managed to disentangle himself from the curtains and out into the hall. The kitchen door was slightly ajar, and he could smell cigarette smoke and hear somebody saying something. He hesitated for a moment, but then he burst into the kitchen, his .44 held out rigidly in front of him with both hands, and screamed out, 'Freeze!'

The two young men in dark glasses were standing either side of the kitchen table. They looked completely unsurprised. One of them was smoking a cigarette, blowing the smoke in thin streams out of his nostrils, while the other one was filing his nails.

Verna Latomba still lay bound tightly to the table, naked, bruised, her ankles and her wrists hogtied up behind her. There was a herringbone pattern of cuts on her back, and her buttocks and upper thighs were splattered with dried white wax.

She tried to look around, to see who it was. 'Patrice?' she called, in a breathy, expectant shrill. 'Patrice, is that you?'

Ralph slowly stepped forward, keeping his gun aimed between Joseph's eyes. When Verna saw who it was, she whispered, '*You?*'

'Let's just say that I owe Patrice a favour,' said Ralph. Bryan stopped filing his nails and dropped his file into the pocket of his coat.

'I said freeze!' Ralph roared at him.

The young man lifted both his hands. 'We're frozen, for Christ's sake, we're frozen.'

'Put your hands on your head,' Ralph instructed them both. 'Put your hands on your head and turn yourselves around. I said, turn yourselves around. *Facing the wall, comprendez!*'

The two young men stared at each other, shrugged, and

then did as they were told. The one who was smoking kept his cigarette in his hand, so that smoke appeared to be ribboning out of the top of his head.

Tense, wide-eyed, Ralph circled around the table. One of the young men glanced around at him but Ralph instantly snapped at him, 'Face the wall, you mother!'

'Pardon me for looking,' the young man replied, almost petulant.

Ralph opened one kitchen drawer after another, until he found what he was looking for – knives. He took out the sharpest-looking, and proceeded to saw left-handed at the cords that bound Verna's wrists and ankles together.

'I don't know what kind of goddamn perverts you two are,' he panted, as he cut through one cord after another.

'Just as well for you,' said one of the men.

He cut through the last of the cords. Wincing with pain, Verna slowly lowered her legs. Ralph dropped the knife, and stood close beside her, his arm protectively covering her back. 'Do you think you can walk?' he asked her.

'I don't know,' she told him. Feebly, she tried to snatch at his sleeve.

'Okay … if you can't walk, I'm going to have to carry you, fireman's lift, okay? Try to sit up, that's all. Just try to sit up.'

The young man with the cigarette turned around to face Ralph, and lowered his hands. Ralph shouted 'Turn around! Turn back around! Are you deaf or something?'

The young man stayed where he was. He took a thin drag on his cigarette and then he said, 'Can we assume from this misguided rescue mission that Mr Latomba is unable to find our money?'

'For the last time, pal, I'm warning you, turn around!'

'My dear sir, I need to know if I've been wasting my time

287

here or not. If we can't recover that money from Mr Latomba, then we're going to have to find out where we *can* recover it from.'

'Turn around!' Ralph repeated.

The young man stayed where he was, smoking, waiting, smiling. Then the other young man lowered his hands and turned around, too, and they both stood watching and waiting, as if they were daring Ralph to kill them.

'Come on, up,' Ralph urged Verna. He went down on one knee beside the table, and managed to heave her onto his shoulder. She wasn't heavy, he could feel her ribcage and her hips, and smell her perfume and her sweat. His arm, however, began to tremble with the strain. He must have pulled his shoulder when he swung out of the balcony, and his right hand was beginning to waver with the strain of holding up his .44 revolver, which weighed over 2lbs.

He climbed to his feet, grunting with the effort, stepping awkwardly sideways to retain his balance.

'Just stay back,' he warned the white-faced young men. 'I don't want to shoot you but I will if I have to.'

'I'm afraid that it's not up to you to decide when we die,' said the young man with the cigarette. He began to edge closer, shifting one of the kitchen chairs that was standing in his way.

Ralph retreated towards the door, hefting Verna higher up. She was hanging on his shoulder as lifeless and unco-operative as a dead antelope, almost toppling him over. Her wrists and ankles must have become so numb that she couldn't even balance herself. For some reason Ralph thought of his father, who had suffered from multiple sclerosis. One day his father had stood in front of an open fire, combing his hair in the mirror on top of the mantel-piece, totally unaware that his slippered foot was buried in the blazing logs, and that he was burning.

He could remember his mother walking into the room and screaming, and that scream could still break his concentration, even today.

Just as Ralph reached the kitchen door, the other young man dodged and whirled and danced his way around the table to block his escape.

Ralph waved his gun at him. 'Just get out of the way, okay? You understand what this is? A .44, it'll blow your head off – shoulders, no head.'

The young man shrugged, and backed away, his hands lifted in a gesture of appeasement. 'It's all right, friend … no need to get over-excited.'

Out of the corner of his eye, Ralph glimpsed the other young man trying to creep closer. He swung around, and the young man went for him, and this time he fired, the good old Ralph Brossard reflex. The gun bucked, and the kitchen seemed to expand with the deafening boom of an overcharged .44 bullet fired at close range. He saw the young man's lapels rip open, tatters of black cloth. He saw smoke, and the young man twisting around in it, falling, dropping to the floor.

But instead of falling all the way to the floor, the young man kept on twisting around, almost like a Cossack dancer, and then he rose again, up through the smoke, smiling, and confronted Ralph with the same insouciance that he had confronted him before.

'I told you,' he smiled. 'It's not up to you to decide when we die.'

Ralph fired again, what the hell. The gun's recoil whipped his arm up and strained his other shoulder. The young man's jacket burst into shreds of black, and he let out a smoky gasp, but that was all. Ralph fired again, although he knew it was useless.

He heard somebody beating on the front door. It

sounded like Patrice. 'Brossard! Brossard! What the hell is going *down* in there, man?'

'It's okay!' he shouted back. 'It's okay! I've got Verna, everything's cool!'

The young man let out an empty laugh. 'Everything's cool? Everything's cool? I don't think so! I think that everything's *hot.*'

He approached Ralph and his coat was still fuming with gunpowder smoke. His eyes were bloody and expressionless. Ralph lifted up his .44 but the young man simply moved away the barrel, and said, 'No, that's not the way.'

'I'm taking this woman out of here,' said Ralph.

'Of course,' the young man agreed. 'You're taking her out of here ... way out of here, and far, far away. Where she'll be safe.'

He reached into the pocket of his ruined jacket and produced a small disc of copper and bronze, which he held up in front of his face between finger and thumb.

'Do you know what this is?' he asked, calmly.

Ralph took an unbalanced step backward. 'I don't give a shit. I'm taking this woman out of here, and that's all there is to it.'

'But look at it ... ' the young man encouraged him, holding the disc higher, in front of his eyes. 'Doesn't it make you feel sleepy ... doesn't it make you feel tired? Doesn't it make you feel like putting Verna down for just a moment, and taking a well-earned rest?'

'You're out of your mind,' Ralph told him. But all the same, he found it impossible to take his eyes away from the copper-and-bronze disc, which seemed to glint at him with knowing simplicity. *All your problems could be copper. All your hardships could be bronze. All of your stresses and all of your strains – every guilt and every anxiety – they could be just as simple as me.*

A circle within a circle. Like every relationship in the galaxy, like planets within planets, like wheels within wheels.

The young man said, 'You're feeling tired, I'll bet.'

'I'm leaving.'

'Sure you're leaving. We don't mind if you leave. What's it to us? Mr Latomba has lost our money, the pigeons have flown the coop.' He slowly blinked his blood-red eyes and in his blood-red eyes Ralph saw birds slowly flying, flapping their wings, slowly turning over blood-red beaches, where congealing oceans glutinously stirred. He couldn't stop himself from staring at the copper-and-bronze disc, and somehow the copper-and-bronze disc seemed to wink and sparkle.

He found himself plunging through the warm and bloody surf, into the sea. The sun shone for an instant through the foam, and the foam was pink; and then it was darkness, an overwhelming darkness, and growing chillier, too, but he kept on swimming deeper, because he had to swim deeper.

'What are you afraid of?' the young man's voice asked him.

'Fire ... my father burned his foot in the fire.'

'Ah, fire! You shouldn't be afraid of fire. Fire is our friend.'

He swam deeper still; and the deeper he swam, the colder he became. He was sure that he could feel his body working, all around him, like a silent, busy machine.

Fire, he thought.

Fire is my friend

– not realizing that he wasn't swimming at all, but shuffling across the Latombas' kitchen in a deep hypnotic trance, bumping into the table, colliding with the chairs, still carrying Verna, helpless, on his shoulder. His right arm dropped down, and his heavy revolver clattered onto the plastic-tiled floor. Neither Bryan nor Joseph made any attempt to pick it up. They didn't have to. It wasn't for anybody else to decide when they were going to die.

'Brossard!' shouted Patrice, pounding at the door. 'Brossard! What's happening in there?'

Bryan smiled at Joseph and Joseph smiled back. Verna started to twist and struggle, trying to wrench herself free, but Ralph was gripping her with unnatural strength – the same strength that had enabled Michael to bend the arm of Dr Rice's chair – and she was weakened and numbed by her long ordeal on the kitchen table.

'– go! Let me – go!' she gasped, but Ralph reached around with his right hand and seized her hair and wrenched her head back so hard that the sinews in her neck made a sharp crackling noise and he almost killed her on the spot. She let out a thin, airless scream – but, lost in his trance, Ralph was unable to hear her.

He believed that he was rising from the sea now, and that he was wading toward the shore. The sky was as black as freshly spilled blood. In the middle distance he could see a fire flickering, and ashes whirling into the wind. A tall man in a grey coat was standing not far away from the fire, his hands in his pockets, his bone-white hair blowing across his face. He had never seen this man before, but somehow he knew who he was, and that they had always been destined to meet.

He walked across the sand and closer to the fire – so close that he could feel its heat against his hands and his face. The man said, '*Hallo, Ralph,*' without even opening his mouth; and Ralph thought, *It's him – it's Mr Hillary*.

At the same time, with Verna grasped tightly around the neck, he was twisting the knobs that turned on the front two burners of her gas hob. They popped alight, and Ralph passed his bare hand across them, back and forth, two or three times, so that he could feel their heat. There was a strong smell of scorching as the hairs on the back of his hand shrivelled and smoked, but he didn't even flinch.

'*It's cold, isn't it, Ralph?*' said Mr Hillary. '*Let's get ourselves warm, shall we? Huddle up to the fire.*'

Ralph held out both hands, as close to the fire as he could. It was burning up fiercely now, a small orange-hot cavern of driftwood and broken packing-cases. He was fascinated by the bright sparks that crawled along the logs and then whirled up into the blood-coloured sky. He felt as if he wanted to pick one of the burning logs up in his hands so that he could watch it more closely.

'*Fire is our friend, Ralph,*' said Mr Hillary.

In the kitchen, he seized Verna by the nape of the neck, his fingers digging deep into her nerves. She tried to escape by scratching furiously at his face, and by hitting him with her elbow, and by groping for his testicles. She screamed again and again, but he took no notice. His eyes were wide open but he didn't blink once, even when she raked his left cheek with her broken fingernails, all the way down from the side of his eye to the corner of his mouth.

'Fire is our friend,' he repeated. Blood ran down his face in four distinct rivulets, and dripped onto his collar. 'Do you hear that? *Fire is our friend!*'

Verna shrieked, '*No!*' and '*no!*' and '*no!*', her face grotesquely contorted with fear and pain. She tried to escape by collapsing onto her knees, but Ralph mercilessly dragged her upright. Then, without hesitation, he slammed her face-down into one of the lighted gas-burners.

And held her there.

And held her there.

Verna's hair flared up. Her whole head became a ball of orange flame. Out of her blistering lips came a cry that didn't sound human at all – a screeching, endless, off-key

293

wail, like somebody dragging a chisel across the entire width of a blackboard – until Ralph briefly lifted her head and slammed it back onto the burner. She breathed in, and she breathed in burning gas.

It took only seconds for her hair to burn into glowing, sparkling clumps. The gas jets roared at her forehead and fiercely consumed her ears. Her cheeks reddened and shrivelled and her skin burst open, like the skin of a roasted red pepper.

All the time she jerked and struggled and thrashed, but Ralph pressed her face hard and unforgiving against the burner, even though his own left hand was burning, and flames were beginning to lick up the sleeve of his coat.

'Fire is our friend,' he kept repeating, with his eyes focused on Mr Hillary's face, fifteen feet away, somewhere in the kitchen wall. 'Fire is our friend.'

The flesh of his fingers swelled and blistered. His entire sleeve was alight now, so that his arm was a column of fire. The distinctive stenches of burning hair and burning wool and burning flesh combined to form a rancid, unbreathable fog, and even Bryan began to cough. Joseph took hold of his arm and began to push him quickly towards the door.

Ralph didn't see them – *couldn't* have seen them, because he was still immersed in a deep hypnotic trance. The trance affected Ralph's nervous system in the same way that multiple sclerosis had affected his father: it made him impervious to pain. He was burning but he didn't feel it, and he knew that fire was his friend.

Verna performed a frenzied dance, an extraordinary arched-back double-hopping dance, and at last broke free. She staggered and fell sideways, away from the oven, her head blackened and smoking, blinded, her nose burned away, her lips smoking and raw. She tried to get up but she couldn't, and she lay on the kitchen floor completely rigid,

294

with only a spasm in her right hand to indicate that she was still alive.

Ralph knew that he was standing too close to the fire. He was far too hot. His left hand felt as if it were blistering, and he lifted it up to make sure that it wasn't scorched.

As he did so, his whole world was engulfed in flame. He screamed, and woke up, and suddenly felt the pain of his burning arm.

What had been strangely enticing – the beach, the night, and 'Mr Hillary's' fire – suddenly became a hell on earth.

His arm – his whole fucking arm was alight. He tried to beat at it, but all he could do was burn the fingers of his other hand. Every beat seemed to do nothing more than fan the flames. What had they told him, in survival lessons? Drop to the ground, roll, smother the fire the best way you can.

He snatched a towel from the hook beside the oven, and wrapped it around his arm. He could see that his hand was gruesomely burned away … a five-fingered pattern of bone and blackened ashes. The pain was more than he could bear, and he staggered stiff-legged around the kitchen in a state of shock, his arm still smoking, trying to find some way to come to terms with the most overwhelming agony that he had ever experienced. He had crushed his fingers in a car door once. He had burned his arm, when he was trying to light a reluctant barbecue with gasoline. He had lost a fingernail in a fight with a violent crack dealer. Pain, all pain. But nothing compared to this. He wouldn't have believed that it was possible for a human being to suffer such pain without dying.

But he wasn't dead. He was still alive. And he didn't even realize that he was roaring out loud.

He heard weeping. He heard furious knocking. Then he heard gunshots, and a splintering sound. He heard somebody arguing, wildly arguing, at the top of his voice. The next thing he knew, Patrice Latomba appeared in the kitchen doorway, panting, sweaty, wearing nothing but a grease-stained vest, and jeans.

Patrice looked down at Verna, lying on her back on the floor, her face still smouldering, her body convulsing in pain, her heels juddering against the kitchen floor. Then he turned back to Ralph. His eyes were white and wild.

'What went down here, man?'

Ralph could do nothing but grin at him, sickly. His pain was misting his eyes with scarlet, and he was right on the point of collapse.

'*What the fuck went down here, man? Where are those guys? Where are those guys?*'

'I – don't know – they're –' Ralph began. Then, in an anguished howl, 'I didn't mean to burn her! I don't know why! I didn't mean to burn her, for Christ's sake!'

Patrice waved smoke away from his face. Suddenly, he looked very serious. '*You* burned her?' he asked. His voice had that terrible coldness of severe shock – a voice that left a taste of oil and metal on the roof of Ralph's mouth.

'I didn't mean to burn her.'

Patrice raised his automatic, stiff-wristed, and fired once. The .45 bullet hit Ralph right on the bridge of his nose, and sprayed his brains all over the kitchen curtains. A flower-basket pattern of beige and bloody red instantly appeared on the window, stencilled at a velocity of 860 feet per second.

Even before Ralph had toppled to the floor, Patrice swivelled around to Verna and shot her in the head, too, one shot, straight into the smoking gristle of her face.

Bertrand appeared in the doorway, and looked around in awe. 'You killed them both, man. What about the law?'

Patrice's eyes were filled with tears. 'No more law,

man. No more fucking law. Not on Seaver Street. No more law.'

Bertrand looked down at Verna, and whispered, 'Mary Mother of God,' and crossed himself.

Patrice pushed him out of the kitchen and across the hall. 'No more religion, man and no more law. No more nothing. This is war, man. This is war! You see one pig inside of a mile of here – you see one white face – you see a Jew, or an Arab, or a goddamned Algonquin Indian – you blow them away! You blow them away, man! With my specific permission! Because *I'm* the law! And what they did here today, that gives me the right!'

Bertrand hefted a nickel-plated .45 automatic out of his red fringed jacket, and fired it into the ceiling. Plaster showered down, and Bertrand brushed off his shoulders, and screamed out, 'Christmas! Christmas come early!'

Michael was sitting in his study when there was a quiet little knock at the door and Patsy came in. It was mid-afternoon now – they had all lunched well, on chicken pot-pie, and Victor had taken Jason out onto the beach so that they could fly Jason's new battle kite.

The sunlight brightened and faded, brightened and faded, as clouds passed swiftly over the shoreline. Michael could just see Victor and Jason in the distance, and the red-and-yellow kite whirling and dipping as they tried to get it to fly. The wind was too turbulent today, too much downdraught.

Patsy came up behind him and massaged his shoulder muscles. She said, 'You're tense! You haven't been tense like this for months.'

'It's the job, that's all. Just as soon as we're done with it, and I've collected my pay cheque, it'll be back to barnacle-zappers, I promise you.'

'I don't know,' she said. 'Maybe it suits you, a little stress.'

He swung his chair around, and took hold of her, and sat her on his lap, and kissed her. Her hair was tied back in a yellow silk scarf, and she was wearing a short cotton dress, yellow as sunflowers, yellow as paint, yellow as I Can't Believe It's Not Butter! Her lips tasted of pink lipstick and freshly-sprayed-on perfume. Her large bead bracelet clattered.

When they had finished kissing they looked each other in the eye, searchingly, unembarrassed.

'You've changed,' she told him, with considerable certainty.

'Changed? I don't think so.'

'No ... I can feel it, you've changed. You're – what can I call it? – *deeper.*'

'Deeper? And up until now, I was shallow? You make me sound like a swimming-pool.'

She flicked the tip of his nose with her finger. 'I didn't mean that. I mean that you seem much more sure of yourself – much more confident. I get the feeling that – all of a sudden – you know exactly where you're going.'

He glanced across at the tattered copy of *Mushing* on the floor beside the couch, and he knew that Patsy was right. He *did* know where he was going, for the first time in nearly a year, and it wasn't the magnetic pole with a team of huskies and four cases of Labatt's.

Ever since Rocky Woods, he had gradually let slip all of his responsibilities as an insurance investigator, and as a husband, too – or even a man. He had tried to pretend that he was capable of being somebody completely different – not just different, but somebody *luckier.* He should have known that he was never lucky, in the sense that he never got anything for nothing. He had never won a competition or a lottery, he had never even made a profit on a slot-machine.

298

Even at work, his most inspired investigation had never won him a raise, or even a modest promotion. Take the Hunt case, for example, three and a half years ago. He had discovered that a wealthy Lynnfield wife had been dead *before* her car had been torched, with her inside it, because there were no smoke inhalation marks around the nose and mouth. Not even the fire department investigators had noticed it. He had saved Plymouth Insurance $1.35 million and won himself a complimentary pat on the back from Joe Garboden, and a thankful memo from Edgar Bedford, and that was all.

But Patsy was right. The John O'Brien investigation had made him deeper. It had made him realize that he was not just an observer, not just a poker-about in the smoking ruins of other people's lives, but an individual who was capable of changing the way things were, starting with the way *he* was, himself.

Some of this new-found confidence had come from the hypnotic trances he had experienced ... the beach and the lighthouse and the bony white-faced man. He had the strongest feeling that the man in his trances was real, and that he was the kind of man who could shape the course of history. He was sure that the lighthouse, too, was invested with some momentous significance. The lighthouse may be real or it may be symbolic. But Michael was determined now to find out *why* it was so significant, and who the man was – and because of his determination, he was beginning to feel stronger.

He could shape the course of history, too.

Patsy kissed his forehead and ruffled his hair. 'So what's this all about?' she wanted to know. 'Who *were* those young men who were hanging out across the street?'

He kissed her back. 'Oh ... they were nobody.'

'They must have been *somebody*.'

Michael swivelled his chair back around again, so that they were both facing his desk. It was strewn with the blown-up black-and-white photographs that Joe had hidden in his magazine. They must have been enlarged to the very limit, because they were grainy and blurred and some of them could have been entered for 'What Is It?' contests in the *National Enquirer*.

'What are these?' asked Patsy.

'You recognize any of them?'

She picked up one of the photographs and frowned at it closely. 'I don't know ... where were they taken?'

She was looking at a picture of a fence, shaded by trees. There were several people standing in front of the fence – a woman in a spotted dress, a man in a suit and a sports coat, another woman in a short-sleeved dress, carrying a hand-bag, another man in a checkered shirt. Behind the fence, however, eight or nine other people were standing, their faces more difficult to distinguish because of the mottled shadow of the trees. On the far right there were three pale-faced young men, all wearing black snapbrim hats, the kind of hats that were popular in the 1960s. All three of them wore dark glasses.

'Well?' asked Michael, coaxing her.

She peered very close, until her turned-up nose was almost touching the surface of the photograph. Then she looked up at him and he could see the little grey flecks in her cornflower-blue irises, and the fine, fine hairs of her eyebrows. 'It's them, isn't it?' she asked.

'I don't know. That's what I'm asking you.'

'It *is* them,' she said, nodding her head. 'At least, those two are. The one on the right and the one next to him, the one in the middle. I don't recognize the one on the left.'

'Are you sure about that?'

She peered at the photograph again, and then nodded.

300

'I'm sure. I'm sure. I'm *positive*. Look at his ears. I mean, he's not exactly Mr Spock, but almost. It's not so much that I recognize them individually, but the two of them together ...'

Michael kissed her ear, curled her fine blonde hair around his finger. 'I wanted to mush to the pole,' he told her. 'I wanted to leave you and Jason, and fly to northern Greenland, and then sledge the rest of the way. I think I was half-hoping that I'd die of hypothermia. It's supposed to be peaceful, dying of hypothermia ... especially with all those loyal huskies licking your face as you go to meet the Great Popsicle-Maker in the Sky.'

'What *you* wanted, honey-pie, was not to think about reality. And don't try to make a joke of it. You suffered, after Rocky Woods, and don't try to pretend that you didn't, because I suffered right along with you.'

'I know,' said Michael, squeezing her hand. 'But *this* is reality.' He tapped the photograph. 'Those were the men who were waiting around outside; and those were the men who followed Joe when he drove away from here. I mean – I want to have these photographs enhanced on Plymouth's computer, but I'm ninety-nine per cent convinced of it.'

'Where was this taken?' Patsy asked.

'Are you ready for this? According to Joe's inscription on the back, it was taken on November 22, 1963, from the east side of Dealey Plaza, Dallas.'

There was a very long pause. Then Patsy looked at the photographs again. 'But Dealey Plaza, Dallas ... that was where President Kennedy was shot.'

'That's correct.'

She thought about that for a moment or two, while Michael watched her. At last she said, 'But ... how could those men have been there ... in 1963, when they were here today, looking just the same?'

'That's what Joe was trying to find out. That's what *I* have to find out.'

'Oh, Michael … they *can't* be the same men. The men I saw were no more than twenty-four or twenty-five … thirty at a pinch. They would have been *babies* when Kennedy was assassinated. Anyway … are you sure these pictures are genuine? They don't look like any pictures I ever saw before. They didn't show them on that Kennedy documentary, did they?'

'No, they didn't. According to Joe, they were taken by a guy named Jacob Parrot, who owned a music store in Grand Prairie. He was one of the few amateur cameramen at the scene of the assassination who didn't have his pictures confiscated by the police or the FBI. When he saw that people were having their cameras taken, he wound on the film, took it out, and dropped it into his pocket.

'Apparently, Jacob Parrot had borrowed the camera from a friend, and he hadn't set the focus correctly. In most of his pictures, President Kennedy is quite blurred, but the people on the grassy knoll and the fence behind it are in pretty sharp focus. And here they are.'

'You really believe they're the same men?'

'Take a look at *this* picture.'

Michael handed her a photograph which clearly showed one of the men in dark glasses with a rifle raised to his shoulder. The other man was turning away, one hand lifted against his ear, as if he were trying to shield himself from the blast.

Patsy had only to glance at it before she dropped it back on the desk and said, 'Yes … it's them. It really is. It's them.'

'Positive?'

'No doubt about it. That's Spock-ears all right. And the other one … there's something kind of *square* about him.

302

Even if I'd seen a photograph of just one of them, I would have said yes. But the two together? It has to be them.'

Michael gave her another kiss. 'All I need to know now is – why did Joe leave these pictures here?'

'To hide them, I guess.'

'Well, that's obvious. But why did he need to hide them *here*? Couldn't have have hidden them at home, or in the office, or in a bus station locker, or something?'

'Maybe he knew they were on to him.'

'All the same …'

'Maybe he knew they were on to him and he simply didn't have the time to hide them anyplace else.'

Michael leafed through the grassy knoll pictures and slowly shook his head. 'I don't know … I hate having these here. These are the kind of photographs that people get killed for.'

'Why don't you discuss it with Joe?'

'With a mobile phone call, that even your kid sister could pick up? You have to be kidding.'

'You don't have to mention "Kennedy" specifically. You could always talk vague … like, "Joe, thanks very much for that interesting file you sent me." Or, "I really enjoyed seeing those pictures of the kids." '

Michael squeezed her, and laughed. 'What do you think this is? *The Man From U.N.C.L.E.*? No … he'll be back at the office soon, I'll call him then.'

Through the window, they could see Victor and Jason walking back to the house. 'Seriously,' said Patsy, 'what are you going to do now? Are you going to call in the police?'

'Unh-hunh. Not yet. We'll have to produce a whole lot more evidence than this. Besides, if these guys get wind of the fact that we're on to them, and that we know who they are, they could very well come after us, too. Look at that guy, what's-his-name, the one who was going to prove in court that Lee Harvey Oswald had a direct connection with Clay Shaw? David Ferrie, that's it.

'David Ferrie "died in mysterious circumstances" before he could take the stand. And so did scores of other people. Anybody who could prove what we can prove … that Lee Harvey Oswald didn't shoot President Kennedy – didn't and couldn't … and that *these* men did. These white-faced guys in their hats and their suits and their weird little shades.'

'Michael … you're not going to try to track them down by yourself?'

'No, Joe and me are going to track them down together … provided we get a little help from the coroner's office and the police department.'

Victor came into the study, his eyes watering from the breeze, closely followed by a grinning Jason.

'Jesus, it's windy out there!' he panted.

'Any luck with the kite?'

'Nosedive City,' said Jason, scathingly.

'That's the story of my life,' said Victor. He sat down and took off his glasses. 'Disappointment at every turn.'

'Jason, you want to get yourself a Coke?' Michael suggested.

Jason had already flung himself onto the couch. 'Oh, I get it. You want to talk adult talk.'

Michael ruffled his hair. 'I never realized that anyone so astute could ever have sprung from my loins.'

'Loins? What are loins?'

'Just get yourself a Coke, okay?'

'I want to know what loins are.'

'Loins are genitalia.'

'Like, your dick, you mean?'

'Yes, Jason, like your dick.'

'Well, why didn't you say so? "Loins." You can just

304

imagine them at school, "Hey, Bradley, put your loins away!" '

'God, thirteen-year-olds,' said Michael, when Jason had left (without closing the door properly).

But Victor had already picked up the Kennedy photographs, and was sorting through them. 'What do you think?' he asked Patsy.

Patsy was tight-lipped. 'I think it's really frightening. I think you should hand it all over to the police or the FBI, let them handle it.'

'I'm not so sure that would be a good idea,' said Victor.

'Oh?'

'Think about it. Joe seems to have found a connection between these men and the killing of President Kennedy. But Joe was also strongly implying that they're tied in with John O'Brien's murder, too – which the Boston police are making every conceivable effort to explain away as an accident.'

'So you're saying that the police are involved in the killings, too?'

Victor shrugged. 'Maybe not directly involved. But they're certainly doing everything they can to cover up the evidence. My advice is that as far as the police are concerned we should tread very, very carefully indeed.'

Michael went to the study door and opened it. Down below, the yard was empty and the street was deserted. Sand sizzled softly through the grass, and swirled across the sidewalk.

'I suggest we go back to Boston and do some more digging,' he said. 'We can trust Thomas Boyle, can't we?'

'I guess so. As much as anybody.'

'We need to talk to Thomas about the official police line on this business. Then we need to go back and talk to Dr Moorpath. We have to have him explain how on God's earth he could have reported that the O'Brien party were killed accidentally. We need to talk to Edgar Bedford, at Plymouth, and ask him why he wants to put a lid on our investigation. We need to talk to Kevin Murray and Artur Rolbein. I've read their reports but I still have plenty of unanswered questions.'

'You're going to be stirring up a whole nest of hornets, if you ask me,' said Victor.

Michael nodded. 'I know that. And I'm going to talk to Joe first. I want to know why he's so frightened … and just how frightened *we* ought to be.'

'I think pretty damned frightened,' said Victor.

Patsy glanced at him anxiously. 'You're not going to go back to Boston *now*?' she asked.

Michael checked his watch and it was eleven minutes after three. 'Not immediately. I have to discuss this with Joe first. I don't want to leave him with his ass hanging out in the breeze.'

Shortly after four o'clock, he phoned Joe at Plymouth Insurance. Joe's assistant said that he hadn't yet returned from New Seabury. It wasn't much more than a two-hour drive, even if the traffic was snarled up, but maybe Joe had stopped for lunch, or maybe he had decided to go home first. Michael called Joe's private number and Marcia answered; but Marcia hadn't seen Joe, either.

She gave him Joe's mobile number and Michael tried that. A flat, nasal recorded voice told him that the mobile phone was out of service.

Michael told Victor, 'He's not at the office yet, and he's not home, and his mobile's on the fritz.'

'Give him another half-hour,' Victor suggested.

Michael called the office again at five, and then at five-thirty. He phoned one more time, at ten minutes to six, and this time the offices were closed and all he heard was the answering machine. '*If you know the extension of the person you're calling, you may press that number now …*'

He pressed Joe's extension and all he got was Joe's desktop answering machine. '*Hi, this is Joe Garboden … I'm away from my desk right now …* '

He held the receiver up so that Victor could hear the message, too. 'Something's wrong,' he said. 'I just hope he hasn't had an accident.'

Victor shook his head. 'I shouldn't worry too much. He probably met somebody and got held up.'

Michael called Kevin Murray, but Kevin Murray's mother said he was away for the weekend in Maine. He called Artur Rolbein, and Artur agreed to meet him at 2 p.m. the following day. All the same, he sounded oddly guarded.

'Is everything okay?' Michael asked him.

'Oh, for sure. It's just that the word is, the O'Brien investigation is firmly closed.'

'Have you seen Dr Moorpath's report?'

'I haven't read it yet but it was mentioned on the four o'clock news.'

'And what do you think?'

'I don't think anything. The investigation's closed. Accidental death, Plymouth coughs up.'

'Do *you* believe that it was accidental death?'

There was a lengthy silence. Then Artur Rolbein said, 'I'm working on something else now.'

'Artur … I need your opinion on this.'

'I'll talk to you tomorrow,' said Artur, and put the phone down so quickly that Michael didn't even have time to say 'Goodbye.'

Victor swigged beer from the bottle and said, 'What did I tell you? Tread very, *very* carefully indeed.'

Twelve

He kept on calling Joe every half hour until well after
midnight. He called the Highway Patrol but the Highway
Patrol had no reports of any accidents in Barnstable or
Plymouth counties involving a metallic-blue Cadillac. A
man and a woman had died on 495 just north-east of West
Wareham in a head-on collision with a refrigerated
Kenworth semi, but they had been travelling in a silver
Lincoln. A Camaro had been found burned out on 151, but
there was no sign of injury, and the Highway Patrol had
assumed that somebody had torched a stolen or broken-
down vehicle, either to hide the evidence or to claim the
insurance. In the end, Michael decided to call it a night.

Victor was already lying on the couch, covered in a
pond-green woven blanket, his glasses folded on the floor
beside him.

'No luck?' he said, as Michael put down the phone.

'I don't know where the hell he's got to.'

'Oh, come on ... we'll find him tomorrow in Boston.
What time do you want to leave?'

'Early. I'm supposed to be seeing Dr Rice at quarter to
ten, but I can cancel.'

'Does that really help you, that hypnotherapy?'

'I don't know. Sometimes I think it makes me even more
screwy than I was to start with. But other times ... well, it
gives me the strength to do things that I might not have
been able to do without it.'

'We were talking about post-hypnotic suggestion this
morning. Does Dr Rice give you any of that?'

Michael gathered together the Kennedy photographs on his desk. 'Only in pretty general terms. You know, like, "today you're going to feel more positive." '

'And you *do* feel more positive?'

'For sure, yes. Some days it works better than others, but it works.'

'He doesn't tell you to do anything specific – like start tapdancing in the middle of the street, or kiss every woman you see wearing a blue dress, or anything like that?'

Michael smiled. 'He'd better not try.'

'He could actually do that, though?'

'Oh, sure. Most people think that they could never be hypnotized, and that they would never respond to post-hypnotic suggestion. But it's incredible what a good hypnotist can make people do. And all that stuff about people not doing anything that's against their inner nature, or anything dangerous or life-threatening ... that's all nonsense. A skilled modern hypnotist could induce you to jump off the John Hancock Tower, or to step in front of a bus, or whatever he wanted.'

'That's what I've been thinking.'

Michael turned to him. 'What do you mean?'

'I've been thinking about Frank Coward, the guy who was piloting the helicopter when the O'Brien family was killed.'

'And?'

'Whatever progress we make with this investigation, we keep coming back to the helicopter crash. Okay – we accept that the O'Brien party were probably murdered, and we accept that Sissy O'Brien was abducted. But how was it done? How did the perpetrator know exactly where the helicopter was going to come down, unless Frank Coward brought it down there deliberately?'

Michael said, 'You think that Frank Coward could have crashed the helicopter under post-hypnotic suggestion?'

'It's a thought, that's all. He wasn't terminally ill. Thomas Boyle told me that the police have been through all of his bank accounts and all of his savings accounts and all of his recent expenditure, and there's no evidence at all that he was bribed. He didn't buy himself a new car or book a holiday to Acapulco or even treat his wife to a side-by-side icebox. Granted – he could have been prepared to commit suicide to kill the O'Brien party. Look at some of those Middle East terrorists who drive trucks of explosives into US Army installations. Look at the woman who killed Rajiv Gandhi. But – I don't know, a suicide mission doesn't really figure, does it? Not by an American pilot, to kill a Supreme Court justice. Doesn't ring true.'

Michael thought about it, and then he said, 'Okay, that's an interesting theory. Maybe I will keep that appointment with Dr Rice tomorrow morning. I can ask him about it.'

Victor lay back on the couch. He crossed himself.

Michael was just about to switch off the light. 'Do you always do that?'

'It's just a habit. My grandmother taught me to do it, when I was a kid. Keeps away the lily-white boys, that's what she said.'

'The lily-white boys? Who were the lily-white boys, when they were at home?'

'I don't really know. Some old Jewish folk-legend from Poland. They came at night and stole your soul, something like that. She would never really tell me. All the time she talked about them, she used to cross herself over and over.'

Michael switched off the light. 'Sleep well, then,' he said. 'And – uh, maybe I should cross myself too.'

Marcia called him at six in the morning and told him in a trembling voice that Joe still hadn't come home. She'd phoned all of his friends, she'd phoned the police and the

Highway Patrol, she'd phoned the hospitals. There was no trace of him anywhere.

'Maybe he got delayed for some reason, and decided to stop off at a hotel,' Michael suggested, even though he didn't believe it for a moment.

'He would have *called*, Michael. He always calls.'

'Well, I'll be back in Boston round lunchtime. If he's not back in the office by then, I'll call round and see you.'

'Oh dear God, I hope he's all right,' said Marcia. 'He's been under such a strain with this O'Brien case.'

'Strain?' asked Michael. He was quite surprised. 'What kind of a strain?'

'It seemed to worry him so much. It seemed to *frighten* him. A couple of weeks ago, he said that there were things going on that nobody knew about. A sort of secret society, that's what he called it. He said that he'd noticed it years ago, and that he hadn't really believed it to begin with, but now he had proof.'

Michael thought of the Kennedy photographs. What on earth had Joe discovered? Maybe it was some kind of connection between the Kennedy assassination and the O'Brien killings? A mob connection, maybe, like Sam Giancana or Bugsy Siegel? Or a secret society of hired political hit-men? Whatever it was, 'He didn't say anything to me,' he told Marcia.

'I know,' said Marcia. She paused, and he could hear the tears in her voice. 'I'm sorry, Michael, maybe he should. But he said he wasn't going to tell anybody until he was completely sure. That's why he didn't want you on the case. He said you were bound to find out what was going on, and that you might blow the whistle before he had enough proof.'

Michael frowned. 'What do you mean, he didn't want me on the case? He came down here and asked me specially. He literally begged me.'

'He had to. Edgar Bedford wanted you, and Joe didn't have any choice.'

Michael was astounded. 'Marcia, I simply can't believe this. Joe actually didn't want me to take over this investigation?'

'He said it was far too dangerous. He said there was far too much to lose. He tried not to show it, but he was absolutely terrified. He used to lie awake at night, shaking. That's why I'm worried now.'

'I'll talk to you later,' Michael assured her, and put down the phone. He was still sitting at the kitchen table staring at it when Patsy came in, wearing nothing but a checkered shirt.

'What's the matter?' she asked him. 'Michael? You look like you've seen a ghost.'

After breakfast, Michael and Victor drove into Hyannis to keep Michael's therapy appointment with Dr Rice. They had tried calling Joe yet again, but he hadn't reached the office and his mobile phone was still dead. It was a hot, bright morning with scarcely any wind, and the streets of Hyannis looked to Michael as if he were seeing them in a highly-polished mirror.

'Maybe he's gone into hiding,' said Victor, his head lolling back against the seat, his arm resting on the open car window.

Michael parked in front of Dr Rice's office. 'I hope so. I'm really worried.'

They walked into the reception area. Inside, it was gloomy and chilly after the heat of the street outside. A large potted cheese-plant dipped and shivered in the flow from the air-conditioner. The receptionist's desk was empty, and the lights on her telephone switchboard were blinking with incoming calls. Her swivel chair was tilted away from the desk at a sharp angle, as if she had got up in a hurry, and her pocketbook was lying on its side on the carpet, with a comb and a lipstick and a set of keys half-spilled out of it.

Michael looked around. 'Strange,' he said.

'Maybe she took five to go to the bathroom,' said Victor.

'Unh-hunh. When girls go to the bathroom, they take their combs and their lipsticks with them.'

'I'm impressed,' said Victor, looking at him sharply. 'You should have been an insurance investigator.'

Michael approached the mahogany-veneered door which led to Dr Rice's office. It was slightly ajar – only an inch or two, but all the same he knocked on it and called out, 'Dr Rice? Dr Rice? It's Michael Rearden. I came for my appointment.'

He pushed the door open and it stuck. He pushed again, but there was something lying on the floor, something soft and heavy which prevented him from pushing it any further – like a mattress, or a –

He pushed again, and saw a stockinged foot.

A stockinged foot that lolled as he pushed against it, lifelessly.

'Jesus,' he said.

'What's the matter?' asked Victor.

'There's a body resting up against the door. A woman's body. I can see her foot.'

Victor peered around the door, and then stood back. 'If the perpetrator left her up against the door, then he's probably still in there. Either that, or he's escaped out of the back.'

Michael felt perspiration crawling down his back, inside of his shirt. 'Maybe we should call the police.'

'Aw, come on,' Victor retorted. 'We practically *are* the police. Leastways, I am.'

Michael hesitated, and then he went back up to the door and called out, 'Dr Rice? Are you there? It's Michael Rearden!'

They waited almost half a minute, but there was still no reply. At last, Victor said, 'We don't have any choice, do we? Let's kick the bastard down.'

They stood side by side in the reception area, holding on to each others' shoulders to balance themselves. For the first time since he had worked with his father, caulking decks and varnishing transoms, Michael felt a strong sense of companionship: this was something that they were doing together, without discussion. Victor was skinny and Victor was wily. He wasn't the kind of guy that Michael normally would have numbered as a friend. But there was something alarmingly direct about him. You knew he wouldn't try to bullshit you, and you knew that if you ever had to call on him, he'd help you, without even thinking about it.

Or not, depending on his mood.

'You ready?' said Victor. 'One, two, three, ready or not – *Kick*!'

Together, they kicked at the door. Their combined strength was very much greater than they had anticipated. The door exploded off its hinges and cracked completely in half, falling into the corridor beyond in a broken, tented shape, covering the body of the woman who lay just behind it.

Michael stepped awkwardly over the door, and Victor followed him. Together, they lifted the door up and pushed it back into the reception area, where it tilted against the receptionist's desk, like a drunk who teeters but refuses to fall down.

On the floor lay the body of Dr Rice's receptionist. Michael recognized her long brunette hair immediately. Her peach silk blouse had been dragged up at the back, and her pantihose had been dragged downward, exposing the small of her back, her bottom and her upper thighs. Her skin was white as pork fat. There were two puncture wounds

314

in the small of her back, not much blood, but very deep, as if she had been attacked with an office hole-puncher.

'It's them again,' said Michael, his voice quiet with shock.

Victor peered closely at the puncture wounds. 'Exactly the same.'

Michael was just about to say, 'I'm going to call Thomas Boyle,' when the offices were filled with a terrible, agonized scream. It was a *male* scream, that's what made it worse – the scream of a man who has been trying not to admit that he is suffering undendurable pain but at last has to let it out.

Without a word, they hurried to the door and Michael kicked it wide open. It slammed back against the wall, juddered, and there was Dr Rice, sitting in his Oggetti chair, his face stiffly crumpled up like an old and filthy handkerchief, his fingernails digging so deep into the palms of his hands that dark red blood was welling up between his knuckles, his whole body bent and crunched-up.

He looked like a medieval cripple, a leper who would drag himself from one market to another, and who would sit on the steps of the Holy Church, crying for mercy, begging for alms. Beside him stood two tall, wary, white-faced young men, their eyes concealed by intensely dark glasses. They wore black, these young men, as if they were priests or morticians or jazz musicians or agents of some Satanic sect. In a frightening way, they were cool. Jason would have said they were cool. But the one on the right was holding up a long-handled pair of industrial bolt-cutters, the really big mothers that could cut through steel bars the diameter of a man's ankles; or *even* a man's ankles.

And they had.

Dr Rice's bloodied feet lay on the floor, ten inches below his ankles. They still wore chestnut-coloured wingtip Oxfords, and they still wore green-and-yellow Argyle socks. One foot lay on its side; the other foot still stood

315

upright. Ten inches above them, his leg-bones protruded from the cringing scarlet flesh of his severed ankles, and blood pumped from his tibial arteries in terrible, rhythmic spurts.

Michael heard himself shout, ' – doing, what are you *doing*!' before he launched himself at the man with the bolt-cutters and seized his bolt-cutters and swung him around so that his back collided with Dr Rice's file-cabinet. The white-faced young man was ridiculously light, and Michael was amazed that he had managed to throw him with such force. The file-cabinet rocked on its base, although it didn't fall over. The young man, however, must have cracked his back, because he lay with his face pressed against the heather-coloured carpet, trembling like a poleaxed calf.

With scarcely a second's hesitation, Michael swung the bolt-cutters around and caught the second young man a sharp glancing blow on the side of the neck, just beneath his ear. He stumbled, overbalanced, and dropped to one knee, holding onto the stereo rack for support. He was just about to get up again when Victor stepped forward with all the intensity of a trained boxer and punched him on the bridge of the nose, and then his right cheekbone, and then his right temple, and then his right temple again. The young man made another attempt to climb to his feet, but then he teetered over sideways, and collapsed onto the floor beside his companion.

Dr Rice had stopped screaming; but his blood hadn't stopped pumping out. The carpet beneath his chair was dark and soaking. He was shaking. In fact he was almost jumping up and down in his seat.

'Call an ambulance!' Victor snapped. He yanked off his necktie and bound it around Dr Rice's left ankle, and knotted it, and pulled it ferociously tight. The flow of blood decreased from a steady, arterial pumping to a slow, thick crimson ooze. Victor dragged off Dr Rice's flowery silk necktie and tied a tourniquet on his right ankle, too, until that had stopped bleeding.

Michael said, 'Ambulance is on its way.'

The first young man was already crawling onto his feet. Michael shouted at him, 'Stay where you are!'

'Are you kidding me?' the young man retorted, although his voice was thick with concussion.

'Just stay where you are, you're under arrest.'

'Oh ... is that it?' the young man mocked him. 'Do I have the right to remain silent? Do I have the right to be represented by an attorney? Do I have the right not to stay here while you hand me out all of that boring flatulent ageist bullshit?'

'You stay where you are,' Michael warned him.

Defiantly, the young man went for the door, but Michael immediately stepped across, snatched hold of his arm, and smashed him up against the wall.

He was immediately ashamed of himself. He hadn't needed to act so violently. He may have looked under-weight; and he wouldn't have been any match at all for anybody who was seriously intent on hurting him. But he was fit; and he had a certain hardness; and, apart from that, he was coming to terms with all of those human bodies that had fallen out of the sky over Rocky Woods. He was discovering a sense of courage that was well over and above anything that had been required of him by the Plymouth Insurance Company, if only they had understood it.

He glanced at Victor and Victor's eyes were gleaming and Michael knew that he felt the same. They had unofficially appointed themselves the Clean-Up Crew.

'Who sent you here?' Michael demanded, of the first young man.

317

'Nobody … no one,' the young man replied. His accent was oddly stilted, a little like Salem or Marblehead or even further north, practically English.

'Call the ambulance again,' said Victor, pressing his hand over Dr Rice's forehead. 'He's going into shock.'

'Hold on,' Michael warned the first young man. He picked up the phone and punched out 911. He repeated his call for an ambulance.

'You want another ambulance?'

'Of course not, for Christ's sake, just tell the first ambulance to step on it.'

'Sir, believe me, they always do.'

Michael put down the phone. As he did so, the first young man said, 'We'll have to go now.'

'What?' Michael retorted. 'You're staying here.'

'I'm sorry, we have to go.'

'You're going to stay and that's final.'

The young man lowered his head and turned his back. For a split second, Michael really believed that he was going to do what he was told. But then he whipped around so fast that Michael didn't even see him, and struck Michael on the collarbone with something hard and heavy – a paper-weight, maybe, or a doorstop, whatever he had managed to scoop up.

The pain exploded in Michael's shoulder like a bomb blast. He fell back against Dr Rice's desk, tried to catch his balance, couldn't, and dropped onto one knee. The second young man, almost simultaneously, had kick-boxed Victor in the left-hand side of his ribcage. Then both of them ducked out of the office door, and dodged right towards the back of the building.

Victor screamed, 'Look after him! Watch his breathing!' and went after the two young men like a terrier. Michael heard the building's back door being kicked open, followed immediately by the ringing of an alarm bell. He heard running and shouting.

Rubbing his bruised shoulder, he climbed to his feet and stood close to Dr Rice. Dr Rice's eyelids had been flickering in shock, but now he opened them, and stared at Michael in agonized recognition.

'The medics are on their way,' Michael reassured him, taking hold of his hand.

'Hope they're bringing some Crazy Glue,' whispered Dr Rice.

'Don't worry ... you'll survive. You may not even lose your feet. It's fantastic what they can do with microsurgery.'

Dr Rice shivered. His nails were very long and dry-ridged, and they dug into Michael's fingers. 'They told me that I wouldn't need feet, where I was going.'

'They were trying to kill you?'

'Of course they were trying to kill me. Just like everyone else who discovers what they're up to.'

'And what *are* they up to?'

Dr Rice gave him a sickly, wavering smile. 'Believe me, Michael, you don't want to know.'

'But why did they pick on you?'

'Why do you think? They picked on me because I was the best. They picked on me because I could use my aura.'

He winced, and coughed, and for a moment Michael thought that he was going to die, right then and there, right in front of him.

But after a while he lifted his trembling hand, and wiped his mouth, and said, 'There are only six or seven of us – as far as I know.'

Michael squeezed his hand. He couldn't bear to look down at his oozing ankles.

'Six or seven of what?' he asked.

'Aura-hypnotists. Didn't you know that? I'm an aura-hypnotist. Something we learned back in the Sixties. Something you can't understand unless you've seen yourself from the outside.'

There was a very long silence. Dr Rice lay back in his chair and it was obvious that he was beginning to feel the pain of his amputation for the very first time. He clutched Michael's hand like a vulture in rigor mortis, and his breathing was shallow and distressed.

In the distance, they heard the wailing of a siren.

'Listen,' said Michael. 'They're on their way.'

Dr Rice gripped his hand even tighter. 'I can't explain everything – there isn't time. But take my notebook … take my Filofax … desk drawer, top right. And take that book on the shelf next to the Sheeler … the green one …'

The ambulance slithered to a halt outside the office. Michael could see its red lights flashing through the half-closed blinds.

'Something else …' Dr Rice whispered.

'It's all right,' Michael reassured him. 'You can tell me later. Let's just get you into hospital.'

'No, Michael … there's something else … something you have to know …'

'Listen … forget it. Tell me as soon as you're well.'

But Dr Rice clung to him, and even tried to pull himself up in his chair. 'The pilot …' he whispered.

'Dr Rice – '

'*Listen to me!*' Dr Rice interrupted him. 'The pilot, Frank Coward … he was one of my patients … they sent him here for Aura Hypnosis so that I could tell him what to do … so that Mr Hillary could tell him what to do.'

'I don't understand,' said Michael.

'Read my diary … read the books … then you'll know.'

'Victor said that Frank Coward could have crashed that helicopter because he was told to, under hypnosis.'

'Well, Victor's right – whoever Victor is. He's on the right track, in any case. But listen – '

At that moment, they heard knocking at the front door, and a paramedic's voice calling out, 'Hallo? Anybody there? Paramedics!'

'In here!' Michael shouted out.

'*Please!*' hissed Dr Rice. '*You have to listen!*'

'Bill, this woman's dead,' said a voice, in the corridor outside.

'*Please!*' Dr Rice begged, clutching at Michael's sleeve, the bloody stumps of his ankles thrashing up and down in anxiety. '*I've done the same to you!*'

'What?' asked Michael, staring down at him in bewilderment.

'I've done the same to you. The same as I did to Frank Coward.'

'What do you mean?' Michael demanded; but Dr Rice didn't answer. Instead, he groped into his pocket with his free hand, and took something out. Something small, about the size of a quarter, only thicker. He pressed it into Michael's palm, and then closed his fingers over it.

At that moment two hefty cropheaded paramedics walked into the office.

'Christ,' said one of them. 'He's lost both of his feet.'

Michael frantically shook Dr Rice's arm. 'What do you mean about Frank Coward?' he repeated. 'What do you mean, you've done the same to me?'

But Dr Rice's eyelids wavered and drooped, and his head suddenly dropped to one side, his upper lip caught on his canine teeth in the faintest parody of a snarl.

'Come on, pal,' said the paramedic, easing Michael away from him. 'This guy needs all the expert help he can get.'

The second paramedic kneeled on the floor and distastefully picked up Dr Rice's feet. 'We've got to get these into ice,' he said. 'Then we've got to get this poor bastard into hospital like five minutes ago.'

Michael heard another siren outside; then another; then car doors slamming. The police had been summoned. At the same time, Victor came in through the back door, gasping for breath. 'Couldn't catch them,' he panted. 'They went around the corner by the Copper Kettle and then they just weren't there any more.'

A heavy-bellied cop in a sharply-pressed uniform stepped into the room, too. He blinked at Victor and then he blinked at Michael and then he blinked at Dr Rice.

'God Almighty,' he said. Then, 'Good God Almighty.'

Thirteen

He met Artur Rolbein at The Rat, on Commonwealth Avenue, which was a dive he hadn't visited in years. It had everything a dive should have: a smoky atmosphere, pounding music, sticky floors, cheap drinks, and the mix of people that a Martian anthropologist would have taken back to the red planet in his flying saucer to demonstrate the breadth and depth of human civilization, from rambunctious Boston College beer-swiller to ultra-cool brother to giggling Inuit.

He was running four hours late. The Hyannis police had interviewed both him and Victor for over two hours each, and had only released them on the condition that they travelled no further than the Hub, and that they were available to return to Hyannis at any time for further questioning.

Dr Rice had been flown to Boston Central for urgent

microsurgery. His feet had been packed in ice and were carried beside him in two aluminium boxes. Fortunately for Michael and Victor, he had given police a description of his assailants and had insisted that neither Michael nor Victor had touched him. 'They came in ... they saved my life.'

Artur Rolbein was wedged tightly into a corner table. He was thin and angular, like an architect's lamp, and his black dandruffy hair was cut into a wavy bowl. His eyes protruded whenever he swallowed, and he had thick, deep-red lips, as if he were wearing make-up.

Michael asked him what he wanted to drink and he said, 'Seven-Up.'

'You're sure?'

'I can't touch alcohol. It gives me hives.'

Michael ordered a Lowenbrau draught. The stereo system was thumping out 'Perpetual Dawn – The Long Remix'. He took a deep, cold drink, and then he said, 'I guess I should have talked to you earlier. Your file on O'Brien was very illuminating.'

Artur Rolbein sniffed and shrugged and looked away. 'Well, as I say, I'm not working on O'Brien any longer.'

'You can't really believe that it was accidental.'

'I'll believe what it's safe to believe.'

'And you don't think it's safe to suggest that this was premeditated homicide? That John O'Brien was assassinated?'

'It's not a word I'd bandy around the office, let's put it that way.'

'Because of why?'

'Because of certain people who come and go.'

'Oh, yes, and who are they?'

Artur Rolbein glanced around the crowded dive with theatrical nervousness, as if he were in a play and had been told to 'act nervous'.

'Joe Garboden can tell you more than me.'

'Joe Garboden's frightened, too, as far as I can tell.'

'Well, so he should be,' said Artur Rolbein. 'I mean, you want to die a horrible death, or what?'

'Artur, this is important,' Michael insisted. 'You have to tell me what this is all about.'

Artur Rolbein took a deep breath, and then he covered his face with his hand, so that his eyes peered out from between his fingers, like a mask. When he spoke, he spoke very quickly, in a low monotonous gabble, and the thumping of 'Perpetual Dawn' made it nearly impossible for Michael to hear what he was saying.

'You read my file. I made a percentage allowance for fate … I mean, that's what insurance is all about. But the odds against the O'Brien helicopter crashing accidentally at a spot on the shoreline where somebody was waiting to kill them were far too great for even a reasonable underwriter to tolerate. And, let's face it, there's no such creature as a reasonable underwriter.

'I went to Kevin with everything I knew … the Masky interview, and all the statistics. Kevin had managed to dig out some of the FAA's technical findings and he agreed with me. So we went to Joe Garboden and he agreed that the whole thing was pretty damned strange, to say the least. On the face of it, it looked as if the O'Brien crash was suspicious death at the very least, and that it could amount to conspiracy to commit multiple homicide.'

'So what happened?' asked Michael. 'You and Kevin were hot on the trail. Why did Joe suddenly take you off it, and offer it to me? He told me himself that he didn't particularly want me to do it.'

Artur Rolbein sipped his Seven-Up without taking his hand away from his face. 'Edgar Bedford told him to do it.'

'But – come on, Artur, it doesn't make any sense. Edgar

Bedford knew that I was invalided out. He knew that I was undergoing therapy. Why did he think that I could handle a major investigation better than you guys?'

'Don't ask me,' said Artur Rolbein. 'But Joe said that even Edgar Bedford was having to obey orders.'

'Edgar Bedford? The great autocratic Boston billionaire? You've got to be joking.'

'Joe was sure of it. He was kind of round-and-about, the way he explained it. He said that there were people who came and went. He'd seen them in Edgar Bedford's office, he'd seen them in the mayor's office, he'd seen them everyplace.'

'What people?'

'I don't know, *people*. He said that once you'd realized who they were, you could always recognize them. He was building up some kind of a file on the subject. Maybe he was paranoid, maybe the job was getting him down. He's my boss, so I didn't try to second-guess him. But O'Brien was a multiple homicide, an assassination, I'm sure of that. I don't know how it was done. The helicopter could have been crashed by remote control, who knows? We live in a technological age, right? If a nine-year-old kid can get to the top level on Sonic the Hedgehog, an adult engineer can find a way of crashing a helicopter wherever he wants to. There's always a way of fixing everything. The *how* of it is not the point.'

'So, what is the point?' Michael asked him.

'The point is, on the afternoon that Joe Garboden told Kevin and me that we were off the O'Brien investigation, he passed a piece of paper across his desk, so that we could read it while we were talking.'

'Go on.'

Artur Rolbein was obviously frightened and upset. He took his hand away from his face and there were tears in his eyes. 'I'll never forget it. The piece of paper said, "Please

Agree, No Arguments, OK, Otherwise They'll Kill You."
Then he turned it over, and on the back he'd written "I'm
Serious." '

'So you agreed,' said Michael, feeling grim. He wished
that Joe were home, so that he could talk to him.

Artur Rolbein wiped his eyes with his fingers and gave
him a bitter smile. 'Wouldn't you?'

They shook hands outside The Rat and agreed to keep in
touch. The evening was warm and Commonwealth Avenue
was thronged with passers-by. Outside the brick façade with
its Germanic *Rathskeller* sign, they could still hear the insistent throb of music. Artur Rolbein said he would probably
walk part of the way home: he wanted to visit a friend on
Boylston Street. Michael hailed a cab.

'Where do you want to be?' the driver asked him.

'Cantina Napoletana, Hanover Street.'

They drove through the evening rush hour. It was almost
dark now, a turmoil of lights and honking cars. Lights
flashed on top of the Prudential Center and Sixty State
Street. Two National Guard Chinooks thundered overhead.
The cab driver glanced in his rear-view mirror and Michael
saw that one of his eyes was darkly bloodshot. 'Looks like
it's war,' the cab driver remarked.

'I didn't hear the latest,' Michael told him. 'Is the rioting
still going on?'

'The cops are still shooting innocent bystanders, if that's
what you mean.'

'Hey,' said Michael. 'I'm not getting political here.'

'Who's getting political?' the driver retorted. 'This is the
day of atonement, aint it? This aint political, this is biblical.'

'Whatever it is, it's a crying shame,' said Michael.

'It's the day of atonement,' the driver repeated. 'I always
knew it was going to come, and now it has.'

He dropped Michael off at the Cantina Napoletana. He handed Michael his change, fixing him with his one good eye and his one bloodshot eye. 'It's a burnt offering, that's what it is,' he said, with aggressive over-emphasis. 'An offering by fire of a soothing aroma to the Lord.'

'A what?'

'A so – o – othing aroma,' the cab driver replied, and steered off into the traffic.

Standing on the sidewalk outside the Cantina Napoletana, amidst all the normality of a summer evening on Hanover Street, with the smells of Italian cooking and gasoline fumes and Boston Harbor and diesel oil and women's perfume, Michael knew for certain that Joe was right, and that Joe had discovered something strange and terrible in the fabric of everyday life.

It must have been like discovering a hideous face in the pattern of a familiar wallpaper. Once you've noticed it, you can never look at the wallpaper again without seeing that same hideous face, endlessly repeated.

He climbed the stairs to his apartment and unlocked the door. All the lights were on, and Thelonious Monk was playing 'Nice Work If You Can Get It' on the CD. Victor was there already, his feet up on the couch, sipping alternately from a cup of espresso and a shot-glass of Jack Daniels.

'I've been waiting for you,' he said, taking off his glasses, and putting down the notebook that he had been reading. Beside him on the couch were the other books that Michael had taken from Dr Rice's office: his Filofax, and the green-bound volume from the shelf beside the Sheeler painting. While the Hyannis police had been helping the paramedics to carry Dr Rice to the ambulance, Michael had simply slipped them into a large manila envelope marked NEW ENGLAND DEACONESS HOSPITAL and walked out of the office with the envelope under his arm.

'It looks like Frank Coward had been a patient of Dr Rice's for quite a few years,' said Victor. 'Dr Rice was giving him hypnotherapy for recurring nightmares and panic attacks. Apparently poor old Frank kept seeing two old buddies from his service days. The unnerving thing was that *he* was twenty years older, while *they* hadn't aged at all.'

'Is there anything to indicate that Frank Coward might have been given post-hypnotic suggestion?'

Victor licked his finger and leafed quickly back through the pages. 'This struck me as a possible clue,' he said, and handed the book over.

There was a short, scribbled entry in Dr Rice's own handwriting, in vivid purple ink. 'April 6, H called 11 am to ask about Frank's progress & gnrl condition. Of course I told him that I am satisfied that Frank is ready to help us and will be even easier to galvanize than Lesley Kellow.'

Michael lowered the book and stared at Victor wide-eyed. 'Lesley Kellow! Do you know who Lesley Kellow was?'

'Should I?'

'Lesley Kellow was the co-pilot of the L10—11 that exploded and crashed over Rocky Woods.'

'You're kidding me.'

'Absolutely not. Not that there was much of him left afterwards. Bits, literally. Little bits and pieces, exactly like a jigsaw, only flesh and bone. In fact, he was more severely injured than anybody else on the aircraft.'

'How did the plane come down?' asked Victor.

'We never found out for sure. But the most plausible theory was that somebody had planted a bomb, somewhere in the mid-section. Not in the hold, but in the passenger compartment, between rows 20-23, right between the wings. The bottom of the airplane opened up like God was shelling peas, and everybody dropped out.'

Victor nodded. 'I remember seeing it on TV.'

Michael said, 'Look at this – a definite connection. Frank Coward and Lesley Kellow were both given hypnotherapy by Dr Rice. And there's another connection, too, that Joe mentioned. It's only a *possible* connection, but it's a connection all the same. John O'Brien was killed in the helicopter crash, and in the Rocky Woods disaster, Dan Margolis died. You remember Dan Margolis, don't you, the guy who was going to clean up the Colombian drugs trade? Two liberal campaigners, both killed in aircraft piloted by patients of Dr Rice.'

'And another connection, too,' Victor put in. 'The men behind the fence on the grassy knoll, when Kennedy was shot. Another liberal campaigner.'

They were both silent for a moment, reluctant to voice the next logical conclusion out loud. It was too far-fetched; too dramatic. It was like finding out that the South Pole was supposed to be at the top of the world, and that the North Pole was supposed to be underneath.

'Conspiracy?' said Victor, at last.

'Pretty incredible kind of conspiracy if it is,' Michael replied. 'And what's the motive? What's the political agenda?'

'That's what we'll have to find out,' said Victor.

Michael read Dr Rice's scribble a second time. 'We could start with finding out who this "H" is. If "H" was interested to know if Frank Coward was ready for action, then it seems likely that "H" is Dr Rice's contact with the conspirators. Always assuming there *are* any conspirators.'

Victor thumbed through Dr Rice's Filofax. 'Hmm – he knows plenty of "H's". Julius Habgood, dental surgeon. Kerry Hastings, florist. Norman T. Henry.'

Michael went across to the table and picked up the telephone. 'I'll give Marcia another call, see if there's any sign of Joe.'

'Mason Herridge, realtor. Ruth Hersov, realtor. Jacob Hertzman, psychiatrist.'

Michael punched out Joe's number and Marcia answered almost instantaneously. 'Joe?' she asked, her voice bleached with worry.

'No, I'm sorry, Marcia, it's Michael. There's still no sign?'

'Nothing. Nobody's seen him, nobody's heard from him.'

'I'm sure he's okay. He probably doesn't even realize how worried you are.'

'You don't believe that, do you? Joe wouldn't just vanish without telling me. He's irritable sometimes, he's impatient sometimes, but he's never cruel.'

'Is there anything I can do?' Michael asked her.

'Joe Hesteren, auto repairs,' Victor intoned. 'Joyce Hewitt. Leonard Heyderman.'

'Just keep in touch,' Marcia begged. 'My sister's coming over tomorrow, but I feel so all alone.'

Michael put down the phone. He was gravely worried about Joe. He had the terrible leaden feeling that Joe was dead; and that he would never see him again, ever, except in his casket.

'Here's an odd one,' said Victor.

'What's that?' asked Michael.

'It's the only entry without a first name, that's all. It probably doesn't mean anything.'

Michael walked around the couch and peered over Victor's shoulder. Victor was pointing to the neatly lettered name and address, *Mr Hillary, Goat's Cape* and then a 508 telephone number.

Michael felt a chilly prickling all the way down his back, and he couldn't suppress an involuntary shiver.

'Mr Hillary,' he repeated. 'That's the man I saw when I was under hypnosis. That's the name that the blind man told me by Copley Place.'

330

Victor turned around. 'Jesus,' he said. 'You're white as a sheet.'

'But I didn't realize that Mr Hillary was real.'

'What are you worried about? It's perfectly explicable. Dr Rice put the name into your mind while he was hypnotizing you. He may not have even mentioned the name to you directly ... maybe he was talking on the phone to Mr Hillary while you were under.'

'But I *saw* Mr Hillary. I know exactly what he looks like.'

'That doesn't mean anything, necessarily. What probably happened was, you heard the name Mr Hillary while you were in a trance, and your imagination fleshed him out for you. I'll bet if you go back into your memory, you'll think of somebody you once knew who looked like that, or maybe a character in a book, or on TV – somebody with a name that sounded like Hillary.'

'I never knew anybody who looked like this guy. And anyway, how come that blind man mentioned his name to me?'

'I don't know. You probably misheard. Or maybe it was a hangover from your hypnotic trance.'

'Who are you, Mr Sceptical or something?' Michael asked him.

Victor smiled. 'I'm a medical examiner. I was trained to be sceptical. I don't mind following clues and connections, and trying to put two and two together. But I don't believe in magic and I don't believe that you can see people under hypnosis when you've never seen them in real life.'

Michael picked up the Filofax. 'Mr Hillary, Goat's Cape. Where the hell's Goat's Cape?'

'I don't know. Do you have a map?'

Michael went down to the street and got his tattered Rand McNally route map out of the glovebox of the car. The sidewalks were still crowded and busy, and across the street a young man with long sweeping black hair was playing the violin – one of those high and hungry passages that always reminded Michael of Gothic movies, with white-faced women in deserted mansions, hurrying in terror from room to room.

Michael was locking the car when he noticed somebody else across the street, too. A man in very dark glasses, standing in the doorway of DiLucca Italian Bakery, which was closed. Michael felt a prickle of apprehension. It was impossible to tell whether the man was staring at Michael or not, but he was standing so still, his arms by his sides, and it was his utter stillness in the midst of all the hurrying and jostling that made him appear so threatening.

Slowly, Michael retreated across the sidewalk, and back to the Cantina Napoletana. He turned around just once, before he went inside, and the man was still there, still motionless.

Back upstairs, he went to the window overlooking Hanover Street, but a large blue van had parked in front of DiLucca's and he was unable to see whether the man was still there or not.

'What's wrong?' asked Victor. He had poured himself another shot-glass of whisky and was reading through Dr Rice's notebook.

'I don't know … there was a guy standing in a doorway across the street. Pale face, dark glasses. He looked just like one those guys who were hanging around at New Seabury.'

'Is he still there now?'

'I don't know … I think he must have gone now.'

'Well … don't let's get paranoid,' said Victor.

Michael unfolded the map and laid it out on the table. He traced his finger all the way up the coastline from Acoaxet in the south to Salisbury Beach in the north.

Victor said, 'Did you know that Dr Rice practised Aura Hypnosis?'

'Yes, he mentioned it today. And he talked about my "aura" a couple of times when I was under therapy. I guessed he meant personal vibes. He said my aura was in pretty lousy shape.'

'That was all? He didn't tell you what he was trying to do?'

Michael looked up and frowned at him. 'He was trying to straighten my aura back into a shape. Kind of a Cindy Crawford workout, with Woody Allenish overtones.'

'But he didn't explain what Aura Hypnosis actually is?'

Michael pursed his lips. He found it irritating that Victor was questioning him so intently on a course of therapy which he, after all, had been experiencing first-hand for almost a year. 'Aura Hypnosis is hypnosis that sorts out your aura, that's all.'

'Well, for sure, it does in a way. But it works in a different way from regular hypnosis. It has the same therapeutic purpose … but the technique is different. Apparently it's much more powerful, much more direct. I was reading an article about it in *New Psychology* a couple of months ago, and if you can understand Advanced Mumbo-Jumbo, it's all explained here in this book.'

'Oh, yes?' said Michael, trying not to be testy. His finger had crept as far north as Priscilla Beach, just south of Plymouth. 'I thought you didn't believe in hypnosis. I thought you said the only hypnosis you'd ever witnessed was on the stage, people being persuaded to take their pants off, stuff like that.'

'Maybe I lied.'

Michael looked up. 'Maybe you *lied*? Why would you lie about something like that?'

Victor took off his glasses. His eyes looked bleary and

unfocused. 'I know what hypnosis did for me. I just wanted to find out what it had done for you.'

'So what did hypnosis do for you?'

'I've never been hypnotized myself. I wasn't lying about that. But my sister was, repeatedly, for months. She was very ill, you understand. It seemed to spare her a whole lot of pain. I suppose I just wanted to know if it was true – and if it really did ease her suffering.'

'Well, it works, I can guarantee it,' Michael told him.

Victor had folded down the corner of one of the pages in Dr Rice's book. 'Listen to this: "Aura Hypnosis was originally discovered by the Marquis de Puysegar in 1782. He was a pupil of Mesmer, the Viennese doctor who invented mesmerism. Mesmer used to use all kinds of elaborate magnetic equipment to hypnotize people, wires and magnets and bowls of water, but the Marquis de Puysegar proved that you didn't need any of this equipment ... all you needed was an optical focus like a light or a coin, and a soothing voice."

'What's more – listen to this – "he travelled to South America in the 1780s and found Peruvian Indians hypnotizing themselves for no other purpose than to let their auras leave their bodies and dance around their campfires to amuse their children." Can you believe that? Early television! "They were even having hypnotic duels with each other ... putting each other into hypnotic trances so that the aura of one warrior could physically leave his body and fight with the aura of another." It sounds like a certain amount of coca leaf chewing was involved in all of this, but basically that's what Aura Hypnotism is all about. The hypnotist's own personal aura actually leaves him for a while, and joins the patient's aura inside of his trance. What you might call "hands-on" hypnotism.'

'Go on,' said Michael, pausing in his map-reading.

Victor said, 'Dr Rice mentions Aura Hypnosis two or three times here. This is, what?, October last year. "*Michael Rearden's trauma is proving so intractable that I decided this session to take him under by Aura. The experience was horrifying. His state of shock is such that his etheric body has formed into dark knots of tension and dread, similar to extreme muscular spasm. It is one of the worst cases I have come across, even more difficult to deal with than Frank Coward's. If it were possible to X-ray his aura, one could identify each and every traumatic experience he had on that night, but as it is I have to do it by 'touch' and by 'feel'. I have never before encountered an etheric body so darkened and deformed.*" '

Michael grunted in amusement. 'He makes me sound like Quasimodo.'

'The Hunchback of Hyannis,' Victor smiled. 'All the same … he seems to think that Aura Hypnosis was helping to straighten you out. I guess you should be grateful, when you consider how dangerous it can be.'

'Dangerous? What do you mean?'

'In regular hypnotherapy, the hypnotist puts you into a light trance which has the effect of temporarily abolishing some of your cortical functions. You become highly suggestible, and so the hypnotherapist can guide you back to your childhood, or whenever your problem started – which in your case was the Rocky Woods air disaster. He helps you to locate and to understand your anxiety, and he simply suggests that it doesn't worry you any more. Wake up, snap, end of problem.'

'But Aura Hypnosis isn't like that?'

'Aura Hypnosis is more like physiotherapy … you know, when you've had an accident or something, and a therapist takes you into a pool and manipulates your muscles. In Aura Hypnosis, the hypnotist puts you into a very deep trance – so deep that your heartbeat slows and your respiration rate is

335

almost halved. Just as you're going in, his etheric body comes in with you. His aura is actually *inside* your trance with you. He can then "visit" your anxieties along with you, and help you to see that you don't have anything to be worried about.'

'What's dangerous about it?'

'For starters, your anxieties could be a whole lot more horrific than your hypnotist's aura is capable of dealing with. Whatever traumas have been distorting *your* aura might distort *his* aura, too. The danger is that the doctor will wind up just as sick as the patient. Even sicker, since his aura is outside of his body, and is much more vulnerable than usual.'

'Do you believe any of that?' asked Michael.

Victor nodded. 'You should have seen Ruth, my sister. In 1967, she contracted stomach cancer. She had the kind of pain you don't even want to think about. The only person who made her last days bearable was her hypnotherapist. She could have spent weeks in agony; instead he gave her weeks of bliss. He took her back through her childhood, he took her back through her wedding day. She relived all of her happiest moments. When she died she wasn't lying in a hospital bed in Newark, she was walking her dog at our uncle's home at Cos Cob, Connecticut.' He tapped his forehead. 'Inside of here, anyway.'

He paused for a while, his eyes glistening a little. Then he added, 'That was Aura Hypnosis, and what I didn't find out until years later was that when the hypnotherapist was taking Ruth under he suffered almost as much pain as Ruth was suffering herself. After Ruth died, he spent seven months in hospital with perforated ulcers. It almost killed him.'

Michael said, 'It's amazing that two people's personalities can be so *intertwined*. You know, so – what's the word – symbiotic.'

'Well, I'm not so sure that I believe in the collective

unconscious,' said Victor. 'But I sure believe that two people can become so magnetically close that they can share the same unconscious experiences. You love your wife. You should know that.'

'Yes,' said Michael, slowly. 'I guess I do. Maybe I forget it more often than I should.'

Victor closed Dr Rice's books and got up from the couch, in a deliberate attempt to break the mood. 'Come on, then,' he said, 'where's this Goat's Cape you're looking for?'

Michael continued to run his finger up the Massachusetts coastline. Past Boston Harbor, past Winthrop Beach and Revere Beach and Lynn Harbor. All of a sudden, there it was, and he was amazed that he had never noticed it before. Goat's Cape, on the southernmost shore of the Nahant promontory, a fragment of land which jutted into Massachusetts Bay at the very end of a three-mile isthmus, like a leaping dolphin on the end of a line.

Nahant – where they had found Sissy O'Brien's tortured body washed up on the beach; and about whose lighthouse Michael had dreamed in his deep hypnotic trance.

'Well, well, well,' said Victor, lifting his glasses on to his forehead and closely scrutinizing the map. 'This is all beginning to make some kind of sense.'

Michael turned away. His shadow on the wall looked enormous and threatening.

'It's real, isn't it?' he said, tightly. 'All this conspiracy stuff. It's real.'

'It's going to bear some further investigation, let's put it that way.'

'Yes,' said Michael, and he could almost feel the floor opening up underneath his feet.

There was nothing much more they could do that night

except drink and watch television and plan what they would do in the morning.

At ten o'clock, CBS flashed a live news bulletin from Seaver Street. There was no sound at first, but the picture told it all. A black reporter was standing in a debris-littered bar with automobiles and trucks burning in the background. Red-and-blue police lights flashed on his sweating face.

They heard him say, ' – *seven National Guardsman killed when their Chinook helicopter came down over Grove Hall, eighteen civilians missing – rioting now totally out of control – governor has declared a state of emergency –*'

'End of the world as we know it,' Victor remarked, drily.

Back in the studio, anchorman John Breezeman announced, 'We have just received a release from the White House that the president is "gravely concerned" about the rioting in Boston and has promised the governor his "wholehearted personal support." '

Michael got up and switched the television off. 'Let's get some sleep. I don't want to face the end of the world with a hangover.'

But that night, in the very small hours of the morning, Michael had the most extraordinary and frightening nightmare. He was falling through darkness, as he always fell, and he knew that other bodies were falling all around him.

But as he plunged through the night, he felt somebody jostling against him. Suddenly, he wasn't falling, but pushing his way through a crowd, and everybody was jostling him. They didn't jostle like a normal crowd, however. They did it stiffly and erratically, as if they were incapable of standing up by themselves, as if somebody was pushing them and pulling them to make them move.

As if they were dead.

338

Through the crowd, he glimpsed a man in a suit, and the man was smiling. He didn't speak, he simply waved; and as Michael pushed his way closer, he held out both of his hands, as if he wanted to catch hold of Michael, embrace him, take him into his arms.

Michael screamed at him, 'No! Don't come near me! Don't come near me!'

He wasn't afraid of the jiggling bodies all around him. He wasn't afraid of the man in the suit.

He was afraid of the harm that he himself was about to inflict. He was terrified of his own murderous intent.

If the man in the suit came any closer, Michael was sure that he would have to kill him. Slice him open, like a ripened canteloupe.

But the man kept smiling, and pushing his way nearer, and Michael couldn't turn around, couldn't escape, because of all of the dead jostling bodies.

He screamed out, '*No, Mr President, don't come near me! No, Mr President, no!*'

Fourteen

Thomas opened the door of his apartment for them and said, 'Come along in.' He was wearing a red checkered lumberjack shirt that showed his greying chest hair. He led the way into a living-room that was prettily decorated but comfortably untidy. There was an aromatic smell of cinnamon and cloves and apple pie, and the sun was shining through the church-like smoke of a recently extinguished cigarette.

'Have you heard the news?' Thomas asked, clearing

339

yesterday's newspapers from the couch. 'Half of Roxbury is burning. Two more National Guardsmen killed. It seems to be getting worse, instead of better.'

'We've got quite a few things to tell you,' said Victor, folding up his spectacles and tucking them into his shirt pocket. 'But first of all you're going to have to suspend your natural policeman's sense of disbelief.'

'Sit down,' said Thomas. 'Victor, you haven't met Megan, have you?'

Megan wheeled her way into the living-room. She was still wearing her off-white broderie anglaise apron, and her nose was smudged with flour. 'I'm so sorry,' she smiled. 'I was trying out an old Irish recipe for apple pie.'

'Hallo, Mrs Boyle,' said Michael. 'I'm Michael Rearden. We met just once, at the farmers' market in Cold Spring Park.'

'Yes, I remember,' Megan nodded. 'How have you been keeping?'

Michael made a wobbly gesture with his hand. 'A little off-balance, but not so bad. I came to have a word with Giraffe here, if that's okay.'

'Of course. Would you like some coffee?'

Thomas impatiently led them through to his den. There was a small sagging green-velveteen couch and a desk that was heaped with files and papers and magazines. On the walls hung scores of framed photographs of Boston Police Department get-togethers – drink-flushed detectives raising their glasses to the camera.

'Sit down,' said Thomas; and he and Victor sat side by side on the couch, rather uncomfortably, with their thighs pressed together. Thomas closed the door, then sat behind his desk and eased himself back in his old-fashioned wooden chair.

'This O'Brien investigation,' Michael began, 'it's opening up a whole great can of worms.'

340

Thomas lifted his hand. 'Before you start, I've had a message from the Barnstable County Sheriff's Department. They've found another body with puncture wounds in the back – just like Sissy O'Brien's and just like Elaine Parker's.'

He took a deep breath. 'You don't know it, but I sent out statewide bulletins that any cases of torture or unusual injury should be reported to the Boston homicide squad immediately. This one came in at 3.30 this morning.'

Michael waited. He could sense that Thomas was finding this difficult; and he had more than half an idea why he was finding it difficult.

Thomas said, in a strained voice, 'The body was found in thick woods about a half mile north of 151, close to John's Pond. There were signs of sexual interference, although I don't have all of the details just yet. But the doctor who examined the body believes that death was caused by the insertion of some kind of needle or needles into the back – needles which penetrated the suprarenal glands. Just the same as Elaine Parker, just the same as Sissy O'Brien.'

Thomas's face was very grey. He hadn't slept since Sheriff Maddox had called him in the early hours of the morning; and in any case he hated to break this kind of news to anyone.

'From – uh – personal documents found nearby – Sheriff Maddox provisionally identified the body as that of Joseph K. Garboden.'

Ever since Thomas had started talking, Michael had suspected that the body was Joe's. But all the same he found that tears were sliding down his cheeks, and that he was overwhelmed by a huge sense of grief and abandonment, almost as painful as losing a parent. Victor, unsentimentally, put his arm around him, and gave him a comforting squeeze.

'What was the estimated time of death?' Victor asked.

'Day before yesterday, just before noon, judging – aheh – by the flesh-fly activity.'

'That means that he probably died only about a half hour after he left Michael's house at New Seabury.'

Thomas nodded. 'I'm very sorry, Mikey. I knew Joe just about as well as I knew anybody in this town; and I liked him a whole lot better than most.'

'Does Marcia know?' Michael asked him, wiping his eyes with his fingers.

'Dick Maddox sent two of his deputies to tell her.'

'Jesus,' said Michael. 'When he didn't answer his mobile phone, and he didn't go back home – I knew that something bad must have happened.'

'I'm real sorry,' said Thomas. 'I know that you and Joe went way back.'

There was a quick rap at the door, and Thomas opened it. It was Megan, bringing a tray of coffee and barmbrack, an Irish fruitcake which she baked herself. She wheeled herself around and set it carefully down on top of a heap of *Guns & Ammo*.

She was just about to leave when she turned and stared at Michael with those green creme-de-menthe eyes and said, 'What did you say?'

At first, Michael didn't understand that she was talking to him. But then he stared back at her, confused, and said, 'I'm sorry?'

'You said something,' she told him. 'I was just setting the tray down and you said something.'

'I'm sorry, I didn't say a word.'

'I've just had to tell him about Joe Garboden,' put in Thomas, taking hold of her hand.

'No, no,' Megan insisted. 'You definitely said something. You said, *Hillary*.'

Michael felt a crawling sensation in his hands, as if he

were holding them, unwillingly, in jars full of yellow centipedes.

'Hillary? You heard me say "Hillary"?'

'I'm sure of it,' said Megan.

'Oh, come on now, honey,' said Thomas, laying his hand on her shoulder. 'I didn't hear Mikey say anything at all.' He turned to Michael and said, 'Megan had her first hypnotherapy session day before yesterday ... ever since then she's been spooked. I know you recommended it, but I don't know. I'm not so sure.'

'You had hypnotherapy?' asked Michael, intently.

Megan nodded. 'I had Aura Therapy with Dr Loeffler at Brigham & Women's. It did a whole lot to ease my pain, but now I keep having hallucinations. Well – not exactly hallucinations, but little odd experiences, like hearing people talking when they're not talking. I keep thinking I have to *go* someplace ... that I ought to be getting myself ready to leave. The trouble is, I don't know where.'

'Have you heard the name "Hillary" before?'

'I don't know. It seems familiar. I don't know why it should.'

Michael turned to Thomas. 'In all of my recent hypnotherapy sessions, I've seen this tall white-haired guy called "Mr Hillary". In every trance, I meet him on the shore at Nahant Bay, and he takes me to the lighthouse. He keeps saying that I ought to join him, that I'm one of his kind. And inside the lighthouse, he introduces me to all of these white-faced young men. The same white-faced young men have been watching my house at New Seabury, and the same white-faced young men have been keeping an eye on Victor and me ever since we got back to Boston, and the same white-faced young men were following Joe when he left us two mornings ago.'

'I've seen them, too,' put in Victor, in case Thomas

thought that Michael was exhibiting the signs of too much emotional stress.

Michael said, 'What we came here to tell you was that we caught two of them cutting off my hypnotherapist's feet.'

'They were doing *what*?' asked Thomas, incredulously.

'Cutting off his feet, with bolt-cutters. They killed his receptionist, and presumably they were going to kill him, too. Fortunately, Victor managed to stop most of the bleeding, and the paramedics flew him to Boston Central for microsurgery. He's there now. He was in shock when we found him, but he managed to confirm what Victor and I had been theorizing already ... that the pilot of John O'Brien's helicopter was flying under post-hypnotic suggestion – and *that's* how the driver of the pick-up truck knew that he was going to crash on Nantasket Beach.

'He also gave us his notebooks and Filofax ... and in his notebooks he makes several references to "H". We looked through his Filofax and came across the name "Mr Hillary, Goat's Cape." Goat's Cape is at Nahant, where the lighthouse stands.'

Megan was holding Thomas's hand and even without her flour-smudged nose she was looking pale. 'The lighthouse. That's right. The lighthouse.'

'You've seen it, too?'

'When I was under hypnosis. Way in the distance. A white, stubby lighthouse.'

Thomas frowned. 'It isn't possible for two people to have the same experience under hypnosis, is it? People can't have the same dreams, can they? How could you two have both seen a lighthouse?'

'It can happen,' Victor put in. 'Both Michael and Megan have been under Aura Hypnotherapy, which is different from regular hypnotherapy. It makes their minds accessible to external influences – to other people's auras. It could be that Michael's therapist and Megan's therapist both had contact with this "Mr Hillary" character, in which case it would have been perfectly feasible for both Michael and Megan to see his lighthouse while they were under hypnosis.'

Megan shivered. 'It's frightening.'

'What's even more frightening is this,' said Michael. He lifted his briefcase off the floor, opened it, and passed over the Parrot photographs that Joe had hidden in *Mushing* magazine.

'What's this all about?' asked Thomas.

But Michael said, 'Just take a look. Read the captions on the back. Then make up your own mind what it's all about.'

Thomas turned the photographs this way and that. 'They're kind of blurry, aren't they? Dealey Plaza, November 22, 1963? But that's –'

After that, Thomas was silent. He scrutinized all of the photographs, read through all of the captions. Megan poured coffee, and they sat together sipping it while Thomas stared at the photograph of the white-faced young men on the grassy knoll and said nothing at all.

'What do you suggest we do?' said Michael, eventually.

'I don't know. I don't know what to say. This is way, way over my head, this kind of investigation.'

'But you're not going to tell Commissioner Hudson, are you? Or the FBI?'

'I don't see what else I can do.'

'You can help us track down this "Mr Hillary".'

'That won't be difficult. We have his address.'

'You can bring him in for questioning.'

'Oh, yes? On what grounds? Suspicion of appearing in other people's hypnotic trances?'

'Giraffe, this is serious,' said Michael. 'Joe died because of it, Sissy O'Brien died because of it, Elaine Parker died because of it. All of those people who were lost at Rocky Woods, *they* died because of it. The evidence here is that JFK died because of it, too.'

Thomas slowly shook his head. He tucked the photographs into their envelope and handed them back. 'It's all guesswork, and wild guesswork, at that. The official autopsy report is that John O'Brien and his family died accidentally – and, let's face it, the only person in the world who hasn't been accused at one time or another of assassinating John F. Kennedy is the Pope.'

The phone rang. Megan answered it in the living-room, and then called, 'Thomas! It's David Jahnke. He says urgent.'

'Pardon me,' said Thomas, and picked up the phone. 'Go – o – od morning, David, what's going down now?' He listened, with a single muscle working rhythmically in his cheek. Then he said, 'Fifteen minutes,' and put down the phone.

'What's going on?' asked Victor.

'You'd better come with me,' Thomas told him. He stood up, and finished his scalding-hot coffee in quick, sharp sips. 'A SWAT team managed to take possession of half of Seaver Street. They've occupied Patrice Latomba's apartment, among others.'

He buckled on his shoulder-holster, and tucked in his service revolver. Victor helped him to shrug on his russet-brown coat.

'They've found some bodies,' said Thomas. 'One of them is Verna Latomba, Patrice Latomba's wife. The other is Detective Ralph Brossard, from the narc squad – the same detective who accidentally shot Patrice Latomba's baby and started this whole war off in the first place.'

Michael asked, 'Can I come along, too?'

'I'm sorry,' said Thomas. 'More than my life's worth, just

346

at the moment. One more civilian dead, and the *Globe*'s going to have us for breakfast.'

Victor gripped Michael's shoulder. 'I'll catch you later. Don't worry – I'm not not going to let you get cut out of this.'

Once they were gone, Megan said, 'What about some more coffee?'

Michael shook his head. 'Thanks all the same.'

'I'm very sorry about your friend Joe,' Megan told him.

'Well, me too. That's why I want to hunt down this "Mr Hillary". '

Megan said, 'How can anybody appear inside a hypnotic trance, the way he did to you?'

'I don't know. But the way Victor explains it, this Aura Hypnosis is very powerful. I didn't even understand that my therapist was using it, until Victor told me.'

'Dr Loeffler explained it a little,' said Megan. 'He told me that everybody has an aura … he said it's like bright coloured light that extends to two or three times the size of your physical body. Some highly-sensitive psychics can actually see it. He said that when he put me under, I would be aware of a white or pink light, and that would be *his* aura following mine, into my subconscious.'

She smiled. 'I suppose it's pretty personal, really – letting a strange man into your subconscious. It's worse than letting him search through your dressing-table drawers.'

Michael said, 'I saw that pink light, too, when Dr Rice took me under. I never knew what it was. I guess that Dr Rice didn't want me to be aware that he was following me.'

'Were you very badly traumatized?' asked Megan. 'I hope you don't mind my asking.'

Michael shook his head. 'I was out to lunch for months.' He took Dr Rice's zinc-and-copper disc out of his pocket,

347

and held it up. 'If it hadn't been for this little baby, I think I would have gradually gone mad. And I mean seriously mad – beyond recovery.'

'Let me see that,' asked Megan, and took the disc in the palm of her hand. She examined it for a while, turning it over, and then she said, 'Why don't we try it together?'

'I don't understand you.'

'Why don't we see if we can *both* go into a hypnotic trance? I mean, the *same* hypnotic trance? Then we could look for this "Mr Hillary" together. If he exists in trances, as well as the real world, then perhaps we can find him without even having to leave the room.'

Michael looked at Megan cautiously. He hoped that her disability hadn't unbalanced her, made her yearn for a freedom of movement which she could never experience again. But she smiled at him, and he couldn't help smiling back. He liked her. She was bright and intelligent and genuine. She wasn't angry at being paralysed, and she didn't seem to crave sympathy, either.

He took the disc, and put it on the table between them, and then pulled out one of the chairs and sat down. 'I don't know whether this is going to work,' he said. 'But I guess it's worth giving it a try. We'll hold hands, okay, and then we'll stare at the disc and induce sleep in each other. Then we'll see if we can get our auras to join together.'

'What if we can't?' Megan asked him.

'Then the worst that can happen is that we both have a well-deserved nap.'

'All right,' she agreed. 'Let's try it.'

Michael took hold of her left hand. 'You ready?' he asked her. 'Stare at the disc. The disc will help us to sleep.'

'We want to sleep,' said Megan. 'We want to sleep, and to see our inner minds.'

Michael gently circled his thumb around the back of

Megan's hand, around and around. 'We want to sleep. Our will is taking us deeper and deeper, into the darkness. Our will is taking us down and down.'

'We *want* to sleep,' Megan repeated. 'We want to rest; we want to swim; we want to leave all of the waking world behind us.'

Michael wasn't aware that he was falling asleep. He could still see Megan sitting opposite; he could still feel the soft warm skin on the back of her hand. But his thumb went around and around, and somehow his mind seemed to follow it, around and around. He felt a warm darkness rising up inside of him, a darkness that was deep and welcoming. The disc on the table winked brightly at him, and no matter how hard he tried, he couldn't take his eyes away from it. He heard helicopters in the distance; he heard traffic; but they didn't distract him. They reminded him of childhood, when he was sick, and staying in bed all day, dozing and dreaming as the sun moved all the way round his bedroom, fading at last into darkness.

'We want to sleep now,' said Megan, and her voice sounded very far away. 'We want to sink back into our minds.'

Michael was about to repeat what she had said, but then he found that he was slowly falling, very slowly, through soft and suffocating darkness. He couldn't hear anything any more – not Megan, not traffic, not even the sound of his own breathing. He was sliding down and down and down, although – unlike his nightmares of Rocky Woods – he wasn't afraid of hitting the ground. He was falling too slowly, as if he were sliding down the side of a black velvet precipice.

With slow, exaggerated movements he turned around, and found that he was sliding down a sand dune, on his back. The dune gradually levelled, and he came to rest, looking up at a sky that was seamlessly black. The sand was sunny, the sky was totally black. He couldn't understand it. Seagulls flew past, dazzling white against the darkness.

In the distance, he could see a woman standing by the edge of the water. She was looking down at the waves as they washed around her ankles. She was reflected in the water, so that it looked to Michael as if there were two of her, one upright and one upside-down, like a playing card. Her hair was blown in the salty sea breeze.

He climbed to his feet, and began to walk toward her. As he did so, she turned, and he saw that it was Megan. She wasn't paralysed any longer. She was standing watching him with regretful but triumphant eyes. *Those things that have passed, have passed. Think of those things that are yet to be.*

He remembered as he approached her that people who lose their mobility often dream for years afterwards that they are still capable of walking. He was meeting Megan as she had been before her accident – something that even Thomas would probably never be able to do. He came up close to her and took hold of her hand, and he could *feel* her, she was real. It was almost impossible for him to believe that he was deep in a self-induced hypnotic trance.

'Hallo, Michael,' she smiled. Her voice didn't quite seem to synchronize with the movement of her lips. 'We did it, then, both of us. We're here.'

'Our auras are here,' he reminded her. 'Our bodies are sleeping in your apartment. Let's hope that Giraffe isn't the jealous type.'

Megan stood on tiptoe and kissed his cheek. 'I trust you,' she said.

Michael looked around. In the distance, way off to the left, he could see the gleaming white stub of Mr Hillary's lighthouse. There was no sign of Mr Hillary anywhere, although there was a greyish bundle lying on the shoreline two or three hundred feet away, a bundle that could have been the body of a young girl. Seagulls were stalking all around it, and now and again one of them would dance in close and peck at it.

'Let's head for the lighthouse,' Michael suggested. 'Maybe we can find Hillary there.'

'Are you sure it's safe?' asked Megan. 'I mean, if somebody injures your aura, what happens to your living body?'

Michael looked around, and ran his hand through his mousy, thinning hair. 'I don't know,' he said. 'There's only one way to find out for sure.'

She hesitated, and gripped his hand more tightly.

'You don't have to do this if you don't want to,' he told her. 'We can always wake ourselves up.'

She stared up at him anxiously, but then she nodded. 'Let's do it,' she agreed. 'We have to do it.'

They walked hand-in-hand across the beach, and then climbed the soft grey slopes of the sand dunes. Behind them, the sea dragged itself wearily back from the shoreline. Above them, gulls still wheeled, searching for fish, searching for carrion. They trod through the lumpy grass until they reached the lighthouse, and then they circled around it until they found the door. A low, thick, solid oak door, with huge iron hinges.

'Perhaps we should knock,' said Megan.

'We're inside of our own minds,' Michael reminded her. 'We don't have to knock.'

'But supposing we're not inside of our own minds. Supposing this is real?'

'Did you ever see a pitch black sky on a sunny day?'

She frowned at him, and looked up. 'The sky's blue Michael. The sky's quite ordinary.'

'I see nothing but black. Maybe Dr Rice was right: maybe my aura's all screwed up.'

'It's a beautiful blue, Michael. I'm amazed you can't see it.'

Michael went up to the door and tried the heavy ring handle. 'Let's just see if there's anybody home.' He twisted the handle, fully expecting it to be locked, but without a sound the door opened, and they found themselves confronting a darkened entrance, chilly and fetid as a cave. They peered inside, but all they could see was part of an iron hand-rail and the first of several wooden steps.

'I'm worried,' said Megan. 'I can feel something not-quite-right.'

Michael didn't reply, but squeezed her hand and listened. He thought he could hear singing, or moaning – very, very faint and echoing.

'There's somebody inside,' he said. 'We ought to take a look.'

'Michael, I don't mind admitting it, I'm scared.'

They listened again. At first they couldn't hear anything at all, only the crying of the seagulls and the persistent fluffing of the wind, but then they heard the moaning again, and this time it was definitely moaning.

'Somebody's hurt,' said Michael.

'But what about Mr Hillary?'

'I don't know. Maybe he won't appear when there's both of us here.'

'Michael, I don't want to go inside.'

'You want to stay out here?'

'I don't want you to go inside, either.'

'Megan, I have to. They killed one of my best friends. They've killed a whole lot more people besides. I can't just let them go.'

Megan gripped his hand tightly. At last she said, 'You're right, of course. Perhaps I'm just a coward, after that accident. The thought of any more pain – '

'I promise you, I won't let anybody hurt you.'

Michael eased open the door, and they stepped cautiously inside. The interior of the lighthouse was intensely gloomy, and there was a strong smell of dead flowers and something else – cinnamon, potash and alcohol – some of the ingredients of embalming fluid. It smelled like a place of death.

Together, they climbed the wooden stairs, which spiralled around to the right. The whitewashed wall beside them was chilly and damp, as if it had absorbed years of seawater. At the very top of the stairs, there was another oak door, which opened outwards, so that Michael had to turn the handle and then step back down the stairs.

They stepped inside, and found themselves in a huge circular library, with thousands and thousands of books arranged on semi-circular shelves. Some of the books were so old that their bindings had worn through to the linen backing, and their vellum spines were worm-eaten. Other books were brand-new, recently published. *The Origins of Sin* by William Charteris. *Social Conscience* by Leah Brightmuller.

The library was illuminated by a single electric bulb which hung from the ceiling. It was a daylight bulb, of the type used by artists to paint at night, and it gave off a cold, frigid light. In the middle of the room there was a couch, upholstered in cracked brown leather, and on it, on all fours, crouched a very thin white young woman, with startling red hair and startling red freckles. She must have been making all the moaning, because she moaned again as Michael and Megan stepped into the room. As Michael circled around the walls of the library, he suddenly saw why she was moaning. Two gingery kittens were dangling from her breasts, each clinging on with its claws, each suckling greedily from her nipples.

Every time the girl moaned, the kittens swayed, and dug

353

their claws in more viciously. Michael could see tears in her eyes; but although her eyes were wide open, she didn't appear to see him.

'What is it?' Megan whispered, in fear and awe. 'What's she supposed to be doing?'

Michael slowly shook his head. 'I don't have any idea, I really don't.'

'God, that must hurt,' said Megan.

They watched the girl a few moments longer, uncertain of what to do. Then Michael whispered, 'I don't think Mr Hillary's here. Maybe we should call it a day.'

But as they turned to go, a cold voice slurred, 'Why call it a day? I should rather enjoy having you here.'

Behind them, tall and skeletal and white-bone-faced, his eyes red, stood 'Mr Hillary'. His long grey overcoat trailed on the floor as he walked toward them, *shush-shush-shush* as if the coat itself were afraid of upsetting him.

He laid one hand on Michael's shoulder and one hand on Megan. Michael noticed that Megan couldn't stop herself from shuddering.

'Why do you leave so soon?' said 'Mr Hillary'. 'The party has barely started yet.'

'I think we've seen enough, thanks,' Michael retorted, and protectively took hold of Megan's hand.

'Enough?' said 'Mr Hillary'. 'You haven't seen anything. This girl is my aperitif, before the real carousing starts.' He walked around the couch, examining the girl from all sides. She was openly weeping now, and there were dozen of scarlet scratch marks on her breasts, but the kittens kept clinging on.

'You're a pretty thing,' said 'Mr Hillary'. He reached in the pocket of his voluminous coat and produced two or three lipsticks. He examined each of them carefully, and then he settled on Strawberry Crush. With great concentration, he leaned forward and painted the girl's lips, even though she was trembling with pain and concentration, and crying.

' "And the sons of Azazel shall paint their women and dress them in great finery, and shall make divine harlots of them, and they shall teach their daughters to be harlots; and all women shall be harlots until the final consuming of the world in fiery hell; and they shall surrender themselves to all who want them, and revel in it." '

'That's not in the Bible,' said Megan, defiantly.

'You're quite right!' said 'Mr Hillary'. He had taken out some eye-liner, and was making-up the girl's eyes. 'Your eyes are beautiful,' he told her, with palpable warmth. 'We have to make them up so that we can see them.'

The girl continued to weep and shake, and the kittens shook, too. Playfully, 'Mr Hillary' slapped at each of them, and they clawed and swung, and the girl screamed out loud. 'Don't do that! Don't do that!'

Without another word, 'Mr Hillary' beckoned, and a thin-white-faced young man appeared from nowhere at all. He was wearing a black suit and dark glasses.

'This is Joseph,' said 'Mr Hillary'. 'Joseph is one of my most senior sons, aren't you, Joseph?'

Joseph said nothing, but reached inside his coat and produced two long thin metal tubes. He handed them to 'Mr Hillary', and then he went up to the couch and without any hesitation whatsoever seized hold of the girl's wrists. She must have known what was coming, because she stopped moaning and began to shriek repeatedly, over and over, although she seemed to make very little effort to get away. None, in fact. Michael had the feeling that Joseph wasn't holding her down because he expected her to escape, but because she was voluntarily going to suffer pain, and needed somebody to hold on to her while she did.

Megan stared at him, shocked; but Michael touched his

finger against his lips. There was a reason why 'Mr Hillary' was showing them this. He could just as easily have captured them, or chased them away, or even killed them – if it were possible to harm anybody's aura.

'Mr Hillary' stood next to the couch and eyed the girl's bare back like a connoisseur. He trailed his finger across her narrow shoulders and down the length of her bony spine, right down to the cleft of her bottom. It was then that Michael noticed that she had two gold studs in her back, one on either side – two gold studs, each with a hole in the centre. He didn't say anything to Megan, but he suddenly realized what these studs were for. They acted like the gold 'sleepers' that women put into their ears after they've had them pierced, to prevent the wound from closing up. This girl had two wounds in her back, which led directly to her suprarenal glands, and she had kept them open so that 'Mr Hillary' could sample her adrenaline again and again.

'Mr Hillary' lifted the first of the thin metal tubes, inserted the end of it into the left-hand stud, and then slid it inside the girl's body, expertly finding the suprarenal gland. The girl shuddered, and uttered another scream, and Joseph lashed at the kittens so that they would claw at her breasts even more viciously.

'Mr Hillary' bent over the girl's back, and took the end of the metal tube between his lips. He closed his eyes, and sucked. Michael could see his cheeks drawing in, steadily and rhythmically. His bone-white hair fell across his forehead, and he reached down and massaged his free hand against his crotch. There was an expression on his face of terrible ecstasy.

Michael and Megan watched this feeding with gradually rising horror. As he sucked at the tubes implanted in the girl's back, 'Mr Hillary' became more and more aroused. His white hair began to rise up on the crown of his head, cockatoo-like, charged with static electricity. His face began to shine white with pleasure, a blurred, dazzling white that Michael could scarcely bring himself to look at.

'Mr Hillary' gradually took on an appalling handsomeness – the kind of handsomeness that could mesmerize men as well as women. He took a final sip from the right-hand metal tube, wiped his lips with his fingers, and then rose up to his full height, well over six feet, and confronted Michael and Megan with a smile.

His white hair shone like the whitest silk. His blood-red eyes glistened with satisfaction and vigour. Although it was so pallid, his skin gleamed on his perfectly-formed cheekbones, skin so soft that Michael had a strong and subversive urge to reach out and stroke it. 'Mr Hillary's' nose was straight and narrow, sharply defined; and his lips were two thin but sensual curves, like the curves of a Stradivarius violin.

He turned back to the girl and gave a dismissive wave of his long-fingered hand. Joseph immediately dragged her off the couch onto her feet. Then he seized each kitten by the scruff of the neck, and tugged them one by one away from her breasts. She didn't cry out, but she covered her breasts with her arms, and covered her face with her hands. Without hesitation, Joseph twisted the kittens' necks, both of them together, as if he were wringing out a wet towel. He flung their bodies into the fire and didn't even bother to watch them burn. Their fur flared, and Michael thought: *How real can this be? Is this a trance or isn't it? How can I smell burning fur, when this is all supposed to be fantasy?*

Joseph covered the girl's shoulders with a loose maroon shawl, and ushered her out of the library. 'Mr Hillary' turned back to Michael and Megan, and he was still smiling, as if something had amused him.

'You're welcome,' he said to Michael. 'This time you came of your own accord.'

'This time I came to see if it was you who murdered Joe Garboden,' Michael retorted.

'Mr Hillary' shook his head. 'You don't understand, do you? Maybe you don't want to understand. A sin is a sin, and has to be punished. There is no such thing as atonement. Your friend was meddling with destiny; and those who meddle with destiny must pay the price.'

'My friend was investigating the assassination of a Supreme Court judge.'

'Mr Hillary' slowly shook his handsome head. He gave off a sexual attraction that was almost tangible – an attraction that made the nerve-endings tingle and the hair stand up on the back of Michael's head. Michael had never been aroused by a man before, and the idea that he might have even the slightest homosexual leanings filled him with dark disgust. But at the same time, he felt an erotic prickling between his legs, as if somebody with very sharp fingernails were delicately cupping his testicles, and stroking the tip of his penis.

He felt himself begin to rise, and he took a step away from 'Mr Hillary' in alarm and revulsion.

'Mr Hillary' said, 'Don't blame me, Michael. I am sin itself – every sin imaginable – but it is you who made me so. I was your scapegoat. I was the one who redeemed you. You poor, weak, confused people! Look what mischief you work, look how you whine and whinge and beg for mercy when your mischief comes home to roost!'

His eyes lingered on Michael for a moment, trawled across his face like a netful of bloodied fish, and Michael felt a shiver of cold sensuality that ran all the way down his spinal column and shrank his prostate gland. His penis was fully erect, hard to bursting, and 'Mr Hillary' hadn't even touched him.

Then 'Mr Hillary' turned his attention to Megan. 'This

isn't the real you, is it, Megan?' he asked. 'This isn't the same you that Dr Loeffler has been trying to help?'

'What do you mean?' asked Megan, her voice tightly constricted with fright. All the same, her face and her upper chest were flushed, and her nipples were jutting stiffly through the thin grey silk of her blouse.

'Mr Hillary' slyly covered his face with his hand, so that all Megan could see was his blood-red eyes, glittering behind the protective cage of his fingers. 'The real you, Megan, is incapable of walking. The real you, Megan, is a poor paralysed scrap of a thing who has to seek fulfilment in cheerfulness, and in cakes and pies.'

He glanced back at Michael, and said, 'You're a good disciple, Michael. I look forward to seeing more of you.'

But then he turned to Megan again and shook his head. 'Don't deceive yourself, Megan. There's far too much deceit in the world. Far too much! And the day is coming soon when all of that deceit is paid for, in full, with two thousand years of interest!'

He reached out with both hands and gripped Megan's shoulders. Michael said, '*Don't touch her!*' but 'Mr Hillary' gave him a glare of such blood-filled ferocity that he hesitated for just an instant, and for Megan that instant was all that was needed to bring her low. Her knees buckled, and she dropped sideways onto the library floor, hitting her shoulder against a small footstool and toppling it over.

'This is the Megan we know and love!' smiled 'Mr Hillary', and knelt beside her, like a lover kneeling beside his paramour, like a supplicant kneeling beside his fallen queen. He lifted her head up in the palm of his right hand, with infinite gentleness, and kissed her lips. At the same time his left hand ran lightly down her side, barely touching her breast, barely touching her hip, barely touching her upper thigh.

Michael stumbled forward, determined to knock him

down, but 'Mr Hillary' turned and raised his hand and simply said, 'Stop,' in the softest of tones; and then 'Wake.'

'*Wake?*' Michael demanded. '*Wake?*'

'It's all over, Michael. Wake.'

Michael looked around him – at the library bookshelves, at the whitewashed ceiling, at 'Mr Hillary', in his soft grey coat, crouching over Megan handsome and evil, his hand still resting on her hip.

He heard a sound like a mirror being stressed, the instant before it breaks.

He felt the world slide from under him, faster and faster.

He saw lights, darkness, and walls rushing past him.

He heard voices and murmurs, thick and slow.

He opened his eyes and he was sitting at Megan's dining-table, blinking in the sunlight, and Megan was sitting opposite him, her hands gripping the arms of her wheelchair. She stared at him. Her eyes were wide and her mouth was open. Her cheeks were two bright spots of pink.

Michael didn't know what to say. He had never in his life been gripped by such a feverish sexual passion. His chest rose and fell as if he had been running, and running hard.

Without a word, Megan lifted herself from her wheel-chair, and slid awkwardly onto the carpet. With one hand, she pushed the wheelchair away, and with the other, she pulled up her skirt.

Michael tugged open the buttons of his shirt, unbuckled his belt, stepped out of his trousers. He was totally aware that what he was doing was wrong. He was betraying Patsy, he was betraying Giraffe. But the blood was pumping through his arteries like rainwater gushing through storm drains, and his head thundered with excitement.

Megan was crying out loud, like a wounded bird. She reached down with both hands and pulled aside her white

360

lace panties. Her vulva was swollen and rosy, and glistening in readiness. Naked, Michael climbed on top of her, his erection held in his fist, and pushed it into her, until their pubic hair was intertwined, and he could push it in no further.

He kissed her and licked her and bit her earlobes. He pulled the buttons from her blouse, and slid his hand into the cups of her bra, and squeezed her nipples. And all the time he forced himself into her, again and again and again, the hugest and hardest and most indomitable erection that he had ever experienced. She didn't have the use of her legs, but she had the use of her lips and the use of her fingers, and she kissed him and nipped at his lips and dragged her fingernails down his back. She pulled apart the cheeks of his bottom and teased him and scratched him and tickled him, until he knew that he couldn't hold himself back any longer.

Megan must have sensed that, too, because she said, '*Here!*' and took hold of his penis in her hand. She pulled him upwards – urged him upwards – until he was sitting astride her. She kissed his penis and rubbed it with her hand, harder and harder, faster and faster. Their combined lust was like two express trains, hurtling toward each other on the same track. Harder and harder, faster and faster.

Michael climaxed, a thick white pumping climax, spurt after spurt. Megan, in the strangest kind of ecstasy, directed his ejaculation all over her face – her eyelashes, her cheeks, her hair, her lips. When it was over, she looked as if she had been decorated with trembling pearls.

Michael, in that empty moment after ejaculation, bent forward and kissed her. She kissed him back, very slowly, very lasciviously, and slid her fingers into his hair.

'You know what happened, don't you?' she whispered, her breath hot and thunderous in his ear.

361

He shook his head.

'It was him, it was 'Mr Hillary', he possessed us both.'

Michael didn't know what to say. He felt desperately guilty already. All he wanted to do was to get up from the floor and put on his pants and pretend that this had never happened. Jesus, he had been unfaithful to Patsy for the first time ever – with the disabled wife of a homicide squad detective. He couldn't believe that he had done it. He couldn't believe that he had *wanted* to do it.

He sat up. He reached over and fumbled in his trouser pocket for his handkerchief. Gently, he wiped Megan's face; and then he kissed her again. 'I'm sorry,' he said. 'I'm really sorry.'

'Why are you sorry? You did what you felt like doing. It wasn't love.'

'I'm sorry because I like you. I'm sorry because you're Thomas's wife. I'm sorry because I'm Patsy's husband.'

'Will you help me back into my chair?' she asked him.

He buttoned up her blouse, and rearranged her panties, and brushed down her skirt. Then he picked her up in his arms, and sat her back in her wheelchair.

'It was him,' she said. 'It wasn't you, and it wasn't me. It was him. He was showing us what our sins are.'

'I still don't understand.'

He reached down to pick up his trousers, but Megan said, 'No … before you dress, come here.'

Naked, he approached her, and stood in front of her. She lifted her hand, and took hold of his softening penis, rubbing her thumb around the glans, and gently massaging the shaft.

'This will never happen to me again,' she said. 'I'm not an adulteress; and I know that you're not an adulterer.' Her eyes sparkled with tears. 'It wasn't us, it was him, and he was sinful. But I don't regret it. I can't. You made me feel

362

whole. For the first time since my accident happened, you made me feel whole.'

Michael leaned over and kissed her forehead. 'I'd better go now. There's a whole lot more for me to do.'

Neither of them noticed it, but a faint pinkish flicker of light passed between them, as one aura reluctantly disentangled itself from the other. What they both felt, as Michael slowly dressed himself, and combed his hair, was a distinct sense of loss, and separation.

Michael picked up the zinc-and-copper disc. He was about to slip it into his pocket, but then he put it back down on the table.

'Souvenir,' he said, and left, closing the door very quietly behind him.

He was manoeuvring his big green Mercury out of the sloping entrance-way in front of Thomas and Megan's apartment when he noticed three white-faced young men in dark glasses, watching him the opposite side of the street. He stopped the car, and trod on the parking-brake.

Instantly, an Italian-looking man in a blue cotton coat came hurrying out of the building, and furiously rapped on his window. Mr Novato, the super that Thomas loved to hate.

'Something wrong?' Michael asked him.

'You can't stop here, sir, this is a private driveway.'

'I'm not stopped here; I'm about to leave.'

'So, leave.'

'I would have left by now if you hadn't stopped me.'

The man lifted one finger, pointing upward to the apartment block. 'You been visiting?'

'That's right, I've been visiting. I'm a friend of Lieutenant Boyle, if you must know.'

'Well, that's-a one sad man.'

'Who? Who are you talking about? Lieutenant Boyle?'

'That's right, that's-a one sad man.'

'Listen, friend, you may be the super here, or whatever, but I'm not going to discuss Lieutenant Boyle's personal feelings with you or anybody.'

'Who wouldn't be sad? His wife so sick. Can't walk, can't go shopping, can't do nothing.'

Michael turned away, and took a deep breath. Then he turned back and said, 'Lieutenant Boyle is very far from sad, I can tell you. And I can tell you something else: Mrs Boyle is worth a hundred of most women that I can think of.'

Mr Novato stared at him beadily. 'Hey … sorry I spoke. No offence meant.'

He retreated, and watched Michael back out of the sloping driveway with an angry little squeal of tyres. Before he drove off, Michael glanced back across the street, to the entrance-way where the three white-faced young men had been watching him, but now they were gone. It was quite possible that he had imagined them – especially after that Aura Hypnosis with Megan.

On the other hand, it was equally possible that they were following him, and that they intended to deal with him in the same way that they had dealt with Joe.

He drove south on Margin Street, crowded and slow, and then west on Copper. The car radio was playing 'Happy Together' by the Turtles. *Imagine me and you, I do, I think about you day and night.*

Jesus Christ, what had he done to his honour? What had he done to his marriage?

He stopped to let a man in dark glasses cross the street, thinking that he was blind. The man had almost reached the opposite kerb when he raised his dark glasses in salute, and smiled.

Marcia was hyperactive. Her face was puffy and her hair was

all flat at the back. She probably hadn't sat down once since the Barnstable County deputies had brought her the news that Joe had been discovered in the woods north of 151, stripped and assaulted, and dead of a massive cardiac arrest.

She talked as if he were still alive. She didn't exactly say 'when Joe gets back' in so many words, but everything she said carried the implication that the Barnstable County Sheriff's Department had made an ugly and painful mistake, and that when Joe did get back, well, heads would probably roll.

Michael sat in the living-room with a cup of cappucino that he didn't want to drink, while Marcia stalked from room to room, talking, arguing, protesting. She had only to stop for a minute and she would have to accept the fact that Joe was dead, and she wasn't ready to do that yet. It was hard enough for Michael to accept it. There were photographs of Joe everywhere he looked. On top of the television, on top of the fireplace. Even when he used the bathroom, there was a photograph of Joe in a yellow wet-suit, lifting up a spider-crab for him to admire.

'I told him not to get involved,' said Marcia.

'You told him not to get involved in what?'

'This conspiracy business. He didn't talk about it much, but I could tell that he was worried.'

'What did he tell you about it?'

Marcia shook her head. 'Hardly anything. Nothing. He said it was safer if I didn't know. I tried to persuade him to forget about it. I'll bet you that none of it's true, that's what I told him. But even if it isn't, you'll still get people coming after you, because they're worried that it might be true, so leave well enough alone.'

'I'm sorry,' said Michael. 'I don't know what else to say.'

Marcia stopped pacing for a moment, and then she said, 'He didn't leave you anything, if that's what you're thinking.'

'I wasn't.'

'There's an envelope, but that's all.'

'An envelope? Do you mind if I see it?'

'Oh … sure.' Marcia disappeared into the room that Joe had used as a den, and then reappeared two or three minutes later with a thick legal-sized envelope. On the front, in Joe's writing, were the words *For Michael Rearden. Only To Be Opened In The Event Of My Sudden Death.*

Michael tore open the envelope and took out the letter. 'This is dated two years ago,' he said, in surprise.

'That was when Joe first came up with this conspiracy theory,' said Marcia. 'Ever since then, life has been very much less harmonious. God – I wish he'd been a streetsweeper, or a school janitor, or an auto mechanic. Why didn't he stick to ordinary, run-of-the-mill insurance investigations? Why did he think that he was going to change the world?'

Michael closed his ears to Marcia Garboden for a moment. He knew how she felt, but she wasn't helping any. Besides, he was trying to make sense of the contents of the letter that Joe had left him. There was a sheet of notepaper, bearing nothing but a typewritten series of names and numbers, with no explanatory notes whatsoever; and then there were twenty or thirty photocopies of engravings and photographs, mostly photographs.

The names and numbers were: 'Lincoln 65 Alexander 81 Garfield 81 Umberto 00 McKinley 01 Madero 13 George 13 Ferdinand 14 Michael 18 Nicholas 18 Carranza 20 Collins 22 Villa 23 Obregon 28 Cermak 33 Dollfuss 34 Long 35 Bronstein 40 Gandhi 48 Bernadotte 48 Hussein 51 Somoza 56 Armas 57 Faisal 58 as-Said 58 Bandaranaike 59 Lumumba 61 Molina 61 Evers 63 Diem 63 Mansour 65 X 65 Verwoerd 66 King 68 Tal 71 NoEL 73 Park 74 Davies 74 Ratsimandrava 75 Faisal 75 Rahman 75 Ramat Mohammed 76 Jumblat 77 Ngoubai 77 Al-Naif 78 Dubs 79 Neave 79 Mountbatten 79 Park 79 Tolbert 80 Debayle 80 Ali Rajı 81 El-Sadat 81 Gemayel 82 Sartawi 83 Aquino 83 Gandhi 84 ...'

It took him a minute or two, but gradually Michael began to understand what the letter was trying to tell him. Every name was the name of an assassinated politician or dignitary or head of state, and the numbers signified the years in which they had been killed.

Then he looked through the photographs. Every one of them was a photograph of the assassination or the funeral of one of the people on the list, or the execution of their assassins. In every one of them, two or three white-faced bystanders had been circled by Joe in red felt-tip pen.

Here was the hanging on July 7, 1865, of John Wilkes Booth's accomplices, after the assassination of Lincoln. Mrs Mary Surratt, David Herrold, Lewis Paine and George Atzerodt hung from the scaffold, their heads covered in sacks, their legs tied together to prevent them from kicking. And there, shielding themselves from the sunlight under large umbrellas, were two of the white-faced men, wearing tiny smoked spectacles, both smiling.

Here was Charles J. Guiteau, who shot President Garfield at the Washington railroad station, arriving handcuffed for his trial on November 14, 1881 – with three white-faced men standing in the crowd, just behind his left shoulder.

Here was the shooting of Egyptian President Anwar El-Sadat on October 6, 1981, at a military parade in Cairo. Most of the spectators were hiding under their seats – but a single white-faced man is watching President El-Sadat's shooting from the far left of the picture, with a faint smile on his face.

Michael asked, 'May I?' and spread out the pictures on Marcia's dining-table. He looked from one to the other –

and although they varied in quality, and some of them had obviously been computer-enhanced, there was no question at all that the same men appeared again and again, unchanged in appearance, from Lincoln's shooting at Ford's Theater in Washington to the killing of Rajiv Gandhi at a political rally in southern India – over 125 years between them. With nothing but names and dates and identifying circles, Joe was giving Michael incontrovertible proof that the white-faced men had been assassinating politicians and heads of state for year after year – regardless of their political points of view.

Some victims were right-wing extremists. Others were left-wing terrorists. There was no political rhyme or reason behind their killing. But Joe was explaining that John F. Kennedy hadn't been the only victim of the white-faced men. They had arranged for all of these assassinations.

Michael stood back and stared at the pictures, so deep in thought that he didn't even hear Marcia when she asked him if he wanted a drink.

What the hell was he going to do now? There was no question at all that the white-faced men would come after him, if they found out what he knew – the same way that they had gone after Joe, and Dr Rice, and maybe everybody throughout history who had witnessed one of their assassinations, or who had put two and two together, like Joe, and realized that the same pallid faces kept appearing about a hundred times too often to be coincidental.

He was seized with such fear and indecision that he could scarcely breathe. This was more than he could handle. Because who could he turn to? Who could he trust? Not the police. Commissioner Hudson had accepted Dr Moorpath's blatantly spurious autopsy on John O'Brien 'with whole-hearted thanks for a difficult job, sensitively carried out'. He couldn't go to the media, either, because they seemed to have accepted the autopsy, too, without a single investigative murmur – even the *Boston Globe*, even Darlene McCarthy on Channel 56.

He couldn't go to Edgar Bedford. After all, Joe had suspected for years now that Edgar Bedford was deeply involved with the white-faced men. What was even more threatening was the way in which Edgar Bedford had accepted Dr Moorpath's autopsy, too, regardless of the fact that it was going to cost Plymouth and its underwriters tens of millions of dollars.

He thought he could trust Thomas Boyle, although he was lacerated with guilt about what he had done to Megan. Pray God that Thomas never found out. And Victor – he could trust Victor, for sure.

Slowly, he collected the photographs together, and slid them back into their envelope. Perhaps, more than anything, he hoped that he could trust himself.

Fifteen

He met Victor and Thomas at Venus Seafood in the Rough, the clamshack on Sleeper Street close to the Northern Avenue Bridge, because Thomas knew Susan Chused-Still, one of the restaurant's partners, or self-appointed 'clam queens'. Victor and Thomas had obviously been disturbed by the morning's events, but they were hungry, too, and ordered fried clams and corn-on-the-cob.

Michael had no appetite at all, and found it very difficult to look Thomas in the eye. He kept thinking about Megan, sliding herself down from her wheelchair, dragging up her skirt, her eyes alight with a lust that wasn't even hers. He

369

toyed with a beer, and ate a few handfuls of smoked almonds, but that was all.

Victor said, 'Verna Latomba was tied up and tortured the same way that Elaine Parker was tortured – the same way that Sissy O'Brien was tortured – except that, with Verna, they didn't have the time to go too far.'

Thomas lit a cigarette, and put in dryly, 'The way we figure it so far is that Ralph Brossard did some kind of a Tarzan act. He swung his way into Patrice Latomba's apartment from the balcony just above. God alone knows why. He was under suspension for shooting Latomba's baby son. I would have thought he would have stayed well clear of Seaver Street, and Patrice Latomba in particular. He made his way into the kitchen, where Verna was tied to the kitchen table. We've established that much – although we don't know who tied her up, or why. There were several witnesses, but they had all vamoosed. Whoever it was, they must have tortured her, because there was blood on the table which has been provisionally identified as hers.

'It looks like Brossard shot one of the perps, because there was blood sprayed all over the window, as well as a bullet-hole, probably caused by a slug from Detective Brossard's .44. There was another slug lodged in one of the kitchen cabinets, another .44, which bore considerable signs of flattening and scoring, as if it might have passed through a soft piece of furniture, or a human body.

'However, the only corpses that were discovered were those of Verna Latomba and Ralph Gossard. Verna's face was critically burned on the kitchen gas ring; and then she was shot at point-blank range with a .45 – not Brossard's gun, for sure. Brossard's left arm was severely charred. It looked like he was responsible for burning Verna. But he was shot by the same .45.'

370

'What's your guess, then?' asked Michael, swallowing more almonds, and almost choking himself.

'Somebody forced Brossard to burn Verna, and then shot the both of them.'

'But why?' asked Michael. 'What was the motive?'

'Revenge, who knows?'

'Revenge? Revenge for what? I can understand somebody shooting Detective Brossard, because of what he did to Latomba's baby. I can understand somebody shooting Verna. An ex-lover, maybe; or a vengeful redneck. But who would shoot both of them? What for?'

Victor put in, 'The other thing that's worrying me is, whose blood did we find on the window? There was no indication that a bleeding body had been dragged or carried through the kitchen, and no further bloodstains in the living-room, landing or stairs. Yet whoever it was that Brossard hit, he must have taken a massively invasive bullet wound, and his chances of staunching the flow of blood and walking out of the apartment must have been absolutely nil.'

Thomas blew smoke out of his nostrils. 'It's bizarre. The whole damn thing's totally bizarre. If I didn't know better, I'd say that we were dealing with zombies. The curse of the living dead.'

Michael said, 'Run that bit by me again – that bit about Detective Brossard burning Verna.'

'Well,' said Victor, 'his left hand was burned right down to the bone, most of the flesh had carbonized. There was severe burning all the way up the forearm, and extensive shrivelling of the skin around the upper arm and shoulder, with second-degree burns to the underarm and left torso and first-degree burns to the left-hand side of the face.

'Judging from the criss-cross hob marks across her face, Verna had been forced right down onto the gas ring, and held there for nearly a minute.'

371

Michael slowly massaged the back of his neck. His muscles were knotted up, and his shoulders were completely rigid. He wished Thomas wouldn't give him such encouraging smiles. He would almost have preferred it if Thomas had been angry with him. At least he would have felt that he was being punished for what he had done.

'Have you ever been burned?' he asked Thomas.

Thomas shook his head. But Victor said, 'I understand what you're driving at. Burns are incredibly painful. They're so painful that burns victims often beg to be killed, rather than suffer.'

Michael nodded. 'So how did these mysterious perpetrators persuade Detective Brossard to hold Verna Latomba's face down on the gas ring while his own hand was being burned off? Even with a gun at his head, I don't think that would have been possible. He couldn't have endured the pain.'

'Maybe he was held there physically.'

'I can't see how. Anybody who forced him to keep his hand on top of Verna Latomba's burning head would have been burned just as seriously themselves.'

Thomas crushed out his cigarette and nodded. 'You're right, of course. So what's your theory?'

'I think he could have been hypnotized,' said Michael. 'He could have burned Verna Latomba under hypnotic suggestion. In a really deep trance he would have felt little or no pain at all.'

Thomas said, 'Do you really believe that's possible? I didn't think that hypnotists could force people to do anything against their nature.' He turned to Victor, and added, 'If I thought they could, do you think I would have sent Megan to see Dr Loeffler?'

It was supposed to be a joke, but it gave Michael an appalling sensation in his stomach, as if he had driven over a humpback hill too fast.

Victor said, 'That's a myth, I'm afraid, that belief that you can't make people hurt themselves, or do anything that they wouldn't normally do. Once you're under hypnosis, you don't feel pain. People have had major surgery under hypnosis, with no anaesthetic whatsoever, and they haven't felt anything.'

'But pushing Verna Latomba's face down onto a lighted gas ring –'

'He may not even have realized that it was a lighted gas ring. He may have been under the impression that he was doing nothing more than effecting a straightforward arrest. Or maybe something totally different. It really all depends how suggestible he was.'

Thomas checked his watch. 'I have to get back to headquarters. I've fixed up a press conference for three o'clock. I think it's time the public were told all of the grisly details of what happened to Elaine Parker and Sissy O'Brien and Joe, too – as well as Ralph Brossard and Verna Latomba.'

'You're going to release *everything*?' asked Victor.

Thomas nodded. 'It can't hurt. I mean, what progress have we made? Absolutely zilch. We've been holding back some of the more bizarre details, like the holes in the back, and the cat thing, in case we made a collar. But we're nowhere. All we can hope for now is that somebody might remember some seemingly irrelevant detail that ties all of these homicides together. Like, where did they get the metal tubes for piercing the victims' suprarenal glands? Like, where do they buy their razor wire? Like, whose cat went missing when Sissy O'Brien was tortured?'

'All right, then,' said Victor, finishing his beer. 'We'll catch you later.'

Thomas picked up the bill. Before he left, however, he turned to Michael and said, 'This hypnosis – do you really think it's going to help Megan very much?'

373

Michael hesitated, and then shrugged. 'It's like any therapy, I guess. It's only as good as the patient's will to get better. But – well, from what I've seen, Megan has plenty of that.'

Thomas thought for a moment, then lifted his hand in a wordless farewell, and walked out of the restaurant.

As soon as he had gone, Victor said, 'Come on – what is it? What are you holding out on?'

Michael produced the envelope that Joe had left for him, with all the pictures of assassinated presidents. 'It's not that I don't trust Thomas. It's just that I wanted you to take a look at these first, and then we can decide what we're going to do with them. Me, I'm fifty-fifty. I mean this is seriously heavy stuff. I'm fifty percent in favour of burning them, and pretending that I never saw them, and I'm fifty percent in favour of keeping them, and using them to prove that John O'Brien didn't die accidentally, any more than Abraham Lincoln died accidentally.'

Victor looked through the photographs with a sober expression on his face. At last he took off his spectacles and folded them up. 'This is either Joe Garboden in the last stages of paranoia; or else it's the most devastating discovery in the history of the last two hundred years.'

Michael nodded, grimly. 'My feelings exactly. But I can't make up my mind which it is. I'm scared that Joe might have been right; but I'm equally scared that he was wrong, and that I'm going to wind up like him, seeing conspiracies in everything that anybody does. Look at those three people, crossing the street together! It's a conspiracy!'

Victor turned around, put on his glasses, peered across the street, and then laughed. 'There's no way that you could know it, but those three people all work for the Boston coroner's office. So, yes, I guess you could say that they were some kind of a conspiracy. A lunch-club, eating fried clams

374

and Misery Island shrimp and talking about diseased liver sections.'

'Exactly,' said Michael. 'You've made your point. But I'm really worried. The O'Brien case has all kinds of weird implications that I don't even want to discuss with Thomas, they're so weird.'

Haltingly, discursively, he told Victor all about the hypnotic trance that he and Megan had put themselves into. Victor listened with his head bowed so that Michael could see that the hair in his parting was thinning. He told Victor all about the erotic feelings that 'Mr Hillary' had aroused in him; and he also told him that Megan must have felt the same way. But he drew the line at telling Victor that he and Megan had made love, or had sex, or whatever it was that they had done together on the floor of the Boyles' apartment. He could see Megan's face now, anointed with his ejaculation, and he felt his cheeks burning with embarrassment.

'Do you think what you saw in your trance was real?' asked Victor.

'Mr Hillary's real. We saw his name in Dr Rice's notebook.'

Victor thought for a while, and then he said, 'I don't know. I think we're getting way out of our depth. The whole key to this matter is who's been pulling the strings. Who insisted that the O'Brien family's remains had to go to Boston Central, so that Raymond Moorpath was in charge of the post-mortem examinations? Who told Raymond Moorpath what the results of those post-mortem examinations were going to be? Who directed Commissioner Hudson and Edgar Bedford to accept Raymond Moorpath's findings?'

'Maybe that was all "Mr Hillary's" doing, too,' Michael suggested.

Victor pulled a face. 'We don't know yet, do we? I believe what you've seen in your trances. I'm pretty sure that "Mr

Hillary" actually exists. But "Mr Hillary" could easily be altering your perception of what's true and what's imaginary, just to put you off the track. We're into the world of hypnosis, now, Michael. You're flying by the seat of your psychological pants.'

Michael looked down at the half-empty dish of almonds, and decided not to eat any more. 'Listen,' he said. 'I think we should talk to Raymond Moorpath.'

'Do you think he'll talk to you?'

'Well ... Raymond's pretty pompous these days, and full of himself. But he and I do go back a few years. Maybe he will, maybe he won't. But it's still worth trying.'

'You're trying to save the world, right?'

'That's it. I'm trying to save the world. Cock-a-doodle-doo.'

They walked out of Venus Seafood and crossed the street to Michael's car. The early afternoon was baking hot, and heat rippled up from the pavement like the transparent ripples of an incoming tide. They didn't notice the two young men in dark glasses standing in the doorway of the narrow brick building opposite. Neither did they notice the saddle-bronze Lincoln Town Car starting up its engine, only three cars away, and nudging its way into the traffic close behind them.

Victor took off his glasses and tiredly pinched the bridge of his nose. 'I feel like I've been awake for ever,' he said.

They drove to Boston Central and parked in the doctors' parking lot. The entrance to the emergency ward was crowded with ambulances and police cars and people rushing everywhere. Michael stopped a thin-faced cop with a droopy Wyatt Earp moustache and asked him what was happening.

'Blue Hill Avenue, it's a fucking war. Seven people hit by

machine-gun fire. Three cops down, two of them dead for sure.'

Michael and Victor walked around to the hospital's main entrance, but even as they did so three more ambulances arrived, their lights flashing and their sirens whooping. Toward the south of the city, more smoke was rising, and there was a rubbery smell of burning on the wind. The rioting had been going on for nearly a week now, and every day the smoke had been rising from Roxbury, and in the way that people quickly learn to adapt to almost anything, the people of Boston scarcely noticed it now, they just went about their business and left half of their community to burn. Call it adaptability, call it cynicism: but it wasn't *their* half, after all.

All the same, there was a feeling throughout the Hub that things were getting worse, rather than better, that the city's foundations were beginning to shift. The president had been interviewed on television this morning, and he had started to talk about 'strong and sweeping action ... to root out urban terrorism ... (which) this is – no more, no less.'

They asked at the desk to speak to Dr Moorpath. The harassed receptionist told them to wait, she didn't know where Dr Moorpath was. He wasn't in his office: maybe he was down in pathology. They sat and waited for almost ten minutes; and then Michael jerked his head toward the elevators and said, 'Time for some independent action, *mon ami.*' The receptionist – answering two telephone calls simultaneously whilst trying to explain to a huge Nigerian woman how to find Liposuction – didn't even see them go.

They rose in the elevator to the eighth floor, and then walked silently along the carpeted corridor to 8202. Michael knocked at the door, waited, and then opened it. Dr Moorpath's grandiose office was deserted, although

377

there was a strong smell of cigar smoke still lingering, and a half-empty glass of Scotch whisky on Dr Moorpath's desk.

'Raymond?' called Michael. He stepped inside, and looked around.

'Some office,' said Victor, with a whistle.

'That's private practice for you,' Michael told him. He looked at the papers on the desk, but they were only estimates for a new set of refrigeration units for preserving human remains, a reminder from *Reader's Digest*, and an invoice for tuning Dr Moorpath's Porsche.

They were just about to leave when a jowly Greek-looking doctor knocked at the door and came in.

'You're looking for Dr Moorpath?' he asked.

'That's right. You haven't seen him, have you?'

'Only two or three minutes ago, on the tenth floor. He's probably still there now.'

'Oh, thanks,' said Michael.

'Tenth floor,' the Greek-looking doctor repeated. 'That's Recovery.'

'Recovery?'

'That's right, where patients go to recover, after major surgery.'

'Not quite the place for Dr Moorpath,' Michael smiled. 'I thought he was only interested in patients if they didn't recover.'

The doctor abruptly laughed, and laid a green manila file on Dr Moorpath's desk. 'Still … there's a very interesting case we've all been taking a look at … a man who had both of his feet accidentally cut off. They've been sewn back on by microsurgery, and of course we're all fascinated to see what kind of recovery he's going to make. Dr Ausiello led the surgical team … he's quite the best.'

Like a small, well-oiled ratchet in a clock, something

clicked inside Michael's brain. It was Dr Rice who had lost his feet – Dr Rice who had been mutilated by the white-faced men. And Dr Moorpath had gone to take a look at him? Dr Moorpath, who was responsible for covering up the John O'Brien helicopter killings?

'Come on,' Michael urged Victor.

'What?' said Victor.

'Come on, that's all! We may be too late!'

The doctor stood staring in bewilderment as they hurried out and ran to the elevators. Michael punched 10 and then they waited and waited, while express elevators whooshed past, or downward elevators pinged and opened up, revealing crowds of chattering nurses and urbane-looking interns. At last, after nearly two minutes had gone aching past, an upward-bound elevator arrived, pinged, and opened up. It was occupied by a single elderly doctor in a three-piece suit.

'Have you tried the Famous Atlantic?' he asked, out of the blue, as the elevator rose toward the 10th.

'Can't say that I have,' Michael replied.

'I had the schrod today, it was excellent. Right off the pier, straight on to your plate. The only way you can get it fresher than that is to swim across the harbour with your mouth open.'

The elevator doors opened, and before the doctor could open his mouth a second time, Michael and Victor were gone. They jogged along the corridor until they reached the reception desk. Under a fluorescent desklamp, a bosomy blonde nurse in a saucy little starched cap was reading the *National Enquirer*. The headline read 'Baby Born With Four Legs'. She looked up and flashed them a wide, dazzling smile.

'Dr Rice?' asked Michael. 'We're friends of his. Intimate friends.'

'I'm sorry,' the nurse replied. 'Dr Rice can't be seen by

anybody right now, not even family. He's just been through major surgery, and he's still very, very sick.'

'Some of the doctors have seen him,' Michael insisted.

'Well, of course. Doctors are doctors.'

'But I'm one of his patients.'

'I'm sorry, sir. You still can't see him.'

'I *must* see him. Dr Moorpath's seen him!'

'I just told you, sir, Dr Moorpath is a doctor. He's entitled to see him. Now, don't give me any trouble, please, or I'll have to call security.'

At that moment, a messenger-boy arrived at the desk with flowers – irises and summer daisies and lilies. 'Rice?' he wanted to know.

'Room 1011,' the nurse told him; and that was all that Michael needed. Without a word he sprinted away from the reception desk, and along the corridor, following the signs that said 1000-1020.

Faster, for Christ's sake, faster! He pumped around the corner, and there was the door of 1011, only thirty feet away from him. The reason he could see the number so clearly was because the door was slightly ajar.

'Sir!' the nurse was calling after him. 'Sir! You can't go in there!'

Panting, Michael slowed down to a hurried walk. But as he did so, the door of room 1011 opened even wider and Raymond Moorpath came out. He was wearing a dark blazer and a dark turtle-neck, and his normally sleek hair was ruffled. He stared at Michael in surprise and displeasure.

'Dr Moorpath – ' Michael began. But in a strange, guarded gesture, Dr Moorpath shielded his face with his hand, and started to hurry away along the corridor.

'Raymond, for Christ's sake!' Michael shouted after him.

Victor caught up with him. 'What's happened? Who was that?'

380

'Raymond Moorpath, acting like the dog that stole the Sunday roast.'

Victor looked into Room 1011, and then he turned back to Michael with a serious expression on his face. 'More like the pathologist who did for Dr Rice.'

Michael stepped into the room. It was one of Boston Central's most sophisticated recovery rooms, with all of the monitoring and life-support equipment that anybody could have needed. Dr Rice lay on the bed in the centre of the room with a cage covering his legs. He was connected to a nasal drip and a McClary vital-signs monitor. His face was yellowy-grey. The monitor was beeping a warning that Dr Rice's pulse, respiration and brain activity had already ceased, and that his blood pressure was taking a long, relentless nosedive.

'Shit,' said Michael. He turned around to go after Dr Moorpath, but he cannoned into two blue-clad doctors, a nurse, and a hospital security guard.

'What the hell's going on here?' one of the doctors demanded. 'Who the hell are you?'

'Victor!' Michael shouted. 'Tell him who the hell we are and what the hell's going on here!'

The doctor stepped back, startled. Michael pushed him in the chest, flat-handed, jostled the security guard with his shoulder, and then started to run off down the corridor, in pursuit of Dr Moorpath.

'Freeze!' screamed the security guard. 'Freeze!' But Michael had already reached the corner of the corridor. He dodged off to the right, almost stumbling over his own feet, and then he was running full-tilt down the corridor, gasping with exertion. His feet thudded on the carpet, doors jiggled past him, lights jiggled past. Somebody opened a door right next to him and shouted, 'Hey!' as he passed.

He reasoned that Dr Moorpath wouldn't try to make it back to the main elevator bank. That would mean doubling-back on himself, with the risk that Victor and he might have split up, to catch him from either direction.

It was then that he reached the emergency stairs – and the pneumatically-buffered door was just closing.

He shoved the door wide open again, and found himself in a gloomy concrete stairwell, with blue-painted metal railings. He stopped still, and listened – and, sure enough, he could hear the echoing chip-chipping noise of Dr Moorpath climbing the staircase to the next storey.

'Raymond!' he shouted, his voice hoarse from running. 'Raymond! I have to talk to you!'

There was no reply. Only the sound of Dr Moorpath climbing higher and higher up the stairs.

'Goddamn it,' Michael breathed. But he had no choice. He started to climb the stairs two at a time, pulling on the railings to help himself up. He passed the 11th floor, and then the 12th. He could still hear Dr Moorpath's footsteps two or three storeys above him, although he was gradually slowing down. Four storeys of twenty-four steps each were enough for anybody who was young and fit, but Dr Moorpath was middle-aged and 40lbs overweight.

Suddenly, up above him, Michael heard a sharp rattling sound. Looking up the stairwell, he saw sunlight flooding in. Dr Moorpath must have reached the roof, and opened the access doors. Michael heaved himself faster and faster up the staircase, chilled with sweat and whining for breath, until at last he reached the final flight.

He hesitated for a moment. The two access doors were swinging slowly backwards and forwards in the warm afternoon wind, so that a parallelogram of sunlight swung backwards and forwards across the concrete walls of the stairwell. Michael glimpsed buildings, rooftops, and smoke. There was no sign of Dr Moorpath. Maybe he had already jumped from the roof. But Dr Moorpath had never seemed like the suicidal type – too proud, too arrogant, too self-assured. It was much more likely that he was hiding behind the doors, waiting to knock Michael down.

'Raymond?' called Michael. 'Raymond, can you hear me?'

The doors swung backwards and forwards, but there was no reply. Michael wiped the sweat from his face with his handkerchief, and then blew his nose. He felt as if his lungs and his sinuses had been scoured out with Ajax.

He heard distant sirens, and the deep beating of helicopters. He also heard a door opening, somewhere far below him, and the distorted sound of people shouting. It wouldn't be very long before the security guards found out where he was – and that would spoil his chance of talking to Raymond Moorpath about the O'Brien autopsy; and 'Mr Hillary'; and the white-faced young men. Not to mention the death of Dr Rice.

Slowly, cautiously, straining his ears for the slightest sound of a footstep, Michael climbed the last flight of stairs to the rooftop. The doors swung and banged, and he reached out with the heel of his left hand and stopped them. He could either ease his way out, or else he could make a mighty leap. He decided, on the whole, that a mighty leap would be better. At least it would give him the advantage of surprise.

He counted to three – and didn't leap. Then he counted to three a second time, and leaped. The instant he did so, the right-hand door swung back in the wind, and the push-bar handle caught him a hard, numbing knock on the elbow. He was thrown totally off-balance, and tripped, and found himself rolling across the gritty blacktop surface of the roof, grazing both hands, and ripping the knees of his trousers – two triangular tears, like a schoolkid.

Panting, panicking, he scrambled onto his feet. He

looked all around him – but Dr Moorpath hadn't been waiting for him behind the doors. He edged backwards a little, so that he could see behind the stair housing, but there was no sign of Dr Moorpath there, either. He glanced down over the parapet, sixteen storeys down to the rear of the hospital, where he could see steam issuing from the kitchen ventilators, and tiny people walking along the pathways. There was no sign of Dr Moorpath down there or any indication that people were hurrying to look at his fallen body, so he must still be up here, on the roof.

Limping a little, his elbow still humming with pain, Michael slowly circled around the elevator tower and the air-conditioners and the grey-painted water tanks. In the distance he could see the sun glittering on the Inner Harbor, and traffic crossing the Northern Avenue Bridge. A warm, animated hum rose from the city, and Michael felt that he could almost hear individual voices: a woman calling her dog on Boston Common; a husband standing at an open apartment window on Branch Street, telling his wife that he loved her; a girl at a telephone booth on Boylston, arguing with her boyfriend.

Over the south-western horizon, however, the smoke still hung, thick and brown, like the smoke of cremated dreams.

Michael had almost completed an entire circuit of the roof when he came around the corner of the water tanks and there was Dr Moorpath. Michael was about to shout, '*Raymond!*' but his voice died in his mouth.

Dr Moorpath was standing on top of the carved stone coat of arms which crested the north-eastern parapet. His arms were spread wide, as if to balance himself, or to simulate crucifixion. His feet were on the very edge of the coat of arms, and below him there was nothing but a drop of 315 feet to the curved stone steps of the hospital's main entrance. He had his back to Michael, his face to the wind. The skirts of his jacket fluttered and twirled.

Michael shuffled as close as he dared. As soon as he sensed that Dr Moorpath was aware that he was there, he stopped. 'Raymond,' he said, trying to sound encouraging. 'You're not going to do anything rash, are you, Raymond?'

Dr Moorpath didn't answer at first, but bowed his head. Then he called back, 'What's the point of living, Michael, if we can't indulge ourselves in an occasional act of rashness?'

'I came here to talk to you,' said Michael.

'You certainly picked your moment. Two or three seconds later, and nobody would have known.'

'You mean you killed him? You actually killed Dr Rice?'

Dr Moorpath didn't turn around. 'Let's just say that I saved him from something far worse.'

'I don't understand.'

'Five hundred milligrams of potassium chloride stopped his heart almost instantaneously. Better than months of torture, don't you agree, with those clammy young men sucking the very soul out of you?'

'Then you know all about them? You know who they are?'

Dr Moorpath said nothing.

'They assassinated John O'Brien, didn't they?' said Michael. 'I saw the photographs.'

Still Dr Moorpath said nothing.

'Tell me that they assassinated John O'Brien,' Michael insisted. 'Dr Rice hypnotized Frank Coward, and Frank Coward brought the helicopter down on Sagamore Point. That's what happened, isn't it? And that's why they wanted to kill Dr Rice, so that he wouldn't tell anybody how it was done.'

'Since you know so much about it, why ask me?' said Dr Moorpath. 'Why not go directly to Edgar Bedford, or to Commissioner Hudson? Why not go directly to the district attorney's office, or His Honour the mayor? Talk to the *Globe*, talk to the *Phoenix*, talk to the *Herald*. Talk to the TV stations.'

Michael waited for Dr Moorpath to say something more, but he didn't. Instead, he remained balanced on that five and a half inches of sandstone, with his arms spread out, like a heavy black rook.

But what Dr Moorpath had already implied had been quite frightening enough. With a feeling of terrible coldness, Michael realized that there would be absolutely no future in talking to Edgar Bedford about 'Mr Hillary' and the white-faced men – nor to the commissioner of police, nor to the district attorney, nor to the mayor or the media.

In fact, if he tried to pursue the John O'Brien assassination any further, he would probably be putting himself in what Plymouth Insurance usually described as 'a calculated and premeditated position of extreme jeopardy'. In other words, his chances of survival would be so small that nobody would agree to insure him.

What Dr Moorpath was telling him was that Joe Garboden had been right in his suspicions, and that those white-faced men had influence that could only be guessed at. They whispered into all the ears that mattered, gave rewards to those of whom they approved, and took terrifying steps to remove those who happened to displease them.

'Raymond,' Michael appealed, 'you have to tell me who they are.'

Dr Moorpath gave him a minimal shake of his head. 'No, I don't, Michael. And believe me, you'd be better off not knowing.'

'Aren't you going to come down?'

'What for?'

'Nobody's going to harm you, Raymond. And if it's true

what you're saying about the district attorney's office, they're not even going to prosecute you, are they?'

'I didn't do what I was told,' said Dr Moorpath. 'I interfered.'

'So? What can they do?'

'What did they do to Elaine Parker? What did they do to Sissy O'Brien? What did they do your friend Joe Garboden? Believe me, Michael, they want me now, and it's better this way, by far.'

He edged a half-inch closer to the brink of the stone crest. He lifted his face toward the sky. 'They showed me something I didn't believe possible,' he said. 'They showed me the power of the human aura in all its glory.'

'You mean hypnosis, is that what you're talking about, hypnosis?'

'Hypnosis is just the beginning. Hypnosis is just the way in, like the hole in the skirting-board through which the mice wriggle in, to discover the wonderful riches of the larder. The human aura is magical, infinite, astounding – and those who learn to use it can command the very substance of life itself.'

Dr Moorpath was almost hysterical now. Michael cautiously reached out his hand and said, 'Come on, Raymond – come down from there. I want to know more. I want you to tell me more. But I can't do it while you're teetering right on the edge there, honestly.'

Dr Moorpath turned around and stared at Michael over his right shoulder. His face was hair-raising. His eyes were staring and his jaw muscles were clenched so tightly that he looked as he might explode from the inside.

'Watch!' he said.

And stepped off the crest.

And *walked*.

He took long, trudging steps through thin air – up from

the parapet, higher and higher, like a man trying to climb up a deep snowdrift.

Michael couldn't move. He couldn't believe what he was seeing. Yet there, ten feet away, now further, and higher, Dr Moorpath was steadily walking away from him – sixteen storeys above the ground.

Michael couldn't call out, couldn't even speak. He was terrified and thrilled, both at the same time.

Dr Moorpath didn't look back, but hunched his shoulders more. It looked as if he were finding his climb harder and harder. He began to slow down, and once or twice he stumbled. He was nearly thirty feet away from the hospital now, and ten feet higher than the level of the roof. Michael saw a pale, pinkish flicker of light criss-crossing Dr Moorpath's back. The same pinkish flicker that he had seen when Dr Rice had hypnotized him. His etheric body. His aura. And as Dr Moorpath struggled higher and higher, the flickering grew brighter, and more frequent, until his heavy black outline was surrounded by dancing, dazzling bursts of energy.

He lifted one leg, then hesitated; then lifted the other – then hesitated longer.

Thin wisps of smoke began to pour from the back of his jacket.

He raised his left hand, as if he were trying to claw himself up a steep slope. Blinding yellow light burst from his sleeve, and smoke began to run from his wrists like blood. He raised his right hand, and heaved himself a little higher, but it was clear that he couldn't sustain this air-walking for very much longer.

There was a moment when he hung in mid-air, clinging desperately to nothing at all, with black smoke gushing out of his clothes. Then he started to scream and scream, and fire engulfed him from head to foot. There was a crackling noise like fireworks, a thick shower of sparks, and Dr Moorpath spun around and around, his mouth stretched impossibly wide, roaring with agony.

For a moment, Michael thought that he would never fall, that he would continue to spin around in mid-air, until he was all burned up. Fragments of burning clothing fell from Dr Moorpath's shoulders, and blazing fat spat from his thrashing feet. But suddenly he dipped sideways, and dropped. Michael took three stiff steps to the edge of the parapet and watched him fall, tumbling over and over, arms, legs, flame, feet, until he hit the ground like a sackful of burning barbecue ash.

Michael was still standing by the parapet watching him burn when Victor appeared, followed by two security guards.

'Jesus,' said Victor, staring down at the crowds and the splattering of ashes. 'What the hell happened?'

'He set fire to himself,' said Michael, dully. 'He jumped. Same way those Japanese students killed themselves, you remember. It was on the news.'

Victor laid his hand on Michael's shoulder. 'Are you okay?'

'Sure I'm okay,' said Michael; although he felt totally empty, totally flat, as if he were standing for the last time in a house that he was about to leave. No furniture, no rugs, no phone, and – surprisingly – no memories.

Victor glanced down at Dr Moorpath's smoking body; then he glanced back at the parapet.

'Where'd he jump from?' Victor asked.

Michael nodded. 'The top of that crest. He was already standing there when I got up here. I talked to him. I asked him to come down. But there was nothing I could do.'

Victor looked down at the body yet again. 'He was standing on top of that crest, and he jumped all the way over there? Come on, Michael, that's at least – '

Michael said, 'Yes?' and stared intently at Victor, and then mouthed 'later' – trying to show him that he didn't want to discuss what had happened to Dr Moorpath in front of these two security guards.

'Oh,' said Victor, looking back down to the ground. 'I see what you mean.'

Two doll-sized medics were hurriedly wheeling a trolley out to the place where Dr Moorpath had fallen. The guards said to Michael and Victor, 'Come on, you two bozos. The police are going to want to talk to you.'

Victor said, 'Listen, friend, you don't call us "bozos". You call us "doctor" and you call us "sir." '

The guard let out a long sigh, as if he really didn't give a shit. 'Come on, then, doctor and sir. The cops are waiting to talk to you two bozos downstairs.'

Sixteen

Michael had just finished making photocopies of Joe Garboden's assassination pictures when his office door opened without warning. He stuffed the last picture into its envelope and switched off the Xerox. To his surprise, it was Edgar Bedford, the grand old man of Plymouth Insurance. Edgar Bedford was stocky, bull-necked, with white crinkly hair. He had a large, handsome head, but his face was marred with crimson-and-white blotches that always reminded Michael of corned-beef hash. Too much sun, too many skin-peels, too many six-ounce martinis.

He was wearing a tuxedo and a black bow tie, and he smelled of Xeryus aftershave, a young man's fragrance which jarred with his appearance. He put his head around the door, and looked this way and that, and then smiled the smile of a man who has no need whatsoever to be ingratiating to anybody.

'Ah, Rearden,' he said. His voice was thick and oddly indistinct, like a poorly recorded soundtrack. 'You've been working late.'

'Yes, sir. I've just been winding up the O'Brien investigation, sir.'

'Well … sad business all around.' Edgar Bedford walked into the centre of the room, and peered at some of the memos on the wall. 'And I'm particularly sad to lose Joe.'

'You heard about Dr Moorpath?' asked Michael, trying not to sound provocative.

Edgar Bedford nodded. 'I knew Raymond for twenty-five years. We used to play golf together. Very sad indeed.'

Michael shrugged and said, 'He'd been under quite a bit of a strain, that's what I heard.' (Watching – in his mind's eye – Raymond Moorpath spinning and burning in mid-air, and screaming in pain.)

Edgar Bedford turned and fixed him with a watery-eyed stare. 'Yes,' he said, after a while. 'That's what I heard, too. You'll – er – finish up this O'Brien thing, won't you, and have it on my desk as soon as you can?'

'I was wondering if you wanted me to stay on,' said Michael.

Edgar Bedford frowned at him, as if he didn't understand what 'stay on' could possibly mean.

Michael took a breath, and then said, 'Now this is finished – this O'Brien thing – maybe you can find me something else.'

'Ah,' said Edgar Bedford. 'That was one of the reasons I wanted to talk to you.'

'Well, fine – I'm willing to take on another case. I think I've got my psychological difficulties pretty well licked.'

391

Edgar Bedford didn't seem to be listening. He looked around until he found a typist's chair, which he rolled across to the centre of the room. He sat down, and folded his arms, and looked up at Michael with an expression that Michael had never seen on anybody's face before. Contemptuous, proprietorial – but anxious, too – as if he didn't hold Michael in any respect whatsoever, but was worried that Michael might upset the carefully orchestrated balance of Bedford life.

'I'm going to tell you something, Michael. My family have dominated Boston society for nearly a hundred years.'

'I'm aware of that, sir.'

'You know how we did that? You know how we acquired such influence?'

'Well, sir, I'm pretty sure that you're going to tell me.'

'We acquired that influence by making the right friends. That's how we did it. We made the right friends. We were good to the people who could help us and we were unforgiving with those people who tried to do us down.'

Michael nodded, as if he fully understood what this lecture was all about.

Edgar Bedford paused for a while, and then he said, 'I'm no fool, Rearden, whatever you take me for. In your own way, you're one of us, and that makes you charmed. But being charmed doesn't mean that you're invulnerable – and being charmed doesn't mean that you can do what you like, and poke your nose into business that doesn't concern you. So I'm telling you now – you wrap up this O'Brien report – accidental death – satisfy the underwriters – and maybe we'll think of keeping you on.'

Michael stood in front of Edgar Bedford with Joe's assassination photographs held behind his back.

'All right, Mr Bedford,' he said. And Edgar Bedford fixed him with watery, washed-out eyes, and Michael knew that the floor was opening up, right beneath his feet, but he refused to look, he refused to fall.

Whether Edgar Bedford had sensed Michael's moment of apprehension or not, he stood up, and rolled away the typist's chair, and tried to smile. 'It's the making of friends, Rearden, that's what makes the world go round. I'll look forward to reading your report. By the way, Joe's funeral is Saturday, 11 a.m. at Wakefield Crematorium. It's odd, that, I wouldn't have taken him for a Wakefield man, would you? But I guess that I'll see you then.'

When Edgar Bedford had left, Michael stood in the twilit copying-room for two or three minutes, and thought of Raymond Moorpath climbing into the air. *That's how we did it*, Edgar Bedford had said. *We made the right friends.*

He called Patsy. He didn't tell her about Raymond Moorpath. She was finding it difficult enough as it was, with his prolonged absences, and Joe being killed, and Dr Rice being injured (he hadn't yet told her that Dr Rice was dead, too). What was more, the television news channels were making a meal of the Boston race riots, and every bulletin was crowded with live footage of firefights and ambushes and buildings burning, and terrified children running for their lives.

The mayor had called in National Guard reserves and SWAT squads, but every new initiative seemed to fuel the rioting more. Decades of anger and malice and alienation were stacked up like a bonfire, and every attempt to suppress them was like throwing on canfuls of gasoline.

'You'll be happy to hear that Edgar Bedford has told me to wrap this whole thing up,' said Michael. 'I should be finished by the weekend. Then I'll come on home.'

'Jason misses you,' said Patsy. 'And I miss you, too. I know what I said about the money ... but somehow it doesn't seem so important any more.'

Michael didn't know what to say. He thought about Megan, sliding down from her wheelchair. He thought about wiping her face. He could have cried, he felt so ashamed of himself.

'Plymouth might give me more work later. I don't know. I'll have to see.'

'Maybe you could finish that board game you were working on.'

He swallowed. He had tears in his eyes. 'Yes, sure. Maybe I could.'

At three o'clock in the morning, the phone rang. He sat up in bed, sweating, frightened. He had been dreaming again. The same dream, with the President walking toward him, smiling, his hand held out. And his own voice, very slow-motion, *Nooooo Mr Pressiddennnt doonnnn't coommme neaaaarrr mmmeeee* –

The phone kept on ringing and it took him a while to realize where he was, and where the phone was, and to pick it up.

'Michael?' said a harsh, Boston-Irish twang. 'This is Giraffe.'

'Giraffe? Do you know what time it is?'

'Three-oh-three. Can you get yourself around to my apartment – like directly?'

'You mean *now*?'

'The sooner the better. This is important, Mikey. This is what we've all been looking for.'

He wasn't confident of finding a taxi at that time of night, so he drove himself to Thomas Boyle's apartment and parked across the street. The night wind was warm, and there were still a few night owls strolling on the sidewalks. A man was standing next to the mailbox on the corner, his face shaded by a hat. He stood with his arms by his sides and he didn't move. Michael hesitated for a moment, and thought about accosting him, but then he decided that it was probably safer not to. What, after all, could he say? 'You look like one of the white-faced men that my friend thinks are responsible for assassinating famous people since way back when? What are you doing here?'

He rapped at Thomas's door with his knuckles in case Megan was asleep and the doorbell woke her; but it was Megan who answered. 'Hallo, Michael, how are you?'

He took her hand and squeezed it. It was an acknowledgement that what they had done together had been induced by 'Mr Hillary', and not by any lust for each other. But it was important for them both to stay friends.

Thomas and Victor were sitting at the dining-table, drinking coffee and talking to a huge, handsome black man in a green djellaba. He rose up when Michael came in, and held out both hands.

'Mikey, this is Matthew Monyatta, of the Olduvai Black Consciousness Group.'

'Pleased to meet you,' said Michael. 'I think I've seen you on television.'

Matthew grinned. 'I expect you have. Now and again they need a black revolutionary to give their programmes some political balance.'

'Do you want some coffee?' asked Thomas. 'Matthew has something pretty important to tell us.'

'It's a little early for me,' Michael told him. 'And, by the way, I think we're being followed and watched. There's a guy hanging out across the street ... I can't be sure, but he looks like the same guy who was watching my apartment, too.'

Matthew said, 'Oh, yes, you're being watched, all right. Everybody who threatens the white-white men is being watched. Twenty-four hours of the day.'

'The white-white men?' asked Michael.

'That's what people call them in Africa and the Middle East. It's because of their faces. Once seen, never forgotten. White, with their eyes shaded.'

'What did you say the other evening?' Michael asked Victor. 'Something about the lily-white boys?'

'The lily-white boys, they're one and the same people,' Matthew nodded. 'It's what you might call an irony. Their faces are white, their skin is white, but their souls are as black as night.'

'Do you know who they are?' asked Michael. He could hardly believe what he was hearing.

Matthew nodded. 'I surely do. That's why I telephoned Lieutenant Boyle here, as soon as I saw his news conference on the television.'

'Tell Michael what you told me,' said Thomas. 'Tell him about the bones.'

Matthew reached into the neckline of his djellaba and produced a soft grey leather bag. He loosened the draw-string that kept it fastened, and spread a dozen small white bones onto the tabletop.

'These are the bones. Witch-doctors used them in Kenya to foretell the future and to divine the secrets of the past. Three weeks ago I cast the bones and the bones warned me that the white-white men were restless.'

'How did they do that?' asked Michael, trying not to sound too sceptical. But it was only four o'clock in the morning, and he had expected something more believable than bones.

Matthew drew the palm of his hand across the bones and they rolled over and changed their pattern. 'I know what's going on in your mind, Michael. You think the bones are primitive; and you think the bones are nothing but black man's superstition. Who can tell the future from a dead rooster? Who can tell the past from bones alone? But I was taught how to use these by a witch-doctor who lived close to Olduvai, and this witch-doctor had been taught to use them by the witch-doctor before him, and so forth, and so on, right back, over a thousand years, the same knowledge, the same psycho-kinetic skill, even before they had a scientific name for it.

'The bones are the same as dowsing-rods; but they don't sense water. Instead, they sense a person's spirit – and when a person's spirit is disturbed, or restless, the bones twitch, and jump, and shift of their own accord. The white-white men have very powerful spirits, spirits which affect the whole of human society, so when the white-white men are restless – well, the bones pretty soon warn you about it.'

'And this is what happened three weeks ago?' asked Thomas, making notes in a springbound notebook.

'This is what *started* three weeks ago,' said Matthew, 'and the bones have been getting more twitchy ever since. I knew that something wicked was coming this way, I knew that somebody important was going to die. But the bones didn't give me no clue as to whom it might be, they were real confused; and so when Mr O'Brien's helicopter came down like that, and everybody was killed, there was nothing I could do but mourn. I couldn't be sure that it was the white-white men who had done the deed, although I had my suspicions, because the bones were literally *leaping* that day, dancing on the table like little dead men. And then, of course, I saw them.'

'You saw them?' asked Thomas. 'You saw the white-white men?'

Matthew hesitated, and lowered his head. When he spoke, his voice was much more subdued. 'I saw them down at Patrice Latomba's.'

Thomas's pencil paused over his notepad. 'Was this before Verna Latomba was murdered, or afterwards?'

'I saw them there, I saw them with Verna. She was all tied up, and they'd been hurting her. Dropping candlewax on her, cutting her with knives.'

Thomas stared at him. 'You saw them with Verna, you saw them doing that, and you didn't call the police? Matthew – you could have saved her life!'

Matthew looked back at him defiantly. 'The white-white men told me to mind my own business. Don't you think that hurt, walking out like that? Don't you think that I was ashamed? Ashamed of myself, ashamed of my race, ashamed of my cowardice?'

'But, Jesus, Matthew –'

Matthew banged his fist on the table. 'You don't know what you're dealing with! These aren't mafiosi, or Yardie gangs, or Chinese tongs! *These are the white-white men*!'

Michael looked away. He was embarrassed by Matthew's outburst, but he was also embarrassed by his own thoughts. The white-white men? For Christ's sake. Was this what Thomas had dragged him out of bed for? To listen to all of this superstitious babble? Yet Matthew seemed like such a proud man, a man of such strength and character.

Thomas said, with great gentleness, 'Come on, Matthew, tell me. What makes the white-white men so much worse than the Mafia?'

Matthew took a deep breath. 'You really don't understand, do you? The Mafia have honour, the Mafia have religion, the Mafia have codes of conduct. Maybe they're killers, maybe they deal in drugs and prostitution and gambling. But they have pride, they have family loyalty, no matter how perverted that pride and that loyalty may be. The white-white men have none of that. The white-white men are guilty of every sin that it's possible for anyone to

398

be guilty of. Every excess. Every cruelty. And that's what they are – the most cruellest creatures on God's earth, the very personification of all evil.'

'And you saw Verna Latomba in the hands of these men, and you didn't make any attempt to save her?'

'No, I didn't.'

'Are you proud of that?'

'No, I'm not. But there was nothing that I could do; and nothing that anybody else could have done. And if I'd crossed them, believe you me, they would have been coming after me, too, like sharks out of hell, for ever and ever, until they got me. I tried to kid myself that it was nothing more than a little bit of drug business between Patrice and Luther Johnson and the white-white men. I don't know whether you even know this, but the white-white men, they're heavily into drugs, not because of the profit, mind, but because of the social disruption that drugs cause. That's why they like to sell to MIT students and Ivy Leaguers … that's what your Ivy Connection is all about. You sell crack to a kid on Blue Hill Avenue, what real difference does it make? He doesn't have no social influence, he's just one more sad statistic. But you sell crack to a physics major or a would-be lawyer or an up-and-coming young politician – then you cause some damage. Then you start destroying hundreds of lives, thousands, for the price of one.'

Victor said, 'What made you call Lieutenant Boyle tonight?'

'Guilt, I guess. And the facts you put out in that press conference of yours, which made me one hundred per cent sure that it was the white-white men who killed John O'Brien and Elaine Parker and that insurance friend of yours. You said that they were all marked in the same identical way, with the puncture holes deep in their backs – well, my blood just turned to ice-water. Because nobody does that, except the white-white men – just like Count Dracula leaving the famous fang holes in women's necks.'

Michael said, 'Where do they come from, these white-white men? I mean, who exactly are they? Are they aliens, or what?'

Matthew gave a loud bellow of bitter laughter, and banged the dining-table with his fist. 'You could say that! You could say that! Aliens, I like that!'

'Come on, Matthew,' said Thomas. 'This isn't a joke.'

'Oh, yes it is,' Matthew retorted. 'It's a joke on you. If you thought that your white Western civilization was free of all of its obligations from times gone by, then it's a joke on you. How many Jewish Americans go back to Israel, to meditate and to pray? How many black Americans go back to Nigeria, and Sierra Leone, to think about their roots? How many Irish go back to Ireland, and Germans to Germany, and Neapolitans to Naples? We are all inextricably entangled, every one of us, in what we are, and what our ancestors were – and that's the fine thing about humanity, and race, and we should all be proud of it, and not ashamed.'

'But what about the white-white men?' Thomas insisted.

Matthew took a sip of espresso and then a sip of plain water. He leaned forward on the table and his face was serious. Michael thought that his face was almost like a landscape – broad and pitted, with veldts for cheeks and high sierras for cheekbones and caverns for nostrils – and above them all, a tableland that formed his forehead.

'The white-white men go back to the days of Leviticus, which was the third book of Moses, and that was written sixteen hundred years ago. The book of Leviticus shows the way in which men could be separated from their sin, and its consequences, and do you know how?

'The Lord ordered his high priest Aaron to "select a goat for Azazel" on the Jewish Day of Atonement. "Aaron shall lay both of his hands on the head of the live goat, and confess over it all the iniquities of the sons of Israel, and all their transgressions in regard to all their sins; and he shall lay them on the head of the goat and send it away into the wilderness by the hand of a man who stands in readiness." And when they talked about sins in those days, they meant every kind of sin … from touching a menstruating woman, to uncovering the nakedness of your brother's wife, to lying with a male as one lies with a female, which is an abomination, and you'd better believe it.

'In other words, Aaron was supposed to choose a scapegoat, and invest it with everybody's sins, and drag it out into the desert, and throw it off a cliff, and from then on, everybody was supposed to be pure, everybody was supposed to be lily-white. I mean, come on, man, all of their sins went over that cliff, along with the goat, now didn't they?'

'Scapegoat,' Michael repeated, and couldn't think why the word sounded so familiar. '*Scapegoat.*'

Matthew said, 'Leviticus is pretty detailed on what kind of goats you ought to use, and which bits you can eat and which bits you ought to burn. But what Leviticus doesn't tell you is that Aaron didn't use no *real* goat. If you look in the Egyptian testaments, if you read the Sumerian stories, Aaron used a *man*, not a goat. Aaron used a man who was supposed to be Azazel, the fallen angel, who walked the earth in those days, the same way that you and me can walk the earth, excepting of course that Azazel was seriously frightening.'

'Excuse me, an *angel?*' Victor asked.

Matthew shrugged. 'That's what people called them, although who they really were, nobody knows. They had human shape, and they spoke human languages, although sometimes they could change their shape, and sometimes they could speak in tongues that nobody had ever heard of. They were easy to recognize, though, because they had tremendous personal auras, and there was usually something significantly different about them, like an extra nipple, or strangely-coloured hair. Azazel was called Goat because his eyes were slitted and he *looked* like a goat.'

Victor sceptically shook his head, but Thomas looked up and said, 'Go on.'

'Well,' said Matthew, 'the people chose Azazel to atone for all of their sins because he was different and because they were frightened of him. Aaron laid his hands on top of Azazel's head, and then a man dragged him out into the desert on the end of a rope and threw him over a cliff. Everybody danced and sang and shouted out the Hebrew equivalent of "terrific, that's the end of it, that's all of our sins atoned for."

'But, as it turned out, they weren't. Because Azazel survived. Injured, broken, but still alive. And Azazel spent twenty years wandering the desert as a nomad, as a tramp, and all the time he had the combined sins of all of those people, the tribe of Israel, locked up inside of him. Through no fault of his own, Azazel was evil incarnate. He killed sheep and camels. He raped women, he raped little girls; he raped dogs, he raped boys; but you can't blame him for it. Blame God, blame Aaron. Blame anybody who still believes in the Lord Thy God. Because Azazel had absolved the Tribe of Israel of *everything*, no matter what it was. Azazel had taken on all of their viciousness, all of their perversion, all of their guilt.

'He was immortal, too, or at least he was unnaturally long-lived. You can raise your eyebrows at that, my friends, but the very plain fact of the matter is that angels are true. Not storybook angels, with wings and haloes and harps; but men who were present in the Days of Magic, when the Lord

God still walked abroad, whatever He was, and miracles and magic were still openly performed.

'They were even supposed to be able to fly – although the expression that you always find in all of the ancient writings is "walk in the air".

'Good God, I don't pretend to know. But I do know that Azazel was real. He's mentioned again and again in different writings from all kinds of different tribes and different cultures.

'According to the stories, he made his way on a Greek merchant ship to the country that we now call Morocco, and started living in an isolated castle overlooking the Straits of Gibraltar. From there, he put out the word that he was gathering around him all those who were magical and disaffected – strange and unnatural outcasts from all over the known world.

'Communications were slower in those days; but they were effective. What you whispered in the Cairo bazaar in September would be whispered into the ear of the Emperor of China the following May.

'The white-white men came from all over Europe and Africa and parts of Asia Minor. Some of them came by sea; others came on trade caravans. Others walked for hundreds of miles.'

'But who were they?' asked Victor. 'Where did they come from?'

'I don't know,' said Matthew. 'I don't suppose we'll ever know for sure. *The Book of Enoch* suggests that they were angels, scattered by the Flood, and in hiding ever since – persecuted because they were different. Hounded because they were magic.

'Maybe that's true, maybe it's just a myth. Whatever they were, they were pretty damned strange, and that was for sure. First off, they never slept. Can you imagine that, *they never slept!* They stayed awake from one year's end to the next, and because of that, their eyes grew totally bloodshot. In the *Book of Enoch*, they're called the Watchers, because they're always watching, never sleeping, never tired – or eternally tired, who's to know?

'In African dialect, in Nigeria and Sierra Leone and Senegal, and in Haiti and Martinique, too, they call them the white-white men. Eyes like rubies, skin like snow. In Europe, they've long-forgotten them mostly, but they still remember "two, two, the lily-white boys, dressed all in green o." '

Thomas said, with complete seriousness, 'What you're trying to tell us, Matthew, is that these white-white men are centuries old? That they never sleep? That they never die?'

'Man, you *know* they never die!' Matthew retorted, his jowls swaying. 'They *never* die! They only die when Azazel *says* they die!'

'Go on,' said Michael. He didn't feel like getting involved in a slanging match, particularly when he had very little idea of what he was talking about.

'The white-white men did everything they could to serve Azazel. But it wasn't easy, because Azazel didn't eat any kind of food, being an angel. All the same, he was here on Earth, on the third stone from the sun, and he did need *some* kind of sustenance.

'The sustenance he needed was human adrenaline. After all, he was carrying around inside of him all of those human evils, all of those human misdeeds, and they burned up inside him, they consumed him. He needed human energy to keep him alive.

'Now – there's been a gross misapprehension that the white-white men drink blood. This is mainly because of their eyes, being red and all. The white-white men gave rise to the myth of vampires, and the Dracula story. But they never happened – vampires never existed! You know what God says in Leviticus? "I will set My face against that person who eats blood, and will cut him off from among his people. No person among you may eat blood. For blood is the life of all flesh."

'Even the darkest of demons obeys that law. But they need adrenaline; they need it real bad. And that's why they kidnap and torture young girls – to frighten them, to hurt them, so that they produce huge amounts of extra adrenaline. The white-white men always carry those thin metal pipes, so that they can slide them into somebody's back, and find their kidneys, and suck their adrenaline before they know.'

'So, Matthew – how do you know all this?' asked Victor.

Matthew slowly turned to him, and held his gaze steady and true. 'I know because I came from Olduvai, and because I've studied religion and anthropology for thirty years, and winnowed the real from the plain fantastic. I know because I believed when traditionalists and sceptics wouldn't believe; and because I had some magic in me. You want me to cast the bones, and see what you've got coming in *your* life?'

Victor gave him an angular smile. 'It's okay, Matthew … I don't think so.'

'Tell me some more about this scapegoat character,' said Thomas.

Matthew finished his coffee and wiped his mouth. 'Well … ever since Aaron first threw Azazel off of the cliff, and Azazel survived, Azazel promised himself that he would give us all of our sins back … the same sins that Aaron laid on him, on the day of atonement. He would keep the world in a state of strife, killing off anybody who looked as if they might bring peace and understanding. His white-white men would breed with human women, so that the world's bloodlines would be permanently contaminated. Like it says in the Bible, "he and his followers saw that the children of men had multiplied and that beautiful and comely daughters were born unto them. They mingled with the women and they began to defile themselves with them."

'The white-white men taught their wives all kinds of enchantments and charms, as well as the science of root-cutting and botany; and Azazel taught their sons the art of war, and the making of swords and shields. He also taught women how to use cosmetics, "the art of deception by ornamenting their bodies", and he revealed the secrets of witchcraft.

'Azazel has been causing chaos, war and social disruption for centuries, turning brother against brother, race against race. What do you think all this rioting on Seaver Street is all about? The white-white men, tearing our community apart. What do you think John O'Brien's killing was all about? Every time that some human being has been fa-voured by God, every time some human being looks like he's going to ease some major problem in the world's condition, Azazel has him killed. Not by the white-white men, not often … but by some kind of stooge, like Sirhan Sirhan, who shot Bobby Kennedy; or James Earl Ray, who shot Martin Luther King.

'Azazel is the Great Goat, Azazel is all the sins of Israel, to the nth power, because we're being paid back for the day of atonement with interest.'

Thomas sat back and tapped his ballpen thoughtfully against his teeth. 'You realize how wacky this sounds.'

Matthew said, 'Of course it sounds wacky. But that's only because the white-white men have kept themselves so well-concealed for so long. I have to call them angels because that's what people called them back in the days of Leviticus and I don't know what else they could be. We used to think that schizophrenics were possessed by Satan, but just because we've learned better, that doesn't stop them being crazy. Maybe these white-white men are nothing more than "differently abled" – maybe they're suffering from some kind of genetic disorder that prevents them from sleeping, and gives them a thirst for extra adrenaline. Until we get a chance to study them, we'll never know.'

'You really think that Azazel is still alive? The same Azazel that Aaron took out into the desert?'

'I don't know. What do you think? Is it possible for any kind of earthbound creature to live for sixteen hundred years? I don't really think that it matters. Even if Azazel himself isn't alive, his name is alive, and his work is alive, and his rituals are still alive.

'Whenever the white-white men assassinate anybody, they always take away a vital piece of that person's body so that resurrection becomes impossible.'

'I didn't know resurrection *was* possible,' put in Victor.

Matthew turned to him, and he made no attempt to hide the scorn in his voice. 'It's obvious, my friend, that you never went to Haiti, nor studied the voodoo religion, because resurrection is not just possible, but common ... and not just in the Caribbean, either. There are dead men walking in Boston, my friend. There are dead men walking in Manhattan. You start looking out for them, you'll see.'

'So they do this with every assassination victim?' Thomas interrupted, trying to get back to the subject.

'That's right, every single one. They took Abraham Lincoln's heart; they took John F. Kennedy's brain. They took the eyes from Martin Luther King and the lungs from Anwar Sadat. If they can't take anything away at the scene of the assassination, they have plenty of doctors and morticians under their thumbs.'

Michael had a vivid mental picture of Dr Moorpath, climbing precariously into the air. Maybe Matthew Monyatta was exaggerating. Maybe he was mixing up fact with mumbo-jumbo. But Michael had seen the power of the white-white men at first hand, the so-called lily-white boys, and he knew that it was frighteningly real.

A power from Old Testament times. A power that had all of the magic and all of the mystery of the Bible itself.

'What did they take from John O'Brien?' asked Matthew. 'You didn't mention on the news that he was mutilated in any way.'

'How do you know that he was mutilated?'

'Because it was the white-white men who did for him, and like I say, the white-white men always take something.'

Thomas was silent for a while, still leaning back, still thoughtful. 'All right,' he said at length. 'They took his head. They decapitated him with Holmatro cutters – the same tool the fire department uses to cut people out of automobile wrecks. There was blood everywhere, but no head. We could only suppose that the perpetrator had taken it away as a trophy.'

'Well, that's half right,' Matthew nodded. 'They took it partly as a trophy, and partly as a precaution.'

Victor said, 'Let me ask you something ... have any of the white-white men ever been known to die?'

Matthew shook his head. 'They keep their secrets well-protected – how they live, how they survive. They have a great many friends in high places, friends who are richly rewarded for helping them. They also have a great many enemies in high places, but almost all of their enemies are far too frightened to touch them. Better to look the other way, if you know what I mean.

'There's a story, though, that one old merchant in Morocco went to visit the white-white men because they had

408

taken his favourite daughter so that they could defile her. He pleaded with the white-white man who had abducted her, but the white-white man refused to give her back.

'But it is a rule of Arab courtesy that a visitor to one's house must never be asked to leave. So the merchant stayed all day and all night at the white-white man's house, pleading with him not to besmirch his daughter's purity, and of course the white-white man had no choice but to sit there and listen to him. The merchant stayed another day and another night, and could hardly keep himself awake, but of course the white-white man never slept. It became obvious to the merchant that he would soon have to sleep, and then the white-white man would have the chance to leave him, and take his daughter. So he began to chant a song that his grandmother used to sing to him when he was a child, to send him to sleep, and he swung his pendant in front of the white-white man's eyes, to and fro.

'The white-white man fell asleep; and as he slept, his real age began to tell on him, and he began to dry up, and shrink, until there was nothing left but a –'

'*Small, curled-up, hairy thing like a swede,*' Thomas interrupted.

Matthew stared at him. 'How did you know that?'

'Because I've seen one. Leastways, I've seen a photograph of one. It was hanging in the hallway of the house on Byron Street where we found Elaine Parker. There were all of these Victorian-looking people standing around a table, and one of these dried-up things was right there on the table in front of them.'

'Then you're beginning to believe me?' asked Matthew.

Victor said, 'I think I need some more coffee.'

Thomas jotted down some more notes. Then he said to Matthew, 'There's something underlying all of this mythical stuff. I'm not sure that I believe that the white-white men were responsible for every major assassination ever. But I think enough of what you've been telling us squares with the facts to make it worth some further investigation.'

'And what that merchant did, that was hypnosis,' said Michael. 'And the only times I've ever seen this "Mr Hillary" character, that was under hypnosis.'

'What name did you say?' asked Matthew. There was genuine anxiety in his voice.

' "Mr Hillary," ' Michael repeated. 'I've been undergoing hypnotherapy, and the past couple of times I've been hypnotized, I've seen this tall white-haired man called "Mr Hillary." '

Matthew touched his hand to his forehead, a gesture to ward off evil.

'Saint Hilary was the only Pope who was known to consort with the white-white men. That was back in the fifth century. There are stories that he was seen with Azazel. There were stories that he *was* Azazel. He was supposed to have come from Sardinia, but some people believe that he came originally from Morocco.'

'Coincidence?' asked Thomas.

'I don't think so,' said Michael. 'There have been too many goddamned coincidences in this case, and all of the coincidences point to one particular party. "Mr Hillary", of Goat's Cape, Nahant.'

'All right,' said Thomas, stretching. 'I think I could use some more coffee, too.'

'What are you going to do?' asked Michael.

'I'm going to have a long think,' Thomas replied.

'Is that all? What about "Mr Hillary"?'

'What about him? He has a name that sounds the same as the name of a fifth-century Pope. He's appeared in your hypnotic trances. He's also appeared in your hypnotherapist's notebook. Oh – and I forgot. A blind man said his name to you in the street. I don't think we have quite enough justification for pulling him in, do you?'

'You could stake out his house,' Michael suggested.

Thomas shook his head. 'I couldn't justify that, either. Not legally, not financially.'

'Then *I'll* stake out his house.'

'You stay away from his house. Keep digging, keep sifting. If and when you find something, let me know.'

Matthew said, 'You're going to go after the white-white boys, lieutenant?'

'If they exist – and if they did what you say they've done, then I'll go after them.'

Matthew heaved his enormous bulk out of his chair, and brushed down his djellaba. 'In that case, a word to the wise. Never let the white-white men in through your door. Never speak to them. Never look at their eyes. And if you see one at night, make sure you have a flashlight or a candle, and never turn your back.'

Thomas showed him to the door. 'I want to thank you for all of your trouble.'

'You don't yet know what trouble is, lieutenant.'

'Well … it sounds like I'm going to find out.'

Matthew touched his forehead again. 'May the good spirits keep you safe from harm, believe me.'

Michael left Thomas's apartment shortly after eight o'clock, after Megan had made them all breakfast and they had discussed the implications of Matthew Monyatta's stories. All three of them agreed that Joe's assassination pictures were *prima facie* evidence that there was some kind of conspiracy behind most of the major political killings of the past 120 years. But they weren't at all sure if the pale-faced men who appeared in all of the pictures were the same men – or if they were Matthew's so-called 'white-white men'

411

– or if they really were the sleepless descendants of Old Testament angels.

'Remember that Matthew's a revolutionary,' put in Thomas. 'He could be setting us up for his own political ends, or simply to make us look like superstitious idiots.'

'I didn't get that feeling,' said Michael. 'I got the feeling that he was genuinely afraid.'

Megan wheeled herself into the room with fresh toast. She laid her hand on Michael's hand, and he could physically feel the warmth of her aura.

'Have you had enough?' she asked him.

He looked at Thomas and Thomas smiled; and Michael felt like the rat that ate the malt that lay in the house that Jack built.

When he got back to his apartment, he tiredly dragged off his sweater and threw it down on the couch. Then he sat down to take off his shoes. The red light on the answering machine was flashing, so he jabbed the play button to hear his messages. There was a click, and a lengthy hiss, and then he faintly heard music playing – strange discordant music, like somebody trying to express a migraine headache on the violin.

Then, very loudly – almost as loudly as if he were standing right next to him – he heard a thick, breathy voice.

'You have tried our patience too far, Michael. We have tried to encourage you, tried to be tolerant. You could have enjoyed a quiet and prosperous life, if only you had looked away. Looking away is no sin, Michael. We have to protect ourselves, you understand that. Every social order has a right to protect itself. That is why we have borrowed your wife and your son, Michael – for no other reason, except to protect ourselves. All you have to do, Michael, is to look away, and never, ever look back.'

That was all. The scraping music continued for a little while longer, and then died away, and the message ended. Michael immediately picked up the phone and jabbed out his home number in New Seabury. The first time, he pressed the wrong number, and he was greeted by a continuous whining tone. The second time, he heard his home phone beeping, but it beeped and beeped for almost a minute and nobody answered.

He phoned Thomas. 'I came back and there was a message on my answering machine. Somebody said that he'd "borrowed" Patsy and Jason. I phoned them but there was no reply.'

'You're sure they didn't go out for a while?'

'Patsy's normally home at this time of the morning. Jason's at school.'

'Why don't you call the school, see if he's shown up. If he hasn't, I'll call my old friend Walt Johnson down at Hyannis and have him check out your house. The main thing is not to panic.'

'Giraffe –'

'What is it, Mikey?'

'I think it was him. The voice on the phone. I think I recognized it.'

'That's a good start. Who do you think it was?'

'I'm ninety-nine percent sure that it was "Mr Hillary."'

There was a very long silence. Then Thomas said, 'Oh, shit.'

'Why, "oh, shit"?' Michael wanted to know.

'Listen,' said Thomas, 'we know where "Mr Hillary" lives, don't we?'

'That's right – so if he's kidnapped Patsy and Jason –'

'He may have kidnapped Patsy and Jason, yes. If he's involved in the John O'Brien killing, then he certainly had a motive to kidnap Patsy and Jason, to stop you from digging

413

into it any further. But I can't search his house without a warrant, and in order to get hold of a warrant I have to show just cause.'

'But I recognized his voice! What more "just cause" do you need than that?'

'Did you ever meet "Mr Hillary"?'

'Well, no, of course, not. But –'

'Mikey – where do you recognize his voice *from*?'

'He talked to me, for Christ's sake! He talked to me when I was under hyp –'

He stopped. He suddenly understood what Thomas was trying to tell him. No judge would grant a search warrant on the basis of an identification that was based on a voice heard in a hypnotic trance.

'Call the school,' Thomas urged him. 'Call the school, then call me back.'

'Okay,' said Michael, and hung up.

He searched through his address book until he found the school's number, and dialled it. But he knew even before he had talked to Jason's class-teacher what the answer was going to be. Patsy and Jason had been taken – by 'Mr Hillary', by the lily-white boys – and all he could think of was Elaine Parker's cigarette-scorched skin and the slimy cat that still grinned in his nightmares from the ruined body of Sissy O'Brien.

Seventeen

There had been an accident on the McClellan Highway at its intersection with Revere Beach Parkway. A huge tractor-trailer had overturned, and lay on its side like a dead bull-elephant, leaking diesel fuel instead of blood. Traffic was backed up as far as Bennington Street, and Michael and Victor had no choice but to wait in frustration for it to edge its way forward.

It was almost four o'clock by the time they reached Lynn Shore Drive and turned south along the Nahant Beach isthmus. The afternoon was warm, and the sea breeze was feather-light, but the sun was obscured by a thick grey haze, which gave the beach the appearance of a black-and-white photograph, drained of colour.

'You realize that Giraffe is going to go apeshit when he finds out that you've come up here on your own,' Victor remarked.

'Giraffe can do what he likes. Giraffe's family hasn't been kidnapped by some gang of white-faced maniacs.'

'You really think that was "Mr Hillary" on the phone?'

'I played it over and over. I'm sure of it. I don't know how I could have heard his real voice when I was under hypnosis, but I did.'

'Well … Aura Hypnosis is a pretty powerful form of human communication. I don't know whether anybody has the mental strength to talk to somebody else over thirty miles, so clearly that their voice can be recognized. But who knows? The whole thing's still in its infancy. It's like virtual reality without the need for any VR equipment.'

'It's like flying without the need for wings,' put in Michael. 'Just like Dr Moorpath.'

Victor said, 'I wish I'd seen that.'

Michael glanced at him. 'Believe me, it happened.'

'Don't get me wrong … I'm not doubting your word. I just wish I'd seen it.'

'Do you think …'

'What?' asked Victor.

'Well … I saw Dr Moorpath walking through the air like

that, and I suddenly thought about Elaine Parker. She fell thousands of feet out of that airplane, yet she managed to survive. I've been having nightmares about that crash for months. I've fallen out of that L10-11 more times than you can count. I've been falling and falling and each time I've been thinking to myself *if only I could fly.*'

Victor raised his eyebrows. 'What you're trying to suggest is – supposing Elaine Parker flew? Or walked in the air? Or whatever it was that Dr Moorpath did?'

'It's a possibility, isn't it? If he could do it, then maybe she could, too. And people have fallen out of airplanes before, and survived. There was some wartime bomber pilot who fell eighteen thousand feet and landed in some trees.'

They drove past the neatly-painted beach houses of Little Nahant, and then turned off down the rough, sandy track that led to the lighthouse at Goat's Cape. The big Mercury bounced and banged on its suspension, and at one point the rear wheels stuck in a slew of gravel and sand. Suddenly, however, they were out in the open, driving over knobbly clumps of sea-grass, and there ahead of them stood the squat white lighthouse which Michael had seen in his hypnotic trances.

'Better park here,' Victor suggested. 'And turn the car around, in case we have to make a quick getaway.'

Michael manoeuvred the Mercury so that it was facing northward. Then they climbed out and walked the rest of the way to the lighthouse steps. There were no other vehicles parked anywhere near, and the lighthouse itself looked deserted. The lamp was grimy and cracked, and the walls facing the sea were badly weathered.

'Looks empty,' Victor remarked. 'Maybe "Mr Hillary" was just a figment of your imagination, after all.'

Michael shook his head. 'Remember that Megan saw him too.'

416

'Maybe he was a figment of her imagination, too.'

'Oh, come on, Victor. You don't believe that two people could have thought about the same imaginary character, do you? We both went to Goat's Cape – in our trance, anyway. We both saw "Mr Hillary," as clearly as if he was real.'

'Why didn't you tell Giraffe?'

'It wouldn't have made any difference. Besides, I didn't want him to get the wrong idea.'

'What wrong idea?' Victor was perplexed. Michael didn't answer, but thought to himself: just because Megan's in a wheelchair, that doesn't make her any less spirited, or any less attractive, or any less sexy.

Victor looked around, and sniffed. 'Why don't you knock at the door? I'll take a look around the back.'

Michael swallowed. The lighthouse remained adamantly silent, and he was beginning to wish that he hadn't come. Maybe Thomas had been right not to rush off to Goat's Cape without any evidence that 'Mr Hillary' might have kidnapped Patsy and Jason. There was still no concrete evidence that Patsy and Jason had been kidnapped at all. The Barnstable County police were out looking for them, but so far they hadn't reported anything suspicious. The house had been empty, but properly locked. None of the neighbours had reported any shouting or struggling; or seen strangers in the neighbourhood.

But he had such a strong feeling that they were gone, and that 'Mr Hillary' had taken them. It filled his mind like a black, unspoken sentence. As if he knew, but couldn't quite understand why.

And even though the lighthouse was silent, without any sign of life, he could sense that there was something here. Something very dark, and something very strange.

Something that drew him nearer, and made him want to stay.

Something that drew him nearer, and made him *need* to stay.

Victor briefly grasped his arm, and then went sliding down the loose sandy slope that led to the seaward side of the lighthouse. 'There's a couple of outbuildings here,' he called back. 'I'll check them out.'

Michael waited for a moment, and then walked slowly up to the solid oak door. There was a rusted wrought-iron bell-pull, with a corroded nameplate underneath that said ' … ARY L… . EEPER.'

It had probably once read 'Mr Hillary, Lighthouse Keeper'. Ironic that it could now be pronounced as 'Airy Leaper'.

He tugged the bell-pull and waited. He didn't even hear the bell jangling. Maybe it was broken. Maybe the lighthouse was derelict, and Patsy and Jason were already back home, trying to get in touch with him. He checked his watch. Four-twenty. He remembered what his mother had always told him about twenty past the hour. That was the time when angels flew overhead. He cleared his throat and tugged at the bell-pull a second time.

'Nothing so far!' Victor called, from the other side of the lighthouse. 'Only the first bicycle ever invented and some crappy old chicken-coop.'

Michael looked up at the lighthouse walls. There was graffiti chiselled just above the doorway, some of it quite old. 'John Feb'ry 1911' and 'I ♥ Anthea, '34'and – rather incongruously 'Andover Newton Theological School For Ever.'

Further up, however, there was even more graffiti, some of it in mirror-writing and some that was nothing more than triangles and squares and zig-zag lines. Michael had to step back to see some of it, because it was so high up, twenty or thirty feet off the ground.

He suddenly thought to himself: how the hell did anybody get up there, to carve all that? They could have used a ladder, but the steps that led up to the lighthouse door had exceptionally narrow treads, too narrow to accommodate a normal ladder. And what lighthouse keeper would have tolerated somebody climbing the side of his lighthouse and banging out lettering and symbols with a hammer and chisel? One of the phrases in mirror-writing was ONE TENTH EPHAH. Another was UNCLEAN. Most of the rest of them were unintelligible gibberish.

Michael was still frowning up at the graffiti when the lighthouse door opened, totally silently. He didn't even notice at first that it had opened – he was too interested in a pattern of hieroglyphs that looked like various birds, ravens and seagulls and hawks and storks. There were insects, too: things that looked like spiders and centipedes and ants.

The lighthouse door opened even further, and it was then that its gradually-widening blackness caught Michael's attention. He jolted in surprise, and almost lost his footing on the steep steps.

A pale young woman was standing in the doorway. Her eyes were mint green. She was wearing a white cotton headscarf that made her look even paler. She wore a thin gold neck-chain, and an ankle-length dress of the same white cotton as her headscarf.

'Are you looking for somebody?' she asked him, in a thin voice, barely audible over the soft sound of the surf.

'I'm looking for "Mr Hillary". Is he here?'

'Of course. He's been expecting you.'

'Is my wife here? Is my son here?'

'Of course. Didn't you expect them to be?'

Michael felt such a surge of anger and panic that he could hardly breathe. 'Tell "Mr Hillary" he has to let them go now. I mean *now*! I want them here, out, *now*!'

The girl smiled at his anger. 'You can come in and see them.'

'All right, then. But I'm taking them away from here, and I'm taking them now.'

'Why not talk to "Mr Hillary"? He's been wanting to talk to you for such a long time.'

'I intend to. I'm not sure he's going to like what he hears. Victor!'

'Ah,' said the girl. 'We noticed that you'd brought a companion.'

'Yes, I have.'

' "Mr Hillary" would prefer it if your companion were to leave.'

'I don't think "Mr Hillary" is in much of a position to tell anybody what to do. The police know that we're here.'

The girl looked him directly in the eyes, and said, without any vehemence, 'No, they don't.'

Michael recoiled, just a fraction. He had felt a coldness somewhere inside his mind, like a cold needle sliding through brain tissue.

'You don't have to lie to us,' the girl smiled.

Victor came around the lighthouse, polishing his glasses with his handkerchief. 'Salt spray,' he said. Then, '*Well*, what's happening here?'

' "Mr Hillary's" here,' Michael explained. 'So are Patsy and Jason.'

'You've seen them?'

'I'm just going in to see them now.'

'Only you,' the girl told Michael. 'We don't want your companion. Your companion must leave immediately, and say nothing to anyone.'

'Now, hold on, sugar –' said Victor. 'Your "Mr Hillary" has committed a serious offence, and so have you. You just let us in there, and we'll take this gentleman's wife and child and be on our way. Otherwise, all you're doing is compounding your felony even more.'

'Only you,' the girl repeated.

Victor came up the last two steps and confronted the girl directly. 'I am an officer of the Boston coroner's department and I am telling you to take us to Patsy and Jason Rearden right *now*. You understand English?'

The girl didn't seem to be focusing on Victor at all. Her green eyes were still looking at Michael, over Victor's shoulder. There was something *concentrated* about them, as if they were filled with lovingly-distilled jealousy – as if every moment of pain and martyrdom that this girl had felt had been reduced to two liquid drops of infinite greenness.

She laid one hand on Victor's right shoulder and Michael couldn't think what she was doing. But then she gripped his shoulder more tightly, and tensed her neck muscles and then Victor suddenly screamed out, 'Christ! Oh, Christ! Oh, Christ!'

He spun around as if he were on a turntable. His mouth was wide open in horror. The front of his shirt was spouting blood – pints of it – which splattered onto the lighthouse steps. Michael tried to catch him, tried to hold him, but he lost his balance and tumbled down the steps, rolling over and over at the bottom.

Michael, stunned, held up both of his hands, both of them bloody. He stared at the girl and the girl smiled back at him, completely calm, completely self-possessed. Her right hand was bloody, too – right up to the elbow, like a single red evening-glove.

She was holding up a small, narrow-bladed knife. She must have cut Victor open from navel to breastbone, without any hesitation whatsoever.

'Victor!' Michael shouted, and started toward the steps. But the girl instantly stepped out of the doorway and stood in front of him, with the knife raised.

'Get out of my goddamned way!' Michael raged at her.

421

'He's hurt, you could have killed him! *Get out of my god-damned way*!'

He tried to dodge around her, but she swayed from one side of the steps to the other. Her eyes were completely emotionless and he was quite certain that she would cut him open, too.

'Joseph!' she called out, her voice piercingly high-pitched.

Michael feinted and tried to dodge around her again, but she whipped her knife diagonally in front of him, and sliced open the knuckles of his left hand, almost to the bone. Blood ran down, dripped all over the steps. He was forced to tug out his handkerchief and bind it around his fist. It turned immediately from white to scarlet.

'Listen,' he told the girl, shaking with shock. 'You can't just leave him there. He'll bleed to death.'

'I'm afraid he should have thought of that when I asked him to leave,' the girl replied. She said it as matter-of-factly as if she and Victor had disagreed over which restaurant they were going to eat in that night.

Michael looked over the girl's shoulder down the steps and saw that Victor was trying to climb to his feet. He was gripping his sliced-open stomach in one hand, and holding onto the railings with the other.

'Victor!' Michael shouted, but Victor didn't answer, didn't even turn around. He was probably too shocked, and hadn't heard.

'You have to let me help him,' Michael insisted.

'It's all right ... Joseph and Bryan will help him,' the girl smiled. At that moment, as if responding to a stage cue, two black-dressed young men came out of the lighthouse door, white-faced, their eyes hidden behind impenetrably black sunglasses. They scarcely glanced at Michael as they hurried down the steps.

422

'For God's sake, treat him gently!' Michael shouted. Then, to the girl, 'You have to call an ambulance. Come on, you have to call an ambulance *now*! Do you have a phone here?'

'Stop worrying,' the girl smiled. 'Come inside, and see your wife and child. Your companion will be taken care of.'

'He has to have an ambulance!' Michael screamed at her. 'He's dying, you've killed him! He has to have an ambulance!'

At the foot of the steps, Victor looked up, and saw the two white-faced young men hurrying down towards him. Michael couldn't guess what went through his mind. He must have been suffering such shock and agony that he didn't know where he was or what had happened to him. Maybe he thought that he was little, and that his grandmother was warning him all over again about the lily-white boys, the pale-faced boys who came when you were sleeping and sucked out your soul. Whatever it was, he let out a cry of such despair that Michael's neck prickled. He let go of the railings, clutched both of his hands to his stomach, and began to hobble away across the clumpy grass.

'Victor! Victor, don't run!' But there was nothing he could do. He tried to push the girl aside, but she swept her knife against his linen coat, and cut right through the shoulder-padding and into his muscle.

Victor hopped and hobbled toward the seashore, bent almost double. Michael could hear him sobbing as he tried to get away. The pale-faced young men didn't even bother to run after him; they followed him at a brisk, relentless walk, only twenty feet behind. The scene reminded Michael of Zybigniew Cybulski, in *Ashes and Diamonds*, staggering shot and bleeding through the wastelands of Warsaw. He felt the same sense of wasted heroism. He also felt the same sense of unreality, as if he were watching yet another movie.

Victor almost made it to the beach. But then he dropped to his knees, and when he managed to heave himself up onto his feet, his intestines suddenly slid out, and hung between his thighs.

Michael knew that Victor was going to die. Clinically speaking, he was probably dead already. But somehow he managed to take one step onto the sand, and then another, his head arched back so that he was staring up at the grey afternoon sky. The whole baggage of his intestines dragged through the sand, gritty and grey and glistening with blood. He stood for a moment or two, while the two pale-faced men stood beside him. Then he fell face-down into the sand.

Without any hesitation, the two pale-faced men knelt down beside him, pulled up his coat and his shirt, and bared his back. One of them produced two long thin metal pipes, which he probed into Victor's flesh. Then the two of them bent over him, and Michael could see them carefully sipping.

He stared at the girl in disbelief. His stomach was churning, and he felt close to vomiting. 'It's true, then,' he said. 'They do exist.'

'The lily-white boys? Of course it's true.'

'If you touch a hair of my wife's head – if you hurt my boy –' He stopped. He knew how stupid he sounded.

'Come inside,' the girl told him. 'You're really in no position to threaten us, are you?'

He took one last look at Victor, lying on the beach, with those two human carrion-crows hunched over him. Then he stepped into the lighthouse, with the girl following him close behind. She silently closed the door, and for a moment they were plunged into complete blackness. But then a heavy drape was drawn aside, and Michael could see a narrow stone staircase leading upward in a lefthand spiral.

424

He knew where to go. He had already visited this lighthouse in his trance.

He climbed, and he could hear the girl's footsteps whispering up the steps behind him. At last he reached a landing, and the girl said, 'Stop.' He stopped, and she passed close by him, her breasts touching his sleeve, her green eyes never leaving his. She unlocked the door in front of them, and said, 'Come on, now. Follow me. It's time you met "Mr Hillary".'

Michael swallowed dryly. He was feeling light-headed from shock, and from witnessing Victor's terrible death.

'Come on, now,' the girl urged him. 'This is a privilege. This is the high point of your entire life.'

He shuffled reluctantly forward and found himself standing in a huge, dimly-lit library. The vaulted stone ceiling must have gone almost all the way up to the light platform itself. The curved walls were lined with thousands of books, many of them new, but some of them so old that they were nothing but worm-wriggled bundles of dusty paper. There were sofas and tables and chairs arranged in a curiously haphazard way, and the floor was carpeted with layer upon layer of different rugs, most of them threadbare. The largest chair was positioned with its back to the door, so that Michael was unable to see who was sitting in it. But he could see a single arm dangling from one side of it, an arm that was sleeved in softest grey wool, an arm with a long-fingered, emaciated hand.

The fingertips were slowly being rubbed together, in persistent circles, in the way that a man might rub silk, or a woman's hair.

The girl circled around the chair until she was facing the man who was sitting in it. 'He's here,' she announced, softly.

The man must have said something like 'What's that

425

blood on your hand?' because the girl answered, 'He brought a companion. We didn't expect him to. Joseph and Bryan have seen to him.'

The man said something else. The girl looked away, as if she were embarrassed.

Michael waited, uncertain what to do next. But his stomach was beginning to settle, and he was beginning to feel a little bolder. After all, if they had wanted to murder him, they probably would have done it already. They wanted him here for a reason.

'I demand to see my wife and son!' he called out, as loudly as he could.

The girl snapped him a sharp, green-eyed look of disapproval. But the grey-sleeved arm waved in a calming gesture, and the man said something else.

Then, at last, he rose from his chair, and walked around it, and confronted Michael in the flesh for the very first time. A grey cat slunk around the man's black boots, watching Michael with cautious hatred.

'*Azazel*,' said Michael. And he was sure of it.

'Mr Hillary' stepped forward with his hands resting on his hips, his coat tails drawn back. He seemed even taller in reality than he had in Michael's hypnotic trance. But he had the same silky white hair, the same chiselled face, the same blood-red eyes. He had the same presence, too – only more powerful, if anything. It was the presence of ageless power, extraordinary wealth, and the erotic but terrifying sensation of being close to the heart of absolute amorality.

His lips slid slowly back across his teeth in a complicated snarl. 'I don't think I know that name. It's "Mr Hillary" to you. This is a secular world now. We have to wear secular names.'

He stepped up closer. He was at least six-feet-three, and

Michael found himself drawing back a little, so that he wouldn't have to crane his neck to look up at him.

'Who have you been talking to?' 'Mr Hillary' asked him. 'Who told you about Azazel?'

'I want my wife and my son back,' Michael retorted. 'You had no right to take them and you have no right to keep them here.'

'Mr Hillary' made a face. 'I think I have a right to protect myself, don't you?'

'Not by threatening my family.'

'Oh, come on, Michael,' said 'Mr Hillary', and reached out with his knuckles and gently stroked Michael's hair. Again, Michael had that alarming homo-erotic feeling. It ran down his spine like centipedes and wriggled between his legs. This man was no ordinary man. This man didn't seem like a man at all. He was something else, something quite *other*. He was like woman and man and beast, all combined into one. And if anything, his aura was much more vibrant now than it had been in Michael's hypnotic trance.

'Mr Hillary' said, 'I don't find you threatening, Michael, but your persistence in investigating John O'Brien's unfortunate death is proving to be highly inconvenient to many of my friends. Your pursuit of poor Raymond Moorpath was the last straw. I liked Raymond. I almost loved him. He was wonderfully corrupt for a man who had taken the Hippocratic oath. He had a highly-developed sense of human frailty.'

'I want to see my wife and son,' Michael repeated, doggedly. 'And don't think that you're going to get away with murdering Victor Kurylowicz. I'm a witness. I'll see those lily-white boys of yours go to the chair. And your girlfriend here.'

'Mr Hillary' paced around Michael thoughtfully, his cat

cringing around his soft black ankle-boots. 'Maybe you'd like to speak to Commissioner Hudson. He's a good friend of mine. I have a house in Amherst, in the Holyoke Range, and he often comes out to visit. Or maybe you'd like to speak to the Boston District Attorney's department. I have all kinds of friends there. I have judges for friends, too, and newspaper publishers, and policemen.

'The advantage of being long-lived, Michael, is that you can weave your influence from one generation to the next, from grandfather to father, from father to son. You can attract a devotion from your friends and colleagues that is quite unique. And from your women, too. Look at poor Jacqueline here. She suffers such pain, just to please me. She suffers such terrors, just to keep me fed. Jacqueline never knows from one minute to the next whether she will live or die. I could kill her now. Cut her open, and rummage in her viscera! You think I wouldn't? And look how her eyes light up!'

Blood from the cut on Michael's knuckles had now soaked right through his handkerchief and was beginning to drip onto the rugs. 'Mr Hillary' stood very still for a while and watched it. Then he said, 'Your life is dripping away, Michael.'

He dragged a white silk scarf from around his neck and handed it to Michael to wrap around his fist. It was charged with static electricity, and crackled as he did so. 'Mr Hillary' looked directly into his eyes and Michael felt all kinds of strange sensations inside his mind and his body, a momentary loss of balance, like a minor earth tremor.

'You shall see your wife and your son, and then you and I shall discuss the way forward.'

He gave an almost imperceptible nod of his head, and the white-faced girl called Jacqueline walked across to the fireplace and pulled a bell handle.

'I don't even know what you want,' said Michael.

'What does anyone want?' said 'Mr Hillary'. There was a touch of wistfulness in his voice. 'Love, excitement, appreciation, comfort, survival.'

'Do you have all of those things?'

'Survival, yes. You would have to ask those around me about love. As for appreciation ... well, yes, there are many who appreciate me. Perhaps they appreciate me more for my influence than they do for my humble self, but –'

The door opened, and five young men came in, all of them wearing black, all of them wearing dark glasses. Their faces were white and chalky and three out of the five were wearing gloves. They gathered around 'Mr Hillary' protectively.

They had an aura like no other that Michael had ever encountered. Deathly, and cold, like dead flowers wrapped in funeral-black tissue-paper.

'My children,' smiled 'Mr Hillary'. 'My lily-white boys. Pale of complexion and perfectly dark of spirit. Pray that you never wake up in the night, Michael, and find one of these young rascals in your room.'

Michael took a deep, steadying breath. His knuckles hurt like hell. 'Can we see my wife and son now?' he repeated.

'Of course. Why don't you come with me? It's a privilege, to see the lighthouse. It's officially out of commission, you know, but I have friends in the coastguard. I call it my retreat. I have houses all over, of course. I have a wonderful ante-bellum mansion near Charlotte, North Carolina. You should visit.'

'Mr Hillary' beckoned, and Michael followed him across the library to a small curtained door on the opposite side. 'Mr Hillary' opened the door, and said, 'Come,' and began to climb the next flight of spiral steps. Three of the lily-white boys followed behind him. One of them took off his dark glasses, and when Michael turned around to glance at him, he saw that his eyes were filled with blood.

'You asked me what I want,' said 'Mr Hillary', as they climbed higher. They passed a small window overlooking the seashore, and Michael could see two children flying a white box kite, and a distant yacht.

'I want only that men should accept the consequences of their actions. I want only that men should take the blame for what they do. Until that happens, this world will remain an evil and chaotic place.

'You are suspicious of me. You are afraid of me. You revile me. But I attract you, too, don't I? And do you know why that is? Because I am the personification of all of your sins, Michael, of everybody's sins. I am the scapegoat.'

He turned on the stairs, and his red eyes glistened. 'Do you love me? Do I frighten you? Good! Then you can have me!'

Michael leaned against the solid stone wall. He was chilled and exhausted, and his hand was hurting so much that he could hardly bear it. 'Mr Hillary's' silk scarf had become drenched in blood, which had then congealed, so that the scarf was stuck to the open wound. He didn't even dare to pull it away.

'Mr Hillary' touched Michael's shoulder, and then continued to lead him upward. At last they reached a narrow, curved landing, and another door. 'Mr Hillary' opened it, and ushered Michael and his lily-white boys inside.

Here was a plain, whitewashed room with a large metal-framed window that looked out over the ocean. It must originally have been a recreation room for the lighthouse keepers, because there was a sagging sofa, two ill-matched armchairs, and a baize-topped table-tennis table which was now crowded with wine glasses and plates and books and magazines. Torn triangles of paper on the wall attested to a large collection of pin-ups, now ripped down, except for one faded 1950s photograph of a heavily-lipsticked blonde, holding her breasts as if she were weighing them.

Patsy and Jason were sitting on the sofa, two or three feet apart. They were blindfolded and tightly bound with cords. Their mouths were covered with sticking-plaster and their ears had been crammed with cotton. Patsy was wearing her pink checkered blouse and blue jeans; Jason was wearing his Red Sox T-shirt and shorts. As Michael and 'Mr Hillary' and the lily-white boys came into the room, they showed no signs that they were aware of their presence. Deaf, dumb and blind.

Michael immediately made a move toward Patsy but 'Mr Hillary' snatched his sleeve, and pulled him back.

'Untie them!' Michael snapped at him. 'Take those gags off! What the hell's the matter with you, that's just a woman and a kid! You don't have to keep them tied up like that!'

'Mr Hillary' pulled Michael even closer. 'It's good for their level of anxiety,' he murmured. 'And it's good for yours, too.'

Michael took two or three more deep breaths. He could feel the floor opening up, and he didn't want that to happen, not now. He needed to be calm and strong and in control. No more plunging through the night. No more Rocky Woods. Patsy and Jason depended on him staying together.

'What do you want me to do?' he asked 'Mr Hillary'.

'Mr Hillary' released his grip on Michael's sleeve, and walked around the sofa, so that he was standing directly behind Patsy's head. He reached out and very gently stroked her bedraggled blonde curls, dreamily, slowly, his eyelids drooping over his blood-red eyes. Patsy twitched her head and tried to shake him off. She made a *mmmfff* of protest, but that was all she could do.

'What I want you to do is very simple,' said 'Mr Hillary'. 'I want you to do nothing. I want you to return to Plymouth

Insurance and file a report saying that the death of John O'Brien, in your expert opinion, was an accident. Then I want you to close the file and forget it.'

'And if I don't? Or if I *won't?*'

'Mr Hillary' carried on stroking Patsy's curls for a while, and then raised his head, and the expression on his sharp, handsome face was terrifying. 'You know what we feed on. You know how we get it.'

One of the lily-white boys, Joseph, let out a high, rustling laugh.

Michael said, 'All right. It seems like you've got me where you want me. I'll agree to that. John O'Brien and his family died by accident. Now, please will you let my wife and my son out of those blindfolds and out of those goddamned gags.'

'Mr Hillary' gave Joseph and Bryan a cursory flap of his hand, and they immediately took out knives and began to cut Patsy and Jason free. When Bryan untied her blindfold, Patsy stared up at Michael and burst into tears, even with her mouth still gagged. Bryan ripped off the sticking-plaster and she sobbed out, 'Michael, thank God! I thought they were going to kill us!'

Michael stepped forward to take hold of her, but 'Mr Hillary' gave him a look which warned him to stay back. Jason was untied, too, and promptly started to sob. 'Dad, my wrists hurt!'

'I hope you're pleased with yourself,' Michael said to 'Mr Hillary'. He was so filled up with rage that he could hardly speak. 'All you had to do was have a quietly threatening word with me – you didn't have to terrorize my family.'

Patsy sobbed, 'They said they were going to cut us open … they said all kinds of terrible things.'

'All right,' said Michael. 'Are you satisfied now? I'll finish my report on O'Brien tonight and I'll have it on Mr Bedford's desk first thing tomorrow.'

'Mr Hillary' smiled archly. 'Oh, come on, Michael, don't be so angry. I was only protecting my own little brood. No harm done. No skin broken. Not yet, anyway.'

'What do you mean – "Not yet, anyway"?'

'You didn't believe that I was simply going to let you walk out of here, and drive off home?'

'Then what?' Michael demanded. 'What else do you want?'

'Michael … you don't seem to know what you are, even now.'

'Maybe not. But I sure as hell know what *you* are.'

'Mr Hillary' ran his hand through his silky white hair, as if he were an actress. 'You have no idea what I am. You have no idea what I was originally, and you have no idea what I am today.'

'I saw what you did to Victor Kurylowicz. I saw what you did to John O'Brien and his family. I saw the victims of the Rocky Woods air disaster. Anybody who could do things like that is a maniac and a sadist, and that's what you are.'

'Mr Hillary's' red eyes flared with anger.

'I was a pilgrim and a being of total purity. I was a messenger of God. In those days, the messengers of God could openly walk amongst men, which they are too afraid to do today. Then I was caught by those superstitious and ignorant Levites and chosen to atone for all of their sins; and my purity was corrupted, and my innocence was stained as black as blood. Do you think your friend Victor suffered? Do you think that Sissy O'Brien suffered? Or any of those people who died at Rocky Woods? You have no conception of suffering, Michael. You have no conception of what it is like to carry the evils of a whole nation within you.'

He paused, and wiped his lips with his fingertips. 'For twenty years I lived as an outcast, in a hell-on-earth. Nobody would accept me, nobody would take me in. But one

433

morning, as I walked toward the sun, I found that somebody was walking beside me. And the next day, another joined us, a little distance off. After a week, there were many of us.

'They were the Seirim. The most primitive of Semitic tribes called the goat-demons, and used to offer them burnt sacrifices. Of course they were not really goat-demons, but *these* people, the white-white men, the lily-white boys. The bastard sons of those beings that you would understand as angels. Sleepless and corrupt. The Seirim, too, were outcasts. They, too, were scapegoats. There had been a time when Rehoboam appointed priests for them – but with the coming of Moses and Aaron, they were hunted and reviled, and Josiah destroyed their encampments and their places of worship.'

'Mr Hillary' spoke even more softly now. 'They are my family; they are my tribe. They took me in when nobody else would take me in; and they walked beside me when everybody else turned their backs on me and made the sign of the evil eye.

'We lived together and the Seirim took wives, and their wives had children. The blood of the lily-white boys runs through many people's veins, Michael. Anybody who dreams of me, anybody who knows that death nestles like a grey spider in the back of his mind, they are descended from the lily-white boys.

'John O'Brien had dreams of me; and so do you. Because I can tell you what you are, Michael, you are a distant descendant of one of these people. It could be Joseph, it could be Bryan. It could be Thomas. But that blood which is dripping from your hand is our blood, too.'

Michael was silent for a moment. Then he said, 'What are you going to do with us?'

'Mr Hillary' gave him his snarling smile. 'I am going to show you what it is like to atone for your sins, and for the sins of other people. I am going to give you the joy of exquisite suffering.'

Eighteen

Thomas was still finishing his breakfast when the telephone rang. He picked up the receiver and wedged it under his chin, and said, 'Boyle,' with a mouthful of muffin.

'Sorry to call you so early, sir.' It was Sergeant Jahnke, sounding unhealthily enthusiastic and boyish.

'What's the problem, David?' asked Thomas. Megan came into the room and lifted the coffee pot, silently offering him more coffee, but Thomas shook his head.

'I came in this morning and there was a fax waiting from the Plymouth police department, in Vermont. They've been tracing James T. Honeyman, DMD, MDS, and Mrs Honeyman – the people who rented the house on Byron.'

'Have they made any progress?'

'It looks like it. Mr and Mrs Honeyman's house at the Hawk-Salt-Ash resort community was purchased not by Mr and Mrs Honeyman but by White Mountain Resort Investments, whose registered offices are at Manchester, Vermont. Actually, this isn't surprising because the records of the US Dental Association show that there *is* no James T. Honeyman, DMD, MDS.'

'That's not too much of a surprise,' said Thomas.

'Ah, but there's more,' said Sergeant Jahnke. 'The chairman of White Mountain Resort Investments is Mr A. Z. Azel, whose address is given as P.O. Box 335, Nahant, Massachusetts. I called the Nahant post office a few minutes ago and they told me that the gentleman who collects the mail from

435

P.O. Box 335 lives in the decommissioned lighthouse on Goat's Cape.'

' "Mr Hillary",' Thomas breathed.

'Just thought you'd like to know, sir,' said David Jahnke, smugly.

'Good work, David. And send my heartfelt thanks back to Plymouth. Tell Warren Forshaw that I owe him a box of cigars.'

'I surely will, sir. You want to put a search warrant in train?'

'You bet your sweet posterior. I'll be down at headquarters in ten minutes.'

He put down the phone and clenched his fist and said, 'Gotcha, you bastard.'

Megan, wheeling herself back into the room, couldn't help smiling.

'Which bastard is this?'

' "Mr Hillary",' he said. 'The prime suspect for the Elaine Parker and the Sissy O'Brien homicides. David's come up with legal justification for searching his house. His *light*-house, rather, up on Goat's Cape.'

Megan's face drained of colour. 'What are you going to do?'

'Megs – I'm going to bust the bastard, that's what I'm going to do. I don't know what time I'll be back. I'll call you later.'

'Thomas –' Megan began. But how could she explain about the self-induced hypnotic trance that she and Michael had entered into? How could she tell him what she had seen and what she had felt, and what had happened between them afterwards? It still made her cheeks burn to think of it. She still fantasized that they might do it again, his ejaculation falling on her face like warm summer rain.

'Be careful!' she called to Thomas, as he left the

436

apartment. She sat in her wheelchair waiting until she heard the sound of his car starting up. Then she pushed herself across to the phone, and leafed through the notebook that Thomas had left beside it, until she found the jotting that she was looking for.

She punched out the number and edgily waited while it rang. Supposing he wasn't at home? What was she going to do then?

But after a while, a cautious voice said, 'Hello? Who is this?'

'Mr Monyatta?' said Megan. 'This is Megan Boyle – Lieutenant Thomas Boyle's wife. Mr Monyatta, I badly need your help.'

Michael was dreaming. He dreamed that he was jostling his way through a crowd of people. They didn't move like ordinary people – they moved as if somebody was pushing and pulling them from side to side. They moved as if they could scarcely stand up.

Through the crowd, inching his way toward him, came a smiling man in a suit. When he saw Michael he held out his hand and said, *'Pleased to meet you – glad you could make it.'*

Michael twisted away from him in panic. But the lifeless crowd kept pressing him closer. He was carried forward against his will, his feet barely touching the ground.

'Don't come near me!' he screamed. *'Mr President, don't come near me!'*

He woke up, sweating and shaking. It was morning, and the room was flooded with sunlight, so bright that it was almost like a dream of heaven.

He was lying on a narrow divan bed in a cramped whitewashed room. There was no other furniture in the room except for a small table with two candlesticks on it, and a

437

faded engraving on the wall of St Christopheros, the Christ-Bearer. Christ was perched on St Christopheros's shoulder in the strangest way, almost as if he were flying rather than sitting, and his face had been darkened by an ink-stain.

Michael stiffly sat up. Through the half-open window a steady sea breeze was flowing, and he could hear the sound of the surf and the crying of the sea gulls. He was wearing his shorts and nothing else, and there was no sign of his clothes. He couldn't even remember what had happened last night. Jason had been taken away to sleep in another room, while he and Patsy had sat on the couch in the recreation room, guarded by Joseph and Bryan.

Joseph and Bryan had played cards on the table-tennis table and said nothing at all. As the night wore on, Patsy had fallen asleep against Michael's shoulder, and the monotonous slapping of the cards on the baize table-top had made Michael feel drowsy, too. But he had been determined to stay awake – if only to see for himself that the lily-white boys never slept.

As far as Michael could remember, they had kept on playing silently and tirelessly until four o'clock in the morning. Not only hadn't they slept, they hadn't even blinked.

Michael could remember thinking: I hope to God they don't hurt Patsy or Jason. Please God, don't let them. But that was all. The lily-white boys must have carried him here and undressed him, and he hadn't even stirred.

He stood up, and as he did so, the narrow wooden door opened. It was Joseph, wearing a loose black-silk shirt. He smiled and beckoned and said, ' "Mr Hillary" is ready for his breakfast now.'

'Tell "Mr Hillary" to screw himself. Where are my clothes?'

'You won't need clothes, Mr Rearden.'

'Either you give me my clothes or else I'm staying put.'

Joseph's smile began to fade like someone's breath on a cold winter window. 'Mr Rearden, your lovely wife is downstairs already. I think for her sake it would be a very good idea if you came down to join her.'

'If you so much as touch her –'

'Loving and touching, Mr Rearden. Loving and touching. They're all part of the same wonderful experience.'

Michael reluctantly followed him out of the door, and along a narrow whitewashed landing, with an oak-boarded floor. Every now and then, Joseph glanced back at him over his shoulder, and grinned.

They passed three windows, and Michael looked out across Nahant Bay and the breeze-blown beach. He could see his car, still parked where he had left it, facing north, in case he needed to make a getaway. No hope of that now.

Joseph led the way down the staircase, and back into the library. There, in his high-backed chair, sat 'Mr Hillary', his legs idly crossed, his hair brushed back and tied with a leather thong into a pony-tail. His blood-red eyes were wide and staring, as if he were working up an appetite; and his lips were stretched back, revealing his teeth.

Behind him – as if they were posing for a family portrait – stood eight or nine of the lily-white boys, some of them dressed in black leather, some of them dressed in black Armani suits, some of them dressed in black brocade waistcoats and black rubber shirts. Black – with white faces, and blood-filled eyes.

Perched on the arm of 'Mr Hillary's' chair was the girl Jacqueline, her coppery hair plaited in fraying braids. She was wearing a gauzy white dress. Over both of her breasts, the dress was stained with speckles of dried blood.

She smiled dreamily at Michael as he entered the library, and nodded her head towards the left-hand side of the room. There, a daybed had been positioned with its head close to the bookshelves. Three more lily-white boys stood beside it, two of them still wearing dark glasses. One of them kept putting his fist up to his mouth and coughing into it, and sniffing.

The daybed had been draped with a fusty bedspread of yellow and red brocade; and on top of the bedspread lay Patsy, completely naked, her wrists and ankles fastened with black silk curtain-cords.

'Patsy!' called Michael, in a wavering voice. 'Patsy – are you okay?'

'Michael – they haven't hurt me!'

Michael stalked up to 'Mr Hillary' and said, 'Let her go. You won't get any kind of agreement out of me, if you don't let her go.'

'Michael,' said 'Mr Hillary', 'you're one of us.'

He was holding a long thin riding crop with a tarnished silver handle. As he spoke, he flicked it against Jacqueline's thigh, for emphasis. Jacqueline flinched with each flick, but she didn't move her leg away.

Michael said, 'Let her go.'

'Mr Hillary' slowly shook his head. 'You've read your vampire stories, haven't you, Michael? Dracula, Salem's Lot, and all the rest of them? How does the vampire spread his contamination throughout the community? He does it by sucking blood, and by infecting his victims with his own disease. They, too, become the Undead.'

He smiled, and twitched his riding-crop even more sharply against Jacqueline's thigh. 'Of course, there is no such thing as a vampire. The Lord thy God forbade the drinking of blood, and not even the most rebellious of his messengers would have *dared* to disobey such an edict. Read your Leviticus.

'But the vampire stories do have some basis in fact. Once one of the Seirim has sucked on your adrenaline, you become something of a slave, something of an addict. You want to give more adrenaline. You feel your kidneys itching, just to give more! Look at Jacqueline here, she adores it, she'd give me some now, if I were to beat her hard enough. Show Michael your studs, Jacqueline. Show him how ready you are, to have me sucking at your glands.'

Jacqueline's eyes flickered green. But without a word, she stood up, and turned around, and lifted her gauzy white dress so that Michael could see her pale bare back.

He knew what he was going to see. He had already seen it in his hypnotic trance. But all the same, those two gold studs in the small of her back still horrified him. They meant that she had deliberately and willingly given herself to 'Mr Hillary', in the full knowledge that he would hurt her, and torture her, and probably kill her, in the end. He had seen her with kittens scratching her bare breasts. God knows what other agonies lay in store for her.

'You can put down your dress now, Jacqueline,' said 'Mr Hillary' – but not before he had struck her a quick, stinging blow across her bare bottom.

He looked up at Michael and wolfishly grinned. 'Your first reaction when you found out what had happened to Elaine Parker and to Cecilia O'Brien was that they had been tortured against their will. Of course! Who would want to be tortured like that?

'But your first reaction was wrong. Elaine Parker begged us to keep her alive longer, so that she could suffer more pain, and give us even more adrenaline. She even suggested tortures herself – like burning her eyelids with cigarettes, like scorching her public hair, like sticking needles through her nipples. She was a devotee, Michael, she wanted to give so much. Just like Cecilia O'Brien.

'It wasn't I who devised the torture that finally killed Cecilia. I would have liked to keep her alive much longer …

as long as Elaine. But she begged us to do it, pleaded with us, *wept*. She couldn't think of anything that would hurt her more.'

Delicately, 'Mr Hillary' licked his middle fingertip, and moistened his eyebrows. 'She was beautiful, in her death throes. Quite beautiful. And she tasted – well, you shall never know. I shan't make you jealous.'

Michael said, flatly, 'You have to let us go.'

'And I *shall* let you go!' 'Mr Hillary' exclaimed. 'But not before you and your beautiful wife feel the same craving that Jacqueline feels ... and that Elaine felt, and Cecilia, too, and *oh* so many more.'

'Don't you fucking touch my wife!' Michael screamed at him.

But "Mr Hillary" stood up to his full height, and adjusted his long grey wool coat with a contemptuous shrug of his shoulders, and glared at Michael with his grisly red eyes, and Michael knew with a terrible feeling of watery helplessness that there was nothing that he could do.

'Come with me,' said "Mr Hillary", and took hold of Michael's arm with a clawlike grip, and pulled him across to the daybed.

Michael was enraged and embarrassed and deeply humiliated. There was Patsy, naked, so that everybody in the room could see her pillowy breasts and her pale pink nipples and the light blonde fuzz of her pubic hair. Patsy's nakedness was private. Patsy's nakedness was something they shared in bed together, when Jason was asleep, and the moon was pinned up in the bedroom window, and the sea was whispering them lullabies.

'Patsy,' he mouthed, trying to explain that he was sorry, that he had never meant this to happen. God almighty, who cared if the world were ruled by lily-white boys, and if presidents were shot, and wars were fought, and neighbourhoods were torn apart? Who cared, if the wife they loved was being shamed?

'You're going to enjoy this, Michael,' said 'Mr Hillary'. 'I don't know how much you associate pain with pleasure, but you will from now on.'

He beckoned to Joseph and Bryan, and they came forward carrying between them a crimson blanket.

'Show him,' said 'Mr Hillary', and they lifted the blanket to reveal a large circular wreath of blood-red roses, stripped of their leaves, but not of their thorns.

Michael stared at him. 'What the hell are you going to do?'

'I'm going to watch you make love to your beautiful wife, that's what I'm going to do. And I'm going to *taste* you, Michael, so that you know what it is to atone for everybody else's sins — so that you know what it is to suffer. You have Seirim blood already … now you're going to join us body and soul.'

He snapped his riding-crop in the air, and without warning Joseph and Bryan seized hold of Michael's arms. He shouted out, 'Get off me!' and 'Shit, get off me!' But then 'Mr Hillary' stepped forward and cracked him across the cheek with his riding-crop, a fierce stinging blow that set the side of his face on fire, and then cracked him again, right across the forehead, almost taking out his eye.

'You're one of us, Michael. Never forget it.'

Michael shuddered with pain and shock. His knees felt weak, but two of the lily-white boys held him up. Another lily-white boy came around and dragged down his shorts, then lifted one heel after the other to tug them clear of his feet.

With great ceremony, Joseph laid the wreath of roses on Patsy's bare stomach. Then he looked up at Michael and smiled mischievously. 'Your second honeymoon,' he said, in that arch, drawling, Marblehead accent. 'Enjoy.'

'Mr Hillary' came forward. 'All you have to do is make love to her. You love her, don't you? Show her how much you love her.'

He slid his fingers into Michael's hair, the way a woman might have done, and in spite of himself, in spite of his fear, Michael felt a thrill of erotic attraction. 'Mr Hillary' caressed his scalp, and twisted his hair, and then he leaned forward and kissed Michael on the mouth.

Michael tasted saliva, and flowers, and death. But he felt his penis rise, and there was nothing that he could do about it. From only two inches away, 'Mr Hillary's' blood-red eyes stared into his – hypnotic, powerful, erotic, commanding – and he was almost tempted to kiss him back.

'Mr Hillary' stood away, just a little. He looked down at Michael's stiffening penis, and he grinned. He teased the end of it with his riding-crop, and then ran the crop all the way down the underside of the shaft, and tickled and probed at Michael's tightening scrotum.

'Now you're ready for her, aren't you?' he breathed, and his voice seemed like six or seven voices, one overdubbed on another. He held Michael's erection in his left hand, and pulled him forward. Then he reached down between Patsy's legs, and parted the lips of her vulva with his right hand. 'Come on, now. Show me how much you love her! Show me how much she arouses you!'

Michael baulked, tried to pull back. 'No! Don't touch her!'

But Joseph knelt down beside the head of the daybed, and produced a long, sharp boning-knife, and held it close to Patsy's cheek. Patsy was trembling and sobbing and her eyes were blurred with tears. 'Michael, just do it, just do it, just do what they want.'

Michael closed his eyes for a moment, which was something the lily-white boys could never do. He didn't say a

444

prayer, he couldn't think of any. But he asked God to keep Patsy safe, and Jason safe; and not to let 'Mr Hillary' hurt him too much. Then he climbed onto the daybed, and looked down into Patsy's eyes, and asked God to kill him, now, on the spot. A heart attack, a stroke, a bolt of lightning. It didn't matter. *Kill me, God. Don't let Patsy suffer.*

But 'Mr Hillary' reached between Michael's legs, and scratched his scrotum with his long, sharp fingernails, and took hold of his penis, and guided it into Patsy's vagina. He even slid two or three of his own fingers into Patsy, alongside Michael's penis, so that he could caress both of them. Michael felt Patsy stiffen rock-hard in revulsion, her pelvic muscles locked, but then 'Mr Hillary' snapped her thighs with his riding-crop, and she flinched, and relaxed.

'You're supposed to be enjoying this,' breathed 'Mr Hillary'. 'All of the pain, and all of the pleasure.'

He drew the tip of his riding-crop down between Michael's buttocks, and poked at his anus. 'All of the pain, Michael, and all of the pleasure. Now – *lean forward.*'

Patsy's stomach and breasts were completely encircled by the wreath of red roses. If he leaned forward, Michael would press them into her flesh, thorns and all.

'I can't,' he whispered.

'What?' asked 'Mr Hillary'.

'I can't, I can't hurt her for anything.'

'Mr Hillary' stepped back, staring at Michael in feigned disbelief. 'You *can't?* Then we shall have to help you! Joseph – Bryan! Help him!'

Laughing, Joseph and Bryan came up to the daybed, and forced Michael down on to Patsy's breasts. The prickling of the rose-thorns was agony. Their skin was snagged, their nerves lacerated. But that wasn't the end of it. Joseph and Bryan forced Michael to ride backward and forward on top of Patsy, pushing him down harder and harder with every

445

stroke. Patsy screamed in pain, and Michael bit the inside of his cheeks so hard that blood poured out of the sides of his mouth.

'In! Out! In! Out!' Joseph and Bryan chanted, and forced Michael deeper and deeper down, until his penis was thrusting right inside Patsy, and the rose thorns were ripping both of their chests into bloody rags. 'In! Out! In! Out!'

Now 'Mr Hillary' stepped forward again, and held out his hand as if he expected Jacqueline to know exactly what he wanted. She did: and passed him two thin tubes of metal.

'In! Out! In! Out!' chanted Joseph and Bryan. And in spite of his tears and in spite of his blood, and in spite of his anguish for Patsy, Michael began to feel a climax rising.

'Faster!' 'Mr Hillary' urged him. 'Harder!' He lashed at Michael's bare buttocks with his riding-crop, and lashed at his scrotum, until Michael didn't know what was pain and what was sexual ecstasy.

Michael felt a clenching feeling between his legs. His spine arched. Then he was climaxing in a way that he had never climaxed before. He felt as if his spine were being dragged out of his back, vertebra by vertebra, and spouted out of his penis.

He dropped heavily onto Patsy and Patsy screamed in pain. She thrashed and twisted and tried to push him off her, but the lily-white boys held him down. Held him down hard, and wouldn't let him move.

They lay on the daybed, bleeding and shaking and crying, and the lily-white boys pressed them harder and harder together. 'Mr Hillary' walked around the daybed and stood over them, gently tapping his metal tubes together, so that they set up a high, tingling rhythm. 'Now what do you think?' he asked them, although Michael scarcely heard him. 'Is it pain, or is it pleasure? Who's to say?'

He reached down between Michael's legs, and hooked

446

his softening penis out of Patsy's vagina with his curled
finger. Then he probed inside Patsy with obscene, obstetric
curiosity, stretching her, watching the semen slide out of
her with remote, blood-red prurience. 'You're beautiful, both
of you,' he murmured, and he ran his fingernails around
Patsy's thighs; and Michael's thighs, too; and it was probably
then that Michael really understood what 'Mr Hillary' was.
A perfect being, perfectly corrupted. A connoisseur of all
things beautiful – of which lovemaking was one – yet a
connoisseur whose taste had become totally depraved.

'Mr Hillary' *was* an angel. Or, at least, the very reverse of
an angel.

Patsy was biting her lips in pain, and sobbing. Michael
said bloodily, 'Let me up. In the name of God, will you
please let me up?'

'Mr Hillary' ran the flat of his hand down Michael's back,
and across his buttocks. 'First, Michael, I have to taste you.
First, I have to contaminate you.'

Michael tried to wrestle free, but the lily-white boys were
far too strong for him. He felt the tip of 'Mr Hillary's' metal
tube digging into the small of his back, and he clenched his
muscles.

'You're going to enjoy this,' said 'Mr Hillary', in an odd
voice. Then he slid the tube into Michael's back and Michael felt pain like he had never felt before – so much that
he writhed and struggled on top of Patsy, and the thorns
tore into her breasts even more savagely, and criss-crossed
his chest with bloody scratches.

'*Don't!*' he screamed, and he was crying like a child.
'*Don't! Don't! Don't! Don't!*'

But 'Mr Hillary's' ice-cold tube probed ever deeper,
through muscle and connective tissue and nerve endings,
until it prodded his left kidney, and then prodded higher,
until it located his suprarenal gland.

447

He felt its sharpness deep inside his back. He didn't even want to die any more, because he could no longer understand what dying meant. He lay on top of Patsy like a dead weight, while 'Mr Hillary' sipped and sipped, and then stood straight, his face transformed, his chest filling with satisfaction.

Jacqueline stood close beside him, stroking his arm, lifting her knee from time to time and caressing his thigh, touching him, nuzzling up to him. *Hurt me, too. Take me, too.* But he drew his metal tubes out of Michael's back, and walked across the room, and stretched, and ran his fingertips down his chest, and down his stomach, and smiled, and looked complete.

The lily-white boys carefully lifted Michael off Patsy, and carried him over to one of the armchairs. They picked up the wreath of roses, and dropped it onto the floor. Then they untied Patsy's bonds, and helped her up, as solicitous and gentle as if she had been involved in an automobile accident, instead of a deliberate act of sadistic perversion.

Patsy said nothing, except, 'Clothes, please, get me my clothes.'

Without turning around, 'Mr Hillary' smiled, and said, 'A true daughter of Eve. "Then the eyes of both of them were opened, and they knew that they were naked." '

Patsy shrieked at him, 'Don't! Don't! What kind of a monster are you?'

'Mr Hillary' swivelled around, his eyes on fire. But then he saw her, naked and scratched and bleeding, and he turned his face away.

'I'm not a monster, Patsy. There are no monsters.'

She dragged on her jeans, shaking and weeping. 'You're evil!'

'Mr Hillary' said, with infinite quietness, ' "The sons of God saw that the daughters of men were beautiful; and they took wives for themselves, whomever they chose. And they bore children unto them. Those were the mighty men who were of old, men of renown. Then the Lord saw that the wickedness of man was great on the earth, and that every intent of the thoughts of his heart was only evil continually. And God said, "The end of all flesh has come before Me; for the earth is filled with violence because of them." '

He was silent for a long time, and then he said, 'Genesis, chapter six. Three thousand years before the birth of Christ. And yet, it seems like yesterday.'

It was then that they heard a high, distant wailing sound. 'What's that?' 'Mr Hillary' asked Bryan.

Bryan went over to the library window and looked out. 'It's nothing,' he said. 'I can't see anything at all.' But then – 'Wait, it's the police. Four police cars. Five. They're coming this way.'

'*Police?*' said 'Mr Hillary', incredulous.

Thomas banged on the door of the lighthouse and waited. 'Can you believe this place?' he asked David Jahnke.

David was combing his hair. 'It's isolated, it's cheap. What more could a homicidal maniac ask for?'

'Don't get smart,' said Thomas. 'This guy Hillary is a lot more than meets the eye.'

He looked around and checked that his six uniformed officers were in position, as well as the two Essex County deputies that his old friend Sheriff Protter had provided – partly out of courtesy and partly to keep an eye on what he was doing. Then he banged on the door a second time.

'There *is* a bell-pull,' David pointed out.

'Bell-pulls are for salesmen,' Thomas retorted. 'Cops knock.'

His knocking seemed to have been heard, because the door silently opened and two white-faced young men stood

449

in the doorway, both of them wearing dark glasses, both of them dressed in black.

Sergeant Jahnke held up the search warrant. 'Is somebody called "Mr Hillary" here?'

The white-faced young men shook their heads.

'Well, even if "Mr Hillary" isn't here, we have a warrant to search these premises, and that's precisely what we're going to do. So if you'll stand aside, please.'

Without a word, the young men closed the door in Thomas's face. Thomas and Sergeant Jahnke stared at each other in total astonishment.

'They didn't even slam it,' said David.

Thomas tugged the bell-pull and hammered on the door with his fist. ' "Mr Hillary"! "Mr Hillary"! Or whoever you are! This is the police! P – O – L – I – C – E, police! And I'm warning you now! Open this goddamned door before I kick it down!'

He banged and banged and then stood back, panting. He was just about to bang again when the door opened and a tall white-haired man stood in front of them, with dark glasses and a long grey coat.

' "Mr Hillary"?' asked Thomas. 'I'm Lieutenant Thomas Boyle, Boston homicide squad. I have a warrant to search this house – uhnh, *light*house.'

'May I see it?' asked 'Mr Hillary.' Sergeant Jahnke passed it to him, and he studied it carefully. Then he handed it back.

'Well?' asked Thomas.

'Mr Hillary' smiled. 'That warrant seems to be genuine. Unfortunately, I can't let you in. We're all quarantined here. Meningitis.'

He had almost closed the door when Thomas jammed his foot into it. ' "Mr Hillary" – meningitis or period-pains, we're still coming in.'

'You can't.'

'You want me to *force* my way in? I have a whole lot of backup here. I wouldn't like to see anybody getting hurt; would you?'

'Mr Hillary' looked testy. 'Lieutenant Boyle, this is my house and I'm entitled to my privacy.'

Thomas held up the search warrant. 'There's an Essex County judge who doesn't think that you're entitled to your privacy.'

'Mr Hillary' was silent for a moment, and stood quite still. Then he beckoned Thomas to come closer, so that he could whisper in his ear.

'Lieutenant,' he breathed, 'I have Michael Rearden and Mrs Rearden and young Master Rearden upstairs. I think they should stay alive and well, don't you? So turn around, and go back the way you came. I'll talk directly to Commissioner Hudson, and by lunchtime you'll be able to drop this case, and carry on with something important, like who sprays all that graffiti on the Hancock Tower, and who's been spitting into the harbour?'

Thomas looked at 'Mr Hillary' narrowly – looked him directly in the eyes, despite the fact that he was wearing dark glasses.

'Are you threatening me?' he wanted to know.

'Mr Hillary' smiled. 'Yes, I'm threatening you.'

'What proof do you have that the Reardens are here?'

'Mr Hillary' gave a nod of his head, over towards the north-west. 'There's Michael's car. What more proof do you need?'

'I'd like to see him, talk to him.'

'I don't think so, Lieutenant. I think the best thing that you can do is to go. Let's just put this down to a little misunderstanding.'

Thomas stood in the doorway and said nothing. But then he turned and waved to two of his uniformed patrolmen and called, 'Officer Wilson! Officer Ribeiro! Come on over here, we're carrying out a search!'

'Mr Hillary' stepped back, stiffening. 'This is not a good idea, lieutenant. You could ruin your career.'

'Well, that's a risk I'm prepared to take,' said Thomas. 'Sergeant Jahnke – a top-to-bottom search, nobody leaves.'

'Yes sir, lieutenant,' said David, springing to attention.

But without saying anything else, 'Mr Hillary' closed the lighthouse door and locked it. Thomas looked at David, and David said, 'Oh.'

Wilson and Ribeiro came hurrying up the steps with their guns drawn. Wilson was ruddy-cheeked and fat, Ribeiro sported a bushy black moustache. Thomas said, 'We're carrying out a search, okay, when we get this door open.'

'We have a sledge in the car, sir,' said Ribeiro.

'This is solid hundred-year-old oak,' Thomas told him. 'We're going to need more than a sledge, we're going to need dynamite.'

'Maybe we can starve them out,' Wilson suggested.

'Oh, yes? And how long is that going to take? They've probably got enough supplies to last them till winter.'

'Maybe we should call in the fire department,' said David. 'They're good at taking out doors. They'll have ladders, too. We could climb up and take the roof.'

Thomas looked up and shook his head. 'We have to think about this. If they really *are* holding the Reardens hostage, then we're in serious trouble. Let's take it a little at a time. Let's set up phone contact first, and see where we go from there. There's no point in trying a full-frontal assault: that lighthouse is built like a fortress.'

They retreated down the steps, and walked across the sandy grass to Thomas's car. 'Wilson, you set up a telephone link,' said Thomas. 'Ribeiro, call the fire department. Tell them we need high ladders and something for knocking out solid oak doors.'

'You got it,' waved Ribeiro.

Thomas eased himself into his car and lit a cigarette. David said, 'This is going to turn out to be one total waste of time, you know that, don't you?'

'Oh, yes? And why should it be?'

'Because this guy "Mr Hillary" has the ear of everybody who's anybody, including Commissioner Hudson. Even if we can produce videotapes showing his personal involvement in all of these homicides – even if we produce eight thousand witnesses, all prepared to swear on the Bible that it was him – do you really think we'll get a conviction, let alone an arraignment, even?'

'We'll see,' said Thomas, tightly blowing out smoke.

It was at that moment that a huge black Lincoln Town Car came bouncing across the tussocks. It was an old model, '72 or '73, glossily polished up, with black-tinted windows. It drew up right beside Thomas's car, and the door opened, and Matthew Monyatta climbed out. He was wearing a flowing green djellaba, and a tasselled green fez. He walked around the car, opened up the trunk, and produced a wheelchair. Then he walked to the passenger door, and opened it up, and there was Megan. Matthew helped her carefully into her wheelchair, his djellaba flapping in the sea breeze.

'Megs?' said Thomas. 'What the hell are you doing here?'

Matthew pushed Megan right up to Thomas, and Thomas couldn't help noticing the look on both of their faces. Determined, serious – but inspired, too.

'Thomas, I know what's happening here,' said Megan. 'I know who "Mr Hillary" is, and how to get through to him. I think I can destroy him, too.'

Thomas knelt down in front of her and took hold of her hands. 'Megs, this man is a homicidal maniac. We've called

453

for back-up, we'll get him out. There's nothing that you can do.'

'Oh, yes there is,' said Megan. 'With Michael's help, and with Matthew's help, I can do anything I want.'

'But Michael's in there. "Mr Hillary's" holding him hostage – along with Patsy and Jason, too.'

'I know. I sensed it, right back on Lynn Shore Drive, over four miles away. It's the aura, Thomas. It's the hypnosis. It gave us a bond. It gave us a mental understanding. Matthew understands it, too.'

Thomas stood up and confronted Matthew and Matthew was impassive.

'Is this true?' Thomas asked him.

'I think so,' Matthew replied. 'Just like God is true and Olduvai is true and the whole damned universe is true.'

'So what do you propose?' asked Thomas.

Megan said, 'Getting in touch with Michael, both me and Matthew, and then using our combined auras to flush "Mr Hillary" out of his lighthouse.'

'Do you think you can do that without anybody getting hurt? Without *you* getting hurt?'

Megan took hold of his hand and squeezed it, and there were tears in her eyes. 'Thomas, my darling, I would never do anything to hurt you. Not willingly, not ever.'

Thomas sensed that she was talking about something else, but he couldn't think what. He took out his handkerchief and wiped her eyes. 'All right, then,' he said. 'If you think it'll work, then try it.'

Megan took hold of Matthew's hand, and then she produced from her pocketbook the zinc-and-copper disc that Michael had left with her. Thomas instinctively stepped away, and he pushed David Jahnke away, too. He didn't believe in any of this, but he didn't believe in crowding people, either, when they were doing their very best.

Megan held the disc in the palm of her hand and the sunlight caught it and made it shine like a distant window. 'Look at the light, Matthew, and relax ... look at the light, and relax. The light is all there is. The light is the centre of the universe. The light is everything. We're feeling sleepy, we're feeling tried. All of our aura is draining out of us, all of our strength ... we're sliding into a trance, Matthew, you and I together, holding hands ... we're sliding into sleep, Matthew, just you and me ... following the point of light, following it, passing right through it ...'

Thomas watched in gradually increasing astonishment as Megan's eyes closed, and Matthew's eyes closed. The two of them remained in a strange tableau, Matthew standing beside Megan's wheelchair, holding her hand, quite natural in every respect except that they were both deeply asleep. Thomas cautiously approached them, and walked around them, and stared into Matthew's face, from only inches away.

'Holy shit,' he said. 'He's gone. I mean, he's completely gone. And Megan, too. I didn't know hypnosis worked that quick.'

David Jahnke didn't know what to say. This wasn't procedure. This wasn't even showing-off. This was just weird.

Megan and Matthew walked hand-in-hand across the grass, and then up the steps to the lighthouse door. The day was grey and colourless, like a black-and-white photograph found in a long-lost shoebox. The lighthouse door was closed, but they passed *through* it, with a rustle of disturbed molecules, and stepped inside. Megan called, 'Hallo, Michael? Hallo?' but there was no reply.

They climbed the spiral staircase to the library door and opened it. Michael was sitting hunched and naked in a chair, his knees drawn up, his chest lacerated and covered in dried blood. But he slowly raised his head as they walked in, and gave them a widening smile of recognition.

'*Meegggaannn* ...' he said, in a slow, blurry voice. '*Matthheeewww* ...'

They saw his aura flickering all around him, pinkish and bright. Their own auras danced across the library like ghosts, unbalanced, furtive, like flames. They joined their auras with his, and all three of them felt a surge of enormous power, of enormous heat, like opening a furnace door and standing bare chested in front of it. Michael rose from his chair, naked, wounded, but almost floating above the floor.

'Azazel!' he shouted, his voice echoing and booming. '*Azazel!*'

'Mr Hillary' appeared at the door, accompanied by Joseph and Jacqueline. He looked different to Megan and Matthew: they could see the darkness of his aura – the glimmering black turmoil that surrounded his physical outline.

But they could see his eyes even more brightly: blazing and red. For a moment they felt genuine, terrible fear – especially since 'Mr Hillary' seemed to sense at once that Michael was different.

'Who are you?' 'Mr Hillary' asked Michael, with suspicion, and that was the giveaway. He must have sensed that Michael had more than one aura within him.

'I'm the one who's come to get you,' said Michael. 'I'm Aaron's friend. I'm man's friend. I'm the friend of all those women you defiled.'

'Mr Hillary' began to laugh. A deep, mocking, knocking laugh, like somebody throwing an empty beer keg down a rubbish chute. But then Michael went for him, hurtling across the dusty rugs and seizing his hair and twisting him around, then kicking the legs from under him, so that he fell heavily onto the floor.

Michael had the power of Megan and Matthew inside him. One magical, one martyred. He burned with power, he exploded with power.

'Mr Hillary' roared *arrrrghhhhhh*, and clambered to his feet in a fury. He lashed at Michael with his riding-crop – once, twice, three times – but Michael was far too quick for him, in the way that Megan had once been agile. Then the strength that had once been Matthew's punched 'Mr Hillary' in the ribs – and punched him again – and punched him again – and punched him again – huge sledge-hammer punches that smashed his ribs and broke his breastbone.

'Mr Hillary' shrieked in rage and pain, and blood flew out of his mouth. He was hysterical, furious, and filled with human adrenaline. But three auras in one body were more than he could handle. He staggered back, tripped on the rugs, staggered again, ran for the door, hurtled down the steps.

Michael went after him. He didn't care that he was naked. He was angelic now, he was superhuman, he was three-in-one. He leaped down the steps in pursuit of 'Mr Hillary', and flung open the lighthouse door. He could see the patrol cars positioned all around the lighthouse, their red-and-blue lights flashing. He could see Megan, head bowed, in her wheelchair, and he could see Matthew Monyatta. And he thought: God bless you.

Because he could see 'Mr Hillary' now, running across the sandy grass, his white hair wild in the wind, his grey coat flapping behind him, and he set off in hot pursuit.

He heard one of the cops shout, 'Freeze! Police!' to 'Mr Hillary', but of course 'Mr Hillary' didn't stop running.

The cop fired a single shot, and 'Mr Hillary's' coat burst open at the back, but 'Mr Hillary' kept on running, faster and faster, towards the shoreline. One of the patrol cars

457

roared into life and started speeding across the tummocky grass towards him.

Michael ran after 'Mr Hillary' like he had never run before. Naked, he ran like a Greek athlete, every muscle tense, every artery pumping. 'Mr Hillary' ran into the surf, his feet splashing in the foam, and now the patrol car was skidding and slewing across the sand, only fifty feet away.

It was then that the impossible happened.

'Mr Hillary' kept on running, but his footsteps splashed less and less heavily into the incoming tide. Then he didn't splash at all, but started to climb up into the air. He was still running, but now he was running six feet above the water. Then ten feet, then twenty feet, then higher still.

The patrol car sprayed to a halt in the shallows, and the two officers climbed out of it, and stepped up to their calves in sea water. They shaded their eyes with their hands and watched in disbelief as 'Mr Hillary' pounded up into the sky, arms going, legs going, running and running, higher and higher.

Michael reached the surf and didn't stop.

Now, he told Megan and Matthew. *Now, for the love of God, now!*

He ran deeper and deeper into the surf, up to his calves, up to his knees, up to his thighs.

Now! he screamed, inside of his mind. *Now!*

And he lifted, he felt himself lifted. He felt the buoyancy, he felt the lightness. His knees surged up through the foam, and then his shins. Then his feet were kicking at the surface of the water, and with one last skip of spray he was up in the air – climbing, higher and higher.

It was desperately hard. It was like running up the side of a mountain that wasn't there. He had to keep on running, he had to keep on pumping his legs and pumping his arms, because every time he eased up a little he could feel himself dropping.

It was his aura that took him up, his human aura, and he could feel the strength and the buoyancy that Megan and Matthew were giving him, too. They were sharing all of their energy, all of their faith. It was the greatest combined act of courage and trust that he had ever experienced – three strangers, working together, and giving their *all.*

He could see 'Mr Hillary' climbing into the air high above him, his feet running quick and furtive, his head hunched, his coat flapping. He tried to run harder, tried to climb higher. The sea was glittering fifty feet below him, then seventy feet. And still 'Mr Hillary' was struggling higher.

Now! he begged. *Now!*

And down on the ground, watched by a serious and baleful Thomas, Megan and Matthew lowered their heads and tightened their hands together and gave Michael everything they could. Matthew was shuddering with the strain. Tears were pouring from Megan's tightly shut eyes. But Thomas knew better than to wake them.

Up above Nahant Bay, one hundred and fifty feet in the air, Michael was close to 'Mr Hillary's' coat tails. He reached out and snatched at them once, and missed. 'Mr Hillary' turned around with fiery red eyes and snarled at him like a wolf, and leaped ahead, and leaped ahead.

'*Azazel!*' Michael screamed at him. But 'Mr Hillary' ducked his shoulders and climbed up even higher, his boot heels kicking in thin air.

Two hundred feet up, and over a half-mile away from the shoreline, Michael thought that he had lost him. He was climbing so high, running so strongly. But then Michael gave one last lunge, and caught hold of his coat, and stopped running, so that he would fall.

459

'*Nooooo!*' ranted 'Mr Hillary.' '*No, you bastard! No, you fool! You're one of us! You're one of us!*'

He dragged at his coat, and struggled and kicked, and tried to gain height. But even the aura of Azazel the Scapegoat wasn't enough to carry two people into the sky, not on a planet where the gravity was so strong, and the weight of human sin was so heavy.

'Mr Hillary's' coat began to scorch, and smoke started to pour out of his boots. His aura was literally overheating. He screamed, and twisted, and lashed at Michael with his fists. He turned over and over, smoking and burning and kicking.

'*You're one of us! You're one of us!*'

But Michael clung onto 'Mr Hillary's' coat tails and refused to let go. And his nightmare of falling came true. He plunged downwards toward the sea, and 'Mr Hillary' plunged too, until they plummeted apart from each other, tumbling over and over, two small black specks against the morning sunlight.

Fifty feet above the ocean, 'Mr Hillary' exploded. There was a soft *ffoommph*, and a brief flare of white flame, and then pieces of charred body and clothing began to fall.

His grey coat fell last of all, floating this way and that on the wind, like a falling leaf, smouldering as it fell. At last it dropped onto the surface, and covered up his burned remains, the way a mother would have done.

Beside it, Michael swam bruised and aimless in the swell, gasping for breath.

Thomas immediately went over to one of the Essex County deputies, who was standing open-mouthed beside his car, and snapped, 'Coastguard, quick. I want both of them out of the water pronto, the dead one and the not-so-dead one.'

Then he went over to Megan and snapped his fingers

right in front of her face. She didn't respond at first, but then he snapped his fingers again, and patted her cheeks.

'Megs! Megs! It's me!'

She blinked at him. She didn't seem to recognize him at first, but then she gradually smiled.

'Megs? You did it! Whatever it was, however you did it, you did it!'

She nodded, and kept on smiling. 'There's just one more piece of unfinished business, sweetheart. The white-white men. The lily-white boys.'

He found Jason locked in one of the small whitewashed rooms at the top of the spiral staircase. As soon as he opened the door, Jason came running across the room and hugged him tight and wouldn't let him go.

'Are you all right?' he asked him. 'They didn't hurt you, did they?'

Jason shook his head. He didn't cry, but he wasn't going to let go.

'You smell like hospital,' he said.

'I got scratched, that's all. The paramedics put some antiseptic on it.'

'Is mommy all right?'

'Mommy got scratched, too. But she's okay.'

Jason looked up at him. 'I saw you through the window. I saw you climbing in the air. How did you *do* that?'

'You can do anything, so long as you try hard enough.'

'But you were right up high in the air.'

'I didn't do it by myself. Megan helped me, and a black man called Matthew. We did it together.'

Jason said, 'What about the other men?'

'The police have got them all rounded up in the library downstairs. You won't have to see any of them again.'

Jason hugged him even tighter.

461

'Come on,' said Michael, ruffling his hair. 'Let's go see mommy.'

They went down the spiral staircase. In the library, the lily-white boys had been assembled under police guard, thirteen of them altogether. Jason averted his eyes as Michael guided him across the room to the opposite door.

'Goodbye, Jason,' said Joseph, taking off his dark glasses, but Jason didn't turn around.

Michael was taking Jason down the stone steps outside the lighthouse when Thomas came out and said, 'Michael! Can you spare me a moment?'

Michael gave Jason a kiss, and said, 'Look after your mom, would you?' Then, to the policewoman standing at the foot of the steps, 'Take him across to the ambulance, would you please?'

Jason said, 'You won't be long, will you?'

'No,' smiled Michael, and kissed him. 'I won't be long.'

He went back into the library. Thomas and Megan and Matthew were standing by the fireplace, looking serious. Thomas said, in a low voice, 'Matthew has suggested something.'

'Oh, yes? What?'

'He says that the lily-white boys are probably going to get away with this, unscathed. They're immortal, to all intents and purposes. You can't kill them, you can't really hurt them. Even if we manage to get them into court, they have far too many friends in high places. They'll walk.'

'So? What do you suggest?'

Matthew said, 'I suggest we try to hypnotize them – put them to sleep.'

'But if we do that, they'll shrivel up, won't they? That's what you said.'

Matthew nodded.

Michael looked at Thomas. 'What's your position on

that? Aren't we infringing their legal rights? I mean, if we kill them, aren't we going to be guilty of homicide, too?'

Matthew said, 'They're not human, in the normal sense. They're just *things*, they're just a disease. A virus doesn't have no legal rights, and neither do they.'

Michael looked down at Megan. 'What do you think?'

She shrugged. 'You saw what we did on the beach. The three of us, all joined together. We made you fly. We could do it again, with the lily-white boys. After all, it isn't a crime to put somebody to sleep.'

'It is if you know it's going to kill them.'

Thomas said, 'You want to be rid of them as much as I do, don't you?'

'More,' said Michael. 'But we're not vigilantes; and we're not murderers, either.'

Thomas checked his watch. 'Then think of it this way. You've got ten minutes to put these characters to sleep. Do it in memory of Elaine Parker. Do it for Sissy O'Brien. Do it for Victor, and for all of those people who died at Rocky Woods.'

Megan reached up and took hold of Michael's hand. 'I think we have a duty, Michael. I really do.'

'All right,' Michael agreed. 'Let's try it.'

Thomas left the library, and his officers reluctantly followed him. One of them said, before he closed the door, 'Any funny business – anything – you just yell out.'

Michael stood up, and walked across to Joseph, who was standing with his hands clasped behind him, and an expression of patient resignation on his face.

'This is the end, then,' said Michael.

Joseph shrugged. 'The end? This isn't the end. This isn't even the beginning of the end. We are very few. There are hundreds more of us. You will recognize us time and time again.'

463

'You know what we're going to do, don't you?' said Michael.

Joseph nodded. 'Yes, of course. And we shall welcome it. None of us have ever known what it is to sleep.' He paused, and then he said, 'You shouldn't look so surprised. The desire for rest is just as strong as any other desire: lust, hunger, greed, revenge.'

'Revenge', said Michael. 'Why do I feel that revenge is something I'm being cheated of?'

'Because revenge is a punishment that you impose on somebody who has wronged you. What you're going to do us now – that's not a punishment. It's a natural consequence of everything that's happened, and we accept it. We could have escaped, you know. Your guns couldn't have stopped us. We decide when our lives are over, not you. And even if you had managed to restrain us, your prisons couldn't have held us – that's if any of your judges would have been willing to convict. "Mr Hillary" may be gone, Michael ... but the influence of the Seirim will last for all eternity.'

Michael looked at Joseph narrowly. Joseph was taunting him, trying to devalue what he had done. In fact, Michael could sense a deep weariness within him, and an even deeper despair. The death of Azazel had taken away the whole meaning of their strange existence. They had lost their leader, their mentor and their inspiration, the being within whose body the sins of the world had burned like blazing tar. Without him, without Azazel, what was left in the modern world for a pack of vicious, anachronistic strays?

'I know why you didn't escape,' he told Joseph, in a voice so quiet that nobody else could hear him. 'You didn't escape because there's nothing for you to escape *to*. No purpose, no future. No apocalypse. Nothing.'

Joseph continued to smile at him. 'You're more complicated than you look, aren't you, Michael?'

'I am now,' Michael replied.

He limped into the middle of the library and held up the zinc-and-copper disc, so that all of the lily-white boys could see it clearly.

'Look at this,' he ordered, and it winked and shone in the sunlight. 'Look at this, and think of sleep. You've never slept, any of you … but think of it now. Think of resting, think of peace. Think of darkness bathing your eyes.'

He paced up and down, holding up the disc so that all of them could see it.

'You're going to sleep now, after months and years and centuries of wakefulness. You're going to sleep now, and rest for ever … You're feeling tired, you're going to sleep. You're feeling tired, you're going to sleep …'

As he recited the monotonous words, an extraordinary shiver passed through the library. Books rustled, dust blew from long-undusted shelves. There was a strong, dry aroma of desert in the air, of endless salt flats and sun-beaten pools. There was a dazzling tingle of sunlight, and desiccation.

Michael felt himself sliding into the darkness of a deep hypnotic trance. As he did so, he felt Matthew close beside him. He could sense his character, proud and primitive and strong. He could sense Megan, too. Softer, but equally determined. The three of them plunged deeper and deeper into their trance – and, as they did so, their auras flickered pinkish-white. It was their combined aura, a high-powered charge of etheric electricity. It danced and dazzled from one to the other, and then gradually died away. Darkness supervened – cold, submarine darkness, in which their auras sank silent and transparent as jellyfish.

Michael found himself walking along the beach. The sun was blinding but the sky was black. Brilliant white seagulls were nailed motionless in mid-air. His feet made a soft, sugary sound in the sand, *pith – pith – pith*.

Amongst the dunes lay hundreds of scattered bodies, their torn clothes flapping in the sea breeze. They were the bodies of all of those people who had fallen victim to the lily-white boys – politicians and diplomats, doctors and lawmakers, men of peace and women of devotion, generation after generation.

Michael discovered that he was weeping, that tears were running freely down his cheeks, and that his throat was constricted with grief. For the first time, he saw the scale of the tragedy. The lily-white boys had ruthlessly killed anybody who had striven to bring people together, anybody who had striven to bring calm and understanding to the world. At the same time, they had also slaughtered thousands and thousands of innocent people, too. All in the name of chaos – all in the name of strife, and jealousy, and cruelty, and war.

He became aware that Matthew was walking beside him, and then – on the other side – Megan. They exchanged looks but they didn't speak. They continued to walk toward the shoreline, across the dry, ribbed sand – and in the distance they could see the black, heat-wavered outlines of the lily-white boys.

They weren't walking across a beach at all, they were walking across a vast, blinding desert. The sea had somehow shrunk away, and the sand was flat and hard. The sun was thumping down on Michael's head, and as he walked he began to feel weaker and weaker, and his mouth grew drier and drier.

The sky remained black. The seagulls remained white and motionless. But somehow Michael felt that the desert was stretching, wider and wider, and that they would never reach the end of it alive. They walked and they walked, saying nothing; but gradually the images of the lily-white boys began to dwindle in the distance, and then they vanished.

'We've lost them,' said Megan, in Michael's head.

'They're playing us for fools,' said Matthew. 'They're stronger than we are ... they're pulling us away.'

'What are we going to do?' asked Megan, anxiously.

'We don't have any choice,' said Michael. 'We're here now, we have to go after them.'

Matthew made a sign with his left hand, an odd, complicated sign that had been used by Olduvai tribesmen to protect them from the evil eye. 'You're right,' he said. 'We don't have no choice. This is our destiny. This is the path we have to walk.'

They walked for hours. Yet no time passed. The sun remained fixed in the same position. The seagulls remained frozen. Eventually, however, they saw smoke on the far horizon. A thick black smudge, against a black sky. They saw sparks whirling, and people running and dancing. With unnatural quickness, they found themselves walking through crowds of men and women, all of them dressed in tunics and turbans and djellabas – dull, simple clothes.

'Biblical times,' said Matthew. 'They've taken us back to the days of Aaron.'

They walked on, through smoke and dust and dancing people, until they reached a huge crude statue of a goat, made out of mud and straw and painted gold. It had been constructed on a brick plinth, and towered thirty or forty feet into the jet-black sky. Its eyes were two tarry fires, pouring out smoke and sparks. Its horns were curled, and hung with hundreds of human skulls – adult and children's. They knocked and rattled in the desert wind.

The lily-white boys were standing on the plinth, silent, waiting, their eyes blood-red, their faces white as kaolin.

Joseph stepped to the edge of the plinth. 'You thought that you could defeat us. You thought that we had given up. But we are timeless. We are indestructible. It is you, now, who are going to become ashes. It is you, now, who are going to meet your Maker.'

He lifted both hands, and a huge, orgiastic roar went up from the crowds of Levites. Michael turned around, and saw them ripping off each other's clothes, and tearing at each other. He saw a naked man gouging out a woman's eyes with his fingers, and cramming them into his mouth, and dancing an obscene, triumphant, hopping dance. He saw six men force a young girl onto the sand, and force themselves into her, all six of them, while she kicked and thrashed and clawed at them.

Drums thundered, trumpets screamed, and dust rose thickly over the desert, mingling with the tarry smoke of the goat-idol's eyes.

'It is you!' screamed Joseph. 'It is you who are going to meet your Maker!'

The ground trembled. The screaming grew louder. Through the smoke and the dust, Michael saw rapes and stabbings and stranglings. Blood flew through the air in a fine, sticky shower.

He closed his eyes in desperation. *They won't sleep* he told Megan and Matthew. *They simply won't sleep.*

The lily-white boys came down the steps at the side of the plinth, and each of them was carrying two thin metal tubes. They tapped them together in a steady, insistent rhythm.

They're going to torture us, said Megan. *They're going to suck us dry.*

Michael turned around, but the orgiastic crowd was pressing too closely for them to escape – just like the crowd in his nightmare. The lily-white boys came closer and closer, tapping their tubes, smiling, their faces as white as fright, their eyes shining red and sleepless and full of revenge.

Joseph approached Michael and prodded his chest with one of his metal tubes. 'You really thought that you could make us sleep so easily? You are far too sinful – and so is this woman, with whom you sinned – and so is this man, Matthew. Sinners can never overcome sinners.'

The lily-white boys gathered around them, and they rustled and whispered and Michael was so frightened of what they were going to do that he couldn't even open his mouth.

The drumming grew louder. The screaming was almost unbearable. Michael saw a woman with her hair on fire, rolling over and over, and a man, castrated, shrieking in pain and desperation.

The oily smoke rolled over them, and hid them.

And out of the oily smoke came the brightest of lights. A brilliant incandescence that Michael could scarcely bear to look at.

At first he thought, *This is it, this is their aura, this is where they kill us.* But then he realized that the lily-white boys were dropping to their knees, one by one, and trying to shield their eyes. Even Joseph finally covered his face, and knelt on the sand, and pressed his forehead against it.

The light hovered over them, dazzling them all, and then a clear young voice said, *Sleep – you have to sleep.*

Michael looked up in astonishment. Every nerve in his body thrilled with pride and recognition. It was Jason, his son, fiery and bright – the force of innocence – the force of sinlessness. He had come to do what his father was unable to do.

Sleep, he said, and smiled at Michael with flawless affection. *Sleep, all of you, sleep.*

One by one, the lily-white boys closed their blood-eyes, and slept. As they did so, they collapsed to their knees, and then to the floor. Dust billowed up, and filled the room, the dust of centuries, mummy-dust, the dust of things that had lived for far too long. Suits were emptied, jackets dropped to the floor, trouser legs flattened.

It took no more than a few minutes; but in those few

469

minutes, Michael had sensed the passing of centuries. He had seen pyramids and Sphinxes, ziggurats and ancient tombs. He had seen red suns rising and red suns sinking. Now there was nothing but discarded clothing, and sinking dust, and some shrivelled-up things that looked like vegetables.

They were back in the library, at Goat's Cape, and the lily-white boys had slept and crumbled.

Jason was sitting in 'Mr Hillary's' chair, his hair electric, his eyes wide.

Michael walked over and held his hand, and he felt his fingers crackle with static.

'You did it,' he said. '*You* did it.'

Jason looked at him, his eyes wide, boyishly triumphant.

Michael limped around and touched one of the dried-up things with his foot. It broke open, and collapsed into ochre dust.

He went over and held Megan's hand.

'Thank you,' he said, and kissed her. She reached up and put her arm around his neck, to prolong his kiss.

It was then that Thomas walked in.

Outside, in the ambulance, Patsy was waiting for them. She had been treated by the paramedics for lacerations and shock, and she was making a statement to Sergeant Jahnke. Jason accepted a Coca-Cola, and stood by the ambulance drinking it, looking tired and extremely grown-up.

David Jahnke climbed out of the ambulance as Michael approached and gave him a one-fingered salute and a funny look.

'That was some pursuit you pulled off there. You're going to have to teach me how to do that.'

'I will,' said Michael. 'Anybody can do it, if they try.'

'You ready to leave now?' Michael asked Patsy. 'It's all over. You won't be seeing those men again, ever.'

470

Matthew Monyatta came up and clapped Michael on the back. 'That was something fine and magical we did there, wasn't it? You and me, and Mrs Boyle, and that son of yours.'

Michael grasped his hand, and nodded. There was nothing he needed to say. Once two men have shared each other's minds, their closeness is complete, no matter what age they are, no matter what race they are.

As the paramedics helped Patsy out of the ambulance, somebody else approached – Jacqueline, with a police topcoat over her shoulders. A policewoman hovered nearby.

'Goodbye,' she said, kissing Michael on the cheek. 'I hope that you can forgive me.'

Michael wiped his cheek with the back of his hand. 'I don't think it's up to me to forgive you. Besides, I don't think I could. Not yet, anyway.'

'I've left something for you,' she said. 'Something you're going to need.'

'Oh, yes? And what's that?'

'Go back to the library. I pushed it down the back of "Mr Hillary's" chair.'

The policewoman took hold of Jacqueline's arm, and led her away. She turned and smiled at Michael over her shoulder, and called out, 'Don't forget! It's something you're going to need!'

'What was all that about?' asked Matthew.

'Search me,' said Michael. But he tossed his car keys to Jason and said, 'Open the car for your mom, will you, Jason? I've left something behind.'

He walked back to the lighthouse and up the steps. In the library, Thomas was standing over the dusty remains of the lily-white boys, while a police photographer was taking pictures. He glanced at Michael and said, 'Hallo, Mikey,' but there was very little warmth in his voice.

471

Michael went over to 'Mr Hillary's' chair and when Thomas had his back turned he pushed his hand down the back. At first he couldn't feel anything at all, but then he suddenly encountered cold, sharp steel, and almost cut his fingers off.

Very cautiously, he lifted the object out of the crack in the back of the upholstery. It was Jacqueline's boning-knife, the same knife that she had used to slice Victor open.

He glanced around to make sure that Thomas wasn't looking, and slid the knife up into his sleeve. He didn't know why. He didn't even want to think why.

As he walked out, Thomas called, 'Take care now.'

'Yes,' he said. 'You too.'

'You're staying at Plymouth Insurance?' Thomas asked him.

'I don't know. I think I might start looking for something a little less exciting.'

Michael had the feeling that Thomas wanted to say something more, but in the end he didn't: he simply turned his back, took out a cigarette, and lit it.

Michael limped off down the steps and went to rejoin Patsy and Jason. In the distance, two small children were flying a kite. It ducked and weaved in the sea breeze as if it were trying to climb the side of an invisible mountain.

Nineteen

Michael and Patsy and Jason went back to New Seabury, and after a week Michael wrote a letter of resignation to Edgar Bedford, and told him that he didn't want to work in insurance investigation any longer.

He started work on a fibre-optic device to create holographic images of bait which would appear on the end of anglers' lines, and attract whichever kind of fish they wanted. Unlike real flies, they would move and change colour and cost less than $10 each.

Most of the time, he seemed happy enough. He no longer had nightmares about Rocky Woods, or about 'Mr Hillary'.

But every now and then, he would come out of his study and watch Patsy at work, and his heart would silently, silently break.

Matthew Monyatta returned to his counselling, although he added a new picture to his office walls: a huge silhouette of a goat, standing against a red desert sky. He never explained to anybody what it meant.

Thomas Boyle quit smoking. Megan Boyle published a paperback called *Challenged Cooking*, a recipe book for disabled men and women.

Detective John Minatello resigned from the Boston police, vacated his apartment on Parkman Street, and went to live in St Cloud, Florida, a small community east of Orlando.

He never opened a bank account. Whenever he needed money, all he had to do was open the sports bag on top of his wardrobe and take out some of the money that Jambo DuFreyne had dropped when he was ambushed on Seaver Street, and John Minatello had later picked up.

The riots on Seaver Street gradually burned themselves out. Patrice Latomba was arrested, but then released for lack of coherent evidence. When he was advised that the risk of further violence was 'minimal', the President arranged to fly in from Washington for a two-hour visit to Seaver Street and Blue Hill Avenue as a show of 'social, racial and emotional fence-mending'.

The day before the President was due to arrive in Boston, Michael reached in the back of his desk-drawer, just to make sure that Jacqueline's knife was still there.

A Selected List of Horror Titles Available from Mandarin

While every effort is made to keep prices low, it is sometimes necessary to increase prices at short notice. Mandarin Paperbacks reserves the right to show new retail prices on covers which may differ from those previously advertised in the text or elsewhere.

The prices shown below were correct at the time of going to press.

☐	7493 0899 0	**The Piper**	Campbell Black	£3.99
☐	7493 0920 2	**The Wanting**	Campbell Black	£3.99
☐	7493 5315 3	**The Horning**	Campbell Black & Jeffrey Caine	£4.99
☐	7493 1372 2	**Burial**	Graham Masterton	£4.99
☐	7493 0950 4	**Prey**	Graham Masterton	£3.99
☐	7493 0963 6	**Black Angel**	Graham Masterton	£3.99
☐	7493 1374 9	**Mystica**	Julia Taylor-Stanley	£3.99
☐	7493 1080 4	**A Reasonable Madness**	Fran Dorf	£3.99
☐	7493 0678 5	**The Devil Rides Out**	Dennis Wheatley	£3.99
☐	7493 0676 9	**Gateway to Hell**	Dennis Wheatley	£3.99
☐	7493 0670 X	**The Satanist**	Dennis Wheatley	£4.99
☐	7493 0679 3	**Strange Conflict**	Dennis Wheatley	£3.99
☐	7493 0677 7	**They Used Dark Forces**	Dennis Wheatley	£4.99
☐	7493 0673 4	**To the Devil – A Daughter**	Dennis Wheatley	£3.99

All these books are available at your bookshop or newsagent, or can be ordered direct from the address below. Just tick the titles you want and fill in the form below.

Cash Sales Department, PO Box 5, Rushden, Northants NN10 6YX.
Fax: 0933 410321 : Phone 0933 410511.

Please send cheque, payable to 'Reed Book Services Ltd.', or postal order for purchase price quoted and allow the following for postage and packing:

£1.00 for the first book, 50p for the second; **FREE POSTAGE AND PACKING FOR THREE BOOKS OR MORE PER ORDER.**

NAME (Block letters) ....

ADDRESS ....

....

☐ I enclose my remittance for ....

☐ I wish to pay by Access/Visa Card Number ⬚⬚⬚⬚⬚⬚⬚⬚⬚⬚⬚⬚⬚⬚⬚⬚

Expiry Date ⬚⬚⬚⬚

Signature ....

Please quote our reference: MAND